PREDATOR™

EYES OF THE DEMON

THE COMPLETE PREDATOR™ LIBRARY FROM TITAN BOOKS

Predator
If It Bleeds edited by Bryan Thomas Schmidt
The Predator by Christopher Golden
& Mark Morris
The Predator: Hunters and Hunted
by James A. Moore
Stalking Shadows by James A. Moore
& Mark Morris
Eyes of the Demon edited by
Bryan Thomas Schmidt

The Complete Predator Omnibus
by Nathan Archer & Sandy Scofield

The Rage War
by Tim Lebbon
Predator™: Incursion, Alien: Invasion
Alien vs. Predator™: Armageddon

Aliens vs. Predators
Ultimate Prey edited by Jonathan Maberry
& Bryan Thomas Schmidt
Rift War by Weston Ochse & Yvonne Navarro

The Complete Aliens vs. Predator Omnibus
by Steve Perry & S.D. Perry

The Official Movie Novelizations
by Alan Dean Foster
Alien, Aliens™, Alien 3, Alien: Covenant,
Alien: Covenant Origins

Alien: Resurrection by A.C. Crispin

Alien 3: The Unproduced Screenplay
by William Gibson & Pat Cadigan

Alien
Out of the Shadows by Tim Lebbon
Sea of Sorrows by James A. Moore
River of Pain by Christopher Golden
The Cold Forge by Alex White
Isolation by Keith R.A. DeCandido
Prototype by Tim Waggoner
Into Charybdis by Alex White
Colony War by David Barnett
Inferno's Fall by Philippa Ballantine
Enemy of My Enemy by Mary SanGiovanni

Aliens
Bug Hunt edited by Jonathan Maberry
Phalanx by Scott Sigler
Infiltrator by Weston Ochse
Vasquez by V. Castro

The Complete Aliens Omnibus
Volumes 1–7

Non-Fiction
AVP: Alien vs. Predator
by Alec Gillis & Tom Woodruff, Jr.
Aliens vs. Predator Requiem:
Inside The Monster Shop
by Alec Gillis & Tom Woodruff, Jr.
Alien: The Illustrated Story
by Archie Goodwin & Walter Simonson
The Art of Alien: Isolation by Andy McVittie
Alien: The Archive
Alien: The Weyland-Yutani Report
by S.D. Perry
Aliens: The Set Photography
by Simon Ward
Alien: The Coloring Book
The Art and Making of Alien: Covenant
by Simon Ward
Alien Covenant: David's Drawings
by Dane Hallett & Matt Hatton
The Predator: The Art and Making
of the Film by James Nolan
The Making of Alien by J.W. Rinzler
Alien: The Blueprints by Graham Langridge
Alien: 40 Years 40 Artists
Alien: The Official Cookbook
by Chris-Rachael Oseland
Aliens: Artbook by Printed In Blood

ALL-NEW TALES FROM THE EXPANDED PREDATOR UNIVERSE

EYES OF THE DEMON

EDITED BY BRYAN THOMAS SCHMIDT

TITAN BOOKS

PREDATOR: EYES OF THE DEMON
Print edition ISBN: 9781803360294
E-book edition ISBN: 9781803360416

Published by Titan Books
A division of Titan Publishing Group Ltd
144 Southwark Street, London SE1 0UP

First edition: August 2022
10 9 8 7 6 5 4 3 2 1

A CIP catalogue record for this title is available from the British Library.

Printed and bound by CPI Group (UK) Ltd, Croydon CR0 4YY

For Jess T. and Johnny Ortiz—fans, friends,
cheerleaders
And for May, who's everything

CONTENTS

INTRODUCTION

BY BRYAN THOMAS SCHMIDT

Thirty-five years ago on Friday, June 12, 1987, action and science fiction fans converged on darkened theatres to see a new science fiction action movie.

The concept of soldiers moving through a jungle was hardly new, but their opponent was the likes of which fans had never seen before. The Yautja, the Hunter, the Predator—he goes by all these names, and what happened next gave birth to a franchise that still thrives three and a half decades later, with a number of films, numerous books, comic books, and more.

On October 17, 2017, I made my first professional contribution to this fantastic universe with the anthology *Predator: If It Bleeds*, celebrating, in part, the thirtieth anniversary of the franchise, so it gives me a thrill and is a high honor to come back now with this new anthology to celebrate the thirty-fifth anniversary.

We've taken a slightly different approach to the stories this time. Almost everything takes place in the present—or close to it—and the future. Yet what these authors did was a lot of fun for me as a fan, editor, and reader. Unique takes that show us new sides of the story. More than ever you will see stories from the Yautja point of view. You'll discover new species that challenge the Yautja like never before. There are new settings galore and several appearances of female predators.

I spent the last four years talking with fans and listening to their wish list, and with *Eyes of the Demon*, I think we've delivered something truly special that will excite and please you like never before. We even have the return of a few old friends and a few connections and expansions of the universe that tie things together in new ways.

I hope these sixteen stories are as fun to read as they were to edit. We worked hard to get the details right, too, so hopefully we succeeded. And in the process we have the Yautja appearing in stories like you've never seen him—or her—and in ways I think you'll find unforgettable in the best way. How better to celebrate thirty-five years of our favorite franchise than with new, unique stories unlike what you've seen before?

So sit back in your most comfy chair, grab your favorite beverage, and get ready for a few hours' reading pleasure as you revisit your old friend, the Predator, sixteen more times. I hope you find it worth the wait, and a worthy successor to *If It Bleeds*, which one fan group graciously deemed "the best *Predator* book ever released." Personally, I hope this one steals that title. But now I leave that up to you.

With humble gratitude to my fellow fans,

Bryan Thomas Schmidt, Ottawa, KS, December 2021

THE TITANS

BY TIM LEBBON

Jeremiah Beck has always enjoyed being a Corporal in "The Unluckies," because he's young and cocky and has delusions of immortality, and he never believes their title might come home to roost. He's proud that countless other regiments know of the 13th Spaceborne by such a name, especially considering the 13th have one of the most successful operational records since the initiation of the marines' Spaceborne contingent. The nickname has become a badge of honour, so much so that at least half of the 13th have various forms of Unluckies tattoos, from the grunts right up to Major Ashley Hughes herself. Beck's tattoo is around his left bicep, fashioned in the stylized mask of a Predator dripping blood both red and green, human and alien. He was inked on Francilia's second moon on his twentieth birthday, three days after he'd helped take out his first Predator in a firefight close to the moon's colony of space archaeologists. That day, he felt like a hero.

Now he might just be the unluckiest motherfucker in his whole squad, because he's the only one left alive.

His tattoo has been ripped by shrapnel and scoured by fire, along with much of the flesh of his left arm and shoulder. His space suit is melted into the mess, torn and leaking, and if it weren't for his combat armour feeding him high doses of trauma suppressant he'd have passed out from the pain.

It would have been better if I had *passed out.*

There's a steady, destructive vibration thudding through Rankin Station's superstructure, and it could be that which is blurring his vision, though he thinks maybe it's the sudden rush of pain-blocker from his suit. Explosions thump in the distance and roar closer by. Once the hull is compromised and starts venting to space, he'll be dead in a matter of minutes.

He makes his way along corridors strobed by emergency lighting. He tries to shake the memory of his fellow Unluckies dying, six of them taken out in the first surprise attack by the band of Predators who'd been hiding on the station, Melton and Lincoln dead from wounds sustained in their decisive and suicidal counterattack.

I should have fought harder by their side. We might have killed them all. Not left that one alive. Luna, carrying the crescent moon wound on her face where my shotgun blast smashed away her damaged helmet.

But he can't forget seeing them die. Their deaths are etched on his memory, just as aspects of their lives together will always be carried inside. They'd been serving together as a platoon of nine on their strike-ship *Aragorn* for over four years, and now they're gone, and *Aragorn* is rolling away from the station with a hole in her belly, spinning for eternity, empty of life and devoid of purpose.

Beck struggles towards Rankin Station's escape hub, hoping there's a pod left for him. And as he hurries through corridors flashing with warning lights and scarred with the echoes of battle, he sees her, the one he now calls Luna. The sight of her pain is the only balm to his loss.

That's not true. I didn't see her. She was already dead from the self-destruct the Unluckies set... fighting fire with fire... or she died when I left the station and it came apart.

She is waiting for him up ahead, badly wounded just as he is, spilling green blood on the same buckled flooring where his own red blood spatters, as if his tattoo is finally coming apart. She sways, taking up the whole height and width of the corridor. Maybe her swaying is the motion of Rankin Station as it shakes itself apart. Maybe it's his own failing eyesight.

Beck raises his gun, though he knows he's out of ammo. Luna steps forward, broken plasma scythe spitting at the air between them.

If I had *seen her on the way to the escape hub, we'd both be dead. I made it there and blasted away like the coward I always feared I might be. Alive, while they were all dead. Alone. Adrift.*

An explosion. Fire dancing in zero gravity now that the station's artificial gravity has malfunctioned, the flames beautiful and deadly as they spread and consume like a burst blossom. Shrapnel flying as the station starts to break up.

An escape pod, targeted away from the planet because there's nothing down there to escape to.

The heavy thud of launch, and then the mechanized prodding and caresses of the robo-pod preparing Beck for hypersleep. The brief engine burn is already over, and he's been accelerated away from the planet and into deep space. Beacon pulsing. Chance of rescue minuscule.

Perhaps that's why he hangs onto his pained, tortured wakefulness—

But no, I did *sleep. I* did. *I wasn't awake for all that time. If I was I'd have been driven mad.*

—for the first few days and weeks, and then the years that start to slip by, frozen into the escape pod and unable to move, simply lying there breathing fluid and hearing nothing, just thinking... thinking... dreaming of Luna and that wound he gave her, and the good, dead friends further behind with every never-ending moment that crawls by.

Beck woke up in the same small room he'd been living and sleeping in for over sixteen years, and for those first few moments it was a strange place, and the horrible memories from five decades before were where he still dwelled. Then his nightmare began to dissipate and reality asserted itself. With a groan, he sat up on the edge of his bed and waited for feeling to return to his aged limbs.

Damn, that was a bad one. He'd had the same nightmare ever since he'd been rescued, though as time went by so the frequency decreased. This was the first in over six months. He was grateful for that. It always left him feeling like shit, and remembering his dead friends from the Unluckies made him sad. He hardly recalled their faces—though fresh in his nightmares, they quickly faded away once he woke up—but their voices were more solid. He stood from his bed and heard his knees click, and Lincoln sang her dirty limericks. He walked into the bathroom pod and took a piss, and Poonam waxed lyrical about the bread her mother used to bake. He heard the heart in Lincoln's voice, smelled Poonam's mother's bread.

Sometimes when he had the nightmare he thought this long life was all in his imagination, and he had spent the last five decades on that shuddering, burning, dying space station.

He went through a morning ritual that sometimes eased the pain of his injuries, sometimes not. His left arm and shoulder had been built back up with artificial flesh, similar to that used for androids. It sometimes itched like hell, but he grudgingly admitted that it was a good match. He moisturised and massaged to get his old blood flowing through this new flesh, enjoying the tingling sensation as feeling returned. He changed his stoma bag. He'd lost half of his stomach in an explosion during his final moments on the burning station and, unable to treat his wounds, the escape pod had put him straight into hypersleep in order to pause any more degeneration to his damaged body. Combined with the medical circuits in his combat suit, it had saved his life. He tended his other wounds, and then last of all he removed his eye patch and chose his eye for the day. Running his hand back and forth over the glass eye box in his bathroom cabinet, he paused over the white orb with a jet-black pupil, and smiled. It was his favourite. He was too old and decrepit to try new things.

Beck left his bathroom pod and something flashed across his vision, a fluid shadow that had once been so horribly familiar. His heart fluttered, and though he knew it was the dregs of his dream, for a moment he saw Luna standing in the corner of his small apartment. She was bent over because she was so tall, her facial wound leaking across his small table and the books scattered there, her breath coming in wet grunts, and for a moment he could even smell her, a sweet-sour tang underlying warm musk. He stared at her and she stared back, and then he blinked and she was gone.

"Fuck's sake," Beck muttered, and he went about preparing breakfast. Powdered egg on toast, coffee strong enough to require a new chemical classification, and a handful of vitamin supplements. Same every morning, same as it had been for the sixteen years he'd lived here. Beck was nothing if not a man of habit.

Ready for work, he opened his apartment door and left that familiar nightmare behind.

Beck took some pride in knowing that out of two hundred permanent residents, he was Hamilton Base's oldest, not only in age but the time he'd been there. Seventy years old, and he'd been Hamilton's librarian for the last sixteen of those years. His younger life was separated from his life now by the nightmare he'd just woken from, and much as he missed his dead marine squad, he was more than happy living out his time in such a safe, familiar environment. *Boring*, he sometimes heard Poonam saying to him. *Alive,* he replied.

He limped along familiar hallways, nodding to people he passed, exchanging brief pleasantries with some. Windows were shielded, as usual, but here and there some of the shading had only half-fallen, and beyond he could see ghost images of Titan's inimical landscape as sharp ice storms pounded from all sides.

There was a young woman waiting outside the library door when he arrived. He didn't recognize her.

"Jeremiah Beck?"

"You can go in, you know," he said.

"It's not locked?" She seemed surprised, which told him immediately that she was a new arrival.

"Why would I lock up a room full of knowledge?"

The woman shrugged. She was nervous, too. Probably facing her first shift on Titan, and if that were the case he understood her nervousness Beck had ventured out from the base and onto the moon's surface a few times, and counted them as a few too many.

"Come on in," Beck said. "It takes me seven minutes to walk to work—though almost eight today, and it's been getting longer lately, which doesn't make me happy—and I'm always ready for another coffee when I get here. You?"

"Me? I only got here two days ago, I'm heading out for the atmos processor in a few hours so... and I came from crew quarters, it's just... " She waved back over her shoulder towards the station's accommodation arm.

"I mean, coffee?" Beck asked.

She smiled, nodded.

"So, you know my name.. "

"Oh, sorry. I'm Bindy."

Beck nodded and entered the base's only library. He liked his apartment, but this was the place where he felt most at home. He'd made it that way. His time as a marine was decades in the past, even though over three of those decades had been spent in hypersleep, and though his experiences had dictated what his life was now, they did not define him. The space was warm and comfortable, and as far from a room on a functioning terraforming base as he'd been able to make it. Genuine old books lining the walls gave the library depth and peace, stealing away all but the deepest purring from life support. Comfortable chairs with sagging upholstery were scattered around the room, and he kept the viewing ports permanently shaded. Old lamps sat on rickety tables. Much of the furniture he'd made himself from scrap metal, painting it to give the appearance of wood. He had a chair of his own, behind a low metal desk, and sometimes he slept in there. He breathed in deeply and the smell of old books made him close his eyes.

"Were you really on the *Aragorn*?"

Beck opened his eyes again, and sighed. He turned around and Bindy stood in the centre of his library, staring at him, focused on the jet-black pupil of his false eye. He wondered if she'd ever held a real book in her hands, let alone opened one. She was about to embark on her first shift out on the surface, throwing her lot in with some of the hardiest grafters in Sol system—braving the ice storms and hostile environment to tend the atmosphere processors, living in small subterranean cells, risking death every moment of their ten-day shift before enjoying three days back at Hamilton Station—and all she could think about was meeting him. He should have felt humbled.

"I was, and my story's archived in the holo room on Deck C. I was going to write a book about it, actually, but—"

"And you really killed seventeen Predators?"

"Me and my platoon, yes." He blinked and saw Poonam again, and Melton, and the others slaughtered in the first surprise attack, and he felt nothing but sadness and a lingering dread. That was the dream, he supposed. Luna's eyes on him as he fled, even though he was certain—reasonably certain—that he'd not seen her again after that time he shot her. She was probably dead before he even turned away. If not, she'd died minutes later in that final explosion when the station came apart. "Soon as we arrived, we knew we could never beat them in open combat. No one had encountered that many before, in one place. So we did the only thing we thought might work and set the station to self-destruct. Last resort."

"It was a great victory," Bindy said with a naive, childlike glee. Beck went from feeling annoyed to sad.

"Not really," he said.

"Huh? But you wiped out a whole load of those bastards! If *Aragorn* hadn't been there, attacked them, just think of the planets or ships or habitats that would have fallen victim to them."

"True, seems they were using the abandoned Rankin Station as a staging post. But I mean it's not a victory. I've told a hundred people the same thing in this very room. The more you defeat them in combat, the more respect they have for you. And the more they keep coming back." Beck went to his coffee machine and pressed a button, enjoying the sound and smell as it brewed.

Bindy stood behind him, motionless and silent. She knew he had more to say.

"I could point you towards a dozen attacks by Predators over the past fifty years that I think might be a direct result of our so-called victory. We wiped them out, yeah, but there's a code of honour amongst their clans. A desire for challenging combat, a need for revenge. How do you beat an enemy like that?"

He handed her a coffee. She was frowning. "Maybe you don't win."

Beck paused with his coffee half-raised to his lips. He'd

never heard that before, from those many fascinated people who'd come to see him and quiz him rather than borrow his precious books. He'd thought it himself, of course, and sometimes he wondered if he really had won. If by surviving, he had achieved anything at all.

Luna, watching him as he staggered with terrible wounds, her own wounds carried with a sense of honour and pride.

"Guess I'll never know," he said. And then fate came to spill his coffee, and shake his hand, and make him and Bindy stagger and fall to their knees, as a powerful explosion ripped through Hamilton Base.

"What?" Bindy said, panicked. "What the hell?"

Between blinks Beck could only see the shimmering corridors of Rankin Station as fire took hold, and the smears of green blood. His own wounds throbbed and sang out.

"What?" Bindy shouted again.

He went to his library's viewing ports and unshaded them for the first time in years, letting the stark reality of outside into this small, comfortable room echoing with the past. And he saw just what he'd always known he would see, one of these days.

On one of the station's landing pads, a Predator ship. It was battered and scarred, like an old relic emerging from the past. As wounded as him.

It's taken her so long to find me.

"Run," he said to Bindy. "Hide."

"What about you?"

He could not answer that. He didn't yet know.

Beck moved against the tide.

"Turn around, Beck!"

"Other way, Jeremiah!"

It was the first time he'd run anywhere in years. His old wounds hurt, a reminder of his violent past, and the artificial flesh of his left arm ached.

"Someone said it's a *Predator*. Beck! You don't wanna be going that way, man."

Beck already knew what it was. *Who* it was. His dreams had told him, her eyes holding him frozen there in the burning, ruined gangways of Rankin Station moments before his escape. Pinned against that vast expanse of space and time beyond the outer reaches of the Heliosphere with a promise that she would see him again. He'd always done his best to persuade himself it was only a dream. And deeper, within that dream, he had always known that she was real.

His life that had been on gentle pause, awake and asleep—a pause he had come to enjoy, over time—was moving on, and now that Luna had come for him, he knew that he could not let her take anyone else.

Chief Stannard hurried towards him, a familiar face, but his usual calm expression had slipped.

"Bill, what's the damage?" Beck asked.

"Infiltration through landing pad three," Stannard said. "Looks like the door was blown open from the outside, no real damage, but..." He shrugged.

"I know what it is," Beck said.

Stannard caught his eye. He knew Beck's history; they'd talked about it a few times over a bottle of bourbon, when the level was closer to the bottom than the top. Beck never wanted to say too much, because he hated the way some people looked at him. Just because he was last survivor of the *Aragorn* didn't make him a fucking hero.

"How can you be sure?" Stannard asked.

I dreamt of her again last night, he could say. Or, *It's just a feeling and I'm old enough to trust them*, or, *I've always known my past would catch up with me*. But he didn't say anything.

"I never thought it'd happen here," Stannard said. "I mean, here. There's nothing here for them. No challenge. We're just a bunch of techies and labourers and..." His eyes settled back on Beck, growing even wider. He was the librarian, and Stannard enjoyed reading old horror novels by Tremblay and Ward, spooking himself in the dead of night. Now it was Beck who had spooked him.

"You have a weapons locker," Beck said.

"In my room," Stannard said. "Box under the bed, locked." He nodded, as if agreeing with some internal dialogue. "Come on, I'll—"

"Bill!" Beck said. "You need to help as many people as you can. You know this base better than anyone. Hunker down, hide. Be no threat."

Stannard only hesitated for a moment before dropping a set of keycards into Beck's hand.

"What'll you do?"

Beck slapped him on the shoulder, then started running against the flow once again towards the landing pad, where he was certain his past had caught up with him at last.

On the way he ducked into Stannard's room close to the central hub tower. It smelled of oil and cigars. He pulled a battered metal box out from under the bed, opened it, found an old pistol that was probably worth a fortune on the collectors' market and a well-maintained knife almost as long as his forearm. He hadn't expected much more, and he knew that more wouldn't matter.

He had no intention of fighting.

Once back out of Stannard's room, Beck found his instincts kicking in without any conscious effort. He could never move like he used to—he was too old, too worn down by his past—but his senses came alight, time seemed to slow, and he stalked forward through Hamilton's emptying corridors with his perception shifting. He knew how to see her, even if she had no wish to be seen.

A scream wailed in from somewhere ahead. Beck froze and raised the pistol. It had eleven rounds in the magazine, and he wondered when it had last been fired. The scream faded quickly, replaced by a silence filled only with the station's steady background hum.

Beck hurried forward, no longer cautious. He was afraid of what that scream meant. Moments later, rounding another corner, he knew.

A woman wearing a surface technician's suit sat against the wall beside an open door. Her stomach was also open, insides turned out, throat slit. A slick of blood was spreading across the floor around her, making an island of the handgun she had dropped. At least she had died quickly. He didn't know her name, but she liked reading old 20th-century history books.

"I'm here!" Beck shouted. Something moved to his right, along a corridor darkened beneath half-faded illumination, and he spun that way. Two small children huddled down in a service nook in the side wall, wide eyes catching the flickering light.

"Go!" Beck said. "That way!" He pointed back the way he'd come, stepping forward so that they could not see the mess of the dead woman. *Maybe she's their mother*, he thought, but he couldn't let that awful possibility shift his focus.

The kids ran. They didn't look back.

"I'm here!" he shouted again. "Come on! This time I'll take your fucking head off."

Past the dead woman, where the corridor curved out of view around the base's large central hub, the air shimmered. Beck blinked and looked again, focusing, seeing the walls bend with fluid grace and then grow solid.

He pointed the gun and pulled the trigger without aiming. It bucked in his hand and the bullet ricocheted from the metal wall with a flash of sparks. The sound shocked him, the smell ignited memories he did his best to veer away from, and as he blinked he saw his old squad laughing together, fighting, dying. The air rippled and then stilled once again as whatever had been there shifted to the left.

Beck stepped right and fired a second shot.

Shouts came from somewhere behind him, and he recognised Stannard's voice. Good. He'd have heard the shooting and would know what to do. Hamilton's command structure would have processes to go through in circumstances such as this, but the terraforming installation had been on site for over two decades without such an incident, and it wasn't only some of the metal doors and staircase treads that were growing rusty.

Beck started along the hallway, watching the doors, sliding close to the wall, gun aimed ahead. He breathed through his mouth, hoping to hear any movement. His heart hammered, pulse thrumming in his ears. *Steady and fast*, Poonam said. *Don't trust two bullets when you can give them ten*, Lincoln said.

The base's audio system crackled and spat, and then a voice said, "All residents secure yourselves, lock yourselves in, there's a Predator in the station and we have to—" The message ended as quickly as it had begun. Crackling, fumbling, as if a hand covered the microphone, and then Stannard's voice came over, low and gravelly.

"Everyone hunker down and stay still," he said. "And friend, there's a Sandbug fuelled and prepped in Bay Two."

Beck paused for only a moment before shooting along the hallway one more time, then turned and ran back the way he'd come. Stannard knew him so well and had guessed what he wanted to do, and why.

And he had given him a chance.

Beck moved through the discomfort and pain, listening for sounds of pursuit and gripping the pistol tight. The long knife in his belt slapped against his leg as he ran, as if reminding him of the wounds put there decades before. He ducked around corners, and along a couple of perpendicular corridors he saw shadows hurrying away and heard doors slamming. He prayed that none of them would be stupid enough to pick up a weapon.

At the wide entry doors to Bay Two of the parking garage, he paused to catch his breath and check behind him.

And there she was.

Luna stood thirty metres away, his nemesis and nightmare, his past and his destiny. She was not as tall or broad as he remembered, nor even as fearsome, but perhaps his memories and dreams had painted her that way. Time had weathered and worn her down as it had him. Her limbs were thin and mottled, her dreadlocks also speckled grey, her torso too small for the armour it bore. Her helmet was skagged and scarred, covering the damage his shotgun blasts had done to her fearsome face all those years ago.

As he thought of that half-moon wound that had named her forever in his soul, the Predator reached up and disconnected tubes and pipes from her helmet. Strange gases hissed at the air and then dissipated as she lifted it from her head. That scar was dark and livid, starting above her left eye and ending in the tattered upper mandible of her monstrous mouth. She breathed, heavy and broken, and stared at him with her one good eye.

We both took an eye, he thought, and held there by her glare, Beck was both a jaded seventy-year-old in pain, and a furious youth filled with rage and the need for revenge.

But it was not he who sought vengeance now.

He gripped the gun, but knew it would be pointless. The moment he lifted it, she would dodge, twist, and slice him in two with a blade from her forearm armour, or scorch him to smithereens with her shoulder blaster.

This was not about fighting.

"Took your time," he said, and then he turned into Bay Two and slammed his hand on the door closure mechanism. As the old metal doors started grinding together, he heard Luna running towards him. He took a few steps back into the parking hanger and aimed at the narrowing gap between the doors. Closing, closing, at the last moment her arm thrust between the doors and bent at the elbow, hand slamming against one door face.

The mechanism grumbled and cranked as she began to push.

Beck shot her three times in the hand and arm. Her screech was loud and awful and sweet music to his ears, and as her arm withdrew the doors slammed shut. A smear of grim green blood dribbled down the tarnished metal.

He put a bullet into the door's mechanism—just one; he didn't want to make it too difficult for Luna to follow him—and then ran for the Sandbug. His footsteps echoed through the hanger, brain racing almost as fast as he considered what he had to do. *Start the Sandbug, drive for the doors, open them from inside the cab, what else, what else?* He thought he had everything covered, and that if he moved fast enough—

A loud explosion boomed behind him, then another, and as he reached the Sandbug a third blast tore the doors' closing edges, willing them apart from their magnetic lock and twisting them from their runners. One bounced and spun past him, missing the nose of the Sandbug by half a metre. He leapt for the open cab and tripped over the sill, landing half on the driver's seat. He reached for the steering handle and pulled himself fully into the vehicle, other hand fumbling across the control panel for the starter button.

I don't have long, seconds, she'll blast the Sandbug and then take her time with me.

He had to get Luna away from Hamilton. He knew these beasts from the short time he'd spent killing them in his twenties, and the longer periods he had spent researching them since he woke from his decades in the escape pod. However long Luna had been searching for him, whatever circuitous route had brought her here, once she had settled her score with him her bloodlust would be up. She would turn back into the base, and if she met any resistance from the residents she would slaughter them. Beck's friends were not soldiers. They wouldn't stand a chance. Beck hit the starter and shoved the driving handle forward, hauling himself up into the driver's seat as he did so. Only then did he risk a look towards the blasted doorway. Luna shoved through the hanging, torn metal doorway into the vehicle bay, her mutilated hand held pressed across her stomach. She glared at him and her blaster shifted his way, but it glitched, stuck in place for a moment or two, before aiming at the Sandbug.

He leaned right and steered that way, and the blast scorched along the side of the Sandbug and slammed into one of the two big Haulers parked in the bay. One of its huge pressurised wheels exploded, throwing a barrage of torn metal tread sections across the hanger to hammer into vehicles, walls and high ceiling. They fell with clangs that faded away with the blast's echo.

Luna ducked from the shrapnel and debris, and Beck took the opportunity to steer for the external doors. He pressed the door operation button on the control dashboard and they began to rumble open, allowing in the violence of the ongoing storm beyond—swirling ice shards, and twisting spirals of noxious atmosphere. The sound added to the chaos in the parking garage, but the doors were opening too slowly. Beck peeked above the control panel and through the windscreen, eased back on the lever, and just as the Sandbug scraped and squealed through the widening opening, a shot from Luna's plasma cannon struck one of the withdrawing doors. The bug's left window shattered and it rocked onto its right wheels, heat blasting through the cabin, and Beck cried out as he nudged the steering lever and managed to bring the vehicle crashing back down onto six wheels.

He was out, into the inimical environment beyond Hamilton Base, and he leaned forward on the stick to accelerate away. He grabbed a mask from beneath the seat and slipped it over his face, clipping the straps behind his ears. It would give him oxygen for a while, but would not protect him from Titan's fury for long.

He switched one of the viewing cameras to the rear and moments later saw what he had been hoping for—Luna running after him. Mask off, body ravaged, tattered hand held across her chest, she sprinted after Beck and the Sandbug, striving to finish the journey of revenge she had begun five decades before.

"Come on," Beck said, and he couldn't help admire the old Predator. Such commitment, such need for vengeance and closure, was as admirable as it was terrifying. "Not long now," he said. A prickle of sadness closed around him as he saw Hamilton behind Luna, swallowed by the violent storms as he lured her further and further from the base. It had been his home for sixteen years and he had made friends there.

That was why he was doing this. Without knowing it, he'd been moving towards this moment since blasting from Rankin Station in that last, desperate escape pod, sleeping on his journey even though he'd had nightmares about staying awake.

A flash of light, and an explosion took the Sandbug in the rear, lifting the vehicle and sliding it forward. Beck fought with the steering, tracked wheels skidded and spun when it crashed back down, and he powered forward even harder, not caring about where he steered or where he was going, only concerned that it was away from his friends and home.

He jigged left around an icy mound, and a blast took the ice apart. He turned right into the settling cloud of vapour and debris, and another shot took out one of the rear wheels, axle snapping and smashing up into the undercarriage.

Ahead he saw the edge of a former, shallow methane lake, at the far side of which was the first of the atmosphere processors. He didn't want to go that far, because there were three shifts of workers down there and Luna might view them as prey.

Here, now, was where he would spend his final moments. And though the old soldier in him wanted to fight his enemy, he knew that there was a more certain way to achieve his aims.

He slowed the vehicle and opened the door to his right, and as another blast smashed into the Sandbug's left flank he threw himself from the open doorway. He hit the cold ground hard, rolled, still grasping the gun even though he wasn't sure how many bullets were left, if any. The Sandbug struck an ice mound sculptured by wind and tilted, balanced on two good wheels, and another shot from Luna sent it tumbling onto its side. Beck felt the wave of plasma heat close around him, hair sizzling, clothing crackling, and he squeezed his eyes closed. For an instant he was back on Rankin Station again, his mutilated arm simmering as the remains of his spacesuit settled into his denuded flesh.

Then he opened his eyes and Luna stood ten metres from him. In her uninjured hand she carried a glaive, heavy blades at both ends so sharp that they cut through time back to an older fight, an unfinished battle.

She watched him with her one good eye. It blazed, but Beck didn't know whether it was with anger or triumph, or some other alien emotion he could not comprehend. Her shoulder weapon still glitched, shifting minutely left and right, but trained mostly on him. Her hand dripped blood onto the icy surface of this strange moon. She carried other scars, but the one that mattered was the crescent he had put onto her face. It hurt her, defined her. It was her fuel, and she had never been so alight.

Luna crouched and aimed her glaive at him, and Beck gripped the pistol.

Then he let the weapon go and held both hands above his head.

Maybe you don't win, Bindy had said.

Luna shouted something in her strange language that he could never know, but he understood nevertheless—it was frustration. She had travelled so far and for so long for this confrontation, and now Beck had thrown up his hands. Surrendered. The old soldier who bettered her last time might have promised the glory of a final fight, but instead he was slouched in the ice, shivering and freezing, gun dropped by his side.

She screeched again, tattered mandibled mouth gaping wide, crouched down, limbs lifted in a spider-like pose, and a chill went through Beck that had nothing to do with the cold.

Luna closed the distance between them with two steps and slammed her glaive into his chest.

Beck stiffened, eyes wide and arms still aloft, waiting for the pain to come in. He looked down at the wide, heavy blade jammed between his ribs, blood blooming, his clothing pinched and wet around the weapon's head. He groaned, and then roared as Luna heaved him aloft with her one good arm. Still he kept his arms raised above his head, fighting against every instinct to grasp the spear to try and ease the pressure, the agony, the flaming sun at the heart of him that ground against his spine and cracked ribs and spewed blood in a steady stream.

Luna growled with a sense of victory. He'd give her that, for now. For this brief moment. He caught her eye and stared, and she jarred the glaive to make it penetrate deeper, sliding him down the shaft closer to her. Even in the swirl of ice and wind he could smell her warm, spicy scent, mysterious and unknowable.

"You win," Beck said, and Luna tilted her head back to roar in triumph.

Beck brought his right hand down. The knife slipped from his sleeve and he gripped the handle, sweeping the blade right to left across Luna's exposed throat.

Stannard kept his knife well-sharpened. It sliced in deep, cutting off Luna's mocking laughter. She dropped him and staggered back a few steps, and then a rush of blood poured from her throat.

Beck landed on his side, pierced all the way through by the cruel spear. His own blood soaked into the icy ground, and perhaps somewhere between them in this alien land their lifebloods might meet.

Luna dropped to her knees and reached for the control panel on her armour's left forearm, and Beck felt a moment of terror and failure, because he had not considered this at all.

Are we far enough away? he thought, but of course they were not. If Luna detonated her suit's device, the blast would take out most of Hamilton and rumble down across the old lake bed. If it didn't completely destroy the atmosphere processing plants, it would still leave the workers who survived down there homeless and doomed to an agonizing death.

Beck tensed, writhed, trying to stand and unable to do so. But there was no need. Luna's right hand was too mangled, her fingers unable to find purchase. She soon gave up. Kneeling there close to him, bleeding, she and Beck stared at each other as time caught up with them, light faded, and eternity welcomed both old warriors into its final embrace.

THE DISTANCE IN THEIR EYES

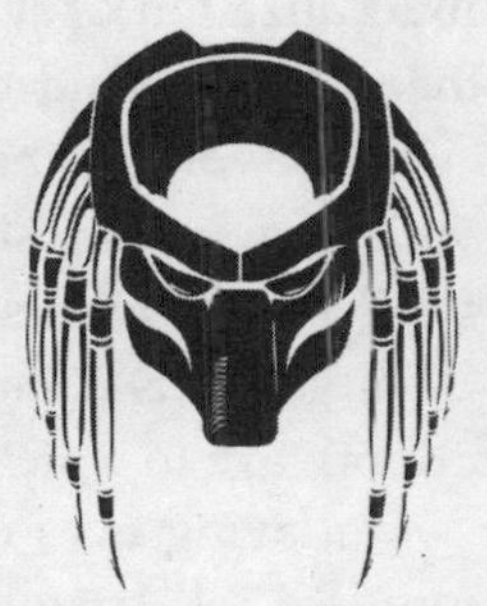

BY STEPHEN GRAHAM JONES

A *good* hunt would be nice.

Or if these planets in this system were closer together.

You can only get your blades so sharp, your targeting sensors so dialed in. And, while stalking back and forth along the lone corridor might feel like movement, Tel isn't really getting anywhere with it, he knows.

But the slog between hunts would be worth it if the prey could just be worthy, could care about its own life enough to, if not fight back, at least run, maybe even hide.

This last drop, though?

Given a cycle or two, Tel could have harvested every individual on the planet. The way they submitted was against nature. He had initially been thrilled that the wavelengths their large eyes evidently had access to negated his cloaking, meaning he was going to actually have to use stealth, and strategy, and skill—one animal hunting another, the primal equation, as it should be.

But whenever one of them saw him creeping in, his presence would immediately circulate through the herd by pheromone or subvocalization or it doesn't matter, and each individual in the village would drop whatever they were doing, look his way in wonder, the foliage transparent to them. Even the children would slow their activities, turn their large eyes Tel's way. His first time stepping into one of their villages, the elders and bedridden had pulled themselves into their doorways to watch his approach.

It was like they were laying eyes on a god. Of course they'd never seen armor like Tel's, painted with the blood of many hunts, and his bio-helmet was, as far as they knew, his actual head, but still, their wonder shouldn't have overridden their instinctual fear, should it?

The one Tel identified as the leader—surely the trophy among them—he crept in close and skewered it with his wrist blades, coming up under the chin, the blades popping the top of the skull loose. This trophy's overlarge eyes had been locked on his until the light glimmered out, at which point Tel was ready to call the hunt done.

Save for a sense that it had been too easy.

Perhaps size and bearing wasn't what counted as the most fierce with this species?

To test it, Tel stalked and eviscerated the smallest and quietest.

Again, those overlarge seemed to look at him with gratitude.

Tel scowled, pushed this one away, and, though this

wasn't practice, the need for a trophy overrode convention, and he waded into the village, hunting right out in the open, taking whatever life presented itself. To an individual, the response was the same. No matter if he used the glaive or the scythe or the scimitar, no matter the iridescent blood of the whole village was pooling around his prey's feet, no matter the stench of ruptured bodies permeating the air, this species never ran away from his blades, but just stood there awaiting their turn, as if he wasn't killing them, but delivering them from their struggles.

What kind of species doesn't protect its own life? What kind of species welcomes death like this?

It was an abomination.

Still, Tel had lined all seventy-four heads up on one of their low retaining walls and walked down that line, finally settling on the most symmetrical skull. Even when dead, this prey's skin flayed from the skull as if in gratitude.

It was sick.

For the first time in all his hunts, Tel had gagged the littlest bit. Moral revulsion finding physical expression.

All he left behind on the planet, aside from the skulls, was a marker rolling along the top of the atmosphere, telling other Yautja not to bother. His sensors alerted him to the low-orbit moths drifting toward the curious aberration the marker must be to their antennae, but the creatures were so gossamer that, even at their size—their wingspan three times Tel's height—they wouldn't be able to alter the marker's centuries-long tumble. Probably it would punch through their wings, send them spiraling down into the gravity that would pull them apart.

Good.

The flashing of their wings had been what had lured Tel in in the first place. Let them all die, and crumble down to the planet.

Tel wiped the holo warning away, stood, and, on the way to the trophy wall, grabbed that one skull he'd kept. Standing there, however, he found there was no place for it. It would disrespect the other hunts already memorialized—this skull wasn't an artifact of another victory, but of a drop with so little challenge that it left a taste in his mouth like defeat.

After the coordinates for the next hunt were locked in—a harsh planet closer down to this planet's star , sure to have spawned a biosphere built to *survive*—Tel tossed this one example of species 76re-0 into the wire basket in the corridor, where he sometimes spat in passing, or crumbled dried blood off his wrist gauntlet.

The specifics of the system 76re-0 hailed from, along with encodings of its genetic parameters and parentage, had already been logged and transmitted, so there was no reason to save the physical proof—this skull.

It *would* be a proper insult for it to fall to pieces in that bin, though, its empty eye sockets staring out, its face coated in spit and dried blood.

Yes, a good hunt would be nice. Some *worthy* prey.

For the first two days of the trip, Tel paced the corridor, for the next three days he watched enhanced particulars of his trophy hunts, and then for the next five days, with ten yet to go, he sat at the controls and stared out into the great emptiness, imagining it as a monstrous mouth he was steering into—the ultimate trophy animal.

Each time he passed the waste bin he now considered

species 76re-0's, he dragged the claws at the end of his glove across the hard wire, loudly.

What he should have done instead of leaving a marker, he knew, was set fire to the endless forest, just to see if that would make this species scurry away.

Next time, he told himself.

Except there weren't going to be any disappointments like species 76re-0 again.

From here on out, it was just challenging prey. No more gambling that some unlikely backwater planet had, over the millennia, evolved something dangerous. No, for the next few cycles—maybe for all the cycles—Tel was only navigating to systems where life had to have evolved claws and teeth in order to survive.

Though, he had to admit, species 76re-0's eyes had been a thing of wonder.

He wondered what they had seen him as, really. If their vision flayed him down to his own skull. If that was why they stared so long: because they were processing his vascular system, his nervous system. Maybe even tracing his synapses out, and tasting his memories.

Put that kind of visual rigging on something with a will to survive, and *that's* a skull Tel would hang on his trophy wall.

If he even survived to take that trophy.

He chuckled to himself, imagining a hunt like that.

Maybe this next system would provide something along those lines, right? It was funny how, when you found yourself navigating along a corridor like he was, that the life on each next planet would share attributes with the last. Perhaps species 76re-0, with different environmental stressors, could become something formidable. Or at least something to get this bad taste out of Tel's mouth.

Passing by that basket again, Tel dragged his fingertips over the wire, rattling the whole apparatus, and he was five or eight paces down the corridor before it registered: where had those large eye sockets been?

Distinctly aware that he wasn't wearing his armor, his helmet, even his dagger, Tel stepped back, confirmed.

The skull was gone.

Tel's every sense came alive. His right hand snapped into a hard fist.

Instead of relying on his display for a reading, he flared his mandibles, sharpened his eyes, tightened his skin.

Nothing.

He was as alone as ever.

Still, the skull that was there before was most definitely not there anymore.

Tel chuckled, even grinned.

But don't get too excited, he told himself. You don't know for sure, yet.

He came back armored up, let his sensors deliver him a reading on the bin, to see if this skull, in keeping with the listlessness of its species, had given up, crumbled to dust.

Aside from Tel's own spit and the dried blood from a nasty race of cave dwellers, though, there was nothing.

All the same, Tel wrenched the bin free from its mooring on the floor and slammed it against the opposite wall, daring this insulting skull to show itself.

His howl of rage filled every corridor of the ship, and came back to him almost as loud, almost as angry.

A hunt on his own *ship*?

Why not.

In the pilot seat, he lit the console up, dialing up every internal and external sensor way past tolerance, insisting they find this lost skull.

Except they didn't. They couldn't.

Tel slammed his gauntlet down on the control board, circuity gel bleeding from the display, and, seeing that weakness, he wanted to crush it into the floor. But if he destroyed his own navigation, that would be letting this skull win. That would be losing to species 76re-0.

And that, simply, was not an option.

For the next two cycles, Tel scoured the ship from nose to tail. Every crevice, every nook, every shadow.

Then, in what felt like desperation, though he would never admit such a thing, he dialed up the internal security feeds, on a different subsystem than the sensors, since... what use is a feed of yourself impatiently waiting for the next hunt?

But, if 76re-0 could see in different spectrums, then maybe it could move among them as well. Specifically, Tel hated to admit: maybe when dead, 76re-0 could move among the less common spectrums.

What kind of a life cycle would that be, though?

It would explain why 76re-0 hadn't fought for its own life, he supposed. Death for 76re-0 could just be elevation to a different state.

If so, then perhaps 76re-0 was worthy prey after all. Perhaps the hunt had felt like failure because Tel had been hunting larvae.

At the control board, the display shuddering now from its uncorrected damage, Tel dialed and zoomed, shifted visible wavelengths, and finally caught up with himself doing this very search.

Which is when he saw it.

Not 76re-0, but the shuddering, partial display over his own shoulder.

For the flashing instant he was able to rewind to and heighten, the data he was being fed on this same screen he was looking at, it... it wasn't what the camera was now seeing. No: what the camera had *just* seen.

This could only mean... Tel shook his head no, pushed away from the console, trying to wrap his hunter's mind around it.

When that first individual 76re-0 had seen him moving in through the foliage, and instantly the rest of the village had known, they hadn't been communicating via pheromones or subvocalization, but mind-to-mind, after some fashion.

And that must be the same ability now being used against him, to obfuscate the very readings he thought he could trust.

More important, on the recording, very partial, there was a holo representation of the skull.

Only now it was encased in some organic body again.

And—how could this be? It was no longer bipedal and upright, but thick, bulging, tapering down to a sharp tail that was probably a stinger of some sort.

Tel activated his vibration scanning.

He was breathing hard now.

The hunt was on. And not only could this prey see him through walls, probably see him down to the molecular level, but it could cloud his mind, too.

Only rarely did a species turn to fight.

Only rarely did Tel ever feel a rush like this.

The profile in his system was woefully incomplete, he knew now. Evidently the seeds of this next form 76re-0 was programmed for had been embedded deep in the bone, deep enough that it went beneath notice of the scans he had made while disappointed, while insulted, while only wanting this drop to be over with.

Tel nodded to himself and lowered his visor, told it to record and then show him that recording a tenth of a second later. This meant Tel would be moving slightly in the past, which would give this next iteration of 76re-0 the advantage, but that was just the way he liked it.

He told the lights in his ship—the ones that could be adjusted—to cycle across all the wavelengths, and keep doing it until he told them to stop. His hope was one of them would throw 76re-0's shadow, which his targeting sensors could lock on.

This was a worthy prey indeed.

Tel stalked from room to room, corridor to corridor, and finally, after half a day of it, his display delivered him what he was looking for: a trail.

76re-0 left a slight depression wherever it went, evidently. As if it were scraping up the usable mass from whatever it came into contact with, and then adding it to its own.

Once Tel understood what spectrum to look for those trails in—they were everywhere.

76re-0 had been crawling over every surface of the ship, it seemed, and hiding in plain sight the whole time.

When Tel checked in on his life's work, his trophies, he could only glare and mutter curses.

All the skulls from his previous hunts were gone, were part of 76re-0, now.

He slammed the side of his fist into the wall, and, to his surprise, that wall crumbled like ash.

Whatever molecular material 76re-0 was taking from the ship was leaving it structurally compromised.

Shaking his head no, Tel raced for the controls, strapped himself into the pilot's seat, and called up readings and diagnostics, then, remembering that he couldn't trust direct data, he pulled his visor down, looked at *recordings* of those readings and diagnostics.

A tenth of a second after it was actually happening, he saw a reduction of his ship coming apart at the seams, its indigestible parts drifting away from each other like an exploded diagram.

The ship was coming apart under him, all around him.

He floated ahead, still strapped into the pilot's seat. He was in open space now.

His helmet sealed him in, fed him what breath it had, but it wasn't going to be much, Tel knew.

What it was, as it turned out, was just enough for him to see the cocoon adhered to the outside of his ship cracking open.

A wet pair of wings flopped out, then spread themselves, pulled what had been the after-death slug of 76re-0 up and out.

There wasn't enough air out here for wings to work, he didn't think, but evidently they could push against something in a spectrum Tel's visor couldn't register.

This giant flying thing flapped once, twice, and then turned, not even bothering to drop the sharp barb at the end of its tail into the chest of this Hunter drifting in open space. It just locked him in its overlarge, iridescent eyes—eyes Tel recognized, having snuffed more than a hundred and fifty of them in a single cycle.

But he could snuff these as well, he knew, take this moth with him, at least.

Working his fingers furiously on his control pad, Tel chose suicide over suffocation, but—

Instead he looked back up to those eyes of many colors, staring into his soul.

It was beautiful. It was like sleeping while awake, his whole self relaxing for what felt like the first time. His fingers slowed on the control pad and he nodded forward against his face-shield, his own eyes open to eternity, now, never to shut again.

It had been a good hunt, after all.

The worthiest of prey.

AFTERMATH

BY BRYAN THOMAS SCHMIDT

SEPTEMBER 1987

By the time he took a seat at the wooden table in the small, windowless room, Dutch Schaefer was soaked in sweat, but it wasn't because of the thirty-foot walk from his hospital room at Mountain Home, the V.A. Hospital in Johnson City, Tennessee. He could do ten times that without a second thought. He groaned and his hand went automatically to his head, even as two men in suits entered, nodding to the exiting nurse. The blond one, bearing the smugness of leadership common to ranking government officials, extended his hand.

"Major, I'm Peter Keyes," the man said, sporting a smile that was clearly intended as friendly but instead looked mildly threatening. "This is my associate, Jim Garber." The tall brunette behind him nodded, not bothering to smile.

The brunette was muscle and had the attitude to match. The blond had the quiet confidence of one in his element.

"What do you want?" Dutch asked, not even bothering with false pleasantries. His head was killing him—radiation sickness from exposure to the alien's nuclear device in Val Verde, they said. He wasn't in the mood to answer questions. Besides, he'd already told them everything he knew. It was a waste of time.

"We want to hear what happened in Val Verde," Keyes said as the two men took seats opposite him at the table.

Dutch stared at them a moment further. He had absolutely no desire to talk with government suits, especially strangers. Escaping it, radiation sickness, and the resulting PTSD—as the doctors called it—was what he'd come here to do. Reliving that nightmare was the last thing he wanted to do.

"We already talked with Miss Gonsalves, but we need to hear your perspective," Keyes continued, unperturbed by his stare.

After a few moments of staring back and forth, Dutch realized they probably weren't going away until he said at least something. *Might as well get this shit over with.* "It was a clusterfuck and I lost my entire team," Dutch growled. "We never should have been there. He lied to us."

The two suits exchanged a look.

"General Phillips?" Garber asked.

Dutch laughed. "We all know who sent me there. Conned me. Hostage rescue. We're not assassins. They sent us in there to die."

"I don't think anyone knew what to expect—" Garber started, but Keyes cut him off with a wave.

"Major, I hear you're sick. Radiation?" Keyes said in a

tone that suggested he cared, but Dutch saw in his eyes it was all an act.

"That's what they say. From the fucking device that bastard set off trying to kill us both." Dutch shifted in the chair, leaning forward on his elbows on the table. "And my head hurts. So trying to remember right now hurts."

"We'll try and make this as quick as we can," Keyes said, nodding.

"Why don't you make it later?" Dutch said, locking eyes with him.

"There may not be a later—" Garber blurted and Keyes cut him off again.

"We'd just like to hear what we can now," Keyes said. "At least get started."

Dutch chortled. It actually sounded sincere.

"But we're willing to come back as often as it takes for you to tell us everything," Keyes added, the look accompanying it making it clear he meant that too.

Dutch looked up at the fluorescent tubes lighting the room, the nondescript ceiling that perfectly matched the bare walls. "Pretty good approximation of an interrogation room considering this is a hospital."

"It's for consults. Doctor–patient privacy," Keyes said.

Dutch smiled. "Don't bullshit me. It's standard for government institutions, especially those with patients having top secret knowledge you're worried might leak."

Keyes shrugged, leaning back in his chair. "Okay, yeah. We like to take precautions. Don't you think that's wise, given what you experienced?"

"Wise was that coward Phillips sending you instead of coming himself," Dutch said. "I'm less likely to fuck you up in a blind rage, I suppose." He stared at Keyes a moment and the lackey held his gaze, unperturbed.

"Why take it out on me? I'm not responsible," Keyes said.

"We're not people you want to fuck with," Garber snapped, clearly irritated with Dutch's attitude.

The wooden chair practically squealed as Dutch pushed it backward and shot to his feet. He leaned forward, planting his fists on the table and glared at them both, his sweaty muscles glistening in the fluorescent light. "Try me, asshole." His eyes locked on Garber's and he sneered, glaring back.

Garber moved to scoot back and stand but Keyes shot him down with a look, hand gripping his forearm hard. "No one's going to fuck with anyone," he said. "We're just talking."

"Fuck you," Dutch said, turning his glare to Keyes before relaxing his shoulders and sitting back down loudly.

"You know, this would be over a lot faster if you'd cut the posturing and answer our question." Keyes showed no irritation, it was all matter-of-fact, but Dutch searched his eyes, hoping for a reaction. Nothing. The man was good, that was for sure.

"We went in to rescue three government officials from guerillas. In and out fast. Minimal contact." Dutch grinned. "Blew the fuck outta that jungle, didn't we?"

Keyes smiled. "You left an impression all right. Tell us about the creature."

Dutch sighed, resigning himself. They wouldn't give up. "That was one ugly motherfucker. Lizard skin. Seven feet tall. Some kind of cloaking device. Armor with matching facemask. And he had some kind of laser cannon—high tech, better than anything we've got—jagged blades on his wrist." He licked at his cracked lips, thinking. The scent of antiseptic and industrial cleaners that hung over everything mixed with the stale smell of dust, the odor of his own sweat, and Keyes' cologne. "He was prepared. We thought we were."

"How did he kill your men?" Keyes asked. There was no delicate way so he just said it.

"Pulverized Hawkins," Dutch said. "He was the first. There was nothing left but a bloody mass really. Not that we could see." He thought back, the images flashing through his mind and causing him to cringe involuntarily as he did. Seven years together, the brotherhood of the six. They'd all come out alive time and again. Until Val Verde. Until fucking General Phillips.

Dutch licked his lips again, his throat dry and hurting. "I could use some water."

Keyes looked at Garber. "Get the man some water."

Garber glared at Dutch a moment, trying to intimidate him, then stood, walked around the table and disappeared out the door.

"Just take your time, okay? Tell us what you remember," Keyes said, leaning back in his chair. And after Garber returned a minute later with a glass of water and a pitcher, Dutch drank, and then he did.

Later, he returned to his room in full PTSD mode, his senses heightened—every sight, scent, and touch intensified. Sitting on the hospital bed, he thought about turning on the TV to distract himself, but wasn't feeling it. He eyed the phone, but who would he call? Who could he tell? Then he overheard Keyes talking at the nurse's station outside his door. "He can't get out, right?"

"He's too sick at the moment," the head nurse said. "But when the doctor thinks he should, yes."

"I mean the doors. They're locked, right?"

"Of course. This is the special ward."

"Good. Keep him here until you hear from us."

Dutch cursed. Sent in to slaughter by a lying general and now he was a prisoner? Fucking U.S. government. To hell with them. They didn't own him. Not anymore. He'd leave any time he wanted. Tuning out the rest of the conversation, he sat up, planting his feet on the cold vinyl tile and stood, wobbling. Instinctively, his hands went to his head again. Maybe later.

Groaning, he lay back down and decided to sleep for a while. There was always later. They couldn't keep him if he didn't want to stay.

The two suits came back several times over the next few days, subjecting Dutch to hours of interrogation, despite his illness, over medical staff's objections.

"We need to know what he knows!" Keyes insisted more than once.

Garber remained hostile and impatient, while Keyes continued playing it like they had all the time in the world, even as his questions took on more and more urgency. His attitude remained respectful, however, unlike his companion's.

Dutch couldn't resist needling them a bit. He smiled and looked straight at Garber. "If this is good cop, bad cop, you suck at it, Garber."

Garber's eyes narrowed with hatred and he opened his mouth to speak.

Keyes cut him off. "No cops. We're all on the same side here, Major. Seekers of truth."

Dutch laughed. "Seekers of truth. Tell that to the General. He seems to have missed that course." Dutch wondered where Phillips was. Probably listening in somewhere close or reviewing tapes a few hours later at least. He'd want to know everything. Dutch looked up at the wall vent where he suspected the camera was hidden. "Do tell him I'd love to debrief personally… when he gets a chance." The pause left it clear the last thing on his mind was debriefing. He smiled for the camera.

The suits asked all the wrong questions, focused on the aliens as a "great find" with technology to study, but ignoring the fact that to the giant hunters, humans were prey, and it was all a game. No matter what he said, he couldn't convince them of the danger.

"There's really no need for this hostility, Major," Keyes said, never losing his cool. "As I said, we're on the same side. We both want to stop creatures like the one responsible for murdering your team from killing again. But I need your help to do it."

"Tell that to Garber here," Dutch snapped. "You're gonna need a lot of men and tech to capture one of those things. The one that got us is dead, but there will be others."

Garber and Keyes nodded in unison.

Garber grinned. "We can't wait to meet them."

Keyes took a deep breath then cleared his throat. "There have been other… encounters."

That got Dutch's attention. He stiffened in his chair. "Hunters? Creatures like that?"

"Hunter? What makes you say that?" Garber asked.

Dutch heard Billy Sole's voice in his head: "Something… in the trees."

"Those fucking eyes…" Mac had said later, when he'd seen it, too—something in the jungle, moving, stalking them.

"I drew down and fired right at it," Mac had said after the creature killed Blain. "Nothin' on this earth could have lived…"

And then he heard Billy again, "There's something out there waiting for us… it ain't no man."

They'd been hunted in Val Verde. Just like prey.

"Something my men said, back in the jungle," Dutch said, shaking off the memories. He turned to Keyes again. "There have been more?"

"We think so." Keyes looked at Garber, prompting him.

"Skinned corpses of animals—wolves, a stag, bears. Laser scorching of foliage and trees similar to those we found in Val Verde," Garber said.

"And we found some blood," Keyes said. "Green blood."

"At least, we think it's blood," Garber added.

Dutch grunted again and nodded. "It's blood. They bleed green."

Keyes smiled, this time genuinely. "Good. We're making progress. So you see, we all want the same thing."

Dutch scoffed. "No. I want my fucking men back."

After that, he resisted further questioning so they surrendered and sent him back to his room. He sat down on his bed and grabbed the tape recorder he'd requisitioned from a friend at the base before they shipped him here. Speaking into the mic, he began, "It's September 12th, 1987. My name is Major Alan Schaefer, also known as 'Dutch'…" For the next several minutes, he recorded his testimony, a kind of insurance against a government he'd once served but trusted no more.

Afterward, he lay awake for half an hour unable to nap before turning on the news while he waited for the nutritionist to bring his dinner. Clicking the button on the remote to unmute the sound, he heard the female anchor saying:

"...reports of a rogue hunter, hunting out of season. Rangers found carcasses of a bear and a mountain lion, skinned, their skulls and spines removed."

"Skulls and spines? What kind of hunters are these?" the nutritionist asked, frowning with distaste as she entered with a tray and set it on the rolling cart, then rolled it in front of Dutch on the bed.

"...Authorities found no shells and no powder on site..."

"Salisbury steak and potatoes tonight. Not bad compared to a lot of it. Should be a nice change." She smiled as she went back and retrieved apple juice, a straw, and a milk from her cart, setting them next to the tray. "Enjoy, 'kay?"

Then she whirled and headed off, closing the door behind her as the anchor finished, "...the Sheriff's office asks you to call this number"—a number flashed on the screen—"if you hear or see anything that might be related to the case."

"Sounds like someone is hunting out of season," the male anchor said with a tsk.

"Some people have no respect," the female anchor added, shaking her head.

Dutch tuned them out after that. Spines. Skulls. Skinned. It had to be. And the legend on screen had said it was taking place in Pisgah National Forest outside Asheville, North Carolina, just an hour or two south of the V.A. hospital.

He had to get out of there, go find the creature. Stop it before it killed humans like his men, maybe get a little revenge in their honor as well.

As he ate the rest of his meal, his mind turned, planning his escape. He left just enough food to enable the first phase, and when the nurse came to check on him and retrieve the tray, he faked an outburst and threw it against the wall in the corner, splattering food and the remainder of his milk and ranting like he was enraged. The nurse told him to calm down and get ahold of himself, then left seeking either reinforcements or sedatives. Dutch made sure to calm himself enough to apologize by the time she got back. Somehow, he convinced her not to sedate him, resting contritely on his bed and awaiting the inevitable orderly who'd be sent later to clean it up.

Subduing the orderly was easy. Dutch pretended to be drowsing in bed, and when the man turned his back to mop, he slipped out and knocked him cold by compressing his airflow for just long enough, then slipped him the tranquilizer Dutch had pretended to swallow earlier for the night nurse. Careful to avoid the window in the door to his room, he dragged the man into the bathroom and laid him in the bathtub, then took his keys, ID, and clothes. Luckily, they'd sent a large orderly so the clothes fit.

Grabbing the bag from the closet containing his civvies and wallet, Dutch then slipped out of the room and hurried off down the hall with a mumbled comment about "What a mess. Gotta change the water," as he hurried away from the nurse's station and out the locked door at the end of the hall. He raced down the stairs as fast as he could, slipping out into the parking lot, and hurried off into the night.

Yuahro left the corpse of his latest kill and carried his trophy off into the night with a satisfied roar. His first solo hunt—a test of his skills every Yautja Youngblood faced—had occurred without problems. His mother had been worried because he was younger than most who went off solo, but Yuahro protested. He was ready.

His father, T'an'tath, had laughed. "He's got the family blood," he roared. Yuahro came from a long line of honored Hunters. No bad bloods or missteps among them. "He'll make us proud!"

So Yuahro had gone solo, and now he would prove himself. So far he'd bagged two large predators—one a cat, and now an antlered animal—and he was feeling quite proud. The next night his father would come back for him and he would be ready with many trophies to prove he'd become an adult… blooded. Other clans had different rituals, but these would satisfy his.

The site had been carefully chosen. A wooded area on mountain slopes far enough from any population centers to make avoiding soft meat not only possible but likely, especially this time of year. Soft meat might be the ultimate worthy challenge, but even T'an'tath had warned him he wasn't quite ready for that prey. The air was filled with the scent of sap from trees, animal dung and sweat, and pollen from whatever grasses and flowers were blooming. The temperatures at night dropped precipitously, and there were traces of white, frozen liquid on the ground in places—a sharp contrast to homeworld that, though Yautja could survive conditions far more extreme than humans might, had forced Yuahro to sleep aboard his shuttle instead of in trees or foliage as warriors did in warmer climes. But it was all part of the adventure, wasn't it? Proving one's mettle? You survived and hunted, whatever obstacles and circumstances arose in your path. You did so without complaint, with honor. And Yuahro had done so. Yes. He could hold his head up strong when his father returned.

Now, winding his way along the already familiar trails he'd hunted the past two days and nights, he chittered happily as he imagined how many more trophies he might acquire before his father's return if he skipped sleep and worked through the night. Could he push through the bitter cold? Perhaps use thermal attachments stored on the ship to warm his armor? The netting on his limbs wasn't keeping him warm. He knew he could while away the coldest hours at rest, but his strong desire was to spend as much time as he could on the hunt while he awaited T'an'tath. And so he determined to push himself to new lengths.

That, after all, was what the first solo hunt was all about.

"What do you mean he escaped?!" Keyes barely managed to hold back from yelling at the head nurse, who sternly stared at him across the nurse's station. Jessica, her name tag read, and though he hardly cared, he knew a switch in tactics was in order if he wanted the information he needed. "Jessica," he took a deep breath, softening his tone. "How did he escape?"

"He knocked out an orderly who was in his room cleaning up a mess he'd made during an outburst after dinner, and took the man's keys and uniform. We suspect he faked the outburst," the head nurse said, her own tone softening in response. "The orderly awoke in the tub and called for help about two hours later, and that's when we discovered the Major had disappeared."

Keyes felt Garber bristle beside him and shot his aide a calming look. "No cameras or personnel reported seeing him?"

She shook her head. "It was late, just before lights out. He was dressed as an orderly. Fewer of them at night. Lighter shifts overall."

Keyes got the message and turned to Garber, who stood at his side, face twisted like he'd just sucked on a lemon. "Get word out to local law enforcement. Anyone sighted hitchhiking, leaving the hospital, wandering the area in an orderly's uniform…"

"Got it," Garber said and reached for the nearest phone.

Keyes had started for the stairs, when he remembered to stop and ask, "How's the orderly?"

Jessica shrugged. "Fine. The Major knocked him out by compressing his airflow and slipping him a tranquilizer but not a scratch."

Keyes grunted. Of course he did. Then he headed for the stairs. It would be a long night for OWLF and local law enforcement.

Mama's Diner was an all-American classic sitting at the corner of Interstate 26 and County Road RR outside Weaverville, North Carolina. Silver metal exterior with red vinyl booths and stools inside, the place smelled of grease, eggs, breakfast meat and coffee, as any good diner should. Dutch entered and made his way to the counter, taking a seat on an isolated stool near the end just to the right of two local hunters.

"Did you hear they found another one?" one said to his companion. "This time a stag."

"Skinned and everything?" his companion asked and received a nod in return. "What the hell does the guy want with hides and spines to leave all that meat wastin'?" He gave a disgusted shake of his head. Porcelain and glass clanked from the kitchen over the sound of sizzling bacon on a grill.

"I heard he takes a little, maybe enough for one meal," said the waitress.

"Who the hell does that?" said the first hunter.

"I don't know, but it gets weirder," the waitress said with a slight twang to her voice. Her ponytail held up in a bun behind her head by a hairnet, she looked to be in her fifties, slightly overweight, and spoke through a huge wad of gum she was constantly chewing. She leaned forward across the counter slightly, her voice lowered to a whisper. "We had Feds in here early this morning, around five, asking some odd questions. Showed up in a helicopter and landed right out there across the highway." She motioned with a nod of her head.

Both hunters looked off in that direction as if the Feds and their aircraft might still be there.

"What would Feds want with a rogue hunting investigation? Thought the rangers and state police were on it?" the first hunter asked.

Dutch cleared his voice and added a slight twang as he said, "I sure hope that bastard doesn't screw things up for the rest of us. I'm just down here for the weekend to get a little quail and rabbit. Last thing I need are cops chasing off the game and hassling me."

The three locals glanced over at him and then exchanged amused looks with each other.

"You just stay the hell away from Mount Mitchell and you should be fine, pal," the first hunter said as the others nodded. "So far, all the finds have been on Mitchell or in the immediate surroundings."

"Plenty of small game elsewhere," his companion added. "Maybe try north of 197. That should be far enough from Mitchell no one will bother you."

"Okay, thanks a lot," Dutch said with a smile as the waitress filled his coffee mug.

"What ya havin'?" she asked as the two hunters launched into a debate of the best spots to hunt various small game.

Dutch ordered and sat there, feeling pleased. Finding his destination had been far easier than he'd expected. Now he just had to find a vehicle to borrow with some hunting gear—a rifle or two. That could wait until he'd eaten.

Two rangers glanced up from their desks as a helicopter landed just north of their parking lot and three men in suits hopped out and ran bent over out of range of the propellers then straight for them. The rangers had been overwhelmed since news of the rogue hunter broke and knew trouble they didn't need when they saw it.

As the three men entered and hurried toward the desk, the rangers quickly went back to work, making it clear they were too busy to be bothered. The ranger station was crowded with desks and file cabinets, paperwork stacked everywhere. It clearly was a place the public rarely visited unless they had a specific need.

The blond leader tossed a photo atop the mess on the

closest ranger's desk. "Federal Agents Keyes and Garber. We're looking for this man."

"Haven't seen him," said Ortiz, the ranger who was sitting there.

"You barely looked," Garber growled.

"We're kinda busy with a bigger problem," said the other, Briggs.

"A bigger problem than a federal fugitive?" Garber snapped.

"Unless the fugitive is an animal killer, yes," said Ortiz.

"Look, the man could be dangerous," Keyes said, still the picture of patience. "He escaped from the special ward up at Mountain Home in Johnson City, and he may have come down this way."

The rangers sighed and looked up at the photo, Briggs even standing and coming over to Ortiz's desk for a better look. "Nope," they both said in unison.

"Where are you looking for that rogue hunter?" Keyes asked.

"Most of the sightings were around Mount Mitchell," Briggs replied.

"But that's a bit off the path unless you have reason to go there," Ortiz added.

"Like hiding from the Feds?" Garber said.

Keyes turned to the third Fed, who was waiting by the door. "Get your men ready. We're going to make a sweep."

The Fed nodded and hurried outside where two black SUVs with tinted windows had now appeared in the lot, not far from the chopper, waiting.

The rangers exchanged an annoyed look, then Ortiz said, "This is local jurisdiction. We'd really appreciate it if you'd stay out of the way."

"We're just gonna make a quick sweep," Keyes said with a grin. "And we have a chopper. Maybe we can help each other." Ortiz started to protest but Keyes cut him off, taking in the name plate sewn onto the right pocket of his uniform, "Besides, Ranger Ortiz, you don't really have a choice." All semblance of friendliness disappeared from his face as he slipped a business card from his pocket and laid it on the desk. "You might want to post that and have people keep a look out. Have someone call us if you see him. Thanks."

And with that he and Garber whirled and ran back out toward the helicopter.

"Fuckin' Feds," Ortiz said, shaking his head.

After leaving the diner, Dutch got lucky and found a pickup with a scoped Remington 700 and ammo parked around the corner out of sight. The owner made it easy. It was unlocked with the keys above the visor. Typical country folk, he thought and laughed. He commandeered it and headed off for Mount Mitchell. As he started it up, the radio blasted country music and he laughed again, and, deciding to go with the flow, sang along with Hank Williams as he took off down the road.

Following blue roads on the map, he was able to avoid the main highway and make his way up onto the mountain fairly quickly and easily, with no sign of pursuing Feds or other authorities. At this point, he cared very little what they did to him as long as he got the chance to stop the alien, if indeed there was one, before it could hurt anyone.

Ditching the pickup on the side of the road as he reached a trailhead that went straight up the mountain about half a mile from the peak, he grabbed the ammo and the scoped rifle and headed off into the woods. The air was cool and crisp and filled with the smell of pines, sap, and the beginnings of spring pollen as plants started to reestablish themselves through the thawing ground. He saw occasional clumps of snow as he climbed. Within half an hour, he'd spotted a patch of snow with red stains and then the corpse of a bear nearby. Overhead was a pattern of broken branches and at the base of one tree an odd footprint with clawed toes.

He bent to examine the footprints and smiled. "Got you, you son of a bitch," he mumbled.

Continuing on, he soon located the flagged location of another of the abandoned carcasses and then another. The alien seemed to be hunting in a circle, sticking to a band about a quarter-mile below the peak and zigzagging across as it searched for prey. He stopped to inspect footprints and odd broken branches overhead, recalling the similar signs they'd found in Val Verde.

"Where are you, motherfucker?" he said aloud at one point as he glanced around, focusing his eyes and trying to note any distortions in the air—signs of the creature in cloaked mode watching him—but saw nothing.

At one point, he stopped and admired the Remington. He hadn't really looked at it closely when he requisitioned it, just made sure it was loaded and in working order. It was a fairly new Remington 700 model featuring a hand-carved wooden stock with symmetrical two-lug bolt action and a black Cerakoted barrel—a beautifully crafted firearm, if you admired such things. Dutch had never used one but noted the safety and this appeared to have the longer 27-inch barrel and be a police issue, so it would be closer to the military-issue weapons he was used to. He felt a bit of excitement at trying out one of the latest models.

Satisfied he was ready for any confrontation, he continued on.

Yuahro finished the last of the fresh deer meat he'd saved from his catch the night before and chittered happily as he glanced again at the trophies adorning his chest and waist. He'd captured three smaller animals and two medium-sized ones overnight, including a very vicious wild dog that fought hard, and a hairy animal with sharp tusks that had managed to gore him once in the thigh. Just remembering, he rubbed at the pain. He'd been able to seal the wound and treat it and it was already healing. He had a scar now, an additional trophy of his first hunt, and one he'd carry with him for life as a constant reminder. He laughed. The first of many trophies made him feel like a real warrior at last.

Hearing bustling in some branches overhead he looked up and spotted a large brown cat slinking along, stalking him. He sighed, chittering. These animals had proven not to be the challenge he'd hoped for. Despite his father's warnings, he wanted prey against which he could prove his mettle—something the others would talk about for years to come. He tossed the remnants of his meal in some brush and uncloaked so the cat could see him better. First, he had to deal with the immediate problem. "M-di h'chak," he whispered. *No mercy*. Then he braced himself for the fight to come.

The cat leaped, flying through the air. Yuahro spread his legs and arms and braced for the impact. It landed at his feet, claws extended. Yuahro grabbed hold of the beast by its flank and shoulders as it scratched at him with razor-sharp claws, snarling and biting. He extended his wrist gauntlet. The cat leapt at him. The blades cut into its flesh immediately, causing it to scream. It writhed, knocking Yuahro off balance. Then they were on the ground, rolling and wrestling. The cat was relentless, ignoring its wounds and going continually for his throat. Yuahro was thankful the bio-helmet and armor protected him.

He felt pain as the animal tore at the flesh of his forearm and scratched his chest and belly. Instinctually, he wished he could use the plasmacaster, but that was impossible at such close range. Instead, he reached toward its belly with his wrist gauntlet, slicing through flesh again. The cat screamed as its stomach ripped open. Despite its thrashing and roars, this prey was no challenge. A true blood warrior deserved better. It was time to find a real challenge, something like he'd never faced before.

Dutch located the third ranger flag and several small animal carcasses within an hour of his arrival, and now he'd found the carcass of a wild boar, skinned and hung from a tree, its spine and skull ripped free. What really interested him was the glowing green fluorescent blood he saw on the bark below the corpse. The boar had wounded the hunter, and Dutch found that pleased him quite a bit.

He'd bent to inspect the site when he heard a familiar chittering and then the scream of a wild cat from not too far away, followed by the sounds of a struggle. He jumped to his feet and raced through the brush, hoping to position himself well with the scope to get his own prey quickly. As he ran, he heard the chatter of human voices approaching through the woods and then the unmistakable beating of air from a chopper's blades and the hum of its engines overhead. The Feds.

Dutch reached the edge of a clearing to see the creature and a bobcat locked in a hand-to-claw struggle on the ground. He looked around but any sniper's roost was too far to get to quickly and he couldn't chance the creature getting away. Here would have to do.

The bobcat had drawn blood like the boar, though it was wounded, its flanks and stomach ripped open. Dutch stayed back, positioning himself with the rifle and taking careful aim. The cat and the creature both paused a moment at the sound of the chopper passing overhead, looking up. And then the voices of men drew nearer, and the creature used the distraction to reach up and slit the bobcat's throat, holding tightly onto it until it ceased its struggle, then pulling to its feet, and ripping the skin from its trophy as it let out a triumphant roar.

Dutch took aim, unnoticed, and fired just as the creature ripped the spine and skull in one piece from his prey with incredible speed. It screamed as a bullet entered its shoulder then turned and saw Dutch as he fired another shot that hit its thigh.

"That's for Mac and Blain and Pancho and Hawkins, you son of a bitch!" Dutch shouted.

The creature dropped its trophy and sprinted toward Dutch with surprising speed. Having faced one of these bastards before, Dutch had no desire to do so up close and hand-to-hand if it could be avoided, so he turned and ran, hoping to regroup or at least get the advantage.

The creature fired blue bursts from its shoulder cannon, and the ground and trees and brush around him exploded, set aflame. Dutch just continued running.

The pilot circled the chopper over Mount Mitchell. Keyes and Garber watched through binoculars, spotting Zeller from the local office and two teams of men, but no Schaefer or alien. Then they heard the distinct sound of a rifle blast as they came over a clearing and the pilot, Percival, shouted, "Down there!"

Both looked down to see the alien scream as it held up the carcass of a bobcat it had just skinned, even as another round struck it again.

Garber spotted the Major in the trees below, holding a rifle, even as the creature sprinted toward him with surprising speed. "Schaefer!" he called and pointed. "And one of the creatures, too! This is our big chance."

"Call in the men," Keyes ordered Garber, who got on the radio as Keyes leaned toward the pilot. "Get us down closer and look for a safe place to put her down."

Percival nodded. "Not much to work with, but will do."

Dutch raced through the trees, hearing branches break and brush crackling behind him as the creature gave chase.

Reaching the top of a rise, he spun and looked back, but the creature had disappeared. Cloaked!

"Come out and play fair, you son of a bitch!" he yelled, then raised the rifle, scanning for any sign of distortion in the air.

The hum and chop of the 'copter overhead continued, even as he heard men shouting orders and calling in response.

"Come on, let's finish this, you ugly fuck!" he taunted.

Then he was tackled from the side, and the rifle flew out of his hands as he struggled against the cloaked seven-foot force of alien muscle that had hold of him and was pushing him down to the ground.

They landed with the alien on top and Dutch reached down to draw the hunting knife from his belt, stabbing at where the creature's arms and chest seemed to be. It screamed and he saw the glow of its green blood, then cried out as its blades cut into his own forearm and the creature was upon him.

"Go to hell, you son of a bitch!"

Dutch grabbed its shoulders and pushed, then they were rolling, still fighting and struggling as they went, each wounding the other. Stabbing, punching, kicking. Pain blossomed all over his body, but Dutch would not lose again.

As they hit a slope, they rolled, picking up speed, and crashed hard into a copse of pines, knocking the wind out of Dutch. The Major rolled off the creature as they both gasped for air, and then turned, noting its cloaked form distorting the air.

"Come out and fight where I can see you, you bastard!" he taunted.

As if it understood, the creature uncloaked and they stared at each other a moment, each sizing up their opponent.

"That's right. I fought your brother," Dutch spat defiantly at the creature. "Or was it your father? He died. Now it's your turn."

The creature emitted a laugh-like chitter and rushed him again, but Dutch bent and grabbed a thick, fallen branch, swinging it around in one smooth motion to slam the alien in the side of the face. It screamed.

Dutch dove to the side and swiped at it with his knife, implanting the blade in its shoulder. It screamed and pounded with its fist at the hand holding the blade. Dutch yanked and pushed simultaneously, forcing the blade in further and the creature's screams grew louder. "I want my men back, you fuck!"

The creature yanked the blade free and threw the knife aside, punching Dutch in the stomach and cutting him across the chest with its wrist blades. Dutch's screams joined that of his opponent as they dove into each other and fell to the ground, rolling again.

Zeller raced through the woods, his team following as two more converged in groups of three from other directions. Topping a rise, he saw Dutch Schaefer and the alien roaring as they rolled and struggled, and grabbed his radio. "We've got Schaefer, confirmed, and the alien, too, sir."

"Don't let them kill each other," Keyes ordered back. "We want that creature alive too!"

Zeller stopped and cocked his M24 sniper rifle, motioning to his two men. "Get in position and see if you can wound or immobilize that creature but don't kill it."

They grunted in affirmation and moved off as he keyed the radio and relayed the same orders to his other teams.

Dutch and the alien spotted the Feds with rifles at the same time and both rolled downhill, seeking to move themselves away and out of range.

"He's mine!" Dutch called out, but doubted they heard him as it came out in a jumble amidst panting breaths and grunts of pain as he rolled against fresh wounds.

"Got it in my sights," called Pereira as he locked his M24 on target.

"Me, too," Clark echoed.

Zeller lined up his own shot as he called, "Fire!"

Green streaks of light appeared and the world exploded around them. A tree beside him burst into flames from an explosion.

"What the fuck?" Pereira said as he ducked for cover.

Zeller and Clark were too busy dodging clear to respond but Zeller looked up and saw some sort of spacecraft hovering overhead, weapons aimed at them, and then the laser cannons fired again. Pereira screamed as his chest exploded open and he fell back, a bloody mass.

"Holy shit!" Clark spat.

"Let's get Schaefer and get outta here," Zeller ordered.

"What the fuck?" Garber yelled as trees exploded below and they saw what appeared to be laser fire.

He and Keyes turned and spotted the alien ship at the same time and then it was firing at them, too. Garber pulled out a rifle and was attaching a scope.

"Son of a bitch!" Percival called out. "Who's shooting at us?"

"Take her back up! Get us clear!" Keyes ordered.

The pilot was complying even before Keyes got all the words out.

Dutch continued punching and stabbing at the creature even as the mountainside around them erupted with laser fire and explosions that set trees and brush ablaze.

"I guess your friends are back," Dutch mumbled as the alien stabbed him again and then he was screaming, "Fuck you!"

"Major!" someone called.

Dutch glanced over to see one of Keyes' men motioning to him. They looked ridiculous traipsing through the woods in suits with rifles. He almost laughed but then the alien punched him again and he rolled, trying to get free.

"If it bleeds, we can kill it!" Dutch yelled, but the Feds were preparing to run, rifles lowered. "God damn it! Shoooooot!"

"We're just here for you. We don't have the firepower," the man yelled back.

The creature, meanwhile, had spotted the alien ship overhead and took off into the trees, headed up hill. A couple of rifle shots echoed from overhead—the chopper shooting after it.

"God damn it!" Dutch yelled and took off in pursuit, the Fed calling after him. As he ran, the creature cloaked again, but Dutch kept his eyes on the movement of brush and branches in its path and followed in its wake.

"Fuck!" Keyes cursed as Garber got off a couple shots from

his rifle. This mission had gone all to hell quickly. As much as he wanted to capture an alien, it might have to wait. His radio beeped. "Go!"

"He declined to come with us, sir," Zeller reported.

"What?" Keyes shouted back. "Where is he?"

"Chasing the alien," Zeller replied, short of breath as if he were running. "And we lost Pereira, sir."

"God damn it!" Keyes shouted as Garber fired again out the open side door.

"Shouldn't we capture the alien, sir?" Garber asked as he lined up another shot.

"There'll be other chances. When we've had time to better prepare," Keyes said, cutting him off, then turned to Percival. "Follow Schaefer up that mountain. I want him. He's the priority."

"What about the alien ship?" Percival objected.

Keyes slammed his fist into the back of the pilot's seat. "It's chasing him, too. Just do it!"

The chopper turned and headed up the mountain, following the Major as he ran through the trees below.

"Shit. I want that alien," Garber muttered, lowering the rifle.

"Me, too, but alive, and with us living to tell about it," Keyes replied.

As they topped a rise and left the cover of trees for a huge clearing, the creature turned and fired laser bursts from its shoulder cannon at Dutch, who tucked and somersaulted to the side, then landed on his feet and started running again. Ahead, the alien craft was lowering to the ground and the creature was heading straight for it. Dutch had to beat it there!

The alien craft began firing bursts from its own cannon, lighting up the ground around Dutch and sending flaming dirt and brush flying around him.

"God damn it! Come back and fight, you pussy!" he screamed as he ran.

Then the chopper was there, hovering, coming lower. And he saw Keyes leaning out even as the air stirred around him from the blades and he felt the ground vibrating.

"It's over, Major," Keyes shouted. "Get to the chopper and come home."

Dutch didn't even glance over. He continued running, shouting, "Fuck you, Keyes!"

"You'll get another chance," Keyes shouted as the chopper's skis touched earth and the ground around it exploded with a near miss from the alien ship's laser cannon. "I promise!"

Dutch hesitated and saw the frightened eyes of the chopper pilot peering out at him through the canopy as the alien ship fired again. The pilot spun the chopper just in time, but the burst sideswiped its tail, shaking the airship and leaving scorch marks on its fuselage.

Keyes leaned out the open rear door, Garber watching over his shoulder. "Come on!"

"Fuck you!" Dutch turned and ran after the creature.

The alien ship set down at the top of the hill and a ramp lowered, another alien appearing.

Dutch grabbed the knife from his belt and stopped, throwing it at the retreating creature's back. It flew through the air almost in slow motion, straight on target, then a blast from the new alien's shoulder cannon knocked it aside. Dutch growled his frustration as the aliens joined each other by the ship and turned back to fire at him with side-by-side cannons.

"Come on, Major!" Keyes called again through a loudspeaker from behind as the whirring of the chopper floated across the clearing.

Dutch ducked and rolled as two more laser bursts exploded at his feet. His weapons were gone and now there were two. Screaming in rage, he turned and ran back toward the chopper.

Keyes grabbed his hand and pulled him aboard even as the chopper started lifting, again swerving violently to avoid a blast from the alien ship's cannons, and they both looked back to see the alien hunter running up a ramp onto its ship, which also took off, firing a couple more warning bursts at the chopper as it raced across the field in the opposite direction toward safety.

"You made the right choice, Major," Keyes said, smiling as Dutch sunk onto the bench across from him, looking defeated.

"Fuck you!" Dutch said, still frustrated and torn. A creature like that had killed the five of the best men he'd ever known, butchered them like animals. He'd wanted that alien so bad. Wanted to hurt it more. Savor its pain. "Take me back! There's more of them out there. We have to stop them."

"That's what we're here for," Garber said and smiled.

"You should work with us," Keyes said. "They formed OWLF just for this purpose."

Dutch glanced over and watched the alien ship disappearing in the distance in the opposite direction from the chopper. He'd lost his chance. His shoulders sank as he finally took a deep breath and leaned back on the bench against the chopper's rear wall. He shook his head. "We want different things."

"It's who we are. Other World Lifeforms Taskforce," Keyes explained. "They want us to capture one of the aliens. Learn everything we can. Capture its technology. Learn to protect ourselves."

Dutch locked eyes with Keyes and saw he was dead serious, then started laughing. "You're fucking insane. You know that?" he finally said.

"We have unlimited resources," Garber said, blanching at the mockery. "Anything we need."

"We can get this done, Dutch," Keyes said, trying a friendlier approach. "But we need your help. Let's work together."

"Hell no. I'm done with the government," Dutch said, shaking his head.

"You don't have to be. You know they'll be back," Keyes insisted.

"And we'll be ready," Garber added.

Keyes leaned forward and tapped the pilot on the shoulder. "Take us to the nearest E.R. so we can get him cleaned up."

"Yes, sir," the pilot nodded and servos whined as the pilot adjusted the controls readying the chopper to lift off again.

Suddenly, Dutch stood and hopped down onto the landing gear of the chopper.

"What are you doing?" Garber demanded, reaching for his weapon, but Keyes reached out a hand to stop him.

"I can take care of myself," Dutch said.

Keyes leaned back in his own seat again and nodded to Dutch. "You think about it. You'll change your mind."

Dutch chuckled and shook his head as he examined himself, checking his wounds. "I don't think so."

"Sure you will," Keyes said. "Where will you go?"

He had to get back to Val Verde, that he knew. He'd heard rumors there were stories about "demons who make trophies of men" and he wanted to hear them for himself. Dutch smiled and thought about his brother John, a cop in New York City. Perhaps he could go there first. The two hadn't seen each other in a long time. His brother would never believe this—whatever Dutch could even tell him since it was technically classified "Top Secret."

He had a sister, too, somewhere. And he had a few friends left. Old buddies from Nam. A few from whatever normal life he'd once had, too. He watched the trees and landscape shimmer below him as the chopper began to hover. Whatever he decided, it wouldn't be today, and it wouldn't be for an asshole like Keyes. Fuck that. He'd had enough of lying government scum.

He focused his eyes on the distance once more and noted no sign of the aliens or their ship. Someday, you son of a bitch. Someday. He promised himself.

"Take us up," he heard Garber order the pilot, circling his index finger in the air.

As the chopper started lifting again, Dutch closed his eyes and stepped off. Fuck talk. It was time to hunt.

PROVING GROUND

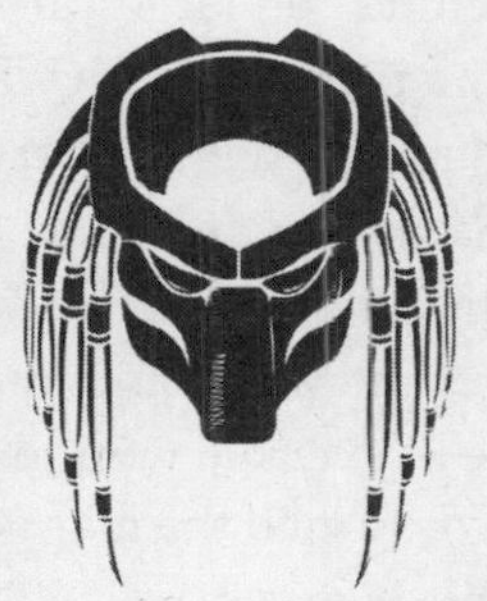

BY LINDA D. ADDISON

A'kael scraped the claws of her feet on the ground and jumped off the highest boulder ledge on the training field. She somersaulted in the air, threw the knife at the target held by the trainee Yautja and landed on her feet. The blade went deep into the wood panel, nicking one of the fingers of the young Yautja, who didn't flinch, but simply pulled the knife out, bowed, and handed it to A'kael as she walked past. A'kael made a note of her calm reaction. Someone to keep an eye on for the next training group she took out for their first hunt.

Jogging on the gravel path back to her clan's stone building complex, she was ready for a meal, but decided to first visit Elder Zan'tih, the clan's leader. Walking through the carved stone hallways, she wanted to ask him about going on a hunt. She had not been off planet for many months and was ready to do more than train first hunters on their homeworld. It was time to add to her extensive trophy collection.

Stepping into the large room where Zan'tih worked, she thought at first he wasn't there, but then got a glimpse of a body on the floor behind the large carved desk. A'kael ran over and checked for a pulse. Zan'tih was thei-de.

A'kael stood and roared with all her breath and strength. Others came running as the death cry echoed through the building. Three elders entered and helped her carry Zan'tih to the examiner's room, who quickly confirmed that his death wasn't because of external wounds. A scan of his blood and internal organs confirmed the manner of death was from a tear in the wall of his heart.

After Zan'tih's death ritual other elders, elite and ancient Yautja gathered in a meeting chamber to discuss who would next lead the clan.

Bachaann, an elite Yautja, took the center of the room. "I am one of the top elite. I want to be clan leader."

A'kael stood. "Zan'tih and I had many conversations about my becoming clan leader one day."

Bachaann said, "He was your great-grandfather."

A'kael's mandibles flared. "Don't disrespect my blood relation to Zan'tih." She turned to the council. "You all know Zan'tih, the warrior he was and the warrior I am."

She stepped toward Bachaann, hand on the knife at her waist. "Do you think I stole my trophies?"

Before Bachaann could react, a smart disc whistled through the air and landed in the ground between them, thrown by Elder Mi'thielth.

"You are both worthy candidates for clan leader,"

Mi'thielth said. "Wait outside while we talk."

In the hallway Bachaann explained, "I meant no disrespect. I was stating a fact."

A'kael leaned against the stone wall, folded her arms, and looked past him at the rising sun framed by the window at the end of the hall. This was too important to be distracted by his words. After many talks with her great-grandfather, A'kael had a feeling about how the council would decide who would be the best clan leader.

Sound dampers kept them from hearing the conversation until an elite Yautja came to the entrance and waved them back into the room.

Mi'thielth stood in the center of the chamber. "Being a leader of a clan is based on leadership skills as well as fighting. There is no doubt you are both fierce hunters and highly valued trainers, but we need to see your decision-making with others. You will each have a team of three first hunters under your guidance. We will look for more than the usual worthy kills and trophies. It is important how you manage your team under conditions that can't be controlled, and the manner of your charges' survival or honorable death. If either of you die, the other will immediately be clan leader."

A'kael wasn't surprised. She also expected Bachaann to accept this approach. Arguing with the council on such an important decision was more than disrespectful, it could result in being exiled.

"Where will this test take place?" Bachaann asked.

"Tomorrow, the clan's mothership will take you to a star system," Mi'thielth said. "You will each take a shuttle to the planet we have selected for the test. You can pick two of the three young Yautja for your team, the third will be selected by the council. You will find out your destination when you arrive. Is this acceptable?"

They both lowered their head and eyes in acquiescence and left the meeting hall.

A'kael paced back and forth in her living space. Her wish of going off homeworld was coming true at the cost of her great-grandfather's life. If she couldn't hunt with him again, she'd perform well in his honor, to become the clan leader.

After contacting her strongest two unbloodied, A'kael packed her weapons and armor, ate a quick meal, and went to bed.

The two young Yautja A'kael chose waited in the hall outside her living space. She waved them in and checked the wristblades and other tools they carried for the trip. She picked a couple of choice trophies to adorn her chest and shoulder plates.

"You are the better leader," Thwutha said. "I will do everything I can for the council to see that truth."

He had always been overly eager. Va'kal'jaad was shorter and quieter, but focused. She knew what he thought without him speaking. Even though Thwutha and Va'kal'jaad were first hunters, they were the best she had trained on Yautja Prime.

"Your words will not prove my skills. Action will." A'kael walked out the door. They followed her to the mothership.

Bachaann stood to the left of the entrance of the mothership talking to his two charges. A'kael and he nodded to each other.

Mi'thielth walked down the ship's ramp, followed by two young Yautja. One joined A'kael, the other Bachaann.

A'kael was pleased it was Pa'jaadh, the young one who had impressed her yesterday on the training ground.

"May you both complete the mission with honor!" Mi'thielth said. He entered the mothership first, both teams following him.

The clan's ship came out of the wormhole into a solar system A'kael recognized, near the third planet from the sun. She watched their approach on the screen of her shuttle inside the mothership. Earth. Zan'tih would have been gratified. He'd collected many valuable trophies from this planet, as had she. The ooman skull on her left shoulder was obtained during an early hunt on this planet with him.

Although most pyode amedha were barely worth killing, there were warriors among them that made the hunts worthy, as well as some of the more fierce wildlife. It had been a while since her last time on Earth; she wondered what new technology they had developed. Like her own people, they were always looking for more efficient, deadly weapons.

"What kind of challenge is this?" Thwutha asked. "I hear these soft meat are easily frightened and killed."

A'kael looked at Pa'jaadh. "What do you think?"

"History has shown that their military continually develop armor, weapons, and surveillance; this makes some of them a worthy challenge."

"That is true," Va'kal'jaad said.

Thwutha's mandibles flared, but he said nothing more.

A light flashed overhead, signaling an incoming message.

"As you see, the test will take place on Earth." Elder

Mi'thielth's voice came through the speaker. "There is a military location where the pyode amedha have been testing newly developed weapons and technology that could make a hunt interesting. The coordinates have been programmed into your shuttles. We will observe your progress from here. Prepare for planetfall."

Both shuttles were released at the same time. As they entered Earth's atmosphere, there was an explosion at the rear of Bachaann's shuttle, causing it to veer off course.

A'kael deactivated the automated navigator and followed his shuttle as it spiraled to the ground. Sensors on her control panel showed major systems were failing from the explosion. She hoped he could find a way to land somewhere safely. This wasn't how A'kael wanted to win, there was no honor in a crash making her leader.

She was relieved when Bachaann's shuttle stopped wildly hurtling to Earth, but clearly he wasn't going to be able to land at the prearranged location. Fortunately it was still cloaked as it crash-landed through the roof of an abandoned building in Salvador, Brazil, a continent away from the chosen military base.

There were no calls for help from Bachaann, as expected for an elite Yautja. Her long-distance scanners detected that he and his three charges were alive, although one of the Young's vital signs were weak. The test would continue.

Bachaann's shuttle broke through the roof and second floor of the building in the shantytown known as Calabar. It settled in the basement. He released his seat restraints and stood to check his charges. Do'tah and Zuhra unlatched their securing restraints and rushed to check on Gan'touh-De, the Young assigned to him by the council, who was pinned to his seat by a large metal shard from the shuttle's ceiling. Green phosphorescent blood was gushing from his chest, even though he was still conscious.

Bachaann checked Gan'touh-De's vitals, but the feedback to his bio-helmet was clear. He might have had a chance on the mothership, but there was no equipment here that could save the young Yautja.

Zuhra pulled out his medicomp, but Bachaann shook his head and said, "Stay with him."

Bachaann turned his attention to the ship's status; the main control panel flashed as multiple systems were offline.

"Were we hit by a weapon from the pyode amedha?" asked Do'tah.

"I don't know." Bachaann quickly studied a three-dimensional view of the engine area. The original explosion started inside the ship. He'd checked every system on the shuttle last night; if there had been a weakness this big the system would have reported it. The next possibility was sabotage!

He didn't believe it was A'kael. Even though he tried to unsettle her yesterday at the council meeting, there was no question she was a top hunter and would never do something so dishonorable and obvious. It had to be one of her charges gone rogue. If this was true both teams were in more danger than they knew.

Suddenly, the command panel began sparking, its display flashing. Do'tah checked the readout. "The shuttle's cloaking function is failing. There are many pyode amedha dwelling nearby."

A familiar beeping started.

Bachaann looked at Do'tah. "Did you active the self-destruct?"

"No, the self-destruct countdown function started on its own." Do'tah pressed several buttons on the command panel. "It's set for implode. I can't stop it."

Gan'touh-De struggled to take off his bio-helmet, letting it drop to the floor. "You have to go," he uttered with difficulty. "The shuttle can't be seen."

Bachaann saw no other choice. "Your clan will know of your bravery."

The other two first hunters turned on their cloaking and quickly exited the shuttle. Before Bachaann left he removed his bio-helmet and touched forehead to forehead with the dying Young. "I believe one of our own sabotaged the shuttle."

"If this is true, the coward will face me." Bachaann rushed out. He climbed with the other two out of the building, putting distance between themselves and the shuttle.

Cloaked, they watched from the small woods nearby as electricity sparked blue inside the building. Bachaann roared as the implosion caused the walls to collapse inward.

Frania held tight onto her grandson's arm as they made their way down the makeshift stone steps to the old church. She had to stop every few steps to catch her breath.

Halfway down, Gino made her sit to rest. "I don't know why you have to come here in the middle of the night, avó."

"I had a dream." She made the sign of the cross. "Something evil is coming. We need to light a candle to pray for protection, for all of us."

"That old church is falling down. It's not safe to go in, especially at night."

"It's holding up, like our homes here in the favela, pieces put together with love."

"Yes, you're right, avó." He sat down next to her.

The full moon made the white walls of the church glow below them. Beyond the church, past the ledge to the beach, the moon was mirrored in the Atlantic Ocean.

Before they could stand up and continue down the stairs there was a loud crash as the roof of the church caved in.

Frania closed her eyes and crossed herself again. "It is too late—it's here."

Gino wrapped his arm around her. "There's nothing here except a building that is tired of standing. At least we weren't in it when…What is that light?" He stared at spots of flashing blue light from the center of the debris.

"We have to go home." She tried to stand up.

He helped her. "Where are the lights inside the church coming from? There's no electricity there."

She pulled at his arm. "Please, Gino. We have to go."

"There's something in there." For a moment he saw the outline of a large object, then the remaining walls violently collapsed into the center. An animal roar echoed in the night air. In his whole life, he had never heard any creature make that sound.

"Yes. Let's go, avó." He helped her up the steps without looking back. Once she was safely home, he rushed out to let the neighborhood security patrol know what he saw.

A'kael landed the cloaked shuttle on top of a tall office

building at the edge of the Calabar area. She watched the recording of Bachaann's shuttle again. There was no energy trail of a weapon from Earth to the ship before the explosion. No matter how much the soft meat technology had advanced, she didn't believe it could evade their detection. Knowing Bachaann, he would have made sure every system was in perfect order the night before they left Yautja Prime, as she did for her shuttle. Was it possible that a Yautja had deliberately set up his shuttle's engine to explode? Could it be one of her first hunters?

A low growl escaped before A'kael could get her anger under control. This was one of the worst rules to break. Now she had twice the reason to keep an eye on them. One could be a code breaker.

"Do we know what caused the shuttle to come down?" Pa'jaadh asked.

"No, but this is where we are now, so the test will continue from here. Bachaann and his team are still alive, as are we. Let's see what we can find of value between here and them to hunt."

They scanned the building for thermal heat sources. There were only a few oomans and even fewer armed. The weapons were simple projectile guns, not military level. As much as the young Yautja wanted their first trophy, these soft meat were barely a threat.

A'kael projected a holographic map of the area, showing where Bachaann's shuttle had crashed and all four Yautja onboard.

Suddenly Bachaann and two of his first hunters quickly moved away from the shuttle, leaving one on board, then the shuttle imploded. This time A'kael didn't hold back an angry snarl. First the shuttle crash, now one of Bachaann's charges was dead.

She understood why they destroyed the disabled shuttle. He wouldn't have left a Young on board unless—

"One of his first hunters must have been badly injured in the crash," Va'kal'jaad said.

"Bachaann should have tried harder to save him," Thwutha said.

"Not if the injuries were too serious," Pa'jaadh explained. "It wouldn't be wise to take a chance on the shuttle being discovered."

"That's one less to worry about," Thwutha added.

A'kael looked at him. This was more than his usual arrogance.

"Let's go," she said to all three.

They activated their armor's cloaking and left the shuttle.

"What do you detect in the area between here and Bachaann, Thwutha?" she asked.

Thwutha studied the holographic map displayed in his bio-helmet. "There are groups of pyode amedha with military-grade weapons moving in the direction of the woods near Bachaann. Someone must have seen the crash."

"Then that is the direction we will go," A'kael replied.

The rooftop entry to the building wasn't locked. They ran down the stairway, taking the steps three or four at a time. When they got to the first floor, the exit door was locked. It was easy for Va'kal'jaad to yank open, but that set off a loud alarm.

Two guards ran toward the broken door, but didn't see the cloaked Yautja. They walked in opposite directions with their guns out, looking for intruders. The guard to the left ran past Thwutha, who started to follow him, while the rest of the team headed to the front of the building. A'kael clicked her mandibles in his direction.

Thwutha turned away from the guard and ran past her to crash through the glass and metal entrance of the building. All four Yautja ran down the paved streets toward the Calabar shantytown.

Bachaann confirmed that A'kael's shuttle landed safely and her team were headed in his direction. Sheltered in a cluster of trees on the hill near the building, he asked what his Young saw in the surroundings with their bio-helmets.

Do'tah pointed toward the water. "The heat signature of a few oomans on the beach, not armed."

Zuhra looked up the hill. "Many pyode amedha in dwellings. Many armed with small weapons, a few with more military-level. Many not. A small group is approaching with better-grade weapons."

"Our crash may have alerted them," Do'tah said. "They are worthy of attention."

"Yes," Bachaann said.

They fanned out and climbed into the trees as four well-armed soft meat came down the stone steps to the rubble. Two pointed high-beam lights down into the pile of bricks and wood. The other two stood on the edge of the woods using bright lights to examine the ground and trees.

Bachaann knew they would find no sign of the shuttle. He had purposely left broken underbrush leading into the thick grove of trees. This kind of settlement on Earth often had their own group of armed military. After the loss of the shuttle and one of the hunting party, his two young Yautja could use a first blooding.

Two oomans entered the trees, and walked in opposite directions with their weapons drawn. Bachaann's bio-helmet vision mode allowed him to watch as his two charges split up to follow them overhead in the trees. The pyode amedha would check overhead when they heard some movement, but the cloaked Young mixed well in the trees' thick canopy.

Do'tah was positioned above his prey. He quietly lowered a razor-edged rope around the ooman's neck and lifted him off the ground into the tree so quickly he didn't have time to call out and warn the others. His gun and light remained on the ground. As Do'tah took the head with a single swipe of his wristblades for his first trophy, Bachaann turned his attention to the other trainee.

Zuhra tracked his prey until it was standing in front of a large tree trunk. He jumped from the tree to the ground and sliced the ooman's neck with his smart disc. The body slid to the ground as the head bounced into the undergrowth. Zuhra caught his returning smart disc, retrieved the head, and went back up the tree.

They were both efficient at silencing the prey in different ways.

The other two oomans finished looking into the fallen building and called out for the two who were already dead in the woods. When no one answered them, they headed into the trees, but didn't split up like the first two.

Do'tah had tied the body on a tree branch, but Zuhra left the headless body on the ground on purpose. When the two pyode amedha found it, they yelled and stood back to back, their weapons ready to fire. One way to easily pick both off was with a single blast from a plasmacaster, but the clan decided young Yautja would not be given that weapon until after a successful first hunt. Instead they were provided with wristblades on both arms.

Zuhra jumped from the tree, landed on both oomans. One started shooting randomly when he fell since he couldn't see the Yautja. The newly blooded hunter grabbed the soft meat shooting, twisted him so his bullets hit the second, then threw him on top of his dying companion and thrust his spear through both of them. They squirmed, still alive, as Zuhra extended his wrist blades and decapitated them both with one strike.

Bachaann and Do'tah joined Zuhra on the ground while he used his flaying tool to quickly peel the flesh from the skulls. Do'tah had tied his cleaned trophy th'syra to his waist.

Now they had completed their first kills Bachaann explained his belief that A'kael might have a coward on her team who was responsible for the shuttle crash and Gan'touh-De's death. They both roared at the same time, a death cry for the young Yautja. Their howl echoed outside the woods.

A'kael and her cloaked team stood in the shadows of a tall building across the street from the beginning of the tumble of homes defining the edge of the Calabar area. The dividing street was brightly lit, and there were surveillance cameras and well-armed military police.

The firearms were technology A'kael recognized. They rushed across the roadway into the shanty town.

The streets were barely defined, twisting and turning

around the uneven living structures, so they climbed to the roof level of a well-built home. From there they used the holographic map of the buildings to run over roofs that were strong enough to support their weight as they jumped rooftop to rooftop toward the woods that faced the ocean.

When they were almost there the roof Pa'jaadh landed on started cracking under her weight. She rolled to the edge of the roof, grabbed the sturdy truss and swung herself into the air to land on an adjacent roof with the rest of the team.

Thwutha pushed Pa'jaadh, almost knocking her off the secure roof. "If you can't run on roofs without falling, you don't belong with us."

A'kael snarled and pointed to the adjacent woods. Once in the thick trees and undergrowth she uncloaked, and the others followed suit.

She looked at Thwutha. "Take off your bio-helmet."

He hesitated, but removed it.

"Thwutha, it is not your place to speak to another Young that way while the hunting party leader is present."

Instead of lowering his gaze as a sign of respect he took a step closer to her. "Her failure would reflect badly on you."

"You would do anything to help me become clan leader?"

"Yes."

"Do you think killing that guard in the building as he walked away from you would have been a worthy first kill?"

"He was armed. What else matters? I do not take the word 'worthy' so seriously for my first kill when it comes to these fragile oomans. There are wild animals on this planet that are stronger."

A'kael aimed her plasmacaster at him; three red dots

glowed on his forehead. "What do you think of the code forbidding intentionally trying to kill other Yautja by sabotaging their shuttle?"

"How do you know it was me? It could have been Va'kal'jaad or Pa'jaadh."

They both stepped next to A'kael, a low growl rumbling under their bio-helmets.

"Thwutha, don't add to your dishonor by accusing others of your cowardly behavior," A'kael countered.

Thwutha's lower mandibles flared as he activated both of his wrist blades and jumped at A'kael, who swung her smart disc, severing one of his arms, followed by a side kick that sent him to the ground. He cried out in pain and rolled up to his knees.

She pointed her disc at his uninjured arm with the wristblade still extended. "Do you wish to lose both arms?"

He deactivated the blade.

"Va'kal'jaad," A'kael said, pointing at the ground.

He picked up Thwutha's helmet and arm, took his combistick and returned to her side.

Thwutha held his bleeding arm, green blood pooling on the ground. "You would kill me?"

"No. Although it would be my right after you attacked me, but Bachaann deserves time to talk to you since your actions caused the death of a young Yautja in his hunting party." She nodded to Pa'jaadh, who used her medicomp to cauterize Thwutha's arm.

A'kael projected a holographic map set to display Yautja in the vicinity. "You will not have to wait long."

The shanty town's community leaders met with three representatives of the city's military police in a building inside Calabar. They showed the police a video on a cellphone.

At first it was hard to make out details, but as clouds drifted away from the full moon the video clearly showed more than fifteen human bodies swinging from tree branches, skinned, some headless.

The military police argued that they were watching special effects until two of the community leaders left the room and returned with a large wrapped bundle. They threw it on the table, and opened it to reveal a skinned, headless human body. The police stood, knocking their chairs over, and backed away from the table.

One of the officers, with a forensic background, examined the body and confirmed that the head had been detached with one perfect cut. He knew of no surgical instrument that could remove all the skin so cleanly.

Three separate groups had gone into the woods, fully armed. None came out, their weapons scattered on the ground, some fired. Who or what killed them had left the woods at some point, but the community leaders believe they were still in one of the woods along the beach.

Rumors of invisible *demonios* were circulating in the neighborhoods. People were afraid to go out of their homes as the sun began to rise.

They all agreed on a plan to have the armed community groups gather on the beach while the military police helicopters would monitor the woods, firing into them to push out whoever was hiding there, toward the ocean. Then they would catch them between the police and groups on the beach.

Thwutha was still on his knees when Bachaann and his two first hunters walked into the woods.

Bachaann took one look at the injured young Yautja. "You sabotaged my shuttle and caused Gan'touh-De to die?"

Thwutha didn't look up.

"He did," A'kael confirmed. "And tried to attack me."

"You let him live?"

"For you," A'kael said.

Bachaann removed his bio-helmet, disabled his plasmacaster, handed A'kael his combistick. "Stand up, code breaker."

Thwutha stood, grabbed his own smart disc with his remaining hand and ran at him. Bachaann didn't move until Thwutha was right in front of him, then he side-stepped, grabbed Thwutha's wrist, twisted his own disc into his throat.

"I would not dirty my blade with your blood." Bachaann pulled the disc through Thwutha's neck, partially decapitating him, and let his body fall.

Do'tah used his blue dissolving liquid to reduce Thwutha's body to unrecognizable sludge, then gathered the remnants of gear, while Bachaann put his bio-helmet and weapons back on.

"I see many new trophies in your hunting party," A'kael said.

"Yes, taken with honor."

A'kael projected a holographic map showing helicopters approaching from the city and highly armed pyode amedha gathering on the beach. "More trophies waiting for everyone."

They activated their cloaking devices and ran toward the beach.

Two helicopters landed on the beach, emptying endless projectiles into the thicket of twisted trees, killing others of their kind between them and the woods. No other helicopters touched down after seeing bodies torn to pieces by unseen forces. Many of the oomans left the fight, running for their lives from the invisible *demonios*.

A'kael used the ship remote in her wrist gauntlet to have the cloaked shuttle fly from the building roof and land on the beach when the remaining soft meat finally fled.

The golden rays of a new day's sun settled on the bloody swatch of sand between the woods and beach. Echoes of weapons fire and screams left Earth and traveled, as all sound does, out and away from the third planet from the sun.

In time, flooding from torrential rain and landslides would clean the sand and woods of the body fluids spilled that day. There were parts of the woods that would not be visited for years, other than to wish peace for the spirits of those upon which unspeakable violence had been delivered.

After the shuttle docked with the mothership, Elder Mi'thielth sat with A'kael and Bachaann in his meeting chamber.

"The council on Yautja Prime and I reviewed the recordings from all of your bio-helmets, including the Dishonorable," Mi'thielth began. "The first hunter, Gan'touh-De, who gave his life in the destruction of the disabled shuttle will be spoken of with honor."

A'kael and Bachaann bowed their heads in agreement.

"A'kael, you made clear decisions even when you

suspected a code breaker was in your team, as well as handing him over to Bachaann.

"Bachaann, you dispensed with him in an acceptable manner. You both returned with two on your teams. These four performed well—their next hunt will be for Hard Meat.

"There are no errors found in your leadership. The final decision of who will become clan leader was very close. In the end, we agreed that A'kael will be clan leader."

Bachaann turned to A'kael and lowered his head and eyes in recognition of her new higher rank.

"It is unfortunate we did not land at the military location on Earth where testing of new weapons and technology was taking place," A'kael admitted. "It could have been an interesting hunt."

Mi'thielth leaned forward. "You are a clan leader, you can assign that hunt to anyone you deem worthy."

A'kael clicked her mandibles and looked at Bachaann. "I know someone very worthy of that kv'var."

LION OF THE HIMALAYAS

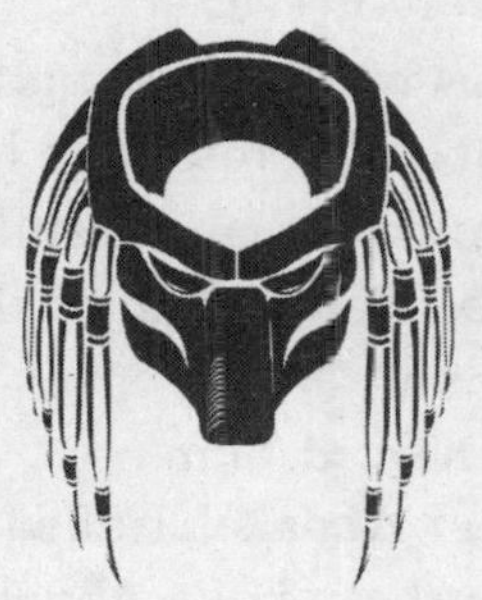

BY AMMAR HABIB

The walls were splattered with blood, the floorboards soaked. The full moon's pale light reflected off it with a sheen. Both corpses were disfigured and hacked to pieces, their faces beyond recognition. However, their hollow eyes remained wide open, staring.

His legs giving in, Abdallah fell to his knees beside them. Streams of tears left his cheeks wet, and snot ran out his nose. As he held the bodies, blood mixed into his clothing and drenched his hands. But he didn't care. Abdallah's body convulsed with his every sob as he pulled both corpses into his chest. Just days ago, he had felt their warmth and heard their voices, but now they were cold, lifeless.

Awaking with a start from the nightmare, Abdallah had to concentrate to slow his breathing. The first thing he heard was the call of a Himalayan Bulbul. Its chirps were quick and short. He didn't move at first. He simply stared at the hut's ceiling as his breathing calmed, and the nightmare's fog was replaced by the new day's light. Sunlight spilled in through the hut's wooden walls and roof, and the outside trees rustled with a soft breeze.

It wasn't until his hunting dog nudged Abdallah's face with his nose that Abdallah rose from his cot. As he sat up, the dog—a fully grown Indian Mastiff—gave his grizzled cheek a lick, and Abdallah couldn't help but chuckle as he pushed the dog off him.

"Alright, Tipu," he said. "I'm up."

Coming to his feet, Abdallah ruffled Tipu's fur. The hut's ceiling hung only inches above Abdallah's head, and the building itself was quite bare except for the essentials. There were some supplies in one corner, including bags of rice and lentils. Nearby sat a chest of clothes, and in a far corner several different firearms leaned against the wall.

Tipu abandoned Abdallah and returned to chewing on his nearly-bare bone. Abdallah peeled off the thin *kurta* he wore while sleeping and put on a *pheran*, but he kept on the same *shalwar* that he slept in. The *pheran* possessed thicker fabric than the *kurta* and offered more protection from the cool weather. Though the tunic and pantaloons he wore were loose, his strong physique was still noticeable underneath his clothing.

Abdallah made his way to his small weapons cache and tied a leather belt around his waist. Grabbing the Remington Model 700 rifle and a sheathed khanda sword, he hung the sword's sheath on his belt before throwing his hunting rifle's strap across his shoulder.

While Abdallah readied himself, Tipu came up to him and rubbed against Abdallah's leg. A trained hunting dog, Tipu grew excited as he saw Abdallah preparing for a hunt. Dropping to a knee, Abdallah smiled and patted Tipu's head. His eyes traveled down the dog's face until it came to his collar. Or, more accurately, until it came to the locket that hung from the collar. The locket had opened, revealing the picture of a woman and a four-year-old girl. The photograph was faded, and the image had started to blur. Abdallah's smile washed away. Running his finger over the picture, Abdallah let out a sigh. That picture of Saira and Little Fatima had been taken just days before…

Tipu whimpered as his nose nudged Abdallah.

"I miss them too, pal. Every day." He took a deep breath, fighting off the visions that haunted his sleep. Abdallah closed the locket. "Every. Damn. Day."

People claimed that Kashmir was created by God's own hand. He molded the high mountains and hills that stretch as far as the eye can see, purified the crystal blue rivers and lakes, and painted the grass and forests with His brush. He'd kept its beauty fresh ever since, a slice of heaven on earth.

Abdallah didn't believe that. God forgot about Kashmir a long time ago. The aesthetic countryside was nothing but a facade. Underneath the land's mirage of beauty lay the truth, and this truth was the one thing the people of Kashmir understood above all else: suffering. The people of Kashmir were all born into the inferno of war, and their lives were molded by its flames. Abdallah knew this better than most.

As soon as Abdallah stepped out of his hut, he was under the shadow of the mountains. These mountains were the start of the Himalayas. For him, they weren't signs of God's majesty; they were sentries to the prison he was trapped within. All his life, no matter where he looked or went, these mountains had followed him as constant reminders of his strife.

The ground outside Abdallah's hut was littered with hunting gear. There were several animal and bear traps that he was in the midst of repairing or building. Most of their metal was rusting, and the traps themselves were weathered. On a clothesline hung some animal skin he would often use for camouflage in the forest and mountains. A small campfire was still smoldering, its odor filling the air.

Coming to a wooden basin filled with water, he removed the heavy lid before leaning down and splashing some water on his face. As the water's ripples dispersed, he got a good look at his reflection. His graying beard and hair were wild, and his face was hard and wrinkled, his eyes tired. He had lived far longer than he deserved. Sometimes his features looked more like an animal's than a man's.

Abdallah's hut offered a perfect view of the valley below, a sea of greenery with streams winding through rolling hills and tall mountains whose peaks stretched to touch the sky. Near the bottom of the valley—amidst the greenery next to a stream—lay a village, a cluster of huts and shops with a small trading post on its north side. At its center stood the largest building: the *masjid.* The structure's green dome rose above the forest surrounding the village, and Abdallah could discern it even from this far off.

The only thing in the village taller than the dome was the *masjid*'s minaret. When the *adhan*—the call to prayer—was performed from there, the voice of the *mu'azzin* would often reach the mountain's foothills. The dome and minaret's paint had faded through the years, and the village itself resembled something from the 19th century. In the faraway city of Dubai, the people had recently built the Burj Khalifa, a building that was said to kiss the heavens; however, this village—just like everyplace else in Kashmir—remained old and weathered. The villagers who lived here were the same. It sometimes seemed as if anything else was forbidden in Kashmir.

A few days ago, people from the village had come to Abdallah. They'd asked him to track down an Asian black bear who roamed the forest near the village. The villagers claimed that the bear had mauled three village men who had ventured into the forest to collect firewood. Nobody had seen the attack, but they claimed the cuts could not belong to anything else.

Hunting was the only thing Abdallah was proficient at. After fighting against the Indian army for decades, there was nothing left for this old man except to scavenge the forest. He often felt more at home in the forest amongst the animals than with people.

With Tipu at his side, Abdallah turned from the village and entered the forest. He was reminded of how old he was by the pain that consumed his joints, but he ignored it. The forest ran through most of the mountain's foothills before the terrain turned rockier. The greenery was thick, and the animals were loud. Asian black bears hardly ever wandered into the mountains, but they enjoyed foraging in the forest.

The forest buzzed with activity, and the calls of birds could be heard as they flew overhead. Two black splotches in the air caught his attention half an hour into his trek.

Abdallah heard their rotating propellers. Helicopters—ones belonging to the Indian army. They were always there, always an ominous presence and menace that loomed in the background. It was like a dam that could burst without warning and drown the land.

It wasn't rare for military jeeps to flood the village, or any Kashmiri village for that matter. They'd come without warning, swarming like vultures onto a dying prey. Towns and villages would be put under curfew. Nobody would be allowed to leave their home, not even for food or medicine. Some villagers would fall ill and die, and others would starve. Village men would be murdered by soldiers for no reason. Women and girls would be abducted by soldiers and never seen again.

Following decades of the Indian government keeping its foot on the throats of the Kashmiri people and years of fighting for independence, the people of Kashmir were no closer to being free. The brave died, the helpless suffered, and the ones who survived—the ones like Abdallah—were the people that truly paid the price. Abdallah knew about the horrors the Kashmiri people faced as much as anyone else.

After all, it was during one such time when Saira and Little Fatima were murdered.

Making his way up a steep hill, Abdallah held his rifle in both hands as he trudged forward. He was surrounded by wildlife, and the calls of the forest animals mixed in with one another. The trees surrounding him were tall, and their greenery thick, seeming to add to the humidity. However, bits of sunlight slipped through between the leaves.

He had set several traps for the bear since getting the request from the villagers. Bears were strong and fierce, but they were also predictable. Abdallah knew where they foraged this time of year, and it was only a matter of time before the bear fell into one of Abdallah's traps.

Arriving at the top of the hill with Tipu close behind him, Abdallah headed toward the Mulberry tree where he'd set a trap.

He stopped dead in his tracks.

Abdallah blinked once. Then once more, thinking that his mind had deceived him. The foot trap was broken. Its metallic jaws were twisted and mangled, mirroring the way wood breaks against stone.

What beast could have done this? Abdallah stared at the wreckage, his mind racing through every possibility. No animal in this valley could break a trap like this, not even an enraged bear. Crouching down next to the trap, he noticed something on one of the blades. It smelt like blood, but it was green. Was this some sort of nectar?

Sensing Tipu tense up, Abdallah looked back at his dog. It was at this moment that Abdallah realized the birds had fallen silent. No, the entire forest had fallen silent, as if every animal had suddenly fled. A stillness had washed over the scene, the sort of calm Abdallah only felt before an ambush.

Tipu's stance grew more aggressive as he let out a growl. His eyes scanned the trees.

"Do you smell something?"

Tipu's posture didn't change as he continued scanning the trees.

"Another animal?"

Tipu's growl heightened.

"Another predator?"

Tipu suddenly took off into the trees. Rifle in hand, Abdallah chased after him. The bushes were thick, and the trees were many, causing Abdallah to quickly lose sight of Tipu. He still heard Tipu, but he was growing further away.

"Tipu!"

Tipu's barks were loud.

"Slow down, boy!"

Tipu's barks grew more violent.

"Slow down!"

And more violent.

"I said slow down!"

Tipu growled, as if he had found something. There was a loud bark, one that seemed to shake the trees, and then—

Silence. The barking stopped.

"Tipu!" Abdallah dashed through the greenery, knocking branches out of his way. His old joints were too slow. "Come here, boy!"

He broke into the clearing. Abdallah froze, and the gun dropped from his hand. There, just a few feet from him was something, something that made his heart stop.

A corpse…a dog's corpse. Tipu was dead.

Abdallah fell to his knees next to what was left of Tipu. The mangled corpse was near the river. The rising sun beat down on Abdallah, and cold sweat streaked down his face.

The corpse had been mauled. Tipu's spine was nearly ripped out, and his skull was deformed, as if it had been crushed beneath a boulder from the mountain. A claw had sliced open Tipu's stomach, and his insides spilled out while his blood painted the grass. Some blood trailed off toward the river, mixing into the sand and water.

But the killer had not taken anything from Tipu. It hadn't slaughtered him out of hunger or self-defense. There was no sign of Tipu having attacked anything. No, this beast—this monster—had killed Tipu for sport. It had killed him for no reason other than pleasure.

Scooping Tipu's body with one arm, Abdallah held it close. He didn't cry. He didn't weep. But his body trembled. Tipu's blood soaked into Abdallah's clothing, but he didn't care. He stared down at Tipu's eyes. They were shut, as if he was sleeping.

Abdallah took the family locket off Tipu's collar. It had been stained with the dog's blood, along with the picture inside. Letting a puddle of Tipu's blood form on the palm of his hand, Abdallah balled his hand into a fist, allowing the blood to run between his fingers.

As Abdallah stared at his bloody hand, his eyes turned red with rage. Over the body of his only friend, his only companion, he swore to track down the killer. He swore it over Tipu's blood. Whether the killer was man or beast, he'd find it, and he'd end it.

Abdallah tracked the killer. It wasn't hard. There were clues—signs that would have been invisible to the common eye, but Abdallah's senses were seasoned. Faint footprints along the riverbank soon turned toward the forest. Broken and disturbed branches showed where the killer had entered the forest and which way they had taken.

As the sun continued rising to its throne, Abdallah drove deeper into the forest. The mountain's shadow enveloped Abdallah, and the further he tracked the killer, the more rage swelled within his heart. Images of Tipu's ripped and mangled form flashed across his mind, and mixed with those images were scenes of Saira's and Little Fatima's death.

The trek became an uphill one, and the trees began to thin as the ground became rockier. The fear of mountain lions didn't stop Abdallah. The scent that he had picked up in the forest was present here, so Abdallah followed it to a ridge. Abdallah kept his senses sharp as he began his ascent.

This mountain was as unsafe as it was beautiful. There were countless ambush points and ledges scattered across its base. If this predator was as clever as Abdallah believed, then he needed to be ready. The ridge became narrower, but Abdallah had scaled this mountain during previous hunts and didn't miss a step. Rifle in hand and khanda hanging from his belt, he kept his ears sharp for any sign of the killer. No matter what it was, beast or man, Abdallah had killed plenty of both.

Abdallah sensed some animals nearby. There was a nest of black kite birds above him and another one up ahead, and he could hear a snake slithering across the rocks below him. A few other birds ascended and descended the mountain, but there was nothing else.

The air turned thinner than it was at the river when Abdallah reached a small cliff that jutted out from the side of the mountain. He heard the river directly below the cliff as the water beat against the rocks. The trail of his target led him here, so he stepped onto the cliff and scanned the area. There were no more footsteps on the cliff. No more scent. No more clues. It all abruptly ended, as if the target had suddenly vanished. Once again, the wildlife fell silent. Even from this high, Abdallah could not sense the presence of birds or animals. It was the same sensation as in the forest before Tipu was slaughtered.

It was then that the truth dawned on Abdallah, breaking through the veil of his rage. He had been led here. The killer had left a trail of breadcrumbs that only Abdallah would follow, bringing him to this cliff. But to what purpose? Was this killer baiting him? Had it lured him into an ambush? Was this—

Abdallah smelt a stench. It was stronger than what he had discerned in the forest. This was an odor he had only ever sensed during the war: the stench of death. His grip around his rifle tightened. Feeling a presence, Abdallah turned around to face the ledge above his cliff…and there it stood.

The demon.

It was not of Earth. It was some sort of *jinn* or otherworldly beast. Those were the first thoughts that rushed into Abdallah's mind. With the high sun behind it, the beast towered over eight feet tall. Though it stood on two legs like a man, there was nothing human about it. It wore armor over its chest and legs, but the demon's torso and arms were bare, revealing reptilian skin with a yellowish cast. Long hair-like appendages hung from its head, and it wore wristblades on one forearm. Sunlight reflected off its metallic hunting mask. Reaching up, the demon took hold of its mask with one hand and removed it, revealing its head. The demon's face was like nothing Abdallah had ever seen. As the demon growled, its insect-like mandibles opened to reveal the beast's fangs.

Abdallah froze as he stared at the demon. Was this some sort of devil conjured up by black magic? In one swift move, the demon leaped off its ledge and landed on the cliff. The ground shook as it landed.

The demon's yellow eyes never broke from Abdallah. As the realization of what stood before him washed over Abdallah, he felt his heart tremor with a fear he'd never felt before.

Abdallah didn't think. He reacted. Abdallah aimed his rifle and pulled the trigger. His ears rang with the deafening gunfire, but his bullets struck air. The beast moved faster than Abdallah could think. The beast was to his left, moving quicker than any tiger or mountain lion. Then it was to his right. Then his left again. Each time it was closer. Abdallah pulled his trigger again. Again. And again.

But it was to no avail.

The demon was upon him. With one strike, its wristblade cut clean through Abdallah's rifle. The gun split in half, and Abdallah stumbled back as the broken rifle dropped to the ground. The next strike from the demon brought its blade a hair's length from Abdallah's throat.

Eyes wide and breathing quick, Abdallah reached for his khanda's handle. But the demon's blade cut into Abdallah's shoulder. Abdallah felt the sharp metal pierce his skin. He bit back his cry, but his arm was ablaze. Gaining control over his fear, Abdallah's used his opposite arm to unsheathe his sword and sent a wild slash. With its blade lodged in Abdallah's shoulder, the demon was too close to avoid the strike. Abdallah's khanda sliced at the demon's unprotected torso. The demon's thick skin absorbed most of the blow, but Abdallah felt his blade cut into something.

Ripping its blade out of Abdallah's shoulder, the demon

moved back and put some distance between them. Blood seeped out of Abdallah's wound, and his injured shoulder began to feel colder as Abdallah's heart beat faster. His ragged breathing was louder than the river below, and his trembling continued to increase.

There was neon green blood dripping from Abdallah's sword. What sort of creature was this? Returning his blurred focus to the demon, Abdallah regained his stance and lifted his blade. The demon made a sound. Chittering followed by something else. Was that a growl?

The demon crouched down, preparing to leap at him. Abdallah barely held his blade steady. He tried to focus his vision and breathing, but he couldn't. The more he looked at the monster, the worse his condition became.

He took a step back. However, when his foot came down, it didn't strike the ground. It only felt air. His eyes widened when he realized that he had retreated too far.

Abdallah was no longer standing on the cliff; he was falling off. The wind rushed by him as he lost sight of the demon and as his head turned toward the heavens. Sword still in hand, the last thing Abdallah felt was falling into the rapids below before everything turned black.

Death. Blood. And misery.

Those three things fueled Abdallah's nightmares. He was back in the past, back in the fateful night where Saira and Little Fatima were murdered. Days before, he had left with the other freedom fighters to battle against the army. However, they were led into an ambush in the mountains. All his fellow warriors were gunned down or blown to bits.

Their cries shook the mountains, and their blood painted the rocks. But Abdallah had survived. He'd woken up underneath a pile of limbs and rotting corpses, drowning in the guts of his brothers-in-arms.

When he staggered into his village a few nights later, it was ablaze. All of it. The inferno reached every corner of the valley. Huts and shops were ashes. The Indian army had come through, killing every Kashmiri in sight. The corpses of women and boys and girls littered the dirt trail. Many had been stripped naked. Many had been mutilated.

Arriving at his home, he found the scene he'd only ever glimpsed in his darkest nightmares. Saira's and Little Fatima's blood sprayed the walls, and they were lying in a pool of it. The Indian soldiers had had their way with Abdallah's wife and daughter before hacking them to pieces. Their corpses were carved up, their faces disfigured, and the foul stench of Hell was mixed into the hut's walls.

Abdallah didn't bury his family that night. His bloodlust didn't let him. He tracked the soldiers to their camp, and he found them in their drunken state under the pale moon. With nothing but his sword, he'd attacked them. Lost in his rage, and blinded by hate, every religious teaching about mercy abandoned him. Nothing was heard in the forest that night except for the cries of soldiers. Abdallah didn't simply kill them; he tortured the soldiers. Slaughtered them. Hacked them bit by bit. By the time the deed was done, Abdallah had bathed in their blood, and his skin was stained by the odor of death. Even the insects steered clear of him.

As Abdallah lived through the nightmare again, something was different this time as he stood in that army camp drenched in the blood of the soldiers. Painted across the moon were the demon's yellow eyes. They watched Abdallah's every move like a wolf hiding in the abyss.

It was after the night ended that Abdallah buried his family. He put them to rest in a grassy field under the mountain's shadow, but he never found any peace. So he retired to the mountains, abandoning any hope in humanity or the cause he'd fought for. The cold mountain became his tomb as he waited for death to overtake him, and now fate had sent this demon as recompense for Abdallah's sins.

The image of the demon was replaced by reality. When Abdallah awoke, the first thing he heard were the distant calls of black headed gulls. He was no longer in the river. He was in a hut, but he was not alone. Pain and soreness consumed his limbs. Coming to his senses, Abdallah shot up and found himself sitting on a cot. He looked to his right and saw a person: a young boy. He was no older than thirteen. Sitting on the floor, the boy's gaze was locked on Abdallah. The boy had rolled up the sleeves of his *kurta,* and there was dry blood on his hands.

Looking toward his injured shoulder, Abdallah realized that his tunic was missing. His bare torso and arms were littered with old scars. Some were made by bullets; others had been created by the blade. However, his shoulder wound was now bandaged. It wasn't professional, but it was efficient. He let his breathing calm a bit before turning to the boy.

"Thank you," Abdallah said, his mouth dry.

The boy didn't reply.

Looking around the small, bare hut, Abdallah could hear and smell the river. It was rancorous as the water beat against the rocks. The sun's dimming light spilled in through an open hole in one of the hut's walls, and Abdallah spotted his khanda in its sheath next to his cot.

"You brought me here yourself?" Abdallah asked.

"Yes. I found you washed up on shore." The boy paused. "I know you. You're Abdallah Khan."

Abdallah remained silent as he slowly rose to his feet.

"You were a leader of the resistance. My father fought for you."

"Your father?"

"Mirza Ullah. He… he died fighting."

Abdallah glanced away. The image of Mirza flashed across his mind, and he remembered the man's warm smile and hearty laugh. He remembered the night Mirza told Abdallah that his son had been born. It all seemed from another lifetime. "He was a brave man," Abdallah responded. "All the people who fought for our freedom were brave."

"And their sacrifices will live on forever."

"Sacrifices?" Abdallah chuckled as he rotated his injured shoulder to make sure it still worked. It hurt like hellfire, but it moved just fine. "We fought, and we lost. Look at how God rewarded our bravery. All the men I fought alongside died. The tyrants still rule our land and people, and the innocent are made to pay the price."

The boy's eyes became a little sullen when he heard Abdallah's words, and he was slow to reply. "Whenever any of our friends or relatives were killed by the Indian army, my father would always recite a line. He'd say, 'To live as a warrior and die as a lion is far better than to live in fear of a tyrant.'"

Abdallah picked up his *kurta* from the ground. It had been haphazardly washed and most of the blood had been rinsed out. He wasn't sure if it was the boy's doing or the river's. Nonetheless, the left sleeve was still ripped.

"He once told me that you taught him that saying," the boy continued. "You taught him that a person who dies in battle is never truly dead. Their deeds echo for eternity."

Abdallah finally responded, "The person who told your father those things is gone. He died the same night your father did."

The boy's face darkened, and a silence followed. His gaze became downcast. When the boy spoke again, his voice was lower than before. "It's called the Predator—the Shikari. That's what the soldiers call it."

"The demon?" Abdallah looked back at the boy. "You know it?"

"I've heard legends. The Shikari comes from distant stars and stalks our lands. The beast often watches the Indian army, picking out the best soldiers. Then it lures them to the mountains and duels them, and only it survives." The boy paused. "It's a hunter, and it looks for worthwhile prey. War zones create the strongest survivors, so that's why it comes here."

"How do you know it's not just some wild animal?"

"Because it has passed by my hut many times. It's seen me, but it never pays me any mind. The Shikari seeks foes worth battling, so it only attacks soldiers…and warriors."

"Then it'll come for me again and again…until I'm dead."

"What will you do?"

Turning from the boy, Abdallah grabbed his sword. "If this Predator enjoys a hunt, then I will give it one. And if it wants to find a worthy foe, then perhaps I should honor its request."

The boy rose to his feet. "You will die. Everyone has."

Abdallah smiled as he stared down at his weapon and replied, "I've got no reason to live but a lot of reasons to die. This is just the best one."

Without looking back, Abdallah departed and headed in the direction of the waning sun.

As dusk drew near and the call to prayer rang across the valley, Abdallah found himself standing in a field next to a Deodar tree. Its leaves like needles, the tree stretched nearly fifty meters tall. The field's grass reached up to his knees, and the air was still. It was beneath this ground that he buried Saira and Little Fatima years ago. His hands had been painted with blood that night, and it seemed as if that blood had never been washed away.

Standing on top of their unmarked graves under the shadow of the mountain, Abdallah felt the sun beat down on his back. How long had it been since he buried them? Time had lost its meaning. If it wasn't for his graying hair, he would've thought that it was just yesterday when they were murdered.

Now he was faced with an unstoppable monster, a beast who was bred to kill. Just like Abdallah was. This Shikari, if the son of Mirza Ullah was to be believed, had slain every foe it had ever faced. Abdallah was simply a man, but the alien hunter was far from it. Its quickness and ferocity were unmatched, and its killer instincts were unparalleled.

Running his hands through the tops of the grass, Abdallah immersed himself in the moment. His entire life had been a war. First, it was against the Indian army. He had fought them for years, fought for his people's liberation. However, ever since he had lost his family and comrades, his fight had been against the darkness. Every night had been a battle against the temptation of ending his own life. If it hadn't been for Tipu, perhaps he would have done it long ago.

What was left now? Would this be the meaningless conclusion to his life? Would his curtain fall quietly, or would he die as a broken scream in the wind? What had he lived for since Saira and Little Fatima were stripped from him? His soul was a shadow of what it once was, and his heart knew nothing but sorrow. It had abandoned any search for light or life.

To live as a warrior and die as a lion is far better than to live in fear of a tyrant.

Abdallah heard Saira's voice whisper in the wind. Her words were faint, almost inaudible. Taking a deep breath, he opened his eyes. Abdallah knew it was only in his mind, but the voice sounded real. It *felt* real. His gaze focused on his khanda's sheath as he placed a hand on his khanda's hilt. He unsheathed his sword and studied the blade.

The edges of Abdallah's lips curled into a small smile.

He had cut the Shikari. He remembered seeing its green blood drip from his blade. And if it could be cut, if it could bleed, then it could be killed. He could not escape his future and could not erase his past, but he could choose his destiny.

Did he stand any chance against this Predator? Perhaps not. But his battle was not with the Shikari. His true war was whether or not he would unleash the lion inside one last time.

The evening turned to night as Abdallah trekked up the mountain. He followed the narrow ridge uphill, and he didn't stop until he was high above the trees. Abdallah didn't keep himself concealed. He knew the Shikari would find him sooner or later. The Predator was an otherworldly hunter, one who had been trained by experiences Abdallah couldn't even begin to conceive.

However, Abdallah knew the land, and he knew the mountains. Knowledge of the terrain was the greatest advantage in any war, so Abdallah would not chase his foe and would not try to outhunt the hunter. Instead, he would wait to be found, and he would trap the Shikari as he'd trapped countless animals over the years.

By the time Abdallah was ready, the full moon and stars provided the night's only illumination. There were no clouds to hinder their light, and the mountain was silent.

Abdallah smelt the subtle scent of midnight as he glared at the heavens. For the first time in a long time, the night was peaceful. The nightmares didn't follow him here. The moon appeared as it did the night he found Saira and Little Fatima butchered. If he closed his eyes, he could feel their faint presence tonight.

Standing at the entrance of a shallow cave, he turned away from the stars. He felt a change in the wind and sensed an impending presence. A moment of tranquility. The mountain suddenly shook as a short blast erupted. Then another. Bursts of pale blue light streaked through the night. Then explosions were followed by a short rockslide. The ground beneath Abdallah's feet vibrated as it occurred, but he didn't react to any of it. However, it was the signal for something: the Shikari was here.

Abdallah walked into the cave. He knew the traps he'd set would not kill the Predator. They'd either soften him up or just make the demon's fury grow tenfold. He picked up his sword and focused on the sheath, reading the faded inscription: *To live as a warrior and die as a lion is far better than to live in fear of a tyrant.*

Shutting his eyes, he remembered Saira and Little Fatima. He let in their warmth and felt it wash away the coldness that had imprisoned him for so long. There was a moment of peace, a moment of serenity where Abdallah shut his eyes and saw a grassy field. The grass swayed in the soft wind, and the sun shined down on Saira and Fatima as they stood at the field's center, beckoning Abdallah to join them.

A foul odor filled the cave. Abdallah opened his eyes and turned around. The Shikari stood at the mouth of the cave. It showed no signs of having fallen into Abdallah's traps. Moonlight reflecting off its yellow eyes, the Predator's mandibles opened as it let out a low growl. If there ever was a manifestation of Abdallah's sins, this was it. The Shikari had a firearm strapped to its waist. However, it now wore wristblades on both forearms and its shoulder canon was readied.

"You're not here to hunt me," Abdallah said. "You came here in search of a duel. Perhaps to prove something to yourself or to someone else. But in doing so, you've given me the chance to earn something as well."

Abdallah unsheathed his khanda. Holding the sword, he let the sheath fall to the ground.

"A chance to earn my place with my family, a chance to earn a warrior's death."

Abdallah's blade was raised. So were the Predator's wristblades. Their eyes locked, Abdallah shifted his right heel across the gravel and changed his stance. The Shikari did the same. Abdallah didn't break his focus from his foe.

The Predator launched itself at him. It moved with all the quickness that Abdallah remembered, its feet barely touching the ground. Abdallah charged forward. He swung his blade at the beast, aiming to cleave off its arm.

Abdallah's blade drew blood. The Shikari's drew more.

Blood trickled from Abdallah's cut ribs, but he ignored it and blocked out the pain. Some of the alien's green blood dripped from Abdallah's sword. Taking a step back, Abdallah planted his feet and regained his posture. The Predator kicked off the cave's wall and leaped into the air, aiming right for him. Abdallah swung his sword with a roar.

Abdallah's blade cut his foe. The Shikari's cut deeper.

With his right thigh cut, Abdallah nearly lost his balance. Blood seeped from the wound, and a part of his muscle had been shredded. Staggering a few steps, Abdallah regained his balance and turned to face the alien. Some of Abdallah's blood trickled from its blade. Tightening his grip on his sword, Abdallah took a deep breath. Then another, focusing his senses on the hunter. He blocked out the pain, blocked out anything other than his foe. It came at him again, this time with a greater fury. One of its blades aimed for his leg, and the other came for his head. Abdallah swung his blade, aiming to split open the Predator's head.

Abdallah's blade sliced through one of the Shikari's mandibles, drawing forth an alien scream unlike any Abdallah had ever heard, but the beast again cut into Abdallah's leg. Abdallah fell to a knee, using his sword to keep himself upright. His injured leg was cut to the bone, and it had all but given in as it grew cold and numb. Blood dripped from the cut on his forehead. It ran down across his eyes, blinding him.

For a moment, he thought the Predator would finish him. Abdallah took a deep breath. Then another. But the blow didn't come. The Shikari stood patiently, as if it waited for him.

"To live as a warrior…" Abdallah forced himself to stand. "And die as a lion…" He wiped the blood off his eyes. "Is far better than to live in fear of a tyrant."

The Predator growled.

"You will not be my death." Abdallah raised his sword. "You will be my rebirth."

Abdallah charged.

When the morning sun rose, the birds returned to the mountain. As did the vultures. The son of Mirza Ullah also found himself scaling the mountain until he came across a cave. He had heard the blasts the night before. When he arrived, the boy saw what lay at the cave's entrance: a corpse.

Abdallah's eyes were shut. In one hand was his sword, and his opposite fist was clenching a blood-stained locket. Crouching over the corpse, the boy ran his hand through Abdallah's hair and whispered a prayer over him. It was when he again looked at Abdallah's face that he noticed something, something he did not expect.

Abdallah was smiling.

THE FIX IS IN

BY JONATHAN MABERRY

1

"You really expect me to sign this?"

Hogarth Fix stared at the military lawyer seated across from him. He wasn't sure the man had blinked once the entire time. The guy was skinny, narrow-shouldered, and sallow, but his eyes were hard as fists. He had the kind of smile Fix was sure they taught in law school. A smile that lacked warmth, and hinted at a disregard for basic humanity. Crocodiles would love to have a smile as unnerving as that. But then, crocodiles had more actual decency than an attorney working for the Department of Defense.

"Whether you sign or not is your decision," said the lawyer, whose name was Pelagatti.

Fix had looked that name up after their first meeting the

week before. It meant 'skins cats.' While that was funny in the abstract, after spending time with the man, Fix wondered if the young Pelagatti took the name as an inspiration. Though, after looking in those eyes, Fix thought this guy probably actually *did* skin cats. Puppies, too. And right now, the bastard was trying to skin a battered old ex SpecOps shooter-turned-cage fighter. And he was doing a good job at it.

Fix tapped a section of the document with a forefinger.

"If I sign this, I'm essentially ceding my constitutional rights," he said.

Pelagatti continued to smile. "Oh, no, Mr. Fix, there's nothing 'essential' about it. If you sign this, you waive all rights of any kind."

"Jesus H. Skydiving Christ."

"Please, let's have no profanity," said Pelagatti primly. "This is the standard contract for certain, ah, *kinds* of missions."

"Why do the phrases 'off the books' and 'plausible deniability' spring to mind here?" asked Fix.

"Because you're more astute than you appear," said the lawyer.

"Okay, ouch."

Pelagatti reached across the table and nudged the document another half-inch toward Fix. He contrived to arrange his features to be sympathetic. It looked like it hurt.

"We are not unaware that your present financial situation gives us a certain degree of leverage," he said. "But we would be fools not to take advantage of any situation that will advance our agenda."

"And which agenda is that?"

"Saving the world, Mr. Fix," he said, and in that moment, he looked and sounded completely honest.

2

Fix signed the document.

3

That night he sat on the couch with his kids watching a holofilm. Even though the vidsystem was old, it still filled the darkened living room with spaceships and planets. Transgenically enhanced actors dressed as superheroes duked it out with fire-breathing space dragons.

As always, Daisy was snuggled up against him. He listened to her breathe, comforted that —if nothing else—the money he'd made fighting on Gameworld had saved her life. Lung cancer of an aggressive kind had begun chewing at her around her fourth birthday. Now she was seven and breathing on her own, though she slept in an Oxy-med tent at night. Surgeries, treatments, and pills cost over a million. Cleaning up some other debts incurred during his wife's illness and funeral, and setting up an account to pay bills, feed and clothe all three kids, and keep the lights on had begun eating up the rest.

There had been more money, and Fix thought he was smart as hell with how he squirreled it away in numbered accounts and even in a box buried in the yard.

He was a great fighter. He'd been a decorated soldier. As a thief, however, he was a borderline idiot, and he knew it. His naivety had come back to bite him in the ass. It took about eight minutes for the IRS tactical squad to uncover the lot. And they took it all.

What little he had left went for his bail and to hire a lawyer who looked like the kind of kitten Pelagatti would enjoy skinning. The trial had been short, and a sentencing hearing was pending.

That's when the Department of Defense sent their cat-skinning heartless sociopath of an attorney to make an offer. Go to jail, have his kids taken permanently by child protection services, and spend the rest of his life digging ore on a penal moon out beyond the ass-end of the core systems… or…

Suit up, gear up, lock, load and join a mission that was likely to have some of the same effects. He'd probably die. He would never see his kids again.

The upside was, though, that his kids would still be his and would be cared for in style and comfort, with college money and medical expenses covered, and the knowledge that their dad died a hero.

Cold comfort, but comfort for sure.

He negotiated one additional clause—that of allowing the kids to stay in the same house and go to the same schools, with a trust set up to hire a live-in nanny. Pelagatti made a big show of exasperation, but Fix figured he'd agree, which he did. After all, the money they dug up in Fix's backyard—money he'd taken from the safe of the asshole who ran Gameworld after a couple of weird-ass aliens chopped the guy up—was more than enough to cover all of that. The Gameworld owner, Sake Chiba, promised Fix a million and a half to fight one of those aliens in the ring. The creature was a kid, though bigger and way stronger than Fix, but then his father showed up and all of Gameworld went straight to hell. In the aftermath of that shit show, Fix had jimmied open Chiba's safe and took what he was owed plus three times as much and smuggled it back to Earth. Now those funds were in some government black ops account.

Pelagatti added the clause and when the revised document was put in front of him, Fix signed it.

He had his big arms around his kids. Daisy, Lucas, and Yee. He pulled them close, kissed their heads, and watched the movie. Tomorrow he would be gone.

He hoped that with all the exploding spaceships and super-heroics, none of the kids would notice the tears in his eyes.

4

Fix sat on the edge of an equipment box, elbows on knees, head drooping between his shoulders, staring down at the patterns made by sweat dripping from his face.

"You getting tired, old man?"

He looked up without raising his head. Corporal Jenks stood there, grinning, fists on hips. Jenks was sweating, too, but the bastard was barely breathing hard.

"Two things," wheezed Fix. "First, fuck you."

Jenks laughed. "And what else?"

"Fuck you," said Fix.

"Yeah, okay," laughed the corporal. He wasn't a bad guy. Just a typical trash-talking NCO with—Fix was positive—an extra lung hidden somewhere. He was also fourteen years younger that Fix. Hell, even the oldest guy on the team, a bruiser named White, was seven years younger. There was no one, not even the pilot or ship's medic, who was as old as Hogarth Fix.

Fix felt he had every right to hate them all and to wish with fervent honesty that they'd collectively trip and fall out of an airlock.

"Oh, and one more thing," said Fix.

"Yeah?"

"Fuck you."

Ginge laughed. "You make a good point, Fix."

"He does," conceded Jenks.

"He also kicked your narrow ass," said Ginge. She was tall, with a gaunt face and hooded eyes beneath the spill of red hair from which she got the inevitable nickname.

"This time," said Jenks, who, despite some new bruises painting themselves on his face and chest, was a good-natured kid. The whole team was. Eleven incredibly fit and well-trained private military contractors, and one older soldier who wanted to push them all out of an airlock and go the hell back to bed.

The team was ramrodded by a solid sergeant, Vasilievici, who looked like he was genetically engineered to be what he was—tough, sarcastic, efficient, and a natural leader. Vasilievici was who the team followed; he was who they looked to very discreetly every time Lieutenant Wilson gave an order. Vasilievici reminded Fix of some of the better sergeants he'd known back when he pulled triggers for Uncle Sam. Without good NCOs the military would crumble. Officers be damned.

There was a *bing-bong* sound from a wall-mounted speaker, and then the LT's voice telling them to report for a mission briefing.

"Finally," said Ginge. "Now we get to know what the hell we're doing out here."

"And why we're hauling old cargo," said Jenks, nodding at Fix.

"Hey," said Fix, "did I mention anything about fuck you?"

They all laughed, and Fix got to his feet, trying not to look as old and achy as he felt.

The team went into a conference room aft of the training bay. They took their assigned seats in rows of chairs, each kitted out with a small monitor. As they sat, Fix and the others tapped the backs of their wrists to a sensor to interface with the small holographic mission computers to the main system. Dozens of tiny nano beads had been implanted along their forearms prior to mission lift-off. With the interface, every critical part of the mission briefing would be stored and accessible to them. With the right combination of fist squeeze and muscle flex the simulated screen would appear above their arms. These were coded to other nano beads attached to their optic nerves so that only each individual team member could see the holographic display. No one else would ever know that a screen had been activated.

This was tech that Fix had never even heard of before, let alone seen in action. It was miles ahead of the standard wrist-mounted tactical computers he wore when he rolled with SpecOps.

A lot of the technology aboard the *Onyx* was like that. The ship was a sleek black torpedo-shape craft longer than three football fields. One of the later generations of high-end cargo ships, the kind used to recover yachts that their rich owners were too drunk or incompetent to pilot. The *Onyx* was massive, richly appointed, and packed with stuff that seemed to come right out of the science fiction movies Fix watched with his kids.

When Fix asked Sergeant Vasilievici about the ultra-sophisticated gear, the sergeant gave him a long five-count stare and said, "Seems to me you're asking about things so far above your pay grade I'm getting a nosebleed just thinking about it. Now, how 'bout you go down to the canteen for a nice big cup of shut the fuck up, what say?"

Which had been the only conversation Fix had about the gear.

As soon as the team were seated and synced in, Lieutenant Wilson came briskly into the room. The man always plowed into any room as if he wanted to bruise the air molecules with his chest. He had a big square hero jaw, cold blue eyes, and no visible sense of humor. Unlike a lot of academy grads, Wilson had plenty of combat experience. However, the officer also had a bad reputation for taking risks that cost lives. Ginge and some of the others called him the Grim Reaper behind his back. Nobody liked him, but then again it was hard to emotionally bond with someone whose career trajectory and bravado racked up body counts among the good guys.

The squad all stood up as he entered, but Wilson waved them curtly back down.

"Shut up and pay attention," he barked, even though no one had said a word. "What I will tell you is what you need to know. However, all of it is above top secret. You will not talk about this mission with anyone. Ever. Do you understand?"

"Sir," they all said.

If some of the squad traded covert eye rolls, that was to be expected. All of them had gotten the security speeches before and after signing the papers.

"Even you mouth-breathers are smart enough to know what will happen if you talk about this with anyone. Ever. Not your spouse, your family, your priest, or your sexbots. Are we in complete harmony here?"

"Sir," they said again.

No one was stupid enough to risk the penalties for loose lips. And none of them were raw enough to make even casual mistakes.

Wilson looked around, though, making sure he had everyone's full attention.

"We are on a salvage mission," he said.

There were a couple of small groans, which he ignored.

"Don't get your panties in a twist," said Wilson. "If the big boys wanted someone to offload cargo from a crashed merchant ship we wouldn't be here. And it's not a rescue mission, either. This is a straight military gig."

That made the groaners shut up and sit forward. Fix did, too.

"Something crashed onto Keiko, an S-type asteroid way out on the far side of the Rocks."

The Rocks was the nickname for the litter between Mars and Jupiter that had once been a planet in ages past. Because of the gravitational forces in the region, wandering comets and asteroids tended to get caught in the mix, bulking it up and frequently changing the patterns. Fix knew a freighter pilot who worked the region and there was no one who drank more after returning planetside.

Satellite cams got enough of the ship still intact to give a sense of its design, but Fix thought it looked ugly as hell. The pieces did not seem to match with any obvious design philosophy. More like it was cobbled together from other craft. The effect was something brutal, with sharp edges and an overall look of a primitive flaked spear point.

"Holy fuck..." someone whispered.

"Permission to ask a question, sir," said Ginge, raising her hand.

"Ask it," said Wilson.

"Whose bird is that, LT? It's not Russian and it's not Chinese. It's sure as heck not ours. Who else is flying stuff that big all the way out here, sir?"

"That," said Wilson with a tight smile, "is a damn good question."

The room went silent again, but now there was a palpable energy in the air. Interest, confusion, and definitely trepidation.

"LT," said Vasilievici, "are we thinking this is someone's stealth craft? One of the Luna conglomerations or…?"

"No, sergeant," said Wilson. "That configuration does not match any design of any terrestrial, lunar, or Martian craft on record. Analysis of the engine structure suggests that it has a propulsion system unknown to modern science."

"Excuse me, sir," said Jenks, "but I don't understand what that means."

Wilson glanced at Fix. "Perhaps you might want to explain that to the team, Mr. Fix."

Every head swiveled toward Fix.

"Um… sure, LT," said Fix. "I could be wrong, but I'm pretty sure that thing is of alien design."

Ginge frowned. "And by alien, you mean…?"

"Alien to our solar system," said Fix. "That kind of alien."

Sergeant Vasilievici peered at Fix. "And how in hell would *you* know that?"

"Because," said Fix, "I met some of those aliens."

There was a beat before Jenks said, "*Met* them…?"

"Yes. Met. Fought against and fought with."

Into the crushing silence that followed that reply, Lieutenant Wilson said, "And now you know why Mr. Fix is accompanying us on this mission."

5

Wilson had Fix explain everything that happened on the entertainment center called Gameworld located in the

Rocks. Fix had volunteered for some no-holds-barred mixed martial arts matches in order to raise the money for his kids. The match they assigned him was not against another MMA fighter, or even one of the transG fighters with special enhancements. No, he was put into the ring with someone called the Nightmare Kid. It was a huge and profoundly ugly monstrosity whose features had no basis in human or Earth animal evolution. A true alien.

The Nightmare Kid was easily twice as strong as Fix, fast as lightning, and very skillfully trained. With all that, Fix won the fight. However, at the end of the bout another alien burst in and began slaughtering everyone. This new monster was considerably larger, stronger, faster, and much better trained. Fix worked out that the new guy was Dad and the Nightmare Kid was junior. Maybe even a young juvenile, approximating a preteen or young teen. Papa was pretty damned pissed that his kid was being forced to fight in pointless matches. Fix reasoned that these monsters were some kind of hunter or predator race, the kind who prized combat ability above all else. Cage matches would have been demeaning to them, as they would have been to, say, the Samurai or Spartans.

In a weird twist of events, Fix wound up siding with the alien hunters against Sake Chiba and the other competitors. It was a bloodbath. At the end of which, Papa Monster seemed to acknowledge Fix's role in saving his son, even though Fix had actually fought the younger creature nearly to death. That part didn't matter. Or maybe it did. In either case, it was like one father acknowledging another and the creatures left Fix alive.

No one else was as lucky.

Fix had robbed Chiba's safe, stolen a ship, and got the hell out of Dodge.

When he finished his story, the other squad members sat staring at him with a mix of admiration, skepticism, and awe.

"Well," said Jenks, "fuck me blind and move the furniture."

Fix said, "Yeah."

What Fix did not tell them was that he had spent a lot of time in an undisclosed location—taken there and returned under sedation—where he was shown photos, vidcaps, and diagrams of the same kind of alien. The unnamed government suits who interrogated him asked him to confirm that these were the same *kind* of alien as Nightmare Kid and his dad. During the briefing earlier, Fix told everyone he hadn't actually seen the creatures' ship, but yes—the armor, weapons and *beings* were the same. Those same suits had leveled a series of threats, phrased as *requests*, that he keep all of this to himself. They floated phrases like 'planetary security' and 'extreme penalties' and then sent him home. They'd even allowed him to keep the money he'd taken from Sake Chiba's safe.

Until that cat-skinning attorney showed up and threatened him with the IRS, jail, and the loss of his kids.

Bastards.

Wilson said, "Mr. Fix's full report, as well as sketches of these creatures based on his description, were in the briefing documents you all got. The codename of 'Hunters' is his and we will use that designation for now. If any of you skipped over it, I suggest you go back and take a much closer look. Fix's assessment of their attitudes and behavior is in there, too."

"Hunters... that's how they seemed to me," agreed

Fix, and the others nodded, accepting it. In the military, everything got a nickname. It was expected.

He wondered, though, if Lieutenant Wilson was in the circle of trust about the government's previous encounters with the Hunters. He doubted it, and he kept that knowledge to himself.

"Our mission," said Wilson, "is in partnership with the Garibaldi Group."

No one balked at that. Since humanity expanded offworld, funding special projects of all kinds was cost-prohibitive for most governments. Multiplanetary corporations had much deeper pockets, and often struck deals based on the corporation paying for 'gas and bullets,' as the phrase went, and in return they retained some or all of the R and D rights. Some of the latter was then sold back to the military at greatly reduced rates. It was a kind of open corruption that kept all the worlds spinning.

The Garibaldi Group was based in what had once been the European Union in the pre-planetary expansion days. They manufactured terraforming equipment, biospheres, and environmental offworld city pods, and were one of the fastest-growing corporations in the rapidly expanding offworld game. Their CEO, Lucy Garibaldi, was one of those trillionaires who joked about one day owning her own moon. Except no one really thought she was joking. She was every bit as ruthless, conniving, and predatory as her competitors, and Fix disliked them all on general principle. The loose change in her purse could pay the medical bills for his kids for ten years.

"Now here's the fun part," said Wilson, and for a moment there seemed to be a species of actual human warmth in his smile. "Should we succeed—and we *will* succeed—then there is a bonus structure in place." That sent up a cheer around the room.

"What's the actual op, LT?" asked Vasilievici.

"Primary goal is to recover that ship," said Wilson crisply. "Which is why we're taking the *Onyx* out here instead of a standard boat. It has a bay big enough, and we have two crane drones and some other gear. And that means we have been directed to collect every scrap, rivet, and piece of debris on that rock."

"And what about those Hunters?" asked Ginge.

"Recovering bodies is our secondary objective," said Wilson.

Fix raised his hand. "And if the Hunters on that ship are alive and don't want us to have their toys?"

Wilson's smile went from genial to arctic in a heartbeat.

"The mission comes first," he said. "All other considerations default to that."

And that, thought Fix, *says it all.*

He glanced at the soldiers and saw the truth register in their eyes. On this kind of black op, far beyond any governmental sphere of legal interest, crews were often of less value than the substance of their mission. Fix had been on gigs like that, and more than once he'd been one of a handful returning.

He was starting to like these kids and wondered now how many of them were going to be alive for the flight home.

His heart sank.

6

The *Onyx* snaked its way through the ocean of floating rocks.

Most of the asteroids were small, but some were actual planetoids big enough to have considerable gravity. The pilots had their work cut out for them. Fix secured permission to sit with them in the cockpit, using the excuse that, because of his previous experience, his first impressions might be of value. That was bullshit, because he had not seen the Hunter ship that took the Nightmare Kid away. But he preferred seeing what was coming.

The pilot drove the boat, and the copilot handled the slicks.

Slicks were a new kind of deflector shield that used jets that created a kind of plasma envelope around the hull. The plasma charge was high and when something came too close it would nudge it out of the way, allowing it to slide down the outside of the energy field. If the object was too big—and the pilot left steering away too late—the slicks were mass-reactive and simply pushed the *Onyx* itself out of the way.

The process was finicky, though, and Fix did not interrupt the work the flight team was doing. He felt his pulse race, though, and more than once he pushed on the arm of his chair as if he could somehow steer the ship out of the path of something dangerous.

But the *Onyx* crew were good at their jobs and despite Fix's pulse rate there was no other drama.

"Coming up on it," said the pilot.

Fix stood and leaned forward between the pilots, peered at a screen that magnified what appeared to be an ordinary rock, bringing it into focus and giving scale and composition in a digital display. It was mostly iron and nickel, with trace amounts of iridium and some methane ice. The surface temperature was not absolute zero, but close enough not to matter.

The cabin door opened and Wilson squeezed in, gave Fix a curt nod, and studied the same magnified image.

"Jeez," he said. "Only thing colder than that is my ex-wife."

When no one laughed at the joke the lieutenant muttered something obscene under his breath.

"The target is on the far side," said the pilot. "I'll overshoot and come up behind it."

"Send this feed to the team," said Wilson.

The *Onyx* braked as it rounded Keiko. The far side was sunward and almost immediately they saw it sparkle on the edges of torn metal.

"There she is," said the pilot. He braked the craft, and they all studied the ship as they drifted toward it.

The copilot licked his lips. "I can't believe this," he said, then he cut a look at Wilson. "Are they *sure* this isn't one of ours?"

"They're sure," said the officer.

"Damn. This is kind of freaking me out here."

"Welcome to my world," said Fix. The pilots looked at him.

The alien ship was a wreck.

"Looks like it was a controlled landing," said the pilot. "Or at least an attempt at one. See those cut marks behind it? They must have been able to slow their speed and then came in low and flat to try and skid to a stop, sloughing off speed through basic friction. There's a bunch of rock broken off, but the hull looks mostly intact. So either they have something like our slicks or that thing is built tougher than anything we have."

The copilot nodded and added, "My guess is that their shielding could only take so much because there's a lot of debris. But it's small stuff. I think maybe the glide angle saved their hull but then their engines failed after the big hit, and that killed their shielding. After that the fragile stuff broke off as it slid to a stop."

"Any signs of life?" asked Wilson.

"Nothing I can see," said the pilot. "However, I'm picking up some electrical pulses. Could be a distress beacon, but it's hard to pin down. It's not static on any one frequency. Keeps sliding across the dial. From the regularity, though, my guess is it's automated."

"Give me a thermal scan," ordered the lieutenant, but the copilot shook his head.

"Already tried that, sir," he said, "but the thermals can't penetrate that hull of theirs."

Fix watched Wilson's face.

The officer was chewing gum and did so very slowly and precisely. *A calming technique,* thought Fix. The lieutenant took his time before answering.

"Okay," said Wilson at last, "Let's get the tethers anchored and reel us in. Mr. Fix, go tell Sergeant Vasilievici I said to suit up. They're not paying us to be tourists."

7

Fix climbed into the combat rig, marveling at how the designs had changed since his days in uniform. The last version he'd worn was a bulky monstrosity with triple shells to prevent atmosphere loss from gunfire or shrapnel, big tanks of compressed O_2, and thigh pads weighted with magazines for the forearm-mounted short-burst minicannons. In normal gravity they weighed over seven hundred pounds, forty of which were little motors to help the wearer move. In microgravity they were only a smidge less cumbersome, but since the bad guys had bigger and bulkier—and older—suits, the good guys tended to win.

But the new generation was constructed according to an entirely different design philosophy. Advances in extra-durable polymers cut the weight down to one hundred pounds, and a whole new generation of nano tech synced to combat AI with learning software allowed the suits to adapt to the individual soldier. It learned from the user during training and adjusted the settings to compensate for different gravities. The arm cannons were slimmer and sleeker, firing much smaller bullets with explosive cores. There were secondary guns mounted on each shoulder, and these had a 30-degree radius, allowing them to literally protect the wearer's back. With a skilled soldier in the saddle, it was possible to fire all four guns separately and in different directions, aided by human–AI software interfaces filtered through an ultra-sophisticated targeting computer. The suits were painted a greenish black, with no military insignia or ID numbers. The color earned them the unfortunate nickname of "cockroaches" or just "roaches," and nothing and no one seemed able to shake that name loose.

Fix's roach was more comfortable than a recliner, with adaptive gel packs to buffer him even if he took an RPG in the chest. The weakest spots were the joints and throat, because the need to bend and move quickly meant that the armor could not be at full thickness. Even so, those spots were made of a fiber based on the genetic composition of spider silk and could stop most bullets and blades.

He sealed the suit and spent a few minutes bouncing around in it. He pivoted, ducked, dodged, punched, and kicked. On the trip to Keiko, he'd trained hard in the suit, but each time he put it on, Fix felt it wise to give it a full test.

Ginge and Jenks watched him, helmets off, looking amused. But then they sealed themselves in and began doing the same. Soon everyone was.

"We're going to kick some alien ass," said Jenks with a laugh.

Fix stopped and turned to him. "Yeah, let's do that, boy," he said, "but believe me when I tell you that you can't underestimate these things. They're big and a hell of a lot faster than they look. And they can fight like nothing you ever saw."

"Yeah, but you kicked one's ass on Gameworld," jeered another soldier.

"I barely won that fight," said Fix. "But the one I fought was a kid. Don't forget that."

The comment stole the fun from the moment, but that was okay with Fix.

Sergeant Vasilievici came to the rescue of his team's morale. "And they're probably all dead." He seemed to think about how foolish a comment that was, and in a gruffer voice said, "So you mean-ass sons of bitches act like the professionals you are. Eyes and ears open. Everyone watches their partner. No one goes wandering off alone. No one takes any fucking chances. We all go in, and we all come home. We get our goodies, and we go back to Earth and get paid, feel me?"

"Hell yes!" they roared in chorus.

"Hell yes," said Fix with much less enthusiasm.

There was a jolt that rippled through the floor—even with the inertial dampeners—as the *Onyx* fired harpoon cannons. Then another softer jerk as the cables began pulling the ship slowly to the surface of the asteroid.

Here we go, said Fix.

Inside his suit he was sweating buckets.

He fell into his numbered place in line as the team marched into an armed rover. It was not a standard military APC. This was a corporate model, which meant that it was sleeker, better appointed, and actually comfortable.

Ginge elbowed him lightly. "You're not used to the good life, are you?"

"Not even a little," he admitted.

"Maybe when this gig is wrapped you should consider signing on permanently. PMCs are the rock stars these days," she said. "The pay and bennies are awesome, and they treat you like you matter."

"Yeah," said Jenks, leaning toward them from across the walkway between rows. "They don't treat you like yesterday's used toilet paper."

Fix smiled. "Works for me."

He glanced at the sergeant seated across from him, and the image of the lieutenant on his helmet's digital display. They were in that odd category of DE/DA, shorthand for dual employment and dual allegiance. They were officially employed by the United Worlds Department of Defense, but they answered to the corporation. Fix had met a few of those types before, and they were either really a-jay squared away, or they were somebody's asshole cousin promoted to rank and sent out where they were likely to get killed. Vasilievici seemed to be the former kind. Wilson was so comprehensively disliked that he could be either. No one liked junior officers fresh from the academy.

The rover moved into the oversized equipment airlock, and as soon as the oxygen was sucked into the tanks, the hatch rolled up.

"Grab your nutsacks," yelled the driver.

"Or whatever," muttered Ginge, though she was grinning.

The rover moved down the ramp and onto the surface of Keiko.

The vehicle had huge low-pressure tires and superb shocks, so even with the uneven surface the ride was not that bumpy. Fix smiled at that, too. Last time he was in a military APC he felt like his fillings were vibrating out of his teeth.

"We're three klicks from the target," said the driver.

"Okay, girls and boys," said Wilson, trying to sound cool, "let's get ready."

"*Let's,*" echoed Jenks silently. The other soldiers traded snarky looks. The lieutenant was safe and snug aboard the *Onyx*.

"Weapons check," snapped Vasilievici. "Then buddy-check left and right."

Everyone went through the routine of checking the seals on the soldiers to either side. This was routinely doubled because one mistake, one loose seal, and somebody would die in the airless vacuum. There were in-suit sensors, too, but eyes-on always made the soldiers feel more comfortable. And, Fix knew, it helped with the bonding process. It reinforced the rule that everyone out there was on the same team, looking out for one another, and depended on each other. The guy next to you was always more important than flags, politics, or corporate interests.

Instead of windows, the armored personnel carrier had

high-def view-screens and they all studied the landscape. Fix picked out landmarks and details, filing them away out of habit. If anything happened, and even if his suit's GPS failed, he was pretty sure he could find his way back to the *Onyx*. He wondered if the others were doing the same. But he doubted it. They were all much younger than him, and his habits were the product of experience.

The faces of his children floated into his awareness, but he forced them back. Sentiment was a deadly distraction. Time enough for loving thoughts when he was back aboard the *Onyx* and heading home.

I'll see your faces as I lie dying.

That thought flitted through his head. Strange and unwelcome. Unbidden. And it gave him a sharp pang of mingled regret and dread. Where had that come from? It was nearly poetic and for a moment he was back in college, studying literature, falling in love, looking at the future as if it was bright and endless.

So much had happened since then.

"No," he said softly.

"What's that?" asked Ginge.

"Nothing," he said.

The rover rolled on.

"There she is," called the driver.

8

The rover stood on a promontory and looked down on something no one else had ever seen close-up. Even the government photos he'd seen had been blurry shots taken from long distance. And those ships looked only vaguely like this one.

"Holy..." began Jenks, but the rest just faded out.

None of the others could frame sentences. There was no trash talk.

This was a moment in history.

Fix touched Ginge's arm. "We need to keep our heads in the game, sis."

She nodded. A few of the others heard his comment, too, and they also nodded. So did Vasilievici.

Then the sergeant unbuckled and stood up. He cleared his throat and pounded his fist twice on the ceiling.

"Time to rock and roll," he growled. If there was less of the hard-edged self-assurance of command in his voice, Fix could forgive him for that. Even if the world already knew about these aliens, this was still a terrifying moment. Anyone who didn't feel it was either immensely stupid or a goddamn fool. "We'll work in teams. First team is Jenks and White. Team Two is Ginge and Mr. Fix; Three is Bagger and Boy; Four is Cho and Singh; Five is Lowell and Garcia; and Six is Tanaka and Krueger. I'll be with Team Two."

Vasilievici gave some additional assignments, though at this point it was all rehashing and reinforcing what they already knew. The weeks of flight time had given them plenty of time to train, and everyone had teamed with everyone else at one time or another. It made the entire platoon flexible. No individual loyalty but instead a mass shared sense of teamwork. Fix was happy to be with Ginge as he had a lot of respect for her skills and her judgment. She was steady, and that mattered. Jenks, though fun to banter with, was a bit more high-strung.

The driver's cabin self-sealed as soon as Vasilievici gave the order to seal face masks. The cabin depressurized and then the door hissed open.

Jenks was first out. Fix was third. Vasilievici was last. The mass and rotation speed of the asteroid gave it enough gravity to hold them on the ground, but Fix felt like he weighed fifty pounds. It made his old joints—which felt decades older that the rest of him—feel young and spry.

Wilson was back aboard the *Onyx*. Safe and sound.

The soldiers lined up on the edge of the promontory, half kneeling, half standing, guns pointed down and also around, covering 360 degrees. Small ports opened on the rover and a dozen tiny drones shot upward, propelled by powerful gas jets. They oriented themselves and spread out, sending real-D images to the tactical computers each soldier wore.

"Vasilievici," said Fix, pointing. "I think that's a body down there. My two o'clock low. Fifty yards from the ship."

One of the drones spun off and headed that way.

Vasilievici split the team into pairs, and they went down, approaching the body as quickly as caution allowed. Bagger, one of the heavy gunners, went around back with his loader, Boyd.

The other heavy gun team, Cho and Singh, trotted over to a ridge and turned it into an elevated shooting nest. The rest moved down to the flat section of what Fix regarded as a plain, which was the area flattened by the ship's belly-surfing landing. They ran toward the ship, keeping their guns moving in sync with line of sight, running with many small steps to prevent jostling the weapons if they needed to fire while in motion. Fix was impressed, because everyone was doing everything right.

There weren't many comforts in combat, but that was a big one.

Vasilievici ran with Fix and Ginge toward the body. They slowed to a careful walk as they approached.

"You're up, Fix," said the sergeant.

Ginge took up a wide-legged stance, her weapons pointing down at the figure.

The body was huge. Bigger even than the Nightmare Kid's father. Maybe eight and a half feet, though some of that was thick-soled boots and a helmet. This armor was necessarily different from the in-atmosphere combat rig like the big Hunter wore when he'd come to rescue his kid. This was a sealed suit, sleek and gleaming. Almost the same color as the roach suits the soldiers wore, except with a sheen of gold over the blackish green. There were devices of various kinds strapped to forearms, shoulders, chest, and helmet. And Fix was amused to see that it wasn't all that different in concept from what he was wearing.

But then his amusement shifted as he thought about what he'd been told by the suits who interviewed him at the black site. They knew about these monsters. Had they seen this kind of rig? The design similarities were more striking the more he looked at it.

He was not a big believer in coincidences.

They have one of these suits, he thought. *Now they want a ship to use as a prototype. Fuck me all to hell.*

Ginge pointed to a device on the thing's left shoulder. "What's that? Is it a scanner?"

"That's some kind of pulse cannon," said Fix, coming quickly back to the moment. "They use a triple laser targeting system and the guns shoot a burst of something so hot it burns through just about anything. Cauterizes flesh."

"Shit," said Ginge. "Wouldn't mind having one of those."

Give it time, thought Fix.

Over the team channel, Wilson growled, "Nobody gets light-fingered. Every scrap you find is to be cataloged. No exceptions."

Jenks coughed but it sounded a lot like *"blow me."*

Vasilievici said, "That's a bad cold you have, soldier. Better see to it."

Ginge grinned at Vasilievici, who winked at her.

Fix did not feel much like smiling.

Suddenly this mission was taking on a new slant. The thought of what the Garibaldi Group could do with a fleet of ships built on alien designs was sobering. Lucy Garibaldi might get her own private moon, and maybe a lot more. Such a fleet would skew the math on the entire interplanetary arms-race and give her corporation a position of dominance whose scope was truly staggering.

It scared him to think that that was what this was really about.

It sickened him to think he was a part of it.

And it terrified him to know that he had no choice. If he didn't do his part in this mission, then he'd lose his kids, maybe forever.

Suddenly, Fix felt terribly trapped. He glanced around as if looking for a way out.

"Tag it," said Vasilievici. "We'll gather up the bits later, bag it all and take it back to the rover."

Fix did not move.

"Hey," snapped Vasilievici, making him jump. "You dozing off, old man?"

Fix forced a smile onto his face. "Good to go, sarge," he said.

Vasilievici paused and gave him a brief scowl of inquiry but said nothing. Then the sergeant tapped his mic for the team channel.

"Let's go see this boat," he said.

They all moved down the slope to where the big, ugly, alien ship waited.

9

The Hunter ship was silent and still.

"Thermal scans are still not getting more than surface temps," said Jenks via the com link.

"That or everyone inside is dead," said Ginge. "Body temps would drop in seconds on this rock."

"Alive, dead, or ghosts," said Vasilievici, "stay sharp and alert."

Fix moved with the rest. He had his shoulder cannons synced with helmet movements. Ginge moved with him, but she had her wrist gun up and out. Fix thought that was a mistake because he preferred to keep his hands free, but each to his—or her—own.

"All teams report in," said Wilson's voice, and they all did. First and fourth teams were on perimeter defense. The other four closed in on the ship, coming in at quarter angles so as not to be in direct line with the hatches.

Fix and Ginge reached the port bow and paused, guns pointed up and down the ship, providing cover as the other teams reached their objectives.

"Team Two," said Vasilievici, "move to objective one."

That was the big hatch on that side of the ship.

Ginge nodded to Fix, and they began to crab sideways, eyes and guns moving to cover everything in their shared field of fire. Fix had been in every kind of environment from the jungles of Central America to the craters of Luna to the icy surface of Europa.

"We got you, Team Two," said Cho, and Fix glanced over to see two ugly yet comforting gun barrels sweeping slowly back and forth.

Ginge knelt and began assessing the locking mechanism on the hatch.

"Never saw this design before," she said. "I mean, obviously, but a door's a door. Same logic. I can see how it works."

"Can you get it open?" asked Vasilievici as he rounded the nose of the ship and hurried to join them.

Fix and Ginge were hunched over, studying the hatch lock.

"Can't run a bypass," said Ginge. "There's no power. We can force it open, but if the inner airlock is damaged that could compromise the whole ship and any crew left alive."

"Maybe we should leave it until we know more about what happened," said Fix.

"The hell else do we need to know?" snapped Wilson via the coms.

"The crash was controlled, sir," said Fix. "There's a corpse out here, but the hull is structurally intact, and the door is sealed."

"Are you at least walking in the direction of a point, Mr. Fix?" demanded the officer.

"Yes, sir, I am," said Fix. "I don't like how this feels."

"You're not here to explore your feelings, Mr. Fix," said Wilson. "Just do your job."

Fix wanted to punch something. Wilson was still aboard the *Onyx* and Ginge was a friend. He very nearly punched the wall of the ship. "There is something wrong about this situation."

Sergeant Vasilievici, to his credit, had all of the teams check in again, but no one else seemed disturbed by the strangeness of the moment. Or, at least, no more disturbed than anyone would be exploring an alien spaceship for the first time.

Vasilievici tapped out of the team channel and directed Fix to a secure private frequency.

"'Something wrong'…? Is this something you know based on having met these freaky sons of bitches?" asked Vasilievici. "Or are you literally having one of those 'I have a bad feeling about this' things? I have to know because we don't want to trip over our own dicks here."

"No, sergeant, we do not," agreed Fix. "And, it's more of the latter. But don't get me wrong, I've been in a lot of different kinds of combat scenarios. I'm not some civilian getting a case of the jumps."

They studied each other and then Vasilievici looked around at the rocky terrain, the corpse, his own soldiers, and the cold, silent ship.

"There's no Plan B here, Fix," he said quietly. "Wilson is just point man for the Garibaldi Corporation. Half the team are probably corporate spooks. We fuck this up and we could both lose our paychecks, let alone bonuses. And… brother, you got kids at home. So do I."

Fix cursed under his breath, but then he nodded.

"Let's hope," he said. "Maybe we'll actually get lucky."

They tapped back into the team channel. Ginge, who had been standing a few feet apart with her hand resting on the locking mechanism, eyed them curiously, but did not ask questions.

Maybe she thought Vasilievici was reading me the riot act, thought Fix.

That thought was followed by another.

Maybe she's a spook for the company.

He turned back to the ship.

"Okay," he said, "let's open this thing up."

Ginge gave him a curt nod. She took several small door-poppers from a pouch and attached them to the hinges and the lock. A couple of button-taps synced them together and she immediately began backing away.

"Fire in the hole!" she yelled and thumbed the device.

The door-poppers were small, but they carried a hefty charge of a mix of chemicals that exploded in airless space. Parts of the lock and doorframe sprayed outward, punching into the rocks behind which she, Fix, and Vasilievici hid. The heavy metal hatch was jolted out of its frame and fell with a soft thud to the surface of the asteroid.

Immediately the team rose up from behind cover, weapons aimed at the open hatch.

"No movement," said Vasilievici. "Perimeter teams stay on station. Everyone else converge on me."

Immediately the rest of the soldiers came running up. Jenks and White were the first to join them, but the others—Lowell, Garcia, Tanaka, and Krueger—were only a few steps behind.

Ginge and Fix stepped into the ship with the others covering.

There was an inner airlock, but it had a manual override in an obvious place, and while Fix watched, Ginge worked a hand-crank. The big inner hatch slid open, belching some gases out at them.

Fix knelt to one side of the open hatch and pointed all his guns inside.

"Black as the pit in here," he said. "Switching to night-vision."

The new combat suits were fitted with Garibaldi Tru-Color sensors that not only allowed them clear sight but assigned colors to everything so that the interior seemed merely poorly lit.

Even with the night-vision software, the ship seemed composed of looming shadows and strange angles. The interior design was as haphazard and frenetic as the exterior, as if every part of the craft was scavenged from something else. There was no real consistency in design or flow of function.

"This is a junk ship," said Ginge, echoing his thoughts.

"Move inside and search by twos," said Vasilievici. He took a position just inside a wide corridor that seemed to run the length of the ship. "Coms on, mouth shut unless you have something you need to share. We are looking for the crew, alive or dead."

The teams moved off, following the corridor and turning down side passages. Jenks and White went aft to check on the engines. Fix nodded to Ginge and they followed the corridor forward toward the bridge.

The interior was lit strangely, with indirect lights that crossed over into several different spectrums. It hurt Fix's eyes until he adjusted his helmet to filter it out.

Different visual spectrum, he mused, but paused at one lamp inset in the steel walls. There was a bulb in the socket, but the light came from a second bulb attached to the wiring by a patch. He tapped Ginge's arm and nodded toward it.

When she shook her head indicating she didn't understand, he went to the fixture across the corridor and showed her the same setup.

She switched to a private channel. "So what?"

"You don't think it's odd?"

"It's a light."

"The lights we're seeing are added. Jury-rigged," Fix said and looked around. "It's adapted to suit the crew, I think, which means this ship wasn't designed for them."

Ginge looked at him, lips parted, but said nothing.

Fix felt it was too important to ignore, though, and he told the rest of the team. There were some snarky comments, and Wilson told him to stop wasting time.

He saw something else. There was a section of the interior that was damaged, with a metal bulkhead broken loose from the wall. Jagged spikes of some steel-like alloy jutted out and one of these was smeared with a luminous green substance. It was something Fix had seen before.

"Guys," he said, "even though the hull's intact, we found a damaged bulkhead. And look at this." He aimed his bodycam toward the green mess. "That's Hunter blood for sure. I saw enough of it firsthand. There's blood trails going everywhere. One or more of these bastards got spiked pretty bad by debris."

"I'm okay with that," said Ginge.

"Might be other damage," said Fix. "My guess is they landed hard and both the ship and crew got knocked around."

Singh said, "I think he's right."

"Why?" asked Vasilievici. "What have you got?"

"We're in the engine room," said Singh, whose MOS—

mode of service—was engineering. His job was to analyze the ship's systems to see if it was fixable or scrap. "Seeing a lot of that green blood. It's on the access panels, controls… all over. Looks like they were working on the engines. There's some power in the batteries, if I'm reading these meters right. And work lights on in here."

"So?" demanded Wilson.

"So, sir, looks like they had life support back online. Wrong gases for us to breathe, but that's fixable. Maybe that was their priority, post-crash. Also, they have a lot of stuff stored here. And a shit-ton of parts. This stuff is exotic, but when it comes down to it, an engine's an engine. I don't see anything that couldn't have been fixed in time."

"Like how much time?" asked Vasilievici.

"Here on the asteroid? Without an actual shipyard? Five, six months." He paused. "Fix said they were fighters. Maybe their engineer was dead. Or maybe none of them were mechanics. I don't know."

"Very well," said the lieutenant. "Continue searching the ship. I need to know what happened to the crew."

Fix and Ginge moved on.

They passed an entrance to what was clearly crew quarters. The door was smeared with green blood. Fix stepped inside and his sense of unease grew.

"What now?" asked Ginge, but then she saw and it stopped her cold.

There were two rows with three bunks each.

Bodies lay on four of the six bunks.

They were Hunters.

And they were dead.

10

"What the hell…?" breathed Ginge.

They stood over the first of the corpses.

The creature was in full armor, but it was of the kind Fix had seen on the father alien back on Gameworld. A mix of armored pieces and also exposed skin covered in a netting material. The hands were folded on the stomach, the fingers curled around the shaft of an ornate club that was etched with obscure symbols. A gauntlet was strapped to each forearm, and from each a pair of razor-sharp blades projected, and these crossed the creature's powerful chest. It wore a helmet that was similar but not identical to what the Nightmare Kid's father wore. Different, too, from the one on the corpse outside. And as he glanced around the room, Fix saw that each helmet was different. Each had some unique features—horns, spikes, beaks, and other things hard to describe. On the shoulder was one of the laser blasters. Dark tendrils that could have been stylish dreadlocks or something mechanical—it was impossible to tell—were arranged over the massive shoulders. Every single one of the Hunters was spattered with green.

"Is it dead?" asked Ginge.

Before Fix could answer, she drew a knife and plunged it into the creature's thigh, then stepped back and swiveled her cannons toward the thing.

There was no reaction of any kind. Although there was more green blood on the knife, none welled from the wound.

"Dead for sure," she said.

"Jesus, Ginge," growled Fix, "what the hell was that?"

She gave him a look that had much less of the affability she'd shown since leaving Earth. Her eyes were cold, calculating.

"We're here for the tech, old man," she said. "Did you miss the briefing?"

"Even so..."

She made a face then reached for the thing's helmet and spent a few moments trying to sort out how it fastened. Then she popped several fittings loose and tore the helmet off. She whistled.

"Cute," she said. "Bet he got *all* the girls."

The monstrous face was similar to the Nightmare Kid's, though much older and slack in the repose of death. The face was scarred and dead, and yet there was a noble, almost regal aspect to it.

In a strange way he felt some remorse for whatever killed the Hunter. He looked down the rows and saw that each figure was laid out like a Viking on his death ship. Surrounded by weapons, ready for war in Valhalla... or whatever passed for it in this alien culture.

Surely, he mused, these Hunters were not dressed this fine all the time. Not in ordinary space flight. Someone had taken time to dress each body and arrange it in this way. Like the heroic dead.

Had it been the Hunter they found outside? Had that been his last act before whatever injuries he sustained in the crash took him? If so, Fix found it sad that no one would show him the same respect.

Instead, the crew of the *Onyx* would load them like so much cold meat into the hold of the corporation ship. Then this craft would be towed into the hold and all of it would go to a Garibaldi lab somewhere sunward of Mars. Everything here would be trophies for some executive and source material for a massive arms-race upgrade.

It all felt wrong.

Ginge walked away from him and checked each corpse in exactly the same way. A stab in leg or belly or arm. Fix did not at all like the vicious and unflinching way she did it.

He trailed along behind her, his sense of dread deepening.

His attention was drawn to the other bunks. The empty ones. One surely belonged to the dead Hunter. But the other…?

Fix looked at the bunk. It was made, but not neatly. As if someone had slept there recently and left in a hurry. There was nothing around the bed except more blood spatter. When he glanced around, he saw that each of the other cots had a metal trunk—probably some kind of footlocker—and their bedside tables had various personal items on them. There was nothing on this one, and no footlocker, but the hastily made bed troubled him greatly.

He was dimly aware of the other team members talking on the team channel as they completed their sweep. White was yelling about a wall covered in grisly trophies—skulls and spinal columns, insectoid heads, and more. The bridge was deserted, as was the rest of the ship.

Fix said, "Who's in the galley?"

"Team Five," replied Garcia. "You should come down for a bite. Looks like they were about to chow down when this ship crashed. Places set for six. Looks like boiled turds. Glad I can't smell it."

"Six…" said Fix softly.

"What's that?" asked Ginge.

Fix felt the floor seemed to tilt under him.

"Vasilievici," he yelled. "Sergeant Vasilievici."

"Right here," said the noncom, and Fix turned to see the sergeant in the doorway. "What have you got?"

"Six bunks," said Fix, his excitement rising with his fear. "Six places for dinner."

"So what?"

"*Five* bodies."

Vasilievici began to say something then looked around. He tapped his coms. "Perimeter teams check in," he ordered. "Tell me what you're seeing outside."

There was no answer.

Vasilievici repeated his order, but all that came back through the communicators was an awful silence.

Fix turned and studied the deck more closely. There was a line of green droplets—thinner than the others—that led toward the door. He hurried over and saw that it wandered awkwardly toward the main hatch.

"No..." he breathed. "Jesus... no." He turned and grabbed Vasilievici's arm. "This is a setup," he growled. "I think we're being played."

"What are you—?"

A scream cut through his words. It came from the command channel and filled all of their helmets with pain and terror and horror.

It was Wilson's voice.

He screamed and screamed and screamed.

And then the channel went dead.

By then Fix was running.

Vasilievici and Ginge were right behind him. The sergeant bellowed for everyone to follow, and the whole platoon bolted from the hatch out onto the surface of the asteroid. They ran to the closest sentry outpost, but even from a dozen paces away Fix could tell they were too late.

Bagger and Boyd lay sprawled.

Torn.

Ruined.

Their bodies were torn to pieces, but each separate piece was fused, cauterized.

"What the fuck?" cried Ginge.

"The rover," snapped Fix. "We need to get back to the ship."

They ran.

In the diminished gravity they took huge bounding steps. They reached the place where the rover had been parked at the top of the promontory.

The rover was gone.

Only faint tracks in the mingled silica and metal dust that covered everything. They stood there, staring toward the eastern stretch of the huge floating rock.

Ginge took a single step in that direction, but she stopped. Her knees buckled and she slowly dropped to the ground.

Over the farthest crest of rock, a shape moved upward. Vast, sleek, and as black as its name.

They all stood and watched the *Onyx* lift off and pass overhead. Fix felt his mouth go totally dry as the ship cruised above them in a dreadful silence.

11

They watched it fly out of sight. That did not take long. The ship was top of the line. Very fast.

Just the thing for stranded survivors of a crash.

"God almighty," whispered Jenks. He sat down hard on the ground and hung his head in total defeat. The others looked at one another as if there was an answer to be found on someone else's face.

Except for Jenks' comment, no one said a word.

Until Fix said, "It was a trick. The whole thing. Just a trick to hijack our fucking ship. One of the crew survived, but he was hurt. Bad, I think. All that blood. Maybe too bad to really fix this ship. And, tough as these sons of bitches are, I think he was too badly injured to risk a fight with us. Then we just came along and provided him a luxury ride. He ghosted us, set the scene here with his comrades in their bunks and all… and was probably watching from the rocks, laughing his ugly ass off as we came in. Then he hightailed it to the *Onyx*."

"God damn!" cried Tanaka.

Krueger had tears running down his cheeks. "We're stuck here. *We're going to die here*."

Fix grabbed him by the front of the suit and shook him. "Shut. The. Fuck. Up."

He rattled Krueger with each word, punctuating them with a rough shake. Then he released him and looked around.

"I have kids at home," Fix snarled. "No way I'm dying on this goddamn rock."

"Well, unless you have wings, I don't know about…" said Ginge, and let the rest hang.

Fix pointed back the way they came. "No wings," he said. "But we have a ship."

"A dead ship," said Jenks. "It'll make a nice goddamn coffin."

Fix ignored him and turned to Singh. "You said you could fix it in five or six months, right?"

Singh looked at him blankly. "Y-yes. I mean, I think so. Maybe."

Fix got up in his face. "Tell me that you can repair that fucking ship. Say it loud enough for everyone to hear. Make us all believe it."

Singh licked his lips. Then he nodded.

"No," barked Fix. "*Say* it."

"Yes," said Singh. He was sweating badly in the suit. "I can fix it."

"Now," said Fix, grinning. "Tell me you can fix it one hell of a lot faster than six months."

The engineer looked around at the faces of his fellow soldiers. There was fear and dread, but also hope. Very little of it. Like a match flickering in a breeze. He straightened his shoulders.

To Fix he said, "You're goddamn right I can fix it. Give me three months and everyone helping? Three tops."

Fix glanced up and away. One of those sparkling white dots up there was planet Earth. He closed his eyes for a moment and conjured the faces of his children.

"Three months," he said. Then he turned to the rest of the team. "Then let's get to work."

Sergeant Vasilievici, who was in command, cleared his throat.

"You heard Mr. Fix," he said. "Let's fix this damn ship and go the hell home."

BITTER HUNT

BY KIM MAY

Ak'kili watched three drop pods descend to the planet below. They were just blips on her screen but seeing the confirmation of her prey's positions made her grip the armrests of the command chair hard enough to leave depressions there. Her hound, Xave, sensed the change in her mood. He sat up and growled at the screen. Ak'kili patted his head until he settled down again. It wouldn't be a good hunt if both of them were agitated.

This wasn't going to be an enjoyable hunt, that was certain, but if they could keep their emotions under control, it would at least be a satisfying one. The law-breaking trio descending to the desert planet below would pay for what they'd done to her.

Her prey left their scout ship in orbit. According to her

sensors they left the pod bay doors open. Ak'kili targeted the top half of their ship and fired a short blast from her ship's plasma cannon. The blast ricocheted off the vessel's shields, going wide into empty space. Ak'kili knew the leader of this group well so she started broadcasting every one of their passwords she knew. The fifth code successfully disabled the scout ship's shields. Ak'kili put a little more distance between her ship and theirs and increased the strength of her forward shields then fired the cannon again. This time she made it a prolonged blast and targeted their fuel tanks. The plasma cut through the hull and ignited the fuel inside. The scout ship exploded, sending fragments of hull in all directions. She watched a singed human skull from their trophy vault float past.

Ak'kili turned her attention back to her targets below. The planet's climate was favorable and the atmosphere tolerable. What intrigued her was that the geological data displayed formidable mountain ranges and caverns that could give them a tactical advantage. If they split up and spread out across multiple canyons, she'd really have an interesting hunt.

They'd picked a good planet for their last stand.

Ak'kili got up and walked to the small armory inside her trophy room. Xave followed at her heels. She gave him an affectionate pat and rubbed one of his locks. Ak'kili pulled her usual assortment from their wall mounts—a plasmacaster, net gun, and smart disc. Her wrist gauntlet, which she already wore, had wristblades and energy flechettes preloaded.

She went back to the bridge and set a brand new security code for her scout ship. Her drop pod already had a new code and it would alert her if someone tried to gain access with an old one. However if anyone tried that with this ship it would autodestruct. If they didn't die on this planet they'd die trying to get away from it. There wasn't another scout ship or mothership for light years.

Ak'kili got into her drop pod. Xave hopped into the pod and settled on her lap before the door closed. Her pod landed beside the nearest drop point. The trio's pods landed in a loose grouping in the heart of a wide valley between two mountain ranges. The pods were far enough apart that she didn't need to scan to confirm that they'd gone separate ways. Any other stratagem would have been unwise. Traveling to a rendezvous point wasted valuable time that they could spend setting up their defenses. She'd taught the trio's leader that.

The sun hadn't reached its zenith yet. There was still plenty of time to hunt all three of them before sundown. Not that it mattered if it took longer. While this planet was hot enough for their kind during the day the nights would be fatally cold, but not so cold that the netting she wore wouldn't be able to compensate. The mesh had proven effective in arctic temperatures multiple times so one desert night would be nothing in comparison. As a precaution she set an alarm on her gauntlet. When it went off, a notification would flash on her helmet's screen to let her know that she had one hour until sunset. She used different techniques when hunting at night. The alarm would give her time to mentally prepare for the shift in tactics.

Ak'kili and Xave headed for the nearest pod. Xave ran ahead. He stopped a short distance away from the lawbreaker's pod and sniffed the ground. It didn't take him long to find the occupant's scent.

Xave led her toward the mountains west of them. Ak'kili pulled up a hologram of the topography of the area. They most likely headed for the foothills. It was rugged enough to provide decent cover. Her prey hadn't been on the planet long enough for them to make it to the mountains or the nearest caves.

Ak'kili walked silently across the red stone valley floor. The sun was high above them in an orange sky that was marred only by their contrails. A light breeze stirred up dust, making her glad of her helmet.

Xave sniffed the ground again and picked up the pace. They were close. Ak'kili grunted a command to Xave to leave the trail and follow her. She walked to a small crag to their left. Ak'kili didn't look to see if Xave followed her. The hound was well trained. He'd follow her across the planet. When they reached the crag, she lay down on her stomach and crawled to the summit. She felt a familiar pressure against her right calf. It was Xave silently telling her where he was.

From this vantage point she could see a good portion of the valley. She did a thermal scan of the area. There were a few hot spots from small wildlife but nothing large enough to be Yautja. Her scanner couldn't penetrate the larger hills and crags so her prey must be in one of the ravines behind them.

She clicked her tusks in irritation. Ak'kili finally understood why the Enforcers hated hunting their kind. It wasn't because of any distaste for the assignment. It was because the prey in question had the same technology and training that they did. Their usual tricks wouldn't work. Anytime prey was intelligent enough to know the limitations of their scanners, they instantly became a much more deadly species. Of course, it also made their actions a bit more predictable.

Ak'kili looked to the right and followed the trajectory that Xave had them on earlier. It led to one such recess behind a large hill. The ravine ran parallel to the valley and judging by the size of the hills on both sides of it this was a fairly deep one as well.

She looked at the far end of the recess. There were some large clusters of rocks that might be tricky to pass through but not enough to make that end inaccessible. Traversing it would be worth the effort. This trio was still young. They'd expect their pursuer to come from the direction of the landing site.

Xave nudged her right arm. The hound looked at a spot near the middle of the ravine. If the breeze hadn't died, she never would have seen it—a thin plume of dust rising into the air. He must be preparing some sort of trap and hadn't noticed that the wind had died.

Perfect.

Ak'kili backed away from her perch. She ran across the valley floor with Xave at her heels. The dense atmosphere made the sprint more difficult but that only made it exhilarating. A hunt that wasn't challenging wasn't worth pursuing. This sprint made her realize that she'd been on the homeworld too long. She missed this. The adrenalin rush of pursuing a prey that knew you were coming for them and was prepared to fight back. There was nothing like it in the galaxy.

A bright flash of light zipped past her and struck the ground to her left. Blasted chunks of rock rained down on them. *Sniper!*

Her skin patterns didn't blend seamlessly with the ground and that gave away her position. Luckily her speed made her exact position difficult to pinpoint and that was the only thing that saved her.

That blast came from a burner. If she was right about his position, then she was just barely in range.

Ak'kili pushed herself harder, sprinting across the open ground. She angled her path away from her prey. Xave matched her angle and moved to her left side to put more distance between himself and the sniper. The hound wasn't being cowardly. He was trained to drag her to safety if she got hurt but he couldn't do that if he didn't protect himself first.

The next blast struck the ground to her right, barely missing her feet. Good. She was out of range. Ak'kili would have to cover more ground to reach him but at least she would survive this crossing.

They ran up the rise and skidded down into the relative safety of the ravine. There wasn't much vegetation here—just some scraggly brush and a thin stream. The greenery thickened a little near her prey's location but not enough to provide full cover. While the low vegetation left her mostly out in the open, it also exposed him. His heat signature was easy to spot and her bio-helmet locked onto it immediately. He knelt on the ridge.

Ak'kili didn't stop when she reached the bottom of the ravine. She dropped into a half-crouch and wound her way through the brush. Xave ran ahead of her. She uttered a series of soft clicks, instructing Xave to stay close to the slope they'd just descended.

Her prey adjusted quickly. The next shot grazed her right arm a heartbeat later. She clenched her jaw. She wasn't going to give him the satisfaction of a hiss.

Ak'kili kept running, varying her path. She clicked once. Xave ran full speed at her prey, growling. Ak'kili threw her smart disc. As her prey aimed at Xave, the smart disc embedded itself in his throat, the force of the impact throwing him onto his back.

Xave quieted and slowed down. The hound wisely kept his distance. Ak'kili didn't give her prey a chance to regroup. She fired her plasmacaster at his chest and torso until it was charred beyond recognition. Ak'kili took a good look at his face. She recognized him. He was one of her spawn's hunt mates. She couldn't recall his name but that hardly mattered.

One down. Two to go.

Ak'kili pressed the recall button for her smart disc. She snatched it out of the air and secured it on its thigh mount. Ak'kili drew her ceremonial dagger and severed the last bits of sinew that kept his head attached. Xave trotted up to the body, sunk his teeth into the body's locks and gave the severed head a fierce shake. Ak'kili clicked a firm order to him to take the head back to her drop ship. The hound reluctantly stopped and obeyed her order. He trotted up the slope and vanished down the other side.

Ak'kili climbed up to the top of the ridge and scanned the area. The only heat signature she saw was Xave's. The other two had hidden themselves well. She switched to a topographic view of the area. There was a small extinct volcano nearby. There was a good chance that there were some caves or old lava tubes in the vicinity. The terrain provided a lot of good defensible places to make a last stand. If she started the next hunt now, she'd have to do it without Xave's help. That was fine. She'd hunted plenty of prey without the hound's help.

Ak'kili took off in the direction of the volcano. When she reached a spot with good cover, she'd stop to scan the area to make sure she wasn't walking into an ambush. The traitor she had just taken down was the most inexperienced of the trio. The other two wouldn't be as easy. Twakese was hot-tempered but a good hunter. The other, Dakdwade, she'd trained herself—a feat she had been proud of until late.

The terrain became much more difficult to traverse as she neared the volcano. Instead of gentle rises and the occasional hill, every step was on uneven ground. The basalt here was smooth and rolled like waves with crevasses between some of them. The inconsistent curvature made it difficult to keep her footing if she didn't pay close attention. But the difficulty it added to the experience made the task more sweet. These law-breakers had created a volcanic anger within her and her clan. Although the anger she felt still paled in comparison to the primal ferocity it took to create the rock beneath her feet.

Violence upon violence.

There was a pleasing symmetry in that. It was as if the planet had created this tectonic battlefield specifically for this hunt. It made her sad that the volcano was long dead. Tracking across an active lava flow would have made it a hunt to cherish.

Ak'kili slowed down. Her attention alternated between the thermal view on her bio-helmet and the terrain. She found a wide opening in the shadow of a small crag. It sloped down at a gentle angle and had enough head clearance for a Yautja to enter without needing to duck. Judging by its smooth sides, this was an extinct lava tube. That explained the terrain. The rolling waves of basalt she crossed were the remnants of at least one lava flow.

She crept up to the mouth of the tube. Her scanners didn't pick up anything, but they also couldn't penetrate deep enough to show her the entire lava tube. The smooth basalt also meant there wouldn't be tracks or any other indication that her prey was inside. Did she dare investigate? If he was inside, she could end this hunt quickly. If he weren't, then she would have wasted precious time. It was also entirely possible that she was walking into her grave. All it would take was one well-aimed shot to bring the entire tube down on her head. She was still outnumbered. Either of her remaining targets could ambush her.

Daylight illuminated the opening enough for her to see that the tube curved to the right. Beyond that was darker than the deepest reaches of space and not even her bio-helmet could decipher what was rock and what was empty air. The dark recesses would have made an excellent hiding spot if it weren't for one thing. The temperature.

It would be much cooler inside—too cool for him to have the slightest chance of thermally blending in. His heat signature would radiate like the sun. If he was in there, he was near the entrance where the outside air kept the ambient temperature warm enough that his residual heat wouldn't give away which rock he hid behind. That made this very simple.

Ak'kili sidled up against the left side of the opening and gave the entrance a thorough once over. Satisfied that he wasn't in the area her bio-helmet could display, she backed away from the entrance. When she was a good distance away, she stopped and watched the entrance. Minutes passed and no one emerged from the lava tube. A prickling sensation on the back of her neck made her spin around with her gauntlet raised.

She didn't immediately spot the threat. Instead Ak'kili acted on instinct. She dove to the side. As she fell, she finally spotted a heat signature close to the ground. Ak'kili fired an energy flechette at the signature and missed. The flechette struck the ground but her message was received. He knew that she'd spotted him.

Ak'kili ran to a small rise and knelt behind it. He was too smart to stay in a compromised location. The question now was which way did he go? Ak'kili peered above the smooth crest. A hint of movement drew her attention to the right. She dropped back beneath the rise. A heartbeat later a smart disc flew through the space where her head had been a moment ago. The disc scraped the stone.

She reached up and snatched the disc from above her head. Instead of stopping it, she pushed it further until it struck the stone behind her and was embedded so deep that the auto-recall wouldn't work. If he wanted it back, he'd have to come and get it.

A loud roar echoed across the landscape. That roar most definitely belonged to Twakese. Ak'kili threw her head back and laughed. Twakese had just realized what she did and would be out for blood. All caution had been launched into orbit.

She ran across the lava field. She didn't make the slightest attempt to be stealthy. There wasn't time for it. She needed to get away from Twakese's smart disc before—

Ak'kili was suddenly thrust forward. It wasn't until she landed and bits of rock rained down on her head that she realized how close she'd come. Twakese hadn't wasted any time targeting his smart disc and blasting it with his plasmacaster. It was a waste of a serviceable weapon but he'd always been the 'if I can't have it then no one can' type of male.

The explosion was small enough that her ears only rang a little. She shook her head to clear it and ran for a nearby fissure. She hopped into it, using her powerful legs to catch and brace herself against the sides. The fissure was very narrow so the fit was tight but tolerable. The important thing was that she got out of sight before the thermal cover the explosion provided vanished.

Ak'kili shimmied along the narrow fissure. It curved slightly, which brought her closer to the site of the explosion. She was too low to see the explosion site so she waited and listened. Enough time had passed for the ringing in her ears to subside. She could hear the faint whisper of soles on pulverized rock. Ak'kili pushed herself up a little, just enough to peek over the top.

Twakese stood near the shallow crater. She could tell by the set of his shoulders he wasn't pleased that there wasn't a corpse. Ak'kili wedged herself into the fissure so she'd have both of her arms free.

Ak'kili drew her smart disc and threw it as hard as she could. She watched it speed through the air in a graceful arc that was high enough Twakese wouldn't see it until it was too late. Her disc struck Twakese in the chest plate, making him bellow. The disc didn't sink in deep enough to kill him. Twakese's chest plate was too strong for it to penetrate. However, judging by his howl of pain right after the impact, her disc hit him with enough force to break a few ribs. That would slow him down. Ak'kili recalled the disc. The second she caught it she dropped back down into the fissure and shimmied back the way she came.

She moved swiftly through the fissure, only stopping when it became too narrow to continue any further. When she reached that point, she climbed out and crept closer to Twakese. He stood near the spot where she'd attacked, staring into the fissure. It would have been so easy to fire her plasmacaster and be done with it but that wouldn't be as satisfying as sinking her blades deep into his flesh. Ak'kili wanted Twakese to know it was her that ended his life.

Ak'kili curled her right hand to release a pair of jagged talon-like blades. They popped out from the wrist gauntlet on that arm. Ak'kili drew her dagger with her off hand. She moved slowly with light steps that even Xave would have had trouble sensing. When she was within striking range she launched herself forward, relying on her memory of his body proportions, since his camouflage was still activated. She slashed his side and back just below his chest plate.

Twakese roared. He turned on her, camouflage deactivating mid-turn. Twakese brandished his own wrist blades. He attacked her with the full force of his rage, slashing and stabbing so quickly that it was all she could do to block and parry.

Ak'kili bit down on her frustration about not being able to get another good strike in. *Be patient. He'll wear himself down soon and then you can…*

Twakese's movements slowed a fraction. Ak'kili kept her guard up. Twakese threw a punch.

Ak'kili caught his wrist blades with hers and twisted his fist to the side. The blow that he'd intended to hit her vulnerable torso with had completely missed instead. His mandibles flared in anger. The outburst made him pause, giving Ak'kili an opening. She thrust her dagger into his lower abdomen and twisted the blade before pulling out. Phosphorescent green blood seeped from the wound.

"How could you?" Ak'kili said. "They were unarmed females and young!"

Twakese fell to his knees. He clutched the wound in his gut. "I don't regret killing them."

"Then I don't regret killing you," Ak'kili said. She kicked him over and used her dagger to sever his head.

She took a step back and cleaned her dagger. Two down, one to go. It figured that the last traitor to take down was the one she was both the most eager to seek out, but the least eager to kill. It had to be done though. There was no other option. They'd repeatedly broken one of their people's foundational laws and because of that she had to kill them.

Movement in the distance drew her attention. A small shape galloped toward her. She zoomed in on the figure with her bio-helmet. It was Xave.

Ak'kili retracted her wristblades and sheathed her dagger. Xave took the head and ran off before she could give him a command. Normally she'd scold him for that kind of willfulness, but this time she'd let it slide. She couldn't take him with her on the next hunt so it was just as well that he left her on his own.

She took a knee to catch her breath. She watched Xave trot back to the ship, dragging Twakese's head by the locks. The head bounced on the uneven stone. Ak'kili's tusks clacked together in irritation. The skull wouldn't be recognizable by the time Xave got it on board. That would make confirming the kill with the elders more difficult. Twakese had an identical twin brother. The only way anyone could tell them apart was a crescent-shaped scar on Twakese's chin. She had planned on taking an image scan before cleaning the trophy but the damage sustained during the trip would probably damage the scar enough to make a scan useless. Unfortunately Xave was already out of earshot. Ak'kili stood up. If she hurried she could catch up to Xave and carry Twakese's head herself to minimize further damage. It would use up what daylight was left, but it was unavoidable.

A notification flashed across the screen of Ak'kili's bio-helmet. Someone was trying to get aboard her pod. The code they'd tried to use was one she hadn't used in decades. Her target would have known that before approaching her pod.

A new notification popped up onto her screen. They'd tried the code a second time. Ak'kili glared at the notifications. There was only one reason he would do that. He was trying to lure her to him. She would have ignored the taunt if it weren't for one thing… Xave was headed straight for him.

Ak'kili ran across the rugged terrain as fast as her legs could propel her. Xave didn't know who the final prey for this hunt was and that was going to cause problems. Her plan was to leave Xave in the drop ship for the final hunt. The hound wouldn't understand why she was hunting this particular individual. She wanted to spare Xave that agony but of course her prey had to ruin that too.

Xave was far enough ahead that she couldn't see him. He was a small dot on the landscape in her thermal view. Ak'kili ran with her heart in her throat. She almost tripped a couple times because she was paying more attention to the horizon than the ground at her feet.

Ak'kili forced herself to stop and catch her breath. She was being reactionary, which was exactly what he wanted. Xave was no fool. If he felt threatened, he'd leave. She needed to be smart about how she handled this. Running up to her ship panicked and out of breath would get her killed. She was better than that and this was her opportunity to prove it to her prey, to her clan, and most of all to herself.

She took a deep breath and started walking back to her ship. It was within sight.

Xave was almost to the ship but there was no sign of her prey. The ground was completely flat there. Where could he be hiding?

The sun was close to the horizon when she reached the landing site. She passed Twakase's head. Xave had dropped it on his way to the ship. Ak'kili grabbed it by the locks and carried it the rest of the way. Xave greeted her and then ran back to the landing gear, where he'd been a moment before.

The law-breaker emerged from behind her drop ship's landing gear. That explained why she didn't see his heat signature on her helmet's screen. Xave sat at the law-breaker's feet, wagging his tail. Ak'kili approached slowly.

"You have my attention, Dakdwade," Ak'kili said. She pointed her gauntlet at him. If he so much as flinched, she'd use energy flechettes to punch him full of holes.

"No embrace for your spawn? I'm disappointed," he said.

Dakdwade glanced at the head dangling from her left hand. He clenched his fists but didn't curse or spit at her. As a mother she was proud of him for not letting an opponent stir his anger. As an opponent, she was eager for this match of skills to commence.

Ak'kili didn't respond. He was deliberately reminding her of their blood relation for the same reason she didn't acknowledge it. Familial bonds were a weakness and they were both going to use it to their advantage—Dakdwade in order to get her to back down and let him go, whereas she was relying on it to get him to underestimate her determination to see this through.

Dakdwade reached down and patted Xave on the head. "What a shame we can't negotiate a truce."

"Don't speak of shame to me," Ak'kili said with a sneer. She tossed Twakese's head toward her ship. It rolled across the stone, stopping near Xave's feet. "My mate won't even look at me because of what you've done." *I will restore my honor and my place among our people at all cost.*

"I don't see what's so shameful about it. We hunted prey like anyone else in the clan."

"You killed unarmed females and young," Ak'kili spat. "It was the first of our people's laws that I taught you and yet you flagrantly disregarded it."

Ak'kili uttered two sharp clicks, commanding Xave to come to her. Dakdwade used a hand signal to command Xave to stay. Xave looked from her to him and back again. The hound whined.

She repeated the command. She put all of the irritation she felt into her voice. Xave's tail stopped wagging and his head drooped. The hound slunk toward her. When Xave was halfway to her, she dropped to one knee and fired her net launcher. The net skimmed the flat rocky plain as it sped across the distance between them. Dakdwade raised his smart disc, prepared to counter. The net didn't come anywhere near him. It hit Xave instead.

The net propelled the hound backward until he hit the landing gear of one of the traitor's drop pods. Ak'kili winced when he hit. The net wrapped around the landing gear, making it impossible for Xave to move until Ak'kili hit the release. She didn't. Instead she used a control on the launcher to release enough tension in the net so that it didn't injure the hound.

Dakdwade threw his smart disc. Ak'kili quickly threw hers to intercept it. Her throw was too hasty so the trajectory was off. Instead of knocking Dakdwade's disc to the ground, it only knocked it off course, but that was enough.

Ak'kili ran. She summoned her disc. It raced back to her. Ak'kili caught it and spun around. She held the disc vertically in front of her. The targeting on Dakdwade's disc corrected the trajectory but her strike had bought her enough time.

Dakdwade's disc struck hers with enough force to make her take two large steps back. It spun and ground down the edge of hers but she held firm. Dakdwade's disc flew back to him. He had an older model that forced him to recall it in order to reset the target.

Ak'kili threw her smart disc but didn't set a target for it. She ran across the empty expanse between them, her wristblades at the ready. Dakdwade started to move and then froze after one step. He couldn't move from that spot until his disc returned. She'd forced Dakdwade to choose between his weapon or avoiding her attacks.

Dakdwade ran toward his smart disc and jumped high into the air. He snatched the disc out of the air, landing with a heavy thud. Ak'kili's disc sailed over his head and struck the stone where he stood moments before. She recalled her disc. Ak'kili clicked her mandibles in frustration. She had hoped he'd be frozen with indecision for a little longer than that. A few more seconds and she would have been in position to finish this quickly.

Ak'kili targeted a spot two steps behind Dakdwade. When her disc returned, she grabbed it and let the momentum spin her around. She added as much momentum as she could into that turn. Right before she completed a rotation, she threw her smart disc at him. She then fired three flechettes at his feet.

The shots surprised him. They also forced him to take two steps backward.

Dakdwade was so focused on her that he never saw her disc come at him from behind. Its angle of descent was steep by design. It didn't strike him in the back. Instead it hit the back of his left heel, slicing through his heavy boots and the tendon beneath.

He hissed and shifted his weight to his other foot. Dakdwade fired energy flechettes at her but she dodged every one. Ak'kili swiftly closed the distance between them. She slashed at his vulnerable midsection. Dakdwade hopped backward, avoiding her attack. He slashed with his own blades. Despite his movement being hampered he attacked with such lethal precision that he managed to slash her left bicep.

Ak'kili ignored the pain. She kicked at his injured heel, not to damage it further but to dislodge and flip up her disc. Ak'kili grabbed it with her left hand. The weight made her injured arm burn. She clenched her mandibles and steeled herself. Ak'kili used the disc like a big knife, slashing and punching at him with it without trying to hit him.

Dakdwade deflected her blows, mostly with the wrist blade on his right gauntlet. The second he deflected with his left Ak'kili struck.

Ak'kili brought down her wrist blade and stabbed his wrist gauntlet, smashing the controls for his self-destruct.

Dakdwade stared at the damaged controls in horror and

confusion. Ak'kili didn't waste the opportunity. She crouched and used the smart disc in her offhand to slice open the thigh of his good leg. Dakdwade crumpled to the ground.

She drove her wristblade through his wind pipe before he could start begging for his life. She forced herself to watch as he started to suffocate. It didn't matter how much her maternal side wanted to look away. She had to bear witness to this.

Ak'kili used her smart disc to bring his suffering to a quick end. She knelt beside him and let the tears flow freely. The mixture of emotions was something she never wanted to experience ever again. She was devastated at having killed her spawn. However, at the same time she was relieved that the day's ordeal was over and happy that her good standing in the clan would be reinstated.

Ak'kili freed Xave from the net when she felt in control of herself again. The hound regarded her with apprehension. She didn't make any move to console him. There wasn't anything she could do to erase the pain he felt. Ak'kili had felt the same way when she found out that Dakdwade and his companions had hunted and killed females and young on several worlds. Xave dragged Twakese's head into the pod and curled up behind the command chair.

She bent down and picked up Dakdwade's head and carried it back to her ship. Her steps were slow. It took several minutes to walk the short distance to her drop pod. She was more worn out than she'd expected and it had nothing to do with her exertions during today's hunts.

The alarm she set after landing flashed across her helmet's screen. One hour until sunset. Ak'kili shook her head and sighed. Her gauntlet's computer was wrong. The sun had fallen and would never rise again.

FIELD TRIP

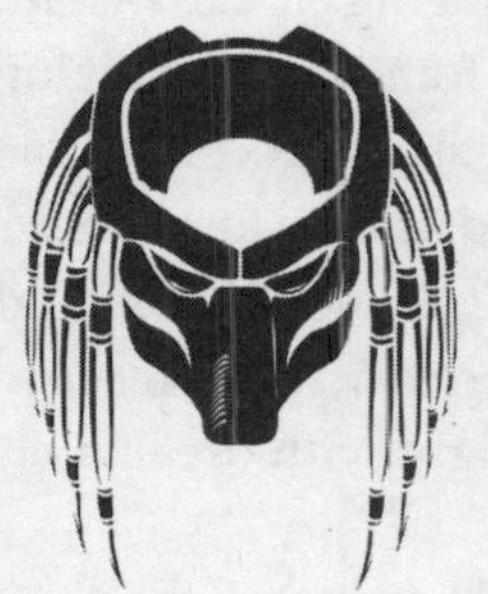

BY ROBERT GREENBERGER

Donatiki found herself sleeping more than she expected, which irritated her because she needed to stay alert. Her mission saw her responsible for four unblooded. They'd been out on a survey mission to Earth for five days, exploring the different terrains and cultures, watching the unassuming oomans go about their business. Each of her charges took notes, reported back after decloaking, and argued which continent looked the most challenging, which people seemed the best to hunt. It was all a simulation to them, preparing them for their first hunts, and showing them a different portion of the universe. All agreed: nothing in the holographic recordings compared with actually feeling the world's gravity, the planet's smells, and sounds.

She'd been assigned this role given her advanced

pregnancy and at first, she chafed at it, but gradually accepted the duty, seeing the value it would bring her charges. They were a fine lot, eager for their first kills; all had successfully completed their lock plating, and after this mission, they would be assigned a Party and sent on their first hunt. For now, they were engaging in claw-challenges after meals to burn off energy. She found herself giving tutorials to sharpen their hand-to-hand skills, becoming a teacher, which was something she would have to focus more on once the suckling was born. It couldn't arrive soon enough so she could nurse it, wean it, and return to action. Her blood was calling to her, keeping her up at night with dreams of past hunts and ones to come.

There were two days left to the survey, an intensive look at jungle terrains in the southern equator and then a final look at the arctic region, which she noted was smaller than her last visit. Back then, she had hunted a large white beast, seeing how long she would last in the frigid environment, and glorying in besting it in close combat.

Her reverie was shaken when the ship rocked violently, throwing her from the chair. As she painfully landed on her knees, the ship was bathed in color signaling an emergency. Her charges were all calling out data, but their overlapping voices confused the situation. She snapped for Tenude, the eldest among them, to report. She regained her footing, steadying herself by holding on against the wall, as he summarized that some relays in the engine seemed to have misfired. She shuffled past him to look at the displays. The readouts were all dropping, and then she felt the ship wobble and begin a descent. She rerouted power to maintain the cloak and then life support. It was clear they needed to land the vessel so it was a matter of finding open space and the most direct descent. The nav came back with an optimal route and she ordered compliance and told the others to buckle in because the landing was likely to be rough. Once they were secured, she harnessed herself, and only then paused to consider the life she was carrying. They had to repair the ship and go home so the baby would begin its life as planned. Earth was no place to raise sucklings.

Jessica Haning felt the baby kick and rubbed her hand across her distended abdomen and smiled. She looked up from her morning Bible study to take in the image of her husband Colin, the Anglo-Saxon warrior, kitted out and looking like someone from a millennia ago. The light brown tunic was worn with a cuirass of leather over it, the long, dark brown cloak was fastened at the shoulder with a brooch in the shape of the sun. The reddish conical cap covered his thinning hair. At his side was a wooden shield with some ancient family's crest on it while the iron sword was dragging along the ground. He had slowly acquired these imitation pieces of combat attire, upgrading over the years, whenever there was spare cash in the account.

She admitted to herself that he looked pretty good, all things considering. He was hitting the mid-thirties, the nights at the pub catching up with him. But he carried the weight well enough and still had the twinkle in his eye that first attracted her to him seven years earlier. He'd already been a regular at the annual reenactment and she went along the first year as a spectator. She'd barely remembered the Battle of Hastings from school and was astonished to see how many people flocked to play fight for a week every October. But if she were to marry Colin, she needed to enter this part of his world, be a part of it. So, before the first visit ended, she bought herself a beautiful red woolen cloak, enduring wolf whistles. Before the second visit, she'd done her research, scoured websites, and read message boards, figuring out the best way to outfit herself to participate.

What surprised her was how much she grew to love this. It was a far cry from her work as a medical administrator at the hospital where dressing up meant cartoon scrubs to entertain the kids.

The next year she kept it simple, adding linen undergarments, leggings, and a shift, playing the role of cup-bearer. She disliked being a mere serving girl, so the following year, she enhanced the outfit, encircling her neck with small glass beads or strands hung on metal rings, strung from shoulder to shoulder over her garments. She had befriended several other women reenactors over the year and decided she was better suited to the role of memory keeper, those who witnessed the battles and mourned the dead. It was a solemn task, but one she was suited for, given her dealing with the sick and the dead every day. That first time in the role, she was there when the princes of Colin's group fell to the Normans and at the feast that night, she told their story to much applause.

Of course, she'd prefer to fight, but the Anglo-Saxon men, male chauvinist pigs that they were, wouldn't let them. While many women arrived and took up swords and crossbows, willingly crossdressing to fit in, this group kept it traditional and while she chafed at it, was willing to play along.

Here they were in the 2020s, another reenactment, another chance to dress up, play fight, party, eat, drink, and screw, although the latter was out for her. She was in her eighth month and needed a modified outfit to be comfortable. At least the cloak mostly hid the ginormous belly that seemed to precede her everywhere.

"I think that belly is coming to rival mine," Jessica said with a smile, earning her a frown.

"Guess I better do something about that before the lad comes," he said.

"No way you can lose that much before she gets here," Jessica countered. "But trying wouldn't kill you. It has to be hard, swinging the sword and running with all that extra baggage."

He frowned again and shrugged. There was a lot of noise outside their tent, others assembling in the field near the camp, where the men would practice before tomorrow's event.

"You know, they think this year'll set a record. Over 3,400 have registered," he said, reaching out to help her up. She had appreciated all the kind gestures he developed as she nurtured the new life. He had certainly done his part and that told her he'd be a great father.

As the ship descended, it rocked back and forth but held together. She wasn't certain if the distress signal to the mothership was properly activated; instead, her focus was on righting the small craft, working hard to ensure the crippled vessel would land as quietly as possible. The last thing they wanted was to draw the attention of oomans, inquisitive, annoying oomans who tended to shoot first before sizing up their prey. Ioniqe reported that the large land space was clear, but close by was quite a mass of life signs which made the landing tricky.

Donatiki snarled in frustration but had little choice because all the extra effort she expended in maneuvering the craft also resulted in the engines overheating. One external thruster was already down, the other two were five minutes from critical and the landing was due in just under that. There was no margin for error.

There was a rattle, a whine, and finally, a solid thump as the vessel contacted the ground. The entire ship seemed to sigh and settle although that did not stop the various alert chimes and signals from shrieking. Donatiki powered down everything but life support and communications.

"What do we do now?" Felke, the youngest and least mature of the group, asked.

"Check all systems, especially comms and see if our distress call was received," she said.

"And then what?" challenged Ekenke. "Sit and wait like insects?"

"What do you propose?" she asked, knowing that every moment could become a teaching opportunity.

"We go hunting," Ekenke said. "Get our first kills while waiting for rescue."

"Just like that? Go out and slaughter the oomans? It'll be a slaughter without glory, not a hunt," challenged Tenude. "Besides, they won't be sanctioned without a Leader to verify it."

"How far are we from the mass of oomans?" Donatiki asked, cutting off the argument.

"About a twenty-minute walk," he replied.

"Fine. If the signal was received, it will take hours before they arrive. We may as well practice our stealth hunting; but for now, we only watch, observe, and there will be no killing at this time."

Various fires crackled outside and would burn continuously over the two-day recreation of the battle. Colin's crew always had a dress rehearsal so they'd not embarrass themselves on the field. They would be among the 1,300 or more foot soldiers, expected to do the dirty work, hand-to-hand combat in the mud. October weather was not kind to the 21st-century reenactors, but it was probably just as messy a field for the real Anglo-Saxons and Normans who clashed, forever changing the island's destiny. An abbey was built to commemorate the battle, which became the site of the recreation battles, but it turned out the real field of battle was nearby, and they left that alone as a heritage site.

Colin headed outside and she could hear him shout greetings to the others, a mix of modern-day English and the Anglo-Saxon tongue. He'd never quite mastered the archaic words and she'd long since stopped trying to correct him. Jessica was adjusting her beads and brooch, this a simple bronze globe. The cloak had worn well and would survive a while longer which was good because any spare cash would be going toward nappies and clothes. Her hands rested on her belly, the baby obliging with a few kicks to remind her he/she/it was awake.

She emerged into a scene from another time. Not an electric line or telephone pole in sight, campfires dotting the row of a dozen tents with a large pit before them. Several women were already wrestling with the day's meat as black kettles burbled, emitting steam in orderly rows. Fifteen teens and men were assembling on the field, all looking rough and ready. Billy was the clan chief, had been for seven years and knew his team well. Many had met on the rugby field during their university days, and here they were, forming another kind of scrum.

Billy, tall and broad, his mechanic's body hard where Colin's was soft, shouted commands, and the others scattered to take up positions. They would practice their swordplay now, and then after lunch would work on their hand-to-hand skills.

Jessica made her way to the nearest kettle to see what help she could be. Liza, another willing spouse, greeted her with a smile. "Come on, have a cuppa, there's a kettle on behind the tent," she said. It was Liza who helped her in the early going, making her feel welcome when this was new and bizarre to her. Her husband, David, was the best of the swordsmen, often giving tips rather than doing his own practicing.

"Year after year, the only thing that changes are the wrinkles," Liza said with a laugh.

"And the weight," Jessica.

They laughed at that, commenting on the changing shapes of the men as they age. They took the time to admire how handsome and sculpted Billy's son, Charles, had become. Some of the girls at the battle tomorrow would be flocking to his side for sure.

Out of the corner of her eye, Jessica thought she saw a shape in the distance, wavery and indistinct. She blinked and it was gone, so she ascribed it to the haze in the air from so much wood smoke. But something in the back of her mind was now on alert and she tensed.

"Is it the baby?" Liza asked, seeing her stance change.

"No, it's nothing," she replied. "I thought I saw something."

Her four unblooded charges were fascinated by what they were witnessing because it didn't come close to matching what they had studied so far. Tenude remarked at the primitive weapons and campsites as opposed to the more modern structures and weapons of war they had seen the past few days.

Felke noted this made them easier to hunt and kill and kept wondering why Donatiki was not letting them loose. Ekenke was practically vibrating, wanting to charge from their tree cover. Thankfully, Tenude was smart enough to realize the number of oomans was a problem not even their superior firepower could handle.

Donatiki was already uncomfortable, coming to regret agreeing to lead the trainee expedition. She wished they had remained in the air, surveyed the planet, and reported back to the mothership. But here she was, stranded on this cursed world with four overeager unblooded and she didn't dare let them loose.

Jessica admired how the men put their all into the mock fighting, training hard to be ready for the real mock fighting the following day. With her cooling mug in hand, she walked the perimeter of the camp, nodding with her friends, but letting her mind wander. The possibilities were not quite endless, but her child could pretty much do whatever it wanted, from plumbing to engineering to poetry.

As she neared the tree line, she continued to fantasize about the future, thinking about what God's plan for their family was to be. He had provided her a good man and together they had a fine life. Sure, there could be more money in the bank, the flat could be a bit larger for a family of three, but they'd manage.

The dreams of the future were shattered when she blinked once and saw something in armor, more of the future than the past. It was larger than a human, with two arms and legs with a fan of dreadlocks across the shoulders. She blinked again and it was gone. Was it a vision, some daydream from the dark recesses of her mind? Shuddering, she crossed herself and hurried back to the others.

"That was foolish," Donatiki chided Ioniqe as he retreated back into the tree covering. "We are not sanctioned to engage our prey. This is a survey mission, a chance to study the people and their various terrains, to see how they behave when not in combat. Why did you decloak?"

The trainee ignored the question, angering his superior, and as he stepped to the rear of the group, he said over his shoulder, "She was like you, with child. It would not have been an honorable kill."

"Have you learned nothing?" she snapped. Donatiki worried about him, his brash way, and callous regard for their ways. A part of her hoped he would fail his first hunt.

To regain order and command of her brood, she asked, "Now, Ekenke, what do you observe?"

"The weather requires them to wear many layers, making them slow," he said. She nodded in confirmation then waited for more. He went on about how the clothing differed from the cities they'd seen while surveying the solar system and Earth's continents. Everything suggested this was how the population lived before technology such as electricity had been introduced. It made them far more vulnerable. Tenude sniffed at making the hunt too easy, even for them.

"What of their activities?"

"They all have a purpose, preparing for something," Ioniqe said, seeking redemption for disobeying her orders. Her nod was slow but he straightened with some regained pride.

"What I don't understand is how many of them seem to fight then fall, but my vision doesn't show a change in the deceased's readings. He still shows being alive," Ekenke said.

"Curious," Tenude said.

"War games," Donatiki said. And as she said that, the discrepancies seemed to make sense. "I do not know why they are doing this, but they are play fighting in costume from an earlier era."

"A religious ceremony perhaps," Ioniqe suggested.

Felke grunted. "For now, stay sharp."

As the morning wore on, that sense of foreboding never faded and she darted her eyes in every direction, scanning for danger. There was nothing more serious than a nick to Roddy's forearm. Thankfully, his wife Doreen had some emergency training and tended to it quickly. Others complained of cramps or tired limbs from swinging heavy blades, many not practicing in the intervening months since the last campaign. Jessica appreciated Colin's effort to stay in practice.

Even as they all sat at picnic tables for lunch, Jessica couldn't shake the sense that something was off. It nibbled at her mind and senses but she kept it to herself, determining it was just nerves over the baby. A month away from arrival and taking more of her mind's concentration by the day, fearing all the usual things new parents fret over. She knew that she and Colin would love the child, be good parents and all, but what if they screwed it up? What if they smothered the child or gave too much freedom? What if, what if, what if… The men were paired up, grappling with one another, practicing their falls to minimize harm during the battle. The outfits weren't padded and the ground, when muddy, difficult to navigate. Still, they shouted and grunted and laughed. All the while, Jessica, nursing another tea, worried.

About an hour into the practice, one of the men had headed into the woods to relieve himself. No one paid any mind to it, resuming their battle. The scream that came from his direction froze everyone. It wasn't a natural scream, but one born of excruciating pain, one that defiantly wanted to live. The sound was cut off but there was still rustling in the woods.

"Lawrence?" someone called.

There was no response.

The ooman had come too close and Donatiki didn't want her group to move, to make a noise that would give away their position. Instead, with a curt hand gesture, she ordered them to freeze.

However, the ooman made too tempting a target and Ioniqe couldn't resist. The ooman was an arm's length away. He had to extend himself given the unblooded's shorter wristblade. With surprising speed, his right wrist gauntlet deployed and he slit the man's throat, slicing through fabric and skin and eliciting a shriek of pain, and then the blood welled into the prey's throat, strangling the sound. The ooman fell, the first to die, and Ioniqe was the first to notch a kill.

"Unworthy," Tenude murmured as Donatiki yanked him back deeper into the tree cover.

"That will alert the others, putting us in danger, you overeager pup," she snarled.

"Good," he shot back, unabashed. "Why wait for the testing when there are so many targets here and now?"

"Because that's how it's done. With an honorable hunt, with sanctioned kills of kiande amedha/hard meat. Not here, not when the odds are against us. If the signal failed and we're stranded, we won't survive long. You have put us all at risk," she continued before smashing him across the bio-helmet, more out of frustration than punishment. But it had the proper effect, staggering him backward so he tripped and fell, an embarrassing sight.

"They'll be coming. We need to be prepared but kill only if there's no choice. We shouldn't be here," she said to the others.

Felke helped Ioniqe up and said, "Worried about us or that thing in your belly?"

"Both," she snapped. "Your disrespect for my rank does not speak well for your future. Think. Then speak and make sure it's worthy of the air you waste." She turned her back on them, engaging her vision to scan for approaching life signs.

"What was that?" Colin cried out. The play fighting had abruptly stopped and all heads turned toward the source of the sound. Jessica could barely glimpse the slumped figure by the trees, not far from where she had been not long before. Whatever sense of danger she had now rattled in her brain, her arms protectively wrapped around her belly.

"Be careful," Billy called, as he and Charles took the lead of the men heading toward their fallen friend.

"You think it's some animal?" Colin asked from behind them.

"Either that or he's had a heart attack," Billy surmised. "It sounded bad."

They neared their friend and saw the blood staining the outfit, turning the grass and dirt muddy red. Lawrence's body was not moving. Paul took one sight of the bodily wounds and turned to vomit.

"So much for the heart attack," Charles said. "And that couldn't have been an animal. Nothing that big is anywhere near here."

"What then? Bigfoot?"

"Don't be so bloody stupid," his father said, scanning the trees. Jessica watched from her tent, not willing to go anywhere near the trees but she could hear the voices carry. Lily had already called emergency services so help should be coming. Of all those assembled, she had the most medical experience, more from osmosis than practical training, but it was clear Lawrence was beyond saving. From her vantage point, the six or seven men and women were moving carefully, none daring to actually enter the forest, but spreading out, craning necks to see what they could see. It was almost comical to note they were carrying their blunted weapons as if they could do anything against whatever killed their friend. Still, they had the courage and she admired that.

Just then, there was some primal cry—not human, not animal—and she once more saw the armored figure charge from tree cover… or maybe it just appeared. She couldn't be sure. It had short blades extending from its wrist gauntlets and was charging Paul and Olivia. Just as it swung at Paul, who twisted away, a second appeared and sliced deep into Olivia's abdomen. She cried out once and collapsed. Two more appeared and everyone backpedaled, stumbling and doing what they could to avoid being struck.

To Jessica, it looked like a bloodbath in the making.

With casual steps, Donatiki followed her loosened charges into the open and walked over to observe the tangled mess. Once Ioniqe killed, the others' bloodlust was overwhelming and she lost control over them. The ooman female's blood was everywhere and she was whimpering, murmuring something only she could hear.

One of the males had seen her over his shoulder and spun on a heel and came rushing back, brandishing a sword, but she didn't fear it. Her maternity armor would protect her from something so primitive. She didn't want to kill him but would if forced to. He swung once, the blade making a dull thud against her shoulder. She twisted about, grabbed the man's other arm, and snapped it, causing him to cry and writhe with pain, dropping the sword.

Donatiki went to reach for him when a shiver washed over her, forcing her to stand still. She backed away, turned on them, and headed back for the trees. She had gone five or six feet when she staggered, went several more feet then fell to the ground, rolling onto her back. *No!* she thought, this was not the time for labor. This was not the world for a new child. But, the ooman triggered something painful within her and the process had begun. None of the unblooded charges knew the first thing about field medicine let alone childbirth. Their training to date was all about the hunt. Quickly, she mentally reviewed what was in her medicomp, prepared specifically with materials for her condition. She would do this herself—somehow—because she would be damned to let the Black Warrior claim her child.

It wasn't just a bloodbath, it was a massacre, Jessica realized with growing horror. These four armored attackers were stalking their prey. One appeared to have a gun of some sort that resembled no pistol she'd ever seen before and it fired some sort of projectile, not a bullet, that seemed to spear her friends. They were all going to die, long before the ambulance arrived, and even then, they'd just be more victims of these creatures.

Aliens. She paused to consider that. She wasn't entirely certain she believed in alien life. The Bible never directly addressed aliens but then again, it never talked about dinosaurs and there was incontrovertible proof they existed. Colossians 1:16 stated He is the creator of all things including the heavens and the worlds. If there *was* alien life, they too would be God's creation. But these aliens were killers, without provocation, so would God truly create such horrible beings?

With growing horror, she saw Nigel speared, the projectile pinning him to the ground. The alien possessing the gun walked casually toward him, straddling the prone figure and studying him. There was a long moment, but then his right wrist emitted a blade and with a single swing, neatly severed the neck, practically decapitating her friend. She bit her lip to stop herself crying out and attracting attention, then the hot tears flowed freely. But, as the killer stood over the corpse, he was bowled over from behind by Billy and Michael. The momentum knocked the armored behemoth to the ground and the two were pounding on the armor with the swords, ineffectually scratching it but also keeping the alien disoriented. Roddy, their rugby captain, rushed over to join in. He was carrying some large stone in his hands and that seemed to actually dent the armor. The focused blows were on the wrist-mounted knives. The constant pounding seemed to do something because one arm sparked and the creature said something inaudible. He righted himself, extending the other blade, causing the three men to back up.

The alien swung in an arc to force them further back, then he stumbled, clearly woozy from the pounding and that emboldened the men. Once more, they took advantage and charged from three directions, Michael pinning the deadly arm, while Roddy took the large, gray stone and pounded against the visor on the alien's helmet, hopefully, blinding it.

Jessica frantically turned her attention elsewhere, seeking Colin, praying he was still alive. She spotted him near one of the cast-iron pots, igniting some broken tree branch in the fire. She doubted it would do any good, but she sensed he had a plan. Aisha and George were grabbing the small cans of kerosene and gas they maintained to help with the fires while Doreen and Judy filled large pots with their intended meal. They were certainly thinking old-school in their defense, but how could they stand against armored giants with deadly weaponry?

She glanced out to see the others using their numbers to try and confuse the two other attackers. Then she looked toward the tree line to make sure no others were coming, which is when she spotted the fallen alien.

Ekenke was chided for bringing the speargun with him on a survey mission, but he claimed it was in case of the unexpected and Donatiki couldn't fault him for that. To see it used so ineffectually made her question his training. He didn't seem to know what to do with it after being knocked to the ground. The whelp was then battered with barbaric weapons and beaten into submission. She was horrified to see one of the oomans actually yank the speargun from his grasp. That would change the battle.

Tenude was doing better, holding off four men and women with his wristblades. All of them had yet to earn their combisticks or plasmacasters that would have destroyed the oomans. As it was, she had left her own on the scout ship and now regretted it, but she was unable to rise and get it. Her body reminded her, it was busy doing other things, taking her out of the fight and making her incredibly vulnerable.

With horror, she watched as the man tested the speargun once then took aim at Felke. He fired once, missing, then adjusted his stance and fired a second time, catching her charge's left leg and forcing him to the ground. As he fell on his back, a man with a flaming stick rushed him and stuck it at the visor, blinding Felke. There was a third shot, and this struck home, piercing the neck, just under the bio-helmet.

Two of her four charges were down, with just Tenude and Ioniqe, the one who instigated this fruitless battle, left against a dozen or more oomans. They hadn't been completely tested against opponents who were fighting for their lives. Training and simulations weren't sufficient.

Jessica looked past them, at the female alien. She hadn't moved since she fell to the ground. On her back, knees up, feet planted firmly on the ground, a hand was on her swollen belly in an all-too-familiar position. Was this woman so foolish as to enter a battle when she was this far along? And if she was presenting as a laboring woman, then biologically, they were not too dissimilar to humans so *maybe* God created them, too.

Despite being amateurs, the group acquitted themselves well so far, stopping two of the four. With the pregnant alien out of action, that left two. Roger cried something guttural. The next sound to be heard was a flight of arrows, fired by crossbows being wielded by several of the spouses—Liza, Lily, and Lara. The shafts all struck the aliens, clattering harmlessly to the ground. It was enough though, to let the others charge from behind, Michael firing the alien weapon and Roddy hurling the great stone, now damp with bright glowing green fluid. Was it blood? Paul came running, crying like a banshee, hefting the multipurpose survival axe he favored. The hatchet struck home against the armor, doing more than a little damage and he kept whaling away with it as the others distracted the alien with whatever tools they could muster.

The final alien had grabbed David by the neck, crushing his larynx as he dangled a good foot off the ground. Charles and Nancy, Roddy's sister, were ineffectually pounding away with stone and stick. Danny rushed into the fray wielding his foot-long heavy-duty flashlight which he used as a baton, battering the left wrist gauntlet. They were like insects, all over the alien, who writhed but couldn't do much but shake them off only to have them attack anew. Harry arrived with a large bottle of scotch which he flung at the alien. As expected, the glass shattered against the armor, coating the alien. While that occurred, Aisha was throwing a metallic bottle, the hiss of escaping gas clear. Colin tossed his flaming stick at the alien. The liquor ignited, setting the creature's chest and webbed arms aflame, which then caught the gas, causing an explosion that knocked the alien clear off its feet.

Both were down, stomped on, and stunned by the onslaught.

Jessica prayed they'd survive this encounter—and then she looked at the fallen alien once more.

Donatiki enhanced her helmet's vision to study her unblooded, and inwardly regretted their performance. They were not doing well at all, and should those four survive the battle to escape, would be denied being taken on the next hunt, losing their place in their training. She was thankful she was not responsible for that aspect of their development.

That was all she could do, though, because right now her body was writhing as she prepared to bring her baby into this alien world. Yet something was wrong and the pain was so severe it hampered her ability to move. She had to risk exposing herself, removing some of her maternity armor, to allow the baby its freedom. But that also made her an easy target.

The problem was compounded, though, by the pain that mostly paralyzed her, so she lay there, grunting with every spasm, unable to even remove a glove.

Jessica looked over and could tell the female was struggling. She paused a moment then made a decision. She snatched a carving knife from the kitchen setup and headed over to the fallen figure, away from the others who were still struggling to subdue the two remaining attackers.

As she neared, Jessica could hear sounds that most definitely suggested the female was in labor and having trouble. Maybe they weren't built to do the job on their own or there was a complication. Still, Jessica had decided, this was a child of God and needed help.

"I'm not going to hurt you," she said as she neared the writhing figure.

Instinctively, she'd extended her wristblade, which was far longer than her charges', and held it above her painful belly, making it clear the ooman female was not to go near her. Instead, the female's action suggested she was not there to claim a victim. She was speaking to her, but she could not translate the words. The tone, though, was not harsh as she was accustomed to. There was something soothing about her, and she could use that right now.

Donatiki considered her situation. Each held a weapon, but only one of them could actually cause harm with it. She cocked her head in confusion at what to do. The ooman was studying her, which she intensely disliked, but it caused her to make a decision. The ooman dropped her knife.

It was a risky act because if she drew closer, Donatiki could actually stab her. Instead, she leaned her head back and withdrew her own blades.

Jessica kneeled before the figure, saying all the soothing things she said when her own sister went unexpectedly into labor on a shopping trip two years earlier. While the alien did or did not understand the words, Jessica hoped the tone would help.

The alien seemed to calm and took in an audible breath, then tried to peel off the armored gloves. Understanding, Jessica worked with the alien, taking off each unlatched piece of the lower armor. There was no way a baby could be delivered when the body was effectively encased in tin like sardines.

She could see the pale, yellowish skin, tendons straining against the rough skin. It was hideous, but this was a living being.

By this point, the others saw what was happening and rushed over, shouting for her to get away. There was fear and anger and hatred written across the faces. It wasn't all of them, as Judy tended to her husband Billy's injuries and Nancy was tending to other injuries. Aisha was crying over Nigel's dead body, comforted by Oliver's wife, now widow, Lara.

"What the bloody hell are you doing?" Colin cried out.

"Delivering that baby," Jessica said as calmly as she could.

"Oh no you're not," he said. "That thing's the devil."

"This is a living being, one who's in labor, so no, there's been enough killing, thank you very much," she said. The alien had unlatched more pieces of the armor and Jessica tugged at them, removing the leg armor. The flexible, golden scale-like coverings were easily rolled off.

No one moved to help.

Jessica reached for the helmet which remained in place. The alien's hands held tight to the helmet and shook. Clearly, the alien woman needed the helmet to breathe. Of course, that made sense now that she considered it. Then again, it was her first alien encounter so what did she know? The body was wracked with labor and she'd been silently counting—these contractions appeared no more than two minutes apart.

Jessica looked at the helmet's ferocious features, and her research flooded back. Could these aliens have been here before? Is it possible they were drawn to their mock army the same way their ancestors were drawn to the Anglo-Saxon warriors centuries earlier? Could they have been here, interacted with the English residents, and given rise to one of the greatest heroic poems of all? Could these aliens have been mistaken for monsters, a mother and son combination immortalized under the name Grendel?

She was exposed to the cold air. The smoky air was distasteful. Everything about this moment was embarrassing and detestable.

Donatiki was surprised that the ooman was able to cow the others with words. Everything suggested she was not a leader, but her actions caused the others to pause.

The pain grew in intensity, and it was getting close.

"No time for modesty," Jessica said to the face. She reached to the waist and undid the rectangular decorated belt buckle then looked for the strap to remove the codpiece.

"Are you really going to bring another one of those into the world?" Harry angrily asked.

"It *is* crazy, Jess," Colin said, trying to be placating.

"Go ask Nancy if the Hippocratic Oath is only for humans," Jessica said. "And while you're at it, see if she's free to do this. I haven't the training."

No one moved.

"Aisha, would you be so kind," she asked. The willowy blond seemed petrified by the sight of the half-naked, fierce alien and was thankful to have a reason to move away.

"We can't let you do this," Charles said, taking a step forward.

"Yeah, you can," Jessica said.

"No," he said with finality and raised the blunted sword, ready to strike the bare flesh.

Jessica whirled about, the carving knife back in her hand. "Don't."

"Move," Charles commanded.

"She's harmless and in distress. It's one thing to do this to protect yourself, but now this would be cold-blooded murder. Twice over. Are you that kind of man?"

Charles hesitated.

"I'll do it, then," Paul said.

"Don't!" Jessica cried out.

The alien chose then to let out an all-too-familiar wail of pain as a fresh contraction wracked her body.

That seemed to decide it for the women. Lily and Olivia stepped forward and stood between Jessica and Paul.

There was a silent standoff so Jessica turned her attention to taking off the leggings and boots. This was nothing she ever imagined herself doing and a part of her felt this was wrong, but her faith carried her forward.

The pelvis was exposed, and to her shock and surprise, between the legs was the appearance of the same mottled head.

"She's crowning," Jessica called out.

"Kill it," cried Danny.

"No," Colin said quietly, stepping to join the women in forming a barrier. "That child has every much a right to live as you and me."

"It'll kill us all," Danny argued.

"Think with your head a moment," Colin said. "We don't know where they're from or if there are more out there. But, if we help bring this one into the world, then maybe they'll show gratitude and leave us alone. Hopefully, even leave altogether. Kill it and the mum, that's a whole other story."

"Nancy can't come," Aisha said, rushing up to the crowd, her eyes taking in the standoff and quickly standing beside Lily, grasping her hand for strength.

"It's just you and me then," Jessica said to the female alien. "I don't know if you push or anything like that, but I'll help however I can."

The alien looked into her face and merely grunted as the body convulsed. Jessica looked down and saw a shoulder.

"You're doing fine. Just fine." She found herself taking the alien's hand—the skin felt rough—and gripping it. The hand gripped back with a strength that threatened to crack her bones.

"So that's it then, we let another be born," Paul said.

The crowd fell silent and when it was clear no one was making a threatening move, watching in horrified fascination, Lily broke free and knelt beside Jessica. Together, they reached down and tried to ease the alien baby out of the body, which wriggled and writhed. There was no clue what was right and what wasn't.

The baby, easily a foot long, narrow, its mandibles wrapped tight against the face, eased out and into their hands. It was coated in something blueish, dripping from the body. There was an umbilical cord, just like theirs, and Jessica looked up at Colin. He gave a heavy sigh then reached down to the carving knife and, with some effort, sliced through the cord. Lily used a strip of cloth to tie it off as Jessica held the baby, looking for a sign of life.

After several seconds, there was a movement and then the top mandible wavered, separating. Then the lower pair. Finally, the tiny mouth parted and it breathed. No crying, just an intake of breath and exhalation. Jessica thanked her lord for letting the baby live and quietly placed the child against the alien's breast. The child's mandibles seemed to wrap around the breast, holding on, and the nursing began.

She was exhausted from all the pain. With a trembling hand, she reached into the medicomp for an analgesic, which helped. Then she unlatched one section of the chest armor and as she felt the child nurse, she was overcome with a wave of exhilaration, shoving aside the embarrassment and everything else. She was a mother, something she'd wanted for so long. All thoughts of her charges were shoved aside. The mothership would come or not. For now, she let the child rest against her, enjoying the slick warmth against her breast.

The oomans would do what they must, but right now, she celebrated the new life.

Lily and Jessica turned their attention to the mother, who seemed exhausted. They had no idea if there was a placenta ejection to come. Liza arrived carrying rags, towels, and a blanket, which Colin used to gently cover mother and child.

Jessica stood up, somewhat dazed by the entire experience. Her heart said she'd done the right thing; her conscience was less certain.

The men and several women went to secure the downed aliens with Noah placing a frantic call to the local police.

Turning back to the newborn, who quietly suckled, Jessica wondered what fate lay in store for him. What would his birth on Earth mean to his worldview? Would he grow up to hunt them? And what of the mother? Was this shared moment a rare instant of peace or a turning point in their lives?

She quietly prayed for guidance, hoping that for now, at least, the killing had ended and new life could take hold. Hers and that of the alien female and her child.

Jessica couldn't believe it but a party of four more aliens arrived well before the local authorities. They appeared just as quietly as those that attacked them. This time, they were not at all threatening. Instead, they collected the downed aliens and gently retrieved the new mother and her infant. Without acknowledging the humans who kept her alive, the collection of aliens disappeared into the woods.

Jessica gazed at the stars, her hands on her own belly, comforted by the kicking within. She wondered what would become of the mother and child. And what these aliens meant for mankind. Was this God's will and if so, what was the grand plan?

CANNON FODDER

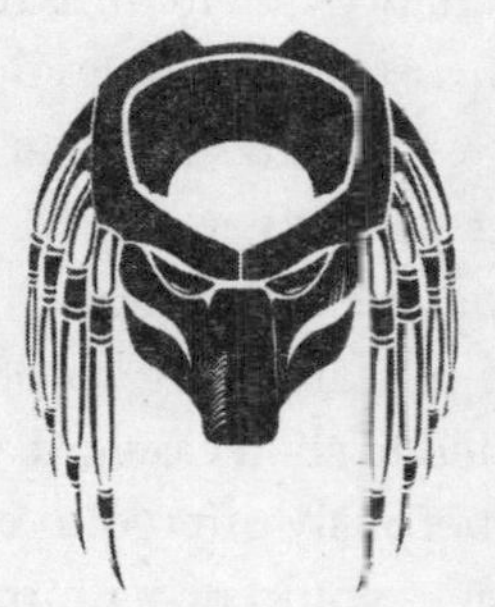

BY GINI KOCH

YEAR 2422, CEVRESAL SYSTEM, PLANET FOURTH—SALTURNA EXODUS

The Yautja scout ship circled the planet.

"Given to us by the oomans," Leader Zalande said gravely. "The gift has been tested by your betters and found worthy. Many Hunts have been successful, many warriors have proven themselves here already." He turned, eyes blazing, mandibles clicking in anger. "So there can be no excuses. You have all failed too often. As our clan demands, this is your last chance to restore honor, to change your Hunt Names."

La'vindi did not look to her right or left. She knew Hekkati and Sula'amini would also be staring straight at Zalande. They were lucky to be given this opportunity, and all three knew it. Clan H'ppattah had once been a weak clan, with many who could not hunt well, looked down upon by the other clans. Over time, they had become fierce and unflinching, and all members accepted death over dishonor, if that was what an elder decreed. Now Clan H'ppattah were among the most dangerous, the most honored, the most feared. Three chances were all that were given to any member. This was their third chance.

Zalande was not who La'vindi had hoped for in their Leader. He was strict and driven and he disliked any trace of weakness. But she desperately wanted to change her Hunt Name—Failure was not anything to be proud of. Hekkati and Sula'amini wanted to shed Coward and Suckling as well, and Zalande had generously offered to be their Hunt Leader. If they succeeded, they would bring him great praise. If they failed, however, they would cause him shame. She knew Zalande would kill them all before he would allow their shame to touch him, to allow their failure to become his.

"Due to your failures, I have decreed that you are required to fight with basic weapons only."

Sula'amini gasped and Hekkati drew in her breath, and only Zalande's look of derision kept La'vindi from doing either. "Will this not make it easier for the oomans to survive?"

"Yes. You have only your plasmacasters, your combisticks, and your armor to use in this fight. You will hunt as our ancestors had to, so long ago, and if you succeed, you will be praised and regain true honor." He didn't need to tell them what would happen if they failed.

Zalande turned back to look at the green planet they were about to land on. "As your first test, we will land close to the ooman spaceport. It is heavily guarded, so we will see how well you can avoid their traps." He said this contemptuously. Zalande had hunted on ooman worlds before and come home victorious with many trophies. Of course, even one trophy would be more than La'vindi, Hekkati, and Sula'amini had acquired.

La'vindi steeled herself. She would show Zalande and all the rest that she was worthy, that she was capable even with the weakest of weapons, no matter what the cost.

The landing ship battered them around as it hit the planet's atmosphere. Cali did her best to keep a stoic look on her face. Scary was managing to look bored. The rest of L-Squad was doing the same, other than Tank and Yolo, who were both whooping it up.

H-Squad were sitting as far from L-Squad as they could get. Not that anyone from L-Squad cared—anyone off the *Landmark* considered themselves far above those assigned to the *Brig*, especially above the lifers, which was what L-Squad was: lifetime members of the "you've fucked up" club.

"Loser Squad, when I say your names, sound off with your callsigns," Captain Joel Haber said with cheerful nastiness. He was from the *Landmark*, so he didn't know them, but he could have asked their sergeant for this information. However, that wouldn't have been nearly as humiliating for all of them. "Master Sergeant William Compton."

"Red Sarge."

Haber smirked. "Dull callsign for a ginger."

All of L-Squad snickered quietly. Red Sarge hadn't gotten that nickname because of his hair, but because of how much blood he'd had on him after he'd gone berserk on a mission gone wrong long before the rest of them had been in the Orbital Marines, let alone assigned to the *Brig* for life. Per Red Sarge, that's what happened when you killed your superior officers along with all the enemy. Of course, there were other reasons to be on the *Brig*, and L-Squad covered all of them.

"I make do," Red Sarge said blandly. He shot the rest of them the "be cool around the asshole" look.

"Alana Gonsalves," Haber said.

She sighed to herself. "Miss California, shortened to Cali."

Haber eyed her. "You're pretty enough."

"Thanks so much." She hadn't gotten saddled with Miss California for her looks but because she'd made the mistake of mentioning how much she missed her home planet and state around the wrong group of marines.

"You're tagged as coming from a long line of military," Haber said. "Back to the late nineteen-hundreds."

"That's us, the Gonsalves Rebels." Her family held the official ancient matriarch from ages ago in high regard. Cali had no idea why other than that "she'd seen some shit in Val Verde and came out clean," per family lore, but she wished she was here right now to punch Haber right in his smug face.

Haber went on. "Sherry Cantrell."

"Scary Sherry. 'Cause I know what we're heading for and I don't pretend I don't."

"Right, you're the one who tells the monster stories." Haber sounded unimpressed.

Scary shrugged. "You want to live? You pay attention." Scary's family had a matriarch from roughly the same timeframe as Cali's. She'd been a police detective in Los

Angeles and, apparently, she, too, had seen some shit and lived to tell the tale in great detail to her family line. "And because I pay attention, my bet is that Salturna's been turned into a hunting ground, and that means we're all heading into some terrifying shit."

Cali and Scary had bonded over California early on. She wasn't sure if Scary's stories had any merit, but there was a lot of bad out there, and a lot of unexplained death and destruction. Her grandfather always told her if she hit the enemy enough she'd be able to see them. Then again, her grandfather had been crazy. But he'd said that even before he'd gone into dementia. Supposedly this was wisdom handed down from the original Gonsalves.

"Right. When I get back to my bunk, I'll pull the covers up over my head. Now, for the rest of the Ladies of L-Squad." He kept on through the list—Yolanda "Yolo" Lopez, Tiffany "Bling-Bling" Lee, Erin "Tank" O'Brien, Jasmine "Dash" Viviers, and Amelia "Booksmarts" Burns rounded out the squad. None of them were spared nastiness from Haber, but none of them expected anything else from the man to begin with.

The ship stopped rocking, meaning they were through the atmosphere. "What's the mission?" Red Sarge asked. "We haven't been briefed."

"Unexplained attacks," Haber said. "Since everyone on Salturna is there because they're all drinking from the same glass and wanted nothing to do with the Expansion Government, we figure that a predatory animal got tossed into the DNA mix for terraformation and has just come to maturity."

Scary nudged Cali. "Predatory animal is right. We have to be hella careful, girl, because all my monster stories are gonna come true."

"When we land," Haber went on, "we'll be met by a group of locals. H-Squad will escort them back to their settlement and maintain a perimeter. L-Squad, you're going to head directly to where the attacks have been centered."

"Great," Dash muttered. "We get to find the tiger someone tossed onto this world."

"Ain't a tiger," Scary said. "A tiger'd be a gift. It's gonna be much, much worse."

La'vindi crouched on the roof of the building the oomans considered a spaceport. It was a big rectangular building with a roof that opened and closed. She was on the edge of it, the part that didn't move, watching.

This planet was almost all jungle—it felt more like home than the ooman world La'vindi had visited for her first, disastrous, Hunt. There were trees and vines everywhere, thick vegetation on the ground, the air was comfortably humid, the smells not too offensive. The oomans had been thoughtful in this gift.

Per Zalande, every ooman here—adult male, adult female, and even young ones—were armed for fighting, making them perfect for the Hunt. While Zalande did not encourage them to kill the young ones, they were allowed to take them as trophies if those young were attacking, but they would receive no disgrace if they left the young ones alone. Pregnant females were, as always, off limits.

As with their own people, males were more predominantly likely to be the fighters, but females were quite capable as well. For their kind, only a quarter of the female population were hunters—for the oomans, it was almost equal. So Zalande would not make any differentiation between male or female kills. And neither would La'vindi.

Zalande had shared that they could breathe this air without their helmets if it became necessary. He was observing them from inside their cloaked ship—they would receive no support until they had each managed a trophy. He had spent the trip here teaching them Hunt basics, and unless they proved that they had learned his lessons, they were less important to him than the oomans. Zalande respected the oomans—unless and until they succeeded, he would not consider respecting those on this Hunt.

Avoiding the traps on this so-called spaceport had been simple so far. Their armor made them blend in with the surroundings, their visors allowed them to differentiate heat signatures easily, and their natural physical prowess made leaping over the paltry explosives that surrounded the spaceport simple.

Hekkati and Sula'amini had chosen to stay in the trees that encircled the spaceport. The three of them were linked via communicators with each other and Zalande. None of them planned to ask for assistance from the others.

La'vindi spotted the ooman ship coming down from the sky—it was small by comparison to their own, but it looked sturdy enough. The roof opened, and she saw some on-planet oomans scurrying about. The ship landed, and the roof closed.

She prepared herself. The oomans would be exiting this building directly under her perch, and she would be ready to begin.

They landed and exited the ship inside Salturna's small spaceport. The locals there to meet them weren't interested in talking to anyone other than Haber, but there was a man with them who didn't fit. He wasn't dressed like anyone else who lived on Salturna—to a person they were in jungle fatigues and armed to the teeth—or any of the OM personnel, who were in standard camouflage body armor that protected and enhanced strength.

This man was in dull-pewter-colored body armor that Cali had never seen before. Like theirs, it was form-fitting and had a full helmet, but it was sleeker and far less bulky, and the helmet looked like a thin, clear piece of strong plasticine that wouldn't stop a rock, let alone a laser shot.

He appeared to have no weapons on him. He looked aloof and amused and, unlike everyone else, he didn't seem to be sweating, but his eyes darted everywhere. He made eye contact with Cali and smiled. It wasn't a nice smile, or an inviting one, either. It was the smile of someone who was happy to see her for all the wrong reasons.

Yolo nudged her. "Who's the Black Ops guy?"

"Fuck," Dash said under her breath. "I know that guy. We're in deeper shit than we thought."

"Who is he?" Booksmarts asked as the man made eye contact with her. If he'd smiled creepily at Cali, it was nothing compared to how he looked at Booksmarts—his expression said that he couldn't wait to watch her die. She was a small, mousy girl, and the rest of L-Squad did their best to protect her. Booksmarts should never have joined the OM and she didn't belong with L-Squad. She'd just politely corrected the wrong superior officer at the wrong time and been sent to the *Brig* for life. That was the downside to signing up with the wrong recruiters—there were clauses some of them added in for "egregious behavior," usually put in for those going with the OM versus prison, which gave the correcting officer the right to send that marine to the *Brig*. And there were plenty of officers who relished enacting those clauses. And once in the *Brig*, never out. The *Brig* sucked, but it was better than planetary prisons, so they all put up with it.

"That, ladies, is Marlon Flucher," Red Sarge said quietly from behind them. "Known as the Mother Fucker. If he's here, it's not for any good reason."

"He's Black Ops," Dash confirmed. "If they're here—we're fucked." She looked at Scary. "He may be black, but he doesn't care that we are, too. That man is equal opportunity about who he fucks over."

"Trust me, we're fucked because we're here," Scary said. "That man isn't going to change anything for us, other than make it harder for us to survive."

"Quiet down," Red Sarge said softly. "I want Bling-Bling to be able to hear what they're saying."

Bling-Bling had been a jewel thief before she'd had to join the OM or spend her life on a prison planet. She had great hearing, which she said had helped her crack safes. She was standing as near to H-Squad as possible. H-Squad were, of course, standing at attention, not moving or speaking.

Bling-Bling moved back to be with the rest of L-Squad as Haber nodded, then turned. "H-Squad is with me," he said. "L-Squad, you will follow Mister Flucher's directions."

"We are so screwed," Dash muttered.

"I think I can take him," Tank said.

"You can't," Red Sarge replied. "Believe me, even you can't."

Flucher crooked his finger at them. "Haber isn't actually in charge," Bling-Bling said as they walked over as slowly as possible. "Flucher is. Flucher has a goal, but no one seems to know what it is other than him. The locals have no idea what's killing them, though their villages seem safe. But in order to survive, they have to leave the villages to hunt, fish, and farm, so that's where they're dying, particularly when they're hunting."

They reached him and Flucher gave them all a feral smile. "I've been advised about L-Squad. Follow me and try not to screw up before we're out of the building."

Everyone other than Tank drew their laser rifles—she went for her plasma launcher. H-Squad had newer, better weapons than L-Squad, but then they also had newer armor and no one on L-Squad was surprised.

They got into formation. Shocking Cali to her core, Flucher was set to lead the way out, L-Squad right behind him. The path was wide enough to walk three abreast, so Red Sarge moved up to Flucher's right, and Tank went to his left.

Scary, Booksmarts, and Cali went behind them and Yolo, Dash, and Bling-Bling brought up L-Squad's rear. H-Squad, flanking the residents, left some space between the squads, with Haber and the head of the reception committee alone in the rear, so they'd be the last ones out of the safety of the spaceport, she assumed.

Cali was relieved Flucher was ahead of them—him behind her would have made her more nervous than whatever they'd be facing once they stepped outside.

But they faced nothing. Just a wide path through an overgrown jungle that made the rainforests on Earth look like deserts.

The spaceport workers slammed and locked the door

behind Haber. Whatever was out here, they were scared as hell of it. L-Squad stayed close together—much closer together than H-Squad was, all of them looking not just ahead of them, but all around.

"I feel eyes on me," Yolo said.

Booksmarts nodded. "Me too." The rest of the squad agreed that they were being watched.

"Something's out there," Red Sarge replied. "That's why we're here. L-Squad, be alert and remember all of our drills." Red Sarge had kept them ready to fight, even though they were supposedly never going to see action again, because he didn't think they were losers—he thought they were capable of overcoming together. It was why they all respected him, because he somehow respected them.

"Be ready," Scary said quietly. "Hell's coming soon."

Cali saw nothing around them, but something made her look up. The trees were tall and thick, with plenty of vines growing up and around them. Leopards and pythons liked trees. So did many other predators. She didn't see anything, though, other than an occasional, fleeting blur which could have been something or just her eyes adjusting to this planet's sunlight.

They were a klick away from the spaceport when Scary's prediction came true.

There was a ruckus behind them and screams and shouts from H-Squad. Cali spun around to see two heads with the spines attached—and nothing else—flying through the air into the trees to their right. The heads belonged to the leader of the reception committee and Haber. The last she saw of Haber was his dead, open-mouthed, wide-eyed face sailing in an up and down pattern into the jungle.

All of H-Squad started firing toward the disappearing heads and spines. As they did so, Red Sarge shouted for them to watch out. Blue plasma fire burst from the top of the building and a different tree. All of L-Squad went down to one knee and into a circle, looking for targets at the spaceport and in the trees.

H-Squad, however, didn't listen to Red Sarge, because they'd been told not to by Haber, meaning too many of them were firing at the trees and not at the closer threat.

"Got it!" Tank shouted as she stood up and aimed for the building.

"Don't destroy the spaceport!" Flucher shouted. She ignored him.

Tank's shot hit something just above the roof of the spaceport, and for a moment Cali saw an outline of a humanoid. Much larger than even Tank, in some kind of armor, with what looked like weird dreadlocks coming out of the helmet, clawed hands and feet, and a strange gun that looked a tiny bit like their laser rifles. The figure also looked feminine—Cali was sure she saw the outline of breasts, a smaller waist, and slightly wider hips. Then the image was gone.

And, as soon as it was, something fired directly at Tank.

La'vindi watched the oomans leave their spaceport. There was something odd in how they did so. All the heat signatures showed three walking side by side other than the first line. That only showed two heat signatures, but the oomans were moving as if someone or something else was there.

The last line had only two, but they were not moving as if

any flanked them. This might mean they were the mightiest of the oomans, and therefore walked last to guard the rear. But she had no time to ponder either oddity.

Hekkati was too intent about regaining her honor, so she struck the oomans first, while they were still in sight of their building. And she did it by leaping down upon them from the trees.

She landed on the two oomans who were in the rear, one foot on each of their backs. She grabbed their heads, and pulled.

Her enthusiasm made her even stronger, and she achieved two trophies immediately. Then she leaped back into the trees, to take those trophies to the ship. La'vindi felt a moment's jealousy—Hekkati had taken the two most dangerous in her first attempt. She was proud for Hekkati and sorrowful for herself, but the Hunt was on and there was no time for self-pity or self-reflection.

Hekkati's attack happened so quickly that the oomans didn't react until she was almost out of sight. Then they started firing at her. La'vindi had planned to wait and follow the oomans, but Hekkati's exuberance now made that plan impossible. So she fired at the oomans.

They were moving around in panic, some flinging themselves down to make themselves smaller targets, so her first shots missed. She ensured that she didn't react to this in any way—Zalande was monitoring, after all, and her expressing dismay would not be wise. Instead, while she aimed more carefully and shot those oomans closest to her, she identified which ooman would be the next greatest prize.

The largest ooman in the front group stood and fired directly at her with a weapon that gave off much heat. La'vindi was hit, but the weapon, big or not, was no match for her armor, though it did affect it some—she felt electricity crackle all around her. But it was over quickly.

She aimed her plasmacaster calmly and fired several times in succession—oomans also had armor, though it was nothing compared to their own. However, she'd learned on her first, failed Hunt that armored oomans usually took at least two shots to kill.

Her shots were on target, hitting the body in rapid succession. The gun her target was holding went off once more. La'vindi avoided the shot by leaping off the building and landing next to her now downed target, in the middle of the clutch of oomans.

She chose to follow Hekkati's example, so put her foot onto the downed ooman's still moving body, grabbed the head, and pulled. The ooman's dying scream was cut off quickly and La'vindi leapt for the trees before the other oomans could react.

Shots fired after her, but she raced off for the ship, behind Sula'amini who had two trophies. No matter—there were plenty of oomans here and their first foray had been successful. More trophies would be a certainty.

"What do we do with the bodies?" Booksmarts asked as they assessed the damage. "What's left of them, I mean."

All of H-Squad was down, two of them without heads and spines, the others just on the ground, some shot up beyond recognition, some down from direct headshots, some looking serenely dead. Most of the civilians were dead like H-Squad, several were injured, one seemed unscathed.

L-Squad had only lost Tank. Yolo was crying angry tears.

"We can't leave her body here like this."

Red Sarge nodded. "Let's get the bodies into the spaceport."

"Leave them," the one unhurt civilian said. "Whatever's hunting us wants the bodies We can use them as bait."

"How do you know that?" Flucher asked, voice smooth as velvet. "And I didn't catch your name earlier."

The civilian shrugged. "I'm Ira Sykes. And I know because we've been dealing with this predator for months now. Killing happens, stops for a bit, then starts up again."

"*Predators,*" Cali said. "There were at least two, probably three. Maybe more."

"You know this how?" Sykes asked.

"I pay attention when things are trying to kill me."

Sykes opened his mouth, presumably to respond, but no words came out. Blood gushed from his mouth as a horrifying sword made from some kind of silver-colored metal stabbed through him. At the same time, four of the dead bodies were lifted into the air, just high enough that two very tall people could be hefting one in each arm. And the bodies—and whatever was holding them—blocked the path to the spaceport.

"Run!" Scary shouted. "L-Squad, run like hell!"

Flucher shouted that they should stand their ground, but none of them, not even Red Sarge, listened to him. Instead, they followed Dash—who was the fastest—down the path, running faster than most of them had ever managed before, Flucher running after them, cursing at their cowardice.

"You are all doing well," Zalande said with the tiniest hint of pride in his voice.

They stood straight and proud before him. La'vindi still held her bloodied combistick in her hand.

They had many kills and trophies hanging in the jungle outside the ship. But they knew they were not done. And they did not wish to be finished. The thrill of the Hunt was theirs and they were not ready to stop.

"Now, the rest of these oomans have fled," Zalande went on. "No more easy kills—they will be in hiding, trying to attack and outwit you. That is their way."

"They will not succeed," Hekkati said firmly.

Zalande nodded and clicked his mandibles approvingly. "No, I now believe they will not. However," he added sternly, "do not allow this first success to cause you to relax your vigilance. The oomans are good prey because they can think. Not as well as us, but well enough. Over the ages they have managed to best some of our greatest hunters. Not many of them and not often, but the feeling of satisfaction you have now must be put aside, so you do not succumb to overconfidence."

They all nodded. "We will not fail you," Sula'amini said.

"We will honor you," La'vindi added.

Zalande nodded gravely. "Now, here are my expectations for the next portion of your Hunt."

They ran until they saw the wooden walls of the first village on this path. Then Red Sarge called for them to stop, and they listened. He was their leader, not Flucher.

"We can't go into that village and say that we want to hide," Red Sarge said when he'd gotten them all back into some kind of order. "We left their dead and ours behind to save our own skins. They won't welcome us." He looked at Cali. "You saw something."

She nodded and described the brief glimpse she'd had. "I don't know if what I saw was real or if I imagined it because of Scary's stories. But if it was real, I think Tank's shot shorted out whatever they use to appear invisible, even though that didn't last long." She'd thought they'd left Tank's weapon behind, but Flucher was holding it. Easily. Meaning his armor had more strength enhancements than theirs did.

Scary snorted. "You saw it, girl. And I'm certain there are three of them, at least, based on what we saw right before we used our brains and ran away."

Flucher seemed intent on something else. He wasn't standing too near and was in profile to them. Cali was sure he was talking to someone, because his lips were moving. Just barely, but she was able to make out the movement.

"We have to get hidden," Scary went on. "Well hidden."

"They're better hidden than we can ever be," Booksmarts said, voice shaking.

"Hit the enemy enough, and you'll be able to see them," Cali said absently, still focused on Flucher. She looked at Red Sarge. "Orders?"

Flucher heard her and spun around. "What did you say? Before you forgot the chain of command."

She shrugged and repeated it. "Family wisdom."

He stared at her. "Yeah. I know who you're descended from." He now looked at Scary. "You, too."

Scary snorted again. "My family's wisdom is to run like hell while throwing everything you've got at things you can't see. Keeping cool is also a good idea, but we're in a jungle, so that's not an option. Being preggers is an asset, too, but none of us are, so we're all targets."

Flucher's eyes narrowed. "Whatever. But I'm in charge here, and you do what I say. And I say we're not going to hide. You do what I say or else."

Cali just stared at him, trying not to smirk. L-Squad hadn't been sent to the *Brig* for life because they were "good" marines. "Or else what? You'll send us back to the *Brig*?" She looked at the rest of the squad and nodded. To a person they all turned their backs on Flucher and looked to Red Sarge. "Orders?" Cali asked again.

Red Sarge shrugged while Flucher cursed under his breath. "Scary's not wrong. We need to get hidden and figure out how to kill whatever these things are."

"How do we hide from something invisible?" Bling-Bling asked.

"By making it visible," Booksmarts replied.

"Then like Cali said," Red Sarge said, "let's figure out how to hit them as much as we can."

La'vindi watched the oomans creeping through the jungle. They were all alert, as they had been before, proving they were the more desirable prey.

Zalande had shared that most of those in this group were females, which made La'vindi feel proud. The group that was all males had been killed by them quickly and easily. But all bar one of the females had survived, and La'vindi's trophy was the one female, meaning her trophy was the best so far. Legend told of female Yautja warriors who'd bested their male Hunt partners, and that was true, even today.

Most males were too arrogant to acknowledge it, though Zalande was not one of those. That the ooman females were the same meant that the rest of their trophies would bring them greater honor, and Zalande would share their glory with pride.

She had repaired her armor back at the ship—the damage had been minimal but she wanted no mistakes, and Zalande had approved. She took his warning seriously and so took her time to assess what the remaining oomans were doing

There was a gap between the oomans, in the middle of their line. Again they acted like someone or something was there, but La'vindi couldn't see it. Neither could Hekkati and Sula'amini, but both of them felt La'vindi was being overcautious without reason.

For this portion, Zalande had demanded they were to use only wrist gauntlets, combisticks, bows, or hand-to-hand combat. This was because it had been too easy for them in the first round, and he wanted to ensure they reclaimed their honor skillfully.

Hekkati was again the first to attack, choosing the ooman at the end of their line, since they all agreed that those in the rear were clearly the best fighters. Her arrow sailed true and she swung down on a vine after it, grabbed the skewered ooman, and swung up to another tree before any of the others noticed.

But they noticed soon enough and stopped moving forward, then began howling—for the missing one, La'vindi assumed. They began to wander about, howling and searching.

Hekkati went again, taking advantage of their confusion. She chose the one that moved the fastest of this group and caught her as she leaped over a fallen tree. It was a successful hit and Hekkati swung after her arrow, not heeding Zalande's warning.

"Bling-Bling, where are you?" Booksmarts shouted.

The rest of them slowed and turned. There was no sign of Bling-Bling.

"She was right behind me," Booksmarts said frantically. "I didn't hear anything, but I don't see her."

"Spread out," Red Sarge ordered. "Look for her."

"Move on," Flucher countered. "If she's gone, she's gone."

They all stared at him for a moment, turned, and started doing what Red Sarge said. Leaving H-Squad and a bunch of civvies they didn't know was one thing. Leaving one of their own was another. Tank had been dead. Bling-Bling might still be alive.

"We all need to stay together," Scary warned. "Or they'll pick us off one by one."

"I'll cover ground the fastest," Dash said, ignoring Scary's warning. She'd had point, but started off at a run toward where Bling-Bling had been, expanding a circle as best she could through the underbrush. "I see blood," she called as she got just out of sight. And then she screamed.

The rest of them ran toward the sound, to find Dash skewered by a huge, metal arrow that had her pinned to a tree. It had missed her heart, but had cut through her body armor like it was made of cotton. Blood was pumping out of her body.

As they neared her, something pulled the arrow out and caught Dash as she collapsed.

Cali spotted what she'd seen before—a sort of hazy blurring of the jungle, but it was next to Dash. She aimed and fired, higher than Dash's head. Her shots hit something, and the others caught on and did the same, forming a semi-circle around where Dash was, ensuring stray shots wouldn't hit the other shooters.

Whatever had Dash ripped her head and spine out of her body. It was horrible, but that just meant they could continue to shoot with less care and more urgency. A metal stick very like the one that had killed Ira Sykes swung toward them, but they were all able to move back, and now they knew for sure where whatever was holding that stick and what was left of Dash stood.

Someone fired Tank's weapon and Cali risked a look—Flucher had decided to get involved. The weapon did what it had done before—caused whatever made this thing invisible to fail. Only this time, the failure lasted.

Sure enough, it was a monster straight out of Scary's stories—seven feet tall if it was an inch, and just as Cali had described. This one looked different from the one she'd seen, though, but only a little. The dreads coming out of its helmet weren't quite the same, the body shape while still feminine was a little less so than the first one. And this one was now down and, she hoped, soon to be dead.

They concentrated their fire at its torso, which seemed to be the weakest part of the armor. The monster dropped what she was holding and tried to reach one gauntleted forearm with the other hand. Flucher fired Tank's weapon again, and the monster blew into bits. So did Dash's remains.

"So, they can die," Red Sarge said finally. "We need to find Bling-Bling."

Cali looked up—she'd seen these things, or their outlines or whatever it was, up high more than once. She pointed to a tree not too far away.

They all saw it, but went closer just to be sure. It was Bling-Bling, or what was left of her. Hanging upside down, a hole through her torso, the last of her blood draining onto the ground.

"Do they eat us?" Cali asked as evenly as she could manage.

"No idea," Scary said. "They kill us for sport, that's all I know for sure." She turned to Flucher. "But I'm just betting you know more about them, Mister Black Ops Man."

Flucher shrugged and handed the weapon to Red Sarge. "Let's keep moving. If Cali's right, there are at least two more of them out there."

La'vindi and Sula'amini did not return to the ship. Zalande would blame them for allowing Hekkati to die without trying to support her, and they needed no lecture. Hekkati had not listened, had been overconfident, and had failed. Her Death Name within the clan would not be a proud one.

"She was reckless," Sula'amini said shortly. "But we will avenge her."

La'vindi said nothing. She thought about their prey. She was certain they felt the same as she and Sula'amini did. Meaning they would want to avenge their dead, too. They had run before, but it was clear these oomans were not going to run again.

And there was more. Their big weapon had fired, seemingly on its own. But the way the other oomans had reacted meant that there was one of their kind holding that weapon. So there was an ooman they couldn't see. She had tested all the options her helmet allowed and the invisible one had remained so. That was problematic, but not insurmountable. But it did mean they needed to be far more cautious than they had been.

"Time to lure them," Sula'amini said, as she leaped for another tree. "Time to pick them off one by one, but this time, without showing off about it."

That La'vindi could agree with. She followed Sula'amini, trying to determine where the invisible ooman was.

They no longer walked in single file, but spread out so they could cover more ground, each of them looking for signs of the monsters, either the blurring Cali had described or the other bodies of the dead.

Red Sarge was on one end, Flucher next to him, then Cali, Scary, Booksmarts, and Yolo. Each made sure they could see the person on either side of them.

Flucher had taken Tank's weapon back from Red Sarge. Cali wondered if it was because that weapon seemed to work best against the monsters. The rest of them only had their laser rifles, but everyone was primed and ready to shoot a lot and never ask any questions now or later.

They'd gone about five klicks when Cali heard screams, rifle fire, and what sounded like Yolo shouting obscenities, which was her war cry. She looked to her right. "I can't see Scary, Booksmarts, or Yolo."

"Go after them," Flucher said. "We'll maintain this location."

Cali moved quickly but carefully, following the sounds of battle, but the jungle went silent before she found anything. She went a good two klicks more without finding any trace of the rest of her squad. She looked up and around. Nothing but jungle.

She swallowed the fear and anger and headed back. Flucher and Red Sarge weren't where she'd left them.

The oomans had changed tactics—as Zalande had expected, it was clear the oomans were searching for them now.

They followed the oomans until they finally began to drift farther apart. "They will find our ship," Sula'amini said softly. "They must be stopped." She didn't wait for La'vindi to comment—she swung down, aiming for the ooman at the farthest side, nearest to their ship.

Only, somehow, she missed and landed near, but not on, her target. The ooman spotted Sula'amini and began howling and firing her weapon. Sula'amini managed to use her wristblades to slice through the weapon, but not before it had shorted out her cloaking. She grabbed the ooman and leaped away as two more of them came after her, firing their weapons.

Faster than La'vindi would have ever believed, the ooman Sula'amini held slashed at her with a bladed weapon. Sula'amini dropped her, but only so that she could then drop upon her, using her weight and claws to crush and rend this ooman.

It was a mistake.

The two others arrived and fired steadily. Sula'amini went down. The bigger female ripped Sula'amini's helmet off, while the other slashed her arms preventing Sula'amini from activating self-destruct. Then the smaller one grabbed Sula'amini's combistick and stabbed her with it, over and over again.

La'vindi readied herself to jump, but as she did so, the bigger female put Sula'amini's helmet on, looked around, and aimed directly for La'vindi—just as Zalande arrived, roaring with rage. The ooman spun to face the greater threat.

La'vindi leaped away, racing for the remaining oomans. She would face Zalande's wrath another time.

Cursing under her breath, Cali started searching again. She found traces of them fast enough—no blood, but footprints. They were together. Maybe they'd spotted one of the monsters and followed.

She heard rifle fire again, from the direction she'd just come from, but Red Sarge was alone with Flucher, and that seemed more dangerous than being alone with one of the monsters.

Cali followed their tracks, going deeper into the jungle, the sounds of fighting getting fainter. She finally found them standing in a small clearing surrounded by giant trees. Flucher seemed to be holding Red Sarge up, but the scene looked wrong. She moved closer, as quietly as possible, staying behind the trees, not moving into the clearing.

The men were in profile to her when she realized what was really going on. Flucher was holding Red Sarge, but that was because he had a huge knife stabbed into Red Sarge's gut. The knife was military issue.

Flucher stood there, a small smile on his face, watching Red Sarge die. "It's for the greater good," he said conversationally. "This planet, peopled by those who oppose the Expansion Government and Orbital Marines, was created to lure the Yautja here, a planet for them to hunt on and enjoy, so that they hopefully leave worlds we care about alone. You and your team are making the ultimate sacrifice for your government and your military order, and we thank you for it. Operation Sidestep has been hundreds of years in the making, and we can't have the cannon fodder screw that up for us, now, can we?"

"Fuck you," Red Sarge managed, as Flucher let him drop to the ground.

Then Red Sarge seemed blurry, and Cali knew one of the monsters was there. Flucher knew it, too. He fired Tank's weapon again and again, and the monster became visible. One more hit, and she was on the ground on her back. Cali was sure this was the first monster she'd spotted, the one that had killed Tank.

Flucher was on top of the monster now, but not trying to kill her. He had a weird-looking collar in his hands and he was trying to get it around her neck. "You be a good girl and come with me so we can learn *all* about you."

Cali didn't hesitate. She aimed her rifle and fired.

La'vindi was down, the invisible ooman on top of her, and she was losing. She would die without honor, just as Hekkati and Sula'amini had, because, though she still fought, the ooman seemed to know her weaknesses, where her armor was penetrable, how to keep her from using her self-destruct, how to immobilize her. If she could not even utilize self-destruct, then her Death Name would be one of shame, of total failure.

There was a loud sound and the invisible ooman stopped

trying to get the thing onto her neck. La'vindi saw an ooman coming toward them, firing, but firing at the invisible one. The invisible one finally let her go, but the other ooman kept on firing. Then she stopped and removed something from the invisible one's head, then from his whole body.

La'vindi scrambled to her feet. The ooman faced her, weapon ready. La'vindi knew she should attack, but this ooman had saved her and she did not know why. The ooman did not fire. Instead she ran past her. La'vindi followed.

Cali knew why she'd let the monster live. Scary said they hunted humans. But humans hunted weaker animals, too. Flucher, however, was a worse monster than these hunters. So were the people who'd hired him. Because all of Scary's stories were true, and they knew it. Hit the enemy enough, and you'll be able to see them indeed—Flucher had been in an advanced-level chill-suit, meaning the monsters hunted by heat. That was why he'd used Tank's weapon, but had done his best not to carry it unless he had to. He wasn't supposed to die, just L-Squad. Flucher had been here to ensure that happened and to capture one of the monsters "for study." Or leverage. Ultimately, it didn't matter.

She ran for where she'd heard the fighting and the monster followed but didn't attack. The jungle was quiet again. "Scary! Yolo! Booksmarts!" she called. No answer.

The monster seemed to know what she wanted and took the lead. In ten klicks, they reached Cali's target. Her friends were all dead, but so were two monsters, both visible, one a female, one a male. The female had both arms cut off, but not the male. The female's helmet was off, revealing a hideous face with a double mouth and four terrible mandibles. Scary had the predator's helmet on for some reason.

Cali took the helmet off Scary, just in case she was still alive. It was then the male moved his hand toward the gauntlet on his other arm, mandibles clicking.

"You are all failures!" Zalande shouted. "Now we must all sacrifice!"

The ooman was too slow, but La'vindi was not. She threw her combistick and pinned Zalande's arm to the ground. Then she grabbed the ooman's weapon and fired, rapidly, at Zalande until she knew he was dead.

Her decision had been made in that moment—she would not return in disgrace or ever, nor would she die here, or anywhere else, at Zalande's hand. She was no longer a member of Clan H'ppattah—she was a lone Yautja, without home, without Clan or Yautja honor. But she now had a ship and her own form of honor, honor she could truly believe in. And possibly more.

She handed the weapon back to the ooman and took off her helmet. "Now we are even. Now we are the only survivors. Now we choose what tale to tell." But she could tell the human did not comprehend her words.

"Cali," she said slowly, as she stood up, holding the helmet, and pointed to herself, as the monster finished making her clicking noises.

The monster made some different clicking noises and pointed to herself.

Cali managed a smile. "I can't understand you, Click-Click, any more than you can understand me."

Click-Click went to the male, searched his body, found a small rectangle, and pushed the button on it. A spaceship the likes of which Cali had never seen appeared above them. The gangplank lowered and Click-Click headed for it. Then she stopped and looked back.

Cali nodded and followed after her. "I see this is the beginning of a weird friendship. Or I'm your dinner. Guess I'll be finding out, won't I?"

The ramp raised, the Yautja scout ship ascended, circled the planet once, then left Salturna in the past, heading for open space, taking the two warriors inside to a new beginning.

LITTLE MISS NIGHTMARE

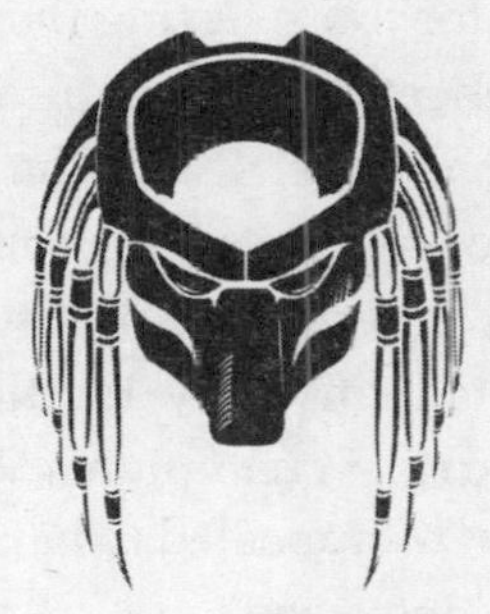

BY PETER BRIGGS

Sheathed in her optical refraction field, R'Kyn of the clan P'Rekh crouched atop the ancient alien slaughter ground. The mighty had once clashed against a bestiary of ferocity here, colored banner fabrics of cruel rulers fluttering above. R'Kyn thought, in essence, it represented the mutation of the ideals the Yautja themselves yearned for.

A garbed custodian passed through, scattered people turning as his voice echoed. "Ladies and gentlemen! It's five p.m. In an hour's time, the Colosseum will be closing for the day..."

R'Kyn gazed across sprawling modern Rome. Beyond the combustion-engine vehicles and the ancient structure they called Constantine's Arch, were the temples and columns of the time-ravaged Forum, and she wondered about the heyday of this fallen empire that had once subjugated all.

Since the scout-probes had spectrographed this backwater exoplanet and discovered its dominant species, the oomans had evolved into a Favored Chosen for the Yautja's fierce pleasures. Their problem-solving and tenacity made oomans especially attractive for those testing their mettle beyond the flashier, brawnier behemoths of a thousand worlds.

In her expeditions here, R'Kyn had noticed troubling societal changes. To make sense of it, she'd researched the popular ooman entertainment distractions from their internet. One depicted this very location in its triumphal glory days. Its warrior champion's defiant utterance—"Strength and Honor"— appealed to her. But did the oomans still believe, truly, in this creed?

One Aberration in particular, R'Kyn had reasoned, might help her understand. The problem this time, was R'Kyn had competition.

Agent Trinh Hue Dang loved monsters. A senior operations manager of one of the United States' diverse anti-terrorism Special Response Teams, monsters motivated and defined who she was. Trinh's Number One freak-show doozy this time had led her a merry chase from Washington itself, through an almost fruitless detour into France, culminating today, in Rome's cheerfully BoHo thirteenth Trastevere district.

Trinh exited the removals truck acting as forward staging post for her modest tactical team. Surveillance had their target well covered with randomized drone fly-bys, but Trinh wanted one more swing-past herself before they sprang the trap.

The Tacs had regarded Trinh earnestly as she'd addressed them. Her face was a contradiction: at once a blade, delicate and fierce, welcoming smile and Bambi-brown eyes. The squad for the most were beefy Midwest farm boys; vested, a handful in armor-concealed civvies. Say what you will about them, thought Trinh, but shooting straight was a necessity of the job, and these boys knew how to hit a target.

Twenty or so were jammed into the boxcar alongside a handful of their Italian equivalents, chomping gum and Red Vines as the air conditioning fought for equilibrium. A couple perspired so freely, Trinh thought their tattoos might drip right off.

"I don't need to remind you all, this target may be a fucking terrorist, but optics still matter to the agency."

Trinh noticed one—a man-mountain named Valtersson—blush at the salty advisory. It'd been gossiped Valtersson was secretly sweet on her, she remembered. She suppressed the urge to smile.

"Even though this is our very own homebrew Osama, remember: a few years, America hasn't been what you might call flavor of the month here. Don't do nothing bad for the Brand. If it goes down, shoot to wound. Leave something for a jury. Legal, legal, legal."

Determined nods. Valtersson, bless his Kevlar socks, tugged his pendant crucifix out for her. "No sweat, ma'am," he pronounced sincerely. "We got Jesus on this job." There were eye rolls, snickers at the back. Trinh looked him in the eye and nodded solemnly. Valtersson reddened again. He was adorable.

Trinh's sneakers went silent on the cul-de-sac's cobbles as she left them to their pre-game talk. Her mind cast eighteen months back to the start.

She'd been stationed in D.C. when the bombing of the Basilica of the National Shrine of the Immaculate Conception happened, during a packed Mass. Response units from a dizzying array of acronymed agencies mobilized for the grim forensic task of sifting bodies and wreckage for leads to the twisted masterminds responsible.

Scarcely had the dust settled when an evangelical megachurch in Houston and a mosque in Michigan were simultaneously rocked by explosions. A catastrophic loss of life.

There was shock, anger, fear, sadness. American bases around the world were placed on high alert as the country's media devolved into noisy, heated pandemonium. The world stood by as the President's heart went predictably out, hollow thoughts-and-prayers uttered by others. The Twitterati's outraged experts, naturally, knew who was really responsible.

Yet time passed, no leads emerged. While America's detractors were secretly pleased, beyond the weeded-out fakers not a single credible group or individual claimed responsibility.

No Jihad rose, and confused White Supremacists were left directionless in their hatred. If there was an upside, it was that badly shaken religious groups across denominations came together, briefly, in a spirit of public sadness and patriotism not seen since 9/11.

Six months passed, and one of the greatest forensic and Intelligence operations in history failed to glean anything more useful than tracing the explosive mix to a discontinued batch of Pentaerythritol from a defunct European manufacturer.

And then thirteen concealed devices of the same PETN cocktail exploded synchronously on remote timer in the middle of a million-strong march of women of differing races and backgrounds, gathered in Washington in defiance of the stripping-away of women's rights. Amongst the nearly seven hundred dead were a Grammy award-winning rapper, a *New York Times* bestselling author, and a self-styled I.T. entrepreneur infamous for sleeping with a married politician.

Trinh snapped to the present. She'd reached the second floor Italian flat, slowed her pace.

On the day of the Million March attack, Trinh had reasoned with panicked superiors convinced the sky was falling in. "A 'Mindset' is the true agenda here," she'd argued. "Not a 'Cause'." The earlier Intelligence Community analysis—that this was another "My Invisible Pal Is Better Than Yours" wingding—Trinh believed was flat-out bogus.

"This is a perp with the kind of serious money and connections to stay comfortably hidden, off the grid. That makes them doubly dangerous," she concluded. "They need taking off the board, stat."

Nobody disagreed.

It wasn't until the Reine Elizabeth II flower market explosion in Paris a year later that they secured a lead that might help achieve just that.

As Trinh neared a parked Amazon delivery van, a chill hit her dead-center. Her eyes flickered. It seemed a regular, leafy street. Normal passers-by, nothing untoward. Yet she'd the weirdest feeling of being watched.

Trinh made a show of fumbling her phone from her olive-green Alexa Chung bag. Pretended to answer, lowering her head while simultaneously glancing upward, faking a grin. "Sì? Oh—ciao, tesoro… !"

She casually panned the terracotta rooftops. Clocked a glint beyond shallow gables. If that was one of her snipers, they'd need to dull that scope-glass shine, pronto, or they'd blow this Op.

Trinh pretend-gabbled, pivoting slowly to glance across the street. "Course, sweetie; I'll grab anchovies from the deli on the way over…" A faint afternoon haze was up there, possibly an extractor vent? Otherwise… nada.

Trinh shook her head, reproached herself for being twitchy.

As Trinh replaced her phone, right in the spot of the presumed heat vent above her acoustic cues were stripped of background noise, analyzed and cross-referenced by a curious R'Kyn of the P'Rekh for their identity, meaning, and emotion. As R'Kyn focused on the ooman, cloaked from sight, she'd the strangest sensation the ooman was peering straight back.

R'Kyn toggled scanning modes. A pheromone tag confirmed the ooman as one of the justice guardians, who cycles ago had followed the Aberration to the City of the Iron Spire. Given the humans' technologies, R'Kyn was grudgingly impressed they'd located this new domicile before her.

The analyzer revealed the female below free of technological enhancements, slight in strength for those of its species' sex. *Is this their Pack Leader? Maybe a scout?* Whatever this meant, R'Kyn would need flexible plans for the Aberration.

R'Kyn was an academic; her specialty based in culturology, hunting patterns. She liked to delve beyond the Code's low-species zoology, deep-profiling the sociological and psychological aspects of more advanced species.

An unexpected byproduct of reasoning in the manner of an outsider ("Thinking Outside the Box" as the oomans phrased it), was that R'Kyn began to correlate subtle-yet-worrying red flags within the Yautja's own factions.

While the Predators had for a millennia occasionally assimilated elsewhere-technologies as their own, when their scientific progression plateaued it was simply because the Yautja required nothing further from their box of tricks. While adding voraciously to their knowledge, it was an oddity that through the years their hardware—plasmacaster actuators, their stellar transition drives—with minor tweaks when the need arose, all utilized the same core technologies their ancestors' had. Like many advanced species throughout the universe who'd achieved harmony, the Yautja were content to fulfill their biological imperative without distraction. If it worked and met their needs, it didn't need changing.

Conversely, here were the oomans. In two hundred stellar revolutions they'd harnessed the electron, achieved flight, left their planet, and were (worryingly) poking at the varied building blocks of the universe. With no signs of stopping, even wishing to slow. Which is why when R'Kyn visited this world in the twilight of their "20th Century", she was intrigued at what seemed to her the overnight creation of an ooman electronic interaction network, unifying planetary discourse.

The internet gave R'Kyn evolving insight into their individual psyches. Prior to its invention, ooman society had maintained an outwardly ordered and intelligent appearance. Fascinated, R'Kyn watched, analyzed… and over decades became disturbed by its "Social Media".

Humanity was manic and intense; self-pitying and self-deluded, powered by a desperate, relentless hunger for attention without either achievement or merit. Constantly envying what they did not possess, increasingly valueless.

The internet generated chaos, fed destructive feedback into ooman society. Disintegrated morality and honor, revealed the unfitness, even insanity, of certain of their leaders, who aired publicly unfiltered sneers and cruelty with ill-judgment.

It was a babbling, gestalt degeneration into madness, broadcast in real-time on a planetary scale. And with shocking clarity, R'Kyn recognized the possible nexus with her own race. Bringing R'Kyn of P'rekh to Rome, Italy.

Watching the ooman peacemaker briskly leave, R'Kyn keyed her wrist bracer for the aerial surveillance she'd placed on her test-subject quarry—Tracey Dahl, formerly of Burlington, Vermont. The ooman Aberration.

Tracey Dahl was dead. And meandering Rome's winding backstreets, thoroughly enjoying her *frutti di scusa* iced cone. Ahead, a murmuration of starlings weaved above the fortress of Castel Sant'Angelo, like a cloud of iron filings swished across paper by a magnet. *The saying was right,* she thought. *All roads did lead to Rome.*

The trick now, Tracey thought, was to not let this heady city lull her into false tranquility. After Prague eight days ago, she needed every ounce of edge she could hone.

Tracey was bullish after her bombing of the Paris flower-market. It was a year since the flight from Vermont to France, via plastic surgery at an expensive and discreet Swiss clinic. Downtime had been dull. Having unlocked her Bonus Life and leveled up, it felt good to be bad again. Hell, she thought. With luck this'd be the first leg of her European Tour. She might even get T-shirts printed.

But then Prague slammed Tracey to the mat. Hard.

On arriving in Europe, Tracey's dark-web contacts had led her to the bomb maker, Horvath. He'd fashioned the stockpile from one of her late father's defunct explosives businesses in Marseille, into something Tracey could effectively use on the Continent. She'd doubted the Slovak was trustworthy. He'd a hinky aura, and Tracey didn't much care for Eastern Europeans. Or anyone else for that matter.

The bells of Sant'Agnese echoed prettily from the Piazza Navona; reminding Tracey of that fateful train journey… holy hell, was she only twenty-two then? She'd nervously clutched her inaugural homemade IED through four states, to a homely Presbyterian church in a run-down Illinois district. Tracey had practiced her monologue all week in front of the cheval glass in the den.

"Forgive me, father. For I must sin…"

The bespectacled priest in the musty confessional was agog. His rote rhetoric continued a full five minutes after she'd thumbed-on the bomb's five-buck Casio timer, then quietly exited. Emergency services had discovered his body still in situ. What was left of it.

Tracey grinned. How far she'd come! How much she'd achieved!

Paris accomplished, Tracey had slipped undetected

through the Schengen travel zones into the Czech Republic, the Europeans' FADO/PRADO border security systems defeated by her dark-web-caliber travel documents.

Facial-recognition paranoia so common these days proved serendipitous. Tracey baffled public camera software using mask-and-sunglasses swaps, drawing not so much as a law-enforcement glance.

Czechia was a convenient one-stop shop for the seedier side of the weapons trade, some of the laxest arms-control in Europe. Years before, ordnance warehouses in the Zlin district of Prague had mysteriously exploded, with much finger-pointing in the direction of Russian GRU agents. The blasts were smaller than one might suppose, as a sizeable portion of their caches were transported discreetly elsewhere just hours before the arson.

Tracey blew her hands for warmth, loitering impatiently at the base of Petřín hill in Prague's Malá Strana Lesser Town. A lime green Škoda Yeti with darkened windows drew up, a compact, clear-cut man with hewn features opening its rear passenger door. "I'm Tamas." Mocking azure eyes regarded her from beneath a slice of blond hair. An alias, she guessed.

"Cathy. Ames," she offered. No recognition. *Not a fan of Steinbeck*, she thought.

"Please. In."

The driver sported a balaclava. Tracey squeezed alongside Tamas, who smelt faintly citrusy. Goutal's Eau d'Hadrien. Classy.

"Your phone, if you will."

She hesitated, passed it over. He slid it carefully into a dark blue Faraday pouch with an RFID logo. Blocking her GPS recording their route.

She shied back as the Czech lifted a black velour bag. Tamas paused, for reassurance. "For your protection only. Okay?"

She acquiesced, a curt nod. He eased the bag over her head.

"Y'know; I usually get dinner and a nice bottle of red to get to this point?" Tracey quipped. Through the scratchy fabric, she heard the driver snort.

Tracey felt the car clunk into gear, DMX on the stereo posing questions about Good Girls and Bad Boys. The bumpy forty-some-minute drive was enlivened by an eclectic playlist, until they reached their destination.

The spiced tang of explosive compounds cut through an acrid base of metal and machine grease. Tracey squinted as the hood pulled free. She was in a medium-sized warehouse; well-lit and pristine, a sprinkler system suspended from a high ceiling. Neatly stacked canisters and crates lined walls, miscellaneous shapes and sizes. An array of rifles, machine guns, and landmines, shelved and organized.

The driver, headgear removed, was a stocky, punky young woman who nodded to Tracey then headed past the well-lit cluster of tables at the warehouse center.

Three men were seated. The youngest spoke quietly into a phone. Another peered over bifocals, pecking numbers into a computer spreadsheet. In a different milieu, they might have been high-school teachers. Machetes and M-26 Tasers lay like an afterthought on a dark fleece blanket nearby. *Maybe a scuzzy high school*, Tracey decided.

The eldest, silver-haired and lanky, rose from his chair. German accent, charmingly urbane.

"Miss... Ames? A pleasure. We're all packed for you, ready for transit." He indicated four Five-Eleven Tactical heavy canvas backpacks in sundry colors. "Would you care to inspect?"

Tracey declined. "I'm sure it's perfect." While the arms business liked to be tightly anonymous, reputations were everything and bad blood traveled fast.

The German nodded politely, scanned a manifest. "Deposit remitted timely, many thanks. Mmm… claymores… oh? The new S-mines? Quite specialized." He briefly studied her, perhaps trying to divine her intentions. Tracey's poker-face was mighty and impenetrable, her smile inscrutable. He shrugged. "There remains only to square the balance. Or perhaps I could tempt you, from our inventory?"

"Maybe another time. 'A gal's got to know her limitations.'"

His mouth quirked, recognizing. "Just so. *Dirty Harry*?"

"*Magnum Force*."

"Ah. The very best. Please, come through. We shall finalize the transfer, then Tamas will carry these for you."

"Thank you."

A piercing metal screech and a woman's yell echoed beyond the furthest aisles. The German frowned, called hesitantly out. "Tracey?"

Silence. Brief swapped looks, then the school teachers reacted as one, lunged for the stun-guns.

"Lloyd? Sicherheit!" the German barked.

Cellphone Lloyd nodded quickly. Thumbed a channel, spoke urgently. "Tamas, Schmidt? Notfall, Lager, jetzt!"

Which is when the overheads extinguished, computers fritzing. Lloyd swore. Bifocals yanked a desk drawer, pulled a handful of Maglites. "Here!" He switched on two, rolled them across the table. Lloyd snatched one. Bifocals grabbed another, hefted his machete and started for the rack-aisles, dust motes dancing in his Maglite beam.

No longer the convivial host, the German rounded on Tracey, savagely grabbed her arm. "Is this you?"

"What?!" Tracey stared, confused.

He tightened painfully on her bicep. "Is. This. A raid?!"

She tore free, indignant. "What… why woul—"

A man's cry pierced the dark. Lloyd whirled his Maglite as Bifocals blurred backward through the air from beyond an aisle rack, entangled in a gridded mesh net. Miniature anchor pitons thunked stacked steel drums, emblazoned with "Hazardous Content" labels. Lloyd cried out in startled horror.

"Werner! Werner!?"

"Holy fuck-a-roni?!" Tracey gaped, while the German fumbled the remaining flashlight.

Werner howled continuously, beyond reason. His right arm flailed; the left, clutching his machete, trapped against his chest by the mesh. White vapor hissed from pierced containers behind, corrosive liquid chewing cloth and flesh as the net contracted around him.

Lloyd bolted to Werner, his eyes wild as the mesh shrank, driving the trapped machete blade into his nose. His bifocals cracked, cartilage snapping as the blade sliced deeper into his skull.

"Gemme… oud! GED ID OF!" Werner burbled, frantic. Tracey watched fascinated as gore fountained down his body, nanofilament slicing shirt and trousers geometrically into cloth swatches, fluttering bloodily to the floor.

Hampered by his Taser, Lloyd tried to drag the net. He screeched instantly, thumb and two fingers falling severed to the floor. Nubs spurting blood.

Tracey watched the macabre slapstick wide-eyed from behind the German as Lloyd turned, clutching his ruined hand. An anodized disc-like device flashed through the Maglite beam, and suddenly a gushing neck-stump and silence was where Lloyd's face had been.

The weapon ricocheted off the mesh with a sharp clink, something thumping to the floor in the darkness. Tracey gasped, dodged as the cutting-disc streaked past on the rebound. The German screamed as it shattered through his left shoulder, carrying on unimpeded somewhere behind. Across, Lloyd's headless body crumpled to the concrete.

That's when Tracey heard the sound. She'd experienced it once before, fleeing Vermont. It was like the sharp, deep ticking of a cooling car on a summer's day, and it made her scalp clench.

The wounded German fell to one knee, keening. Shakily swung his Taser and Maglite to the noise's source.

The disc hung impossibly midair, short of a shelf of grenades. The space around blurred and distorted. Tracey struggled to comprehend what she was seeing, when two… eyes? *Were they?...* flared brightly a moment, proportionately where a head might be.

The German jolted; thumbed the Taser's safety, a red LED glowing. Quick as a flash, the unseeable "whatever" drew the disc back as the German fired. Which is when reality waved bye-bye.

Tracey yelled, ducking as the space flooded with light and sharp cracks. Bloodied and cursing, the driver stumbled unsteadily down the aisle, blazing away with a small-caliber tactical handgun held Weaver stance. *"Meurs, espèce de salaud de fils de pute!"*

She was aiming at the same target-space the German had just Tased. Fifty thousand volts coursed down his wires, and what appeared unsettlingly at their ends made Tracey nearly pee.

Maglite beams and weapon flashes revealed a helmeted humanoid giant with mottled, pebbledash skin. A round sparked from one of numerous segmented armored plates, strapped around limbs to put a bodybuilder to shame.

Another bullet nicked its arm, luminous green fluid spurting from the wound. The being staggered, grabbed shelving as it convulsed from the Taser. Savage crackles like St Elmo's fire coursed across a type of fishing-net body stocking it wore. *"Not human"* flashed through Tracey's mind.

It raised an arm down the aisle, made a twisting motion. Something metallic shot from its wrist vambrace and punky-girl grunted in the darkness. The shooting stopped.

The warrior-giant grasped the Taser wires, helmet swiveling to Tracey. As the German tumbled to the floor next to her, Taser falling from his grip, only then did she notice he too was decapitated. She was Last Gal Standing.

Tracey's gut tightened in fear She stumbled against a table, fingers closing on one of her backpacks. The being rose to full height, tugged the wires away. Its form pulsed oddly, and it winked from existence.

Tracey shrieked as she was grabbed bodily from behind and hauled unexpectedly backward.

"Out, out, 'raus'!"

Tamas barged past Tracey with a crew of burly men, their barrel-slung LED flashlight beams raking the warehouse space. More hands took over the relay and tossed Tracey toward an open door as the fire ignited the drums behind

Werner into flame, what was left of him imploding across the floor in a pool of viscera.

Tracey gasped as Tamas abruptly vanished into blackness with a surprised croak, something harpoon-like powering through his gut. As she was shoved roughly into the safety of an exterior corridor, the overhead sprinklers popped.

She gulped for breath on the passage floor. She heard shouting; random, hesitant shots. Protruding through the inner warehouse wall was the business end of the weirdly intricate harpoon she'd seen in action seconds before. Blood glazed its tip, raining down in a pitter-patter spray from above.

She startled as a circular wall portion on the doorway's far side vaporized outward. Fast-disintegrating cinders of what might have been a human crashed at force into the ante-corridor. The harpoon-tip suddenly vanished, jerked back inside.

She was in an explosives warehouse, and it was on fire! Tracey one-shouldered the backpack, made a staggered run for the dark corridor's end. Slipping as sprinklers slickened the floor. She heaved the armored sliding fire-door open, the muted boom-crump of something igniting behind.

Cool night air hit her. Monolithic concrete blast barriers encircled the warehouse, the parked Škoda visible through a gap. Tracey ran for it, legs feeling not her own. She made the car, wrenched the handle. Unlocked. She piled in, relief crashing down as she found the key in the ignition.

With no idea what was stored back at the arsenal—nerve-agents, God alone knew what—Tracey bore down on the accelerator. Car safeties pinged warnings as she fast-flicked the main beams, zigzagged a concrete bollard springing from the dark. Roaring steeply downhill toward the security entrance, she fumbled her safety belt home, looked quickly into her rearview.

In rapid succession, brilliant blue pulses like ball-lightning flared from some unseen source, far back and dead-square where the Škoda was parked, the blasts streaking for the warehouse.

Tracey poured on the juice, rammed the gate as the universe behind whited-out. It gave violently, bottom hinges popping bolts. She exclaimed as the driver's airbag deployed in her face; miraculously guided the Škoda blindly through. Wrought-iron screeched the roof, monstrous thumps of the warehouse's girder frame landing in her wake, propelled through the air by insanely powerful detonations.

She wrestled the safety-bag from her vision, its rubber and baby-powder odor clogging her nostrils. She wrenched the car around a tight bend, nearly rolling it.

Tracey chanced a look at the tree line above and behind. It had taken the brunt of the shockwave's impact. Fully ablaze, she thought it sublimely beautiful.

Rattled, she took tributary roads. At a brief roadside stop, Tracey burned her passport; destroyed the retrieved cellphone. The Škoda was a goner: front end impacted, hood protruding at a weird angle. Scorched, it was nothing short of a wonder she'd survived.

Tracey coaxed the wreck toward Prague's lights, dumping it into a quiet stretch of river. She lucked out with a passing taxi. As they drove in mutual silence, a pall of noxious smoke and flames lit the horizon behind, a continuous wail of emergency services echoing into the night.

Returning to her Airbnb was out, too risky. Tracey wrote

off her belongings there. Luckily, she'd the forethought to keep a rented locker in the city.

After switching to her next emergency-stash passport, Tracey purchased rail tickets from Czechia with cash (the Euro was a boon to cross-border terrorism), jumping trains for random connections to confuse anyone predicting her destination.

She reached Rome. Navigating its streets in the days ahead, Tracey failed to notice a curious V-shaped wedge of nothing momentarily part the flocking starlings above. An autonomous copper-toned alien arrowhead flitter, not much larger than the birds and optically cloaked, had cruised the city for days, diligently sifting the millions of pheromone signatures below. Having now located the Aberration, her every move was being relayed to its waiting mistress.

Trinh Dang buzzed into the trattoria's innocuous side door to find six-foot-three of frustration at the rack-gate elevator. "Javazilla! Aren't you too old to play coffee-boy?"

Two trays high with drink-cups, Agent Johnny Ortiz turned, played wounded. "Dang, Dang. You cut to the quick. I just try be popular. Industrial brew, top left, yours. Get the button, would ya?"

Ortiz' laid-back drawl you could drizzle on flapjacks. He didn't need to try; his people loved him, so did she. He'd bounced through a slew of Government agencies in the decades since starting as a Ranger in North Carolina, finally sticking on Domestic Counterterrorism in 1999. After 9/11, Ortiz was evangelical about his calling, and decades later (like many contemporaries from those grim days) resisted notions of impending retirement.

Trinh jiggled her offering from the tray and thumbed the control. Ortiz had been with her when Sky News broke the Île de la Cité flower market bombing in Paris. Exotic orchids blasted into the air on a packed family Saturday, fallen like vibrant confetti on mangled Art Nouveau ironwork. Hundreds killed or maimed. It'd been a year's respite since Washington, and Trinh and Ortiz had turned wordlessly to one another, suspecting suddenly why.

Trinh rattled the elevator gate open to a murmur of headset communications; ripe with the scents of danger, anticipation, and Axe body spray. "Morning, each," she offered.

The dozen or so earnest perspiring young faces in the makeshift first-floor operations center glanced across laptops and desk-fans, brightened as they saw Ortiz.

"Champagne of workers, chicas," he announced. "Name 'em, claim 'em."

Eyebrows upraised, fingers eagerly waggled.

"Chewy."

"Soy Boy Ice?"

"Yeah, maybe in the cup this time, Boss?"

Trinh passed an assault-rifled agent, Powell, tiptoed through snaking extension cords. The place was a former videogame development gone bust, convenient to place rooftop antennae for the drones. Banks of chunky UAV hardware were set up in the glass conference annex ahead.

Giovanni, head Italian liaison, smiled as she passed. She nodded back. The Italians had been loosey-goosey about allowing a U.S. Tac Team on their soil. Trinh secretly suspected they'd passed the buck in case anything went wrong.

Trinh thought back to when the Paris bombing had occurred. Immediately, they'd contacted UCLAT, their French opposites. Unbelievably, the French had already mined two slices of luck. Ion Mobility Spectrometry confirmed explosive residue from the market bombing, consistent with the American attacks. Better, recovered fragments of a bomb casing had gleaned partial fingerprints.

Trinh had been at her office vending machine, thinking about heading home and contemplating a life-changing Baby Ruth decision when Ortiz rang her cell excitedly.

"We hit a break. Interpol's AFIS drew a match on the bomb-maker. A Slovak, Stefan Horvath. They'd had him earmarked already on something else."

The air-conditioning buzzed a tad louder. "For reals?"

"Reals 'n' a half. They're holding the creep right now, in solitary."

The U.S. bombings didn't correspond to the Slovakian's movements, eliminating him as the triggerman. Nonetheless, after strained negotiations Ortiz accompanied Trinh on a whistle-stop red-eye for Paris. Via a doubly annoying lawyer/ translator process, ninety minutes in a bright interrogation room with Horvath had produced a monotonal minimum of sentence-reducing cooperation.

Pissed, Trinh snapped. "Last time, or your deal flies south. Your employer? Name." After some more whispered three-way, the bomb maker nodded wearily, muttered something.

The translator turned to Trinh. "The name my client was given, was Mallory Knox. This is all he has."

Trinh blinked hard. A female bomber was unusual. Ortiz looked away, hid a smile. Further back-and-forth, she pried a reluctant half-description before Horvath clammed.

"Can you believe this?" Trinh hissed to Ortiz, as they exited.

He smirked, nodded. "The Mallory Knox thing?"

"No... What?" asked Trinh, genuinely confused. Ortiz raised eyebrows.

"Mallory Knox. She used the name of the crazy chick, in *Natural Born Killers*. Y'know? Tarantino? We've got ourselves a peach, here."

Trinh and Ortiz pulled tablet duty on the flight back, scouring Horvath's downloaded surveillance footage. Nobody matched the given description. Trinh thumbed interrogation notes, looking for a clue while trying to wrap her head around it all.

The carnage this woman caused. The delight in what she did, with the drive to continue? Why? It was unfathomable to her.

Trinh stopped. She'd found something. The Slovakian had met "Mallory" at a Moroccan restaurant, just south of the Seine and across from the bombing.

Before they'd landed, Ortiz pinged an email requesting the Paris authorities pull local CCTV and ATM footage. With a mental sigh, Trinh felt fairly clairvoyant they'd draw a fat nothing.

Back in her glass corner-office, Trinh was deflated the trail had run cold. Twenty minutes on, Ortiz strutted in like hell's own hard-on. "Dang, Dang! That's a 'phone-a-hotline' look, ever I saw one."

Trinh looked at him, dejected. "You know the test dummies, headbutt windshields? It's how I'm feeling."

Ortiz raised his cellphone, smirked. Made a show of pressing a button, said nothing.

"What?" Trinh asked, curious. Her computer chimed an incoming mail. She frown-smiled, opened an attachment sent from Ortiz. Clicking through, her eyes grew to saucers.

"Oh, you are wanging my eight-ball!"

"I ain't much famous for my comedy stylings, Dang."

They were traffic camera shots. A sidewalk bistro, identifiers situating it on the Boulevard Saint-Germain. And sat across a gingham tablecloth from Horvath, an above-average-height brunette sporting a hellish amount of foundation. Maxine Factor must have caught a fleck of something in her eye, because her sunglasses dropped momentarily as the shots progressed... and there was Little Miss Nightmare for all the world to see. Neither plain, nor especially striking, "Mallory Knox" could have merged into any crowd. To Trinh, as she clicked back and forth, devouring her, she was the most goddamned beautiful thing in the world. *Who was this person?*

"She must layer that makeup with a trowel... God, these are clean for biometrics. We sure this is her? We gotta ID."

Johnny's smile broadened. "Buttons have been pushed."

Although avians gave R'Kyn painful memories of her clutch-sibling R'Hyn, she still enjoyed watching them wheel intricate patterns in the Roman skies. Even by Yautja standards, R'Kyn was a gifted mimic, and she'd passed the afternoon imitating some of the Earth species she'd encountered.

R'Kyn's trophy accomplishments through life had been modest. A veteran of multiple hunts (continued survival was the most rewarding achievement of all), despite the heightened aggression of the female Yautja, R'Kyn had by choice matured away from sport hunting at an early age.

The loss of R'Hyn had chosen her path.

Every Yautja hunter, by Code, collated their own

intelligence. Failure to prepare, was preparing to fail—overeagerness led to bad decisions, endangering the Pack. *"Be Diligent, Or Be Dead,"* warned the Code. A lesson hard-earned when as Youngbloods, R'Kyn and R'Hyn made an unsupervised quartzpike ascent to ensnare an Arcturian Sickleridge.

The siblings had poorly researched a narrow geode fissure, becoming snarled in a patch of parasitic Arcturian serraweed, high in the clouds of the four-mooned world. Unseeable within her optical field, yet unable to call out for risk of detection by the circling scavengers, R'Kyn had no option but to watch helplessly until a rescue craft answered her distress call. All the while, the Sickleridge brood squabbled viciously for the right to hammer their scythe-edged beaks over and over into R'Hyn, visible just above. Draining him of his life.

Vengeance burning, R'Kyn had returned. She'd gutted the Broodmother and tore free its serrated bill, as long as R'Kyn's body was tall. Used it to slaughter its enraged offspring. Later, on pondering the mounted trophy in her den, R'Kyn regretted her uncharacteristic fit of pique.

R'Kyn learnt from this worst of errors. Groundwork and research became her life, mentoring Youngbloods for Hunt survival, while quelling her blood-rage with therapeutic sorties. Certain tenacious critters proliferated like wildfire across the universe (one loathsome exoskeletal race stood out for her), and R'Kyn found their efficient culling to help conserve the Lower Species, sometimes whole ecosystems, ethically gratifying. So why, after her recent melee in the ooman arsenal did R'Kyn feel so unfocused? Maybe for the first time since R'Hyn's death, she found herself... *actually enjoying all this?*

She rechecked tracking on the Aberration. Her quarry was crossing the river. Not long now.

Headphones jammed in, Tracey Dahl strolled the Ponte Sisto bridge to the Trastevere. She was thinking Rome at Golden Hour could be very pretty, when Cyndi Lauper complicated her day.

While churches had been Tracey's thrill in the States, Paris made markets her new hunting ground. She'd spent today in a mindless Brownian motion of tourists scoping a potential. Losing three-quarters of her supplies in Prague was a blow, but she'd improvise.

Tracey had been trying not to think about events at the arsenal as she crossed the Tiber, when her phone's playlist randomized. That danged song took her back a year, to the day she learnt she was dead.

In the wake of her Million March bombing, the manhunt for the attacker had become a hungry, circling shark. Tracey was no dummy. She watched the news. Law enforcement was pouring insane resources into finding the perpetrator, and pointlessly remaining in Vermont was courting fate.

Parry Mendoza was her late father's fixer. When Tracey had told him she needed to disappear permanently, he'd promptly arranged for a corpse-dupe that'd pass muster, and a bent coroner to fix the DNA and dental checks. She reiterated to Mendoza there couldn't be loose ends, and he'd smiled indulgently. It had cost a fine penny, but every scrap of Tracey Dahl's traceable identity was expunged from Federal databases. Mendoza's unquestioning efficiency made Tracey wonder at the unsavory acts Andrew Dahl must have committed to amass their family's fortune.

Tracey had been driving when the call came in, interrupting Cyndi singing about boys who hid girls from the world. Mendoza's reportage was matter-of-fact. Tracey's Bentley Continental had tumbled a precipice on a notoriously poor stretch of the VT-9, paramedics pronouncing the driver dead on impact. The coroner ran the paperwork. There was, of course, no next-of-kin.

Tracey felt a teensy twinge of remorse. She'd loved that car.

With Tracey's "death", the Dahl trustee board would now be liquidated, the public fortune dispersed. The Dahl family had been more savvy investors than entrepreneurs. Mutual funds, broadband, demolition. While not the elite of the elite, they'd amassed, through fair means and foul, a fortune the average layperson might wrestle to comprehend. As with any tax-avoiding billionaire-bastard worth their salt, simple mechanisms had been put in place to make substantial finances tiptoe invisibly offshore for a rainy day. Allowing Tracey to do precisely that.

Light-headed like a champagne-high, the newly dead Tracey Dahl had driven the east bank of Lake Champlain, supposed home to "Champ", the Adirondacks' very own Loch Ness Monster. Heading for the private boathouse the Dahls kept there, she didn't imagine she'd be seeing monsters today, herself and Mendoza excluded. Now he was her only remaining loose end.

An hour further, Tracey pulled the Ford Raptor into a shadowed parking lot, deserted aside from Mendoza's five-year-old white Chevy. Vanity's "Nasty Girl" on the speakers cut out with the ignition. She slid out, the ketamine hypo she'd practiced palming all week ready in her pocket. Tracey smirked. In her belted yellow Bottega Veneta coat, she visualized herself as Cruella De Ville.

Tracey had began the eight-minute trail-walk to the shore, chest pounding as her mind ran last-minute scenarios. She'd been fairly confident how this'd go. Once she'd jabbed Mendoza with the ketamine, even if he ran full-pelt to the Chevy he was unlikely to make it in the three minutes the drug would weaken him. She'd picked this route perfectly. Her concealed-carry SIG nine-millimeter was ample insurance against the certainty Mendoza was packing. The lake would do the rest.

Tracey reached the old boathouse, pushing back at nostalgia. The long wooden jetty was empty, creaking softly. The flute-like chirp of an evening Hermit Thrush carried on the still water. She peered up at the trees' vivid hues, muted in the gloaming. *It'd be Stick Season soon*, she thought ruefully. Winter's cusp, when nature flipped a switch and fall's red-yellows suddenly ceased. When she reached Europe, she'd miss this.

Tracey frowned, glanced at her watch. She'd ran late, but Mendoza ought to be here. He'd a mania for punctuality. "Parry?" Tracey's voice was unwavering, carried strong. No reply. She turned an unhurried circle, not wanting to seem an amateur if Mendoza materialized from the murk. Tracey called again. This was freakin' peculiar?

She pulled the burner phone she kept specially for Mendoza, slotted its SIM back. She auto-dialed, switched to speaker. As the ring played into the night, a faint musical twanging niggled at the edge of her hearing. Tracey's brow creased. As she incremented her phone volume down, the new sound got correspondingly louder. It was the intro to the *Better Call Saul* TV show theme. Mendoza's own ringtone.

"Yo? Mendoza...?" Tracey's voice sounded strained as she turned, stepped back. Her neck prickled, and she felt oddly exposed. Had Mendoza suspected?

Splat. Something noxious from above blotched her ten-thousand-buck shearling collar, smaller spatters following. Tracey went to rub them, thought better. She squinted upward. And, mouth suddenly drying, pressed her cellphone's "disconnect." Above, Little Barrie's guitar licks ceased.

As a kid, Tracey had been fascinated by an old model kit called "The Visible Man." A plastic human-shaped shell with veins and bones and organs exposed beneath, what she saw above now felt like its real-world analog.

Still wearing trousers and Salvatore Ferragamo loafers, someone was artfully suspended upside-down from a high tree bough, their stripped-to-the-waist torso flayed bare to bloodied nerves and tendons. Black liquid plinked down, dribbled between the planks. It was Mendoza. Only, without a head.

That's when Tracey first heard the same peculiar rhythm she'd encounter later at the Prague warehouse. Like a woodpecker, echoing deeply through the trees. And close behind, a guttural woman's voice. Vibrato, yet raunchy. A deep chill ran through Tracey, familiar words raising goosebumps.

"Do you think... I'm a... nasty... girl?"

Tracey bolted.

R'Kyn couldn't say why a setting sun, on any world, made her feel reflective. Poised high on the Trastevere rooftops, waiting for her quarry in the shadow of a brickwork chimney, thinking about the Aberration forced her to admit she'd made poor decisions.

Any ooman CSI would have admired the efficiency with which R'Kyn had processed the crime-scene data, connecting the bombings to Tracey Dahl. For a time, R'Kyn had imagined purging the Aberration's proxy at the boat lake would send a message, force it to alter its nihilism. But with the further slaughter of the innocents at the City of the Iron Spire, R'Kyn grudgingly accepted her quarry was merely a rabid animal. Killing without honor, unable to cease.

She'd seen the parallel. There'd been civil discord on Yautja core worlds. Fractures had appeared, younger dissenters from the Lesser Clans exhuming nanosciences long-quashed as dangerous. In a subversive quest to "upgrade," these Rebel Clans practiced merging their DNA with aggressive genome traits from off-world races. They became Aberrations. Bigger, brutal. Intent on slaughter for slaughter's sake.

Insane.

Unhindered by politics or religion, Yautja Clans weighed the Aberrations as dishonorable, and with unusual solidarity moved as one to crush them. The internecine conflict to restore the Yautja's pride was long and costly. Planets died in the process. Some Lower Species were collateral damage, wiped from existence, to the anger of the Yautja Elders. In its aftermath, the victorious hunter wasn't overly concerned with the "why" of the vanquished Clans' behavior. But R'Kyn was.

She'd dug forensically into the conquered Clans' lineages and hunting records, finally realizing with a thrill of discovery most had been hunt veterans… of Earth? *Was it coincidence?* Or, were the Chosen somehow contaminating Yautja with their madnesses? When humanity gained a foothold, would it spread across the stars?

Should the oomans be stopped before it could happen?

A rose-ringed avian hopped the roof ridge, broke R'Kyn's reverie. It couldn't see the Predator through her cloak, yet cocked its head and squawked.

R'Kyn mischievously projected a perfect imitation at the bird. It hopped back, confused by this reply from nowhere.

Something spooked the avian, and it took flight. A proximity sensor tripped in R'Kyn's bio-helmet display. She fancied it might be the Aberration returning, but saw to her annoyance it was a drone, and not hers, circling her position. Somebody was persistent.

"So, I'm looking at a parrot?" Trinh was in the drone control annex, staring dubiously over Quinn's shoulder.

The baby-faced drone pilot sported a Powerpuff Girls tee, her afro cocooned in a silk wrap. A plastic '60s-era Godzilla scowled grumpily alongside her Piccolo avionics station monitor, currently live-feeding a parakeet taking flight. Emma Quinn's brow creased. "Nah, he's just livin' his best life. This is the feed off Louie, Drone Three, right opposite the target. I keep sweepin' this one roof, 'cause… well, I can't shake the feeling somebody… something, is up there? Only I'm seeing squat, and it's kinda drivin' me nuts." She tugged at her T-shirt collar, blew out her cheeks. "Jeez—Italy? How is there no concept of A.C. here?"

"Try infra-red?" Trinh queried.

"Tap-danced the spectrum," nodded Quinn. "Zippo. There's a cellphone tower, but shouldn't be interference this range."

Trinh nodded, thinking. "I'll get someone up for a once-over. But—" Her phone rang, halting her. She answered. "Yello?"

It was Ortiz. "It's Johnny. She's back."

Tracey was puzzled as she set her groceries next to the Backpack of Doom, flipping on the table lamp. Coming in, she could've sworn she'd heard the incongruous trill of a Hermit Thrush. She shook the notion. Wishful thinking the Vermont State Bird somehow found itself four thousand miles west. Maybe she was homesick?

She crossed to the window of her well-appointed first-floor apartment. While money didn't necessarily buy happiness, it did net you a plusher standard of misery.

At school, her classmates envied her family's wealth, despite themselves. Tracey's effortless athleticism and academic excellence could have crowned her the all-time Sorority Princess. Instead, her catnip people skills cast her as the shunned weirdo. Tracey could give an atheist's amen: she'd engineered it that way. While other little girls' hearts were filled with kittens and love, Tracey's was fueled by napalm and frivolous malice.

Her mother having died spawning her, a father forging his empire, Tracey was a preordained vacuum of neglect, foreseeing a depressing metamorphosis of her white-bread pampered life, decade by decade.

Boys were not her speed, girls either. Sex was an

inconsequential biological function oversold to the masses, and she'd long ago excised the craving mechanisms of intimacy as an annoying scratch to be itched when necessary. Tracey Dahl had a different calling.

Her first big score was aged nineteen. She'd cut the brakes on a family's Winnebago as they'd dined at a Bob Evans window booth, sat with her Baskin Robbins on a bench across the road, listening to Courtney Love on her mp3 and watching in fascination at happy faces, the youngest's Pikachu smushed against the glass. Later that night in bed, Tracey listened in breathless anticipation to her police scanner through headphones, collapsing finally into disappointed exhaustion as the sun began to rise.

The next day in the cafeteria, students glanced up puzzled as Tracey squeed from across the room. Local news carried an account of a New Hampshire intersection pileup, a Winnebago shredded in a head-on pileup with a Freightliner. All killed instantly. Tracey's eyes were rapt at the somber screen closeup of a yellow anime toy lying wretchedly in a puddle beyond yellow-black police tape. To this day, the velvet-sweet of Pink Bubblegum ice-cream made Tracey squirm.

Tracey's mind snapped to the now. *Hell with Prague*. She scrolled her phone to its afternoon playlist, switched the sound to the apartment speakers. Cyndi always set her to rights.

Tracey frowned. The street below was quiet for the time of day. Unusually so? No cars, pedestrians. The sports-fiend across the way ordinarily had his TV obnoxiously loud. Today, curtains were closed and all silent. Tracey felt weirdness encroaching. She thumbed "play," then slowly back-stepped from the window, reaching for the earplugs in her denim shirt's breast pocket.

Preoccupied with the ooman drone, R'Kyn missed her flitter returning. It took station, fixed a sound-conductive beam on the apartment window. R'Kyn's mandibles clacked in annoyance as the audio feed transmitted the Aberration's ritual musical choice.

R'Kyn edged over the rooftop. Seeing nothing at the apartment below, she paused scan-modes as rooftop movement caught her eye. Toggling to thermal, the heat-bloom of an armored ooman in concealment emerged; similar Snipers on balconies close by.

With a rush of understanding, R'Kyn went quantum, deep-scanned the surrounding domiciles. The buildings were empty. No families, no occupants. *This is a trap. But not set for me.* She opened her wrist bracer, primed the flitter. It was time. Quantum-fixing the Aberration, she observed human-shapes separating position either side of the hallway entry.

Then R'Kyn heard the creak of hinges behind.

Mouth like sandpaper, Trinh was glued to the Ops room camera feed, confirming each agent's readiness. It'd taken a heap of preparedness to discreetly evacuate the residences. Over her headset, she heard Ortiz' whispered "In place." Her support team shot expectant looks across screens.

External cameras registered the target's retreat. Trinh bit her lip. Looked to Giovanni who nodded, gave a thumbs-up. *Now or never.*

"Very good," she ordered crisply. "Insert."

An ooman appeared on the rooftop behind R'Kyn. Her threat sensors locked his weapon, plasmacaster swiveling. She clicked her mandibles to cancel the shot, irritated. There were bigger Gorthunds to flay. R'Kyn launched from the rooftop, actuated her flitter-drone's electromagnetic chirp.

"There's something up here!" the ooman behind yelled. "Some... *thing*!?"

A powered battering-ram splintered the lock right off Tracey's door. She slowly turned, brought hands up as the Tac Team swarmed in, much shouting and the business ends of serious weaponry.

"Armed agents! Hands in the air, onto your knees! To the ground—now, now!" hollered their lead.

Luck was a finite resource after all, Tracey thought, wondering if she could break for the backpack without being cut down. She carefully knelt. "Okay. Sir, see? I'm complying..."

As the Tacs edged closer, the table lamp unexpectedly extinguished and the music stopped.

The Predator flitter's disruptive pulse fried the American drones, sent them crashing unseen to road and rooftop.

"Ops? Respond please, come in?" The armed ooman straddling the apartment's side window fiddled with his earpiece. A shiftsuited R'Kyn pounced for him. The ooman jumped as a powerful impact vibration shivered his balcony, twisting frantically about, as R'Kyn moved in unseen. And then he screamed.

Hubbub broke out as the Ops Center went black. Trinh raised her voice, tried to calm its edge. "Where's the power? What... *happened*?!"

A junior agent shook her head, her desk fan slowing. "The batteries should've been backup? It's not the power?"

Another nodded urgent agreement. "She's right. Comms are out, everything's fried!"

Trinh's phone was a brick. "Shit, shit, shit!" She rounded to the annex: the drone equipment was military-hardened against an electromagnetic pulse. Quinn fast-nodded, equipment lights indicating a reboot.

Horrified, Trinh's mind raced. Her op was hanging, mid-execution. She had to do something? On impulse, she snatched up her firearm holster, bounded for the exit. Yelled "Powell, with me!" at the flummoxed armed agent in passing.

Tracey was prone on the carpet. Agent Valtersson drew a cable tie, bent to her. "Ma'am, I'm securing your hands. Do not—" A boom and crash of shattering window glass in the hallway cut him off. Tracey jerked her head to look while everyone stood, stupefied.

"Jesus jimpnuts!" someone yelled. Then she heard sounds of men, crying out and dying.

Valtersson glared down at Tracey. Yelled, "Stay put! Don't—" Which is when the wall blasted inward, sending him sprawling.

The Tacs were on the ball. Their leader launched sideways for cover behind the kitchen island as his men loosed rounds, although with no idea at what. Grapefruits in Tracey's groceries exploded to pulp, bounced and scattered on the floor.

The Tac leader suppressed a teeth-gritted curse from hiding as shelf jars above were raked, showering him in glass and splintered pasta. He saw his men fall like ninepins; one with his jugular impossibly cut from nowhere, others downed by lethal bladed pucks of some unknown design.

"Get some, you coward!" a fourth agent roared, blocking his unseen adversary and firing short bursts. With a high-pitched whine and blazing light, he and the flatscreen TV behind suddenly had gaping cavities cindered right through them, the Tac's corpse crashing back through the glass coffee table.

Tracey was motionless on the floor, mind whirling. This was Prague all over, and this fucker was intent on nailing her. She spotted Valtersson's dropped HK416 a few feet off, scrambled for it. Instantly, three bright red points of light bloomed on her arm.

The Tac leader leapt from cover with his MP5 submachine, snapping open and whirling an expandable steel riot-baton with a cry. It hit a spot mid-air with a dull clang, a visual "judder" affecting some invisible outline before him. The agent made to strike again, but with a scything hiss the top two-thirds of his nightstick was sliced clean away. Abruptly, he shuddered, blood gouting from his mouth. His finger contracted on his MP5's trigger, bullets stitching the ceiling plaster.

Tracey dived through the gap where the wall used to be, let-rip the HK416 over her shoulder, the invisible attacker jerking the pinned agent around as a human shield. Tracey's rounds thunked into the twitching body, finishing the job the unseen foe started.

R'Kyn's plasmacaster tracked and fired, but the fleeing woman had defeated its firing angle and the energy bolt sizzled through the rent to blow out a neighboring apartment wall.

A nearby ooman shook himself, spotting the bullet-riddled leader hanging impossibly mid-air, curving scimitar blades exploding from his back below his shoulder blades, then launched up from the floor with his combat blade.

R'Kyn's bio-helmet possessed excellent field vision, yet still had blind spots. Distracted, the reduced distance failed to trip her proximity sensors and she missed the ooman's thermal blur from below, catching a glimpse of the swinging knife.

Jinking aside, she swatted the blade from his grip. The squat ooman struck out with punches, yelling "Down, down, down!" and R'Kyn staggered, irritated at her concentration lapse. His ferocity caught her off-game. She rallied; tightened her core strength, planted her balance, grabbed the ooman by the neck with her right claw, tried to shake the impaled corpse's deadweight.

The ooman's neck bones crunched, but he kept whaling. A blow connected with the being's fishnet body-cabling, its appearance glitching. R'Kyn heaved mightily, and the ooman flailed wildly through the air, met the wall head-on.

Beneath the bio-helmet, R'Kyn's mandibles stretched wide, something like a wince in a human. Her abdomen twinged. No cracked rib, but the ooman's pummeling had torn some combination of her dorsals and obliques. He'd impressed her enough that had she time, she'd have made a point to return and claim his cranial trophy.

The Code frowned on Yautja technology being lost to the Chosen. With no opportunity to clean the scene and locate her throwing projectiles, R'Kyn shook the corpse free, then clicked the timer on a low-yield plasma grenade.

She tossed it behind her, launched back out in pursuit.

Rome's Trastevere was a cubist architectural hodgepodge of varying heights, gentrified and ramshackle. No parkour athlete, Tracey ran on pure adrenalin across the rooftops. She slid tile slopes, bounced flat garden terraces. Terracotta shattered as she put distance between herself and the apartment.

She crashed onto the table of an upmarket rooftop bar, yelling as it overturned to send cutlery and glassware scattering. "*Spostare*! Move, move!" she screamed. Patrons around the central pool started angrily, then registering her machine gun shied back in alarm. Tracey picked herself up, scrambled to the wrought-iron balcony.

As she debated the merits of a parked garbage truck below, something cannonballed the pool at huge velocity. Displaced water drenched the clientele and Tracey. Shocked yelling behind, she didn't look back. Soaked, she leapt the rail.

Tracey clanged to the truck's roof. Despite a cockroach resilience for survival, she'd an inner calmness about her fate. Her outlook for a long time had been that all existence was a nihilistic struggle. The Earth—its hurricanes, 'quakes, floods—was out to get humanity, individually and en masse. Eventually the sun would boil and the universe succumb to heat-death or some other quantum finality. The reality was that John and Jane Q. Schmuck were only the tiniest transitory morsel, and life in its myriad forms, down to the vilest tiny bacteria, would always consume them in the end.

Tracey winced as she jumped quickly to the truck's hood. Her exertions taking their toll.

"It Is Healthy To Have Future Goals," Tracey's favorite-ever fortune cookie had once advised. So why not Do Unto the Universe, Before It Did Unto You? Just get in there first… and fuck everything up? Tracey Dahl had a very positive attitude about her destructive outlook.

Tracey grunted down to the street—and into the path of a speeding yellow Fiat 500. Its female occupant glanced up from phone-texting, her expression shifting to one of horror. Tracey saw her body stiffen as she gripped the wheel and jammed the brakes just before they crashed.

"*Cagna*!?" The woman stumbled furiously from the Fiat, yelling as Tracey stomped toward her. "*Che cazzo era*?!" She gestured angrily, missed Tracey's weapon flush against her leg.

"Yeah, friggety-frag," Tracey commiserated, nodding sympathetically as she shot the skank through the forehead, clambering over her body into the tiny car. She hurled her backpack to the passenger side, gunned the engine.

It'd taken three attempts for Trinh to find a vehicle that'd start. She'd wound zigzags through the Trastevere, Powell riding literal shotgun. They'd made the three blocks to the apartment, which looked as if a giant charring dessert scoop had dipped into the building, inexplicably not even debris left. Johnny Ortiz sat woozily near the destruction, no clue what had happened. The only shielded working sat-phone crackled in Trinh's lap, linked to Ops through their one functioning drone.

"Tell me good things?" Trinh pleaded, flatly.

"Got her!" Quinn announced triumphantly. "Yellow Fiat Five Hundred, three roads west your position."

Tracey had swung the Fiat onto the main thoroughfare, when suddenly its metal roof buckled heavily inward. She shrieked then ducked instinctually as short barbs perforated the ceiling, hollered as far-larger blades punctured through, scratching her cheek. They abruptly withdrew, and Tracey scrabbled for the Heckler, which had slipped into a leg-well. She was driving one-handed when the blades speared again. "SONUVABITCH!" she screamed, alien steel bayoneting into her shoulder. Through searing pain, she glimpsed a side alley ahead and wrenched the wheel fiercely aside.

R'Kyn lost balance, floundered as the automobile veered sharply across oncoming traffic. Vehicles screeched to a halt, collisions ensuing. Horns furiously honking.

The car plunged into the alley mouth, laundry lines of cheerfully colored fabrics crisscrossing all the way down. R'Kyn balled her fist and shattered the driver window, hearing the ooman driver cry out as her clawed fingers grasped urgently. Sheets and clothes slapped annoyingly at R'Kyn, disoriented her. She tried slashing, but the fabric snarled about her. Her arm twisted, and suddenly a line caught her bio-helmet's lip under the chin, wrenching it savagely free from her face. The line gouged excruciatingly into her mouth's soft tissue, snagged a mandible. She felt the powerful cords in her neck whiplash as she was jerked savagely rearward from the vehicle.

Tracey's head tilted at the clattering on the roof, a loud bang following from the region of the trunk. "Gotcha, BITCH!" she bellowed triumphantly as the Fiat roared from the alley end, turning the corner.

Then a military Iveco Massif four-by-four broadsided into her with a metal-on-metal screech.

"Think we found her!" Powell exclaimed emphatically.

"Great!" Trinh shouted back, feeling the burn. She wrestled the wheel, heart hammering her ribs as she drove for dear life. *She was here. This was it.* "Let's give 'er a ticket!"

The cars careened the narrow street, jockeying position. Tracey drew fractionally ahead, felt every crack in the badly maintained surface. She hit a bump, strayed into the Massif's path. Its fender jarred her rear quarter, and Tracey gritted her teeth. She glanced annoyed in the rearview.

"Shake this flea," she muttered. She whirred down the broken fragments of her side window, glass shards tinkling into her lap.

Back in the Massif, Powell leaned from his side, tried to steady his Remington 870 pump-action.

"Tires!" Trinh yelled. "Take out her tires!"

As Powell nodded and aimed, the rifle's wicked tip appeared, spitting death. The fusillade blew open Powell's skull, splintering the Massif's windshield until Trinh could see nothing across one whole half of its blood-spattered glass.

Too focused on her pursuers, Tracey dared a look forward and momentarily lost control. She weaved badly, wresting the wheel back hard, oversteering. The mistake cost her.

The road narrowed to an archway ahead, and Tracey hit its inner wall at an angle. With a grinding crunch, the Fiat corkscrewed uncontrollably into the air. Forward motion carried it into the picturesque piazza beyond, where it slammed onto its roof to skid sparks along the cobbles. Groaning to a stop, to preposterously interrupt the wedding reception ahead.

A truck came unexpectedly out of a side-road into Trinh's blind spot, blaring its horn. With a curt "Shit!" Trinh swerved. The Massif clipped the sidewalk, flipped onto its side to plough into a glass-and-metal-frame bus-stop.

Upside down, blood rushing to her head, Tracey was seriously thinking of pressing "Unsubscribe" on this whole day. There was a clamor of excited Italian voices, running footsteps. Her backpack and gun still within her grasp, Tracey braced for a fall and slowly unbuckled her belt. Somebody tried to open the Fiat's door, but it was jammed and made a grinding racket. Questing hands tried to grab her.

Trinh leaned against the Piazza entrance, all she could do to stay upright. Hearing shots and screams, she sucked up her resolve and limped forward as fast she was able. Shards of pain stabbed through her leg. She was pretty sure it was broken.

Illuminated garlands were strung about the bubbling fountain at the square's center, panicked people in hire suits and fetching dresses fleeing every direction.

Trinh spotted the tall American, facing away near the upended car. As a machine gun was tossed away with a clatter, Trinh raised her own SIG Sauer P226. She fired a warning shot into the air, exacerbating the wedding party's exodus.

"American… agent!" Trinh called haltingly across, as authoritatively as she could manage through spasms. Her target stiffened.

"Hands… in the air. Turn slowly… around!" Trinh shouted. A backpack dropped from the woman's hands, clanked to Roman stone. Teeth gritted, Trinh cautiously closed the gap while the other woman pivoted unsteadily.

Tracey's head was badly gashed, blood matting her face. She held a manual-trigger mechanism in one hand, a rectangular claymore explosive device in front of her at chest level. Trinh could clearly see the raised words "Front Toward Enemy" on its metal surface. They were pointing toward her.

"Ma'am. You need… to put that… down," Trinh ordered unsteadily, blinking sweat. "And you need… to surrender."

Tracey snorted. "Dream on, toots. We got live TV."

Trinh heard the whirring, peered up. There was Quinn's surveillance drone, holding position on the scene. She bit back a curse. She didn't need to give this fruit-loop an audience.

"Give it up." Trinh's voice broke. "And… we can talk?"

Tracey shook her head, dismissive. "You know how this is gonna go. Someone's not walking away today. Maybe nobody, right?"

Trinh sagged. Her gun wavered. "Why?" she croaked, plaintively. She felt blackness nibble at her, thought she'd pass out. Staring into Tracey's eyes, all she got back was cold, glittering madness. "Why do… any… of this?"

Tracey smiled pityingly. "You stupid, dumb bitch. You just really don't get it. Girls—"

There was a whine like an overstressed dynamo, and Trinh and Tracey jolted simultaneously as the drone disintegrated to atoms. With a final confused look, Tracey's toxic white privilege was taken away with swishing finality. Both the explosive mechanism and her headless torso thudded to the cobbles.

Trinh gasped to her knees. A hulking humanoid nightmare appeared over the woman's corpse, its face all teeth and terrifyingly wrong angles. It stepped forward, cocked its head at her.

"*—Just wanna. Have… fun,*" the alien finished. Almost apologetically.

Trinh Dang fainted.

THE TROPHY

BY A. R. REDINGTON

The repetitive beeping from the alert message board on the console of Rhea Ortega's intergalactic hunter spacecraft wrenched her from a light slumber. With a jump, she slid forward from her leather pilot's chair, pressing a calloused finger against the red, blinking light on the screen. A message blipped across the left side monitor:

ATTN: Elite-Opp Hunters
Grade: Class A.
Job: The Exterminator
Location: Zoam-9, Prynaerus star system
Time: SOS beacon activated 14:53.
Reward: 50,000,000 Gal credits.
Note: Proceed with caution. Expert assassin gone

rogue—serial killer, mass murderer, human trafficking, illegal extraction of organs for black market. Wanted in five galaxies.

Drop-off point: Gal-Sar Bastion, Headhunters Assoc.

Requirement: Wanted dead. Acquiring whole body, head, or functioning data chip with deceased log will be accepted for reward.

Rhea pressed against the job name, and a hologram appeared, the image streaking with static as the feed focused on the target. He seemed to be in his forties, looking worse for wear. A series of scars marred his left eye, which had a bionic ocular replacement. Along his neck were what appeared to be acid burns and a thick, ugly red line that revealed he at one time had his throat slit and managed to survive.

"Ugly son of a bitch," Rhea muttered.

She thumbed the location link, and the map appeared on her front window, tracing a blue dotted line across multiple star systems. A brand-new network of dropholes—contained wormholes extensively used to travel vast distances in seconds—lay not too far away. Prynaerus lay along the far end of drophole 4. It would take her one jump to be within the star system. However, Zoam-9 was an uninhabited planet. To be there served little to no purpose. There were no victims there for the Exterminator to claim, and no desirable treasures or resources lay within the gaseous planet. To be so highly sought out, someone like the Exterminator would never risk being found, which meant only one thing—the target was either pulling some trick or had actually crash-landed on the planet.

"What the hell are you doing there?" Rhea whispered, staring at the hologram of the filthy man.

The job details were suspicious as hell, but the reward was worth the risk. With that price, everyone within the surrounding systems would be on the hunt. Rhea had to be careful. The Exterminator was a cruel individual. He was also an expert pilot, having served in the air brigade in his younger years, where he first got the taste of death during the countless dogfights of the Gal-Sar wars. From there, he turned to murder after an insidious discharge from the military. His history was well known among the hunters. The Exterminator had had a bounty on his head for many years. Still, any hunter that risked capturing him arrived at the Headhunters Association in pieces within a box, sometimes in separate orders strung throughout weeks. It was a message to them all—don't even bother trying.

However, if he were such an expert pilot, what would cause him to send an SOS while stranded on a volatile planet? Rhea had an idea, but she needed further evidence. Kicking on the Magnetic Flux Induction Generator, the zero-point induction rod gushed aetheric energy to the engines. With an enormous hum and crackling burst, the spacecraft zipped in a brilliant line toward drophole 3, which would connect her to number 4 of the Prynaerus system. Rhea awaited no orders and passed through the gate with a flash. The tunnel of light absorbed her ship, temporarily blinding her as it pulsed through the wormhole. She sped through the opposite side with a clatter and pressed on at high speeds toward Zoam-9.

A message alert popped on her console, and, expecting an update on the target, she accepted the note to run across her screen.

"Heya, sweetheart," a familiar and much-unwanted

voice drawled from the speakers. Rhea's nostril turned up at the sound, and she barely tore her gaze away from the window.

"I don't have time for your bullshit, Alek," she snarled.

"My, my, testy as usual. I was checking in to see if ya caught wind of the latest Class A assignment from headquarters. Judging by your intense concentration outside the ship instead of the loving one I so desired in my direction, I assume you're already up to date on current affairs." Alek was a sweet-talking narcissistic, sociopathic asshole who had ruined a few missions for Rhea in the past and even claimed more than one of her kills.

"Fuck off, Alek. This one is mine," she snapped.

"Not if I get there first," he said with a laugh.

"We both know my ship is faster," she retorted.

"Yes, but I was already in the Prynaerus system when I got the assignment."

Rhea risked a look, glaring at the screen. Alek smirked, pleased he had finally gained her full attention, if only for a moment. "There's my beauty queen. My goodness, you age like a fine wine. Tell ya what, when I claim this kill, we can both retire. With that many Gal credits, I'll be one of the richest men in this quadrant of the Milky Way. I'll buy you a nice little cottage beside my mansion. We can have parties together, and when your bed gets a little too cold at night, you can keep warm in mine."

Rhea ignored his antics, clicking on her panel. She ran a scan of the system and held back a grin.

"I see you like the sound of my proposal," he smugly stated.

"You've always liked flashy things, right?"

Alek nodded, chuckling as he chewed on a metallic stick full of tobacco-flavored mist. "Always."

"Then take a look at my flashy ass passing you now." She pressed against the injector button, allowing an additional intake of aether into the engines. The ship jerked forward, pressing her back into the seat. Unable to lift her head away from the leather cushion, she eyed the monitor to the side and caught sight of Alek's dumbfounded expression as she sped past his ship and the planet he floated by.

"You goddamn bitch!" he snarled.

"Cut transmission," Rhea called out. Alek's video promptly ended, and the woman reveled in the pleasant silence. "Idiot," she said with a smile.

The enjoyment of her victory was cut short as something clanged against her shields. Her ship wobbled side to side, debris colliding against the energized partition protecting her vessel. Rhea promptly cut the engines to a quarter speed. What she expected to be an asteroid belt was a graveyard of obliterated spacecraft. Taking over the controls, she bobbed and weaved through the mess, scanning the area.

"Analyze wreckage," she ordered.

A voice from her console spoke. "Five civilian vessels, three class A ships, two Gal-Sar elite craft, and fragments belonging to the potential target."

"Shit... Did he do all of this?" Rhea muttered, eyeing the wreckage that lay scattered along the edge of the never-ending horizon. "Any survivors?"

"None."

"Scan for a potential SOS."

"One SOS found. Belonging to an alias known as the Exterminator."

"What a stupid name," Rhea moaned. "Playback message."

A static noise filled the air, followed by a series of beeps. No sound followed for a moment, but a strange clicking chittered for a second before a panicked voice called out.

"Send help! Ah—" It played on a loop, not giving much information. It was dreadfully ominous, especially the terrifying scream that abruptly cut off at the end.

Rhea shrugged, halfway expecting it to be an act. "Stop playback. Location of message transmission?"

"Zoam-9, southern hemisphere," the computer droned.

"He must have received some damage in a fight and went down." Rhea drifted through the clutter, nearing the orbit of the projected planet. "Scan world."

"Oxygen and nitrogen make up much of the atmosphere. The crust is thin, pockets of methane contained within. Multiple geysers exist on the surface, highly flammable. Use of explosives is not advised."

Rhea peered at the blue, swirling planet below. It was tiny, one of the smallest she had dealt with. If not for its thin crust, one could claim it was a gaseous form. The fact that the Exterminator's ship had landed while damaged without creating an explosion was amazing. After analyzing the data, she concluded the man's vessel was indeed impaired and that his foolish SOS may have been warranted after all.

"Still," she exhaled sharply, shoving her hands on her hips, "it could be a ruse." She read the planet's atmospheric composition report once again—highly flammable, no explosives. "What weaponry would you recommend? Are projectiles safe?"

"Sparks and ignitions can potentially create fires and explosions if near pockets of gas. Recommended weapon would be the plasma rifle. Though electrically charged, the emissions are non-flammable, providing efficient and accurate ammunition that will not hazard the environment. Other choices would be non-flammable, non-electrical, projectile weaponry. And last case, blades."

Rhea didn't like her options. especially when it came to dealing with someone so deadly. However, it also meant that the Exterminator was also limited in his capabilities.

"I'll go with the rifle and my trusty knife." She grunted.

"Shall I take us planetside?" the computer asked.

"Take us in nice and slow. Activate the energized partition and cloaking and park a few klicks from the target's ship. I don't want him to know we're coming."

Rhea strolled toward the back of the ship, opening an armored closet holding an assortment of weapons and armor. As she suited up, she eyed her arsenal. How badly Rhea wanted to use her deadly explosives. She had just purchased a cohesive working set from Altar-Senti—projectiles that worked as miniature claymores—with the name of the Little Destroyer, which reminded her of the cheap fireworks her father bought when she was a child. One could fire and mark a target and later detonate the ammunition from a safe distance. It was enough to bring down a skyscraper, something that could easily take out the Exterminator's ship and most likely the entire planet if used. The Little Destroyer, the perfect weapon to take out a target with an equally stupid name. Rhea sighed with longing as she slipped on her helmet. She could try it on her next job.

The bounty hunter's vessel lowered through the atmosphere, silent in its cloaked mode. Swirls of blue and teal stretched across the window while she armed herself with the Noland-80 Plasma Rifle. As the ship passed through the atmosphere, the world quickly mucked into shades of yellow-green and then reached the dusty ground of red and orange. Noxious gases escaped from beneath the surface, creating mustard plumes that eddied their way into the contrasting hues far above. From space, it looked beautiful. But up close, the planet appeared unstable.

"Looks like shit," Rhea muttered, closing the visor to her helmet. Her filtering systems activated, and a monitoring system for vitals and data scans scattered across her visual field, analyzing her surroundings.

With clomping footsteps, she exited the back of the craft, down a ramp. The transition from the artificial gravity on her ship to the planet's almost made her knees buckle. Immediately, she smelled and tasted the difference of the filtered oxygen—a metallic hint that eventually dissipated. Her visor examined the area, detecting no nearby lifeforms. The ship remained cloaked, additionally shrouded by a cloud of yellow smoke. Rhea made a mental note of how toxic the area was and second-checked her plasma rifle before trudging along the chalky terrain. The data log recovered a map, showing the Exterminator's craft rested on lower ground, about a fifty-minute walk away due to the harsh terrain, surrounded by rocky hills and a short drop-off roughly fifteen feet high. Luckily, she had the higher ground and could better view the situation before moving in. However, it also meant she would lose valuable time against the other bounty hunters, but Rhea would rather be safe than sorry. Surely none of them would be bold enough to park close to the Exterminator's vessel.

The planet's gravity made her feel heavier and more

tired than usual, but her cybernetic enhancements quickly adjusted to the change. It seemed everything about the mission was against her so far, and she only hoped it didn't mean things would only get worse. And just as she thought it, it began to rain toxic chemicals upon her suit, the droplets sizzling. A quick scan revealed that her armor was strong enough to endure the damage, as long as she didn't stay out for longer than two hours.

"Just keeps getting better," Rhea grumbled, climbing atop a stack of rocks. Looking over the short cliffside, she immediately took cover, peeking over the top of a chemically stained boulder. With a press against her helmet, her view zoomed onto the Exterminator's ship that lay within the valley. It was damaged, the nose buried in the dirt. However, a group of bounty hunters already had the craft surrounded, five in total. "And better and better...."

Sometimes hunters worked together and split the reward, but Rhea never teamed up. It usually ended in betrayal, the hunters picking each other off to enlarge their shares. She kept watch, curious as to how the attack would play out. If they claimed the kill, she remained far enough away to avoid detection. Undoubtedly, if they discovered her, they would slaughter her too.

An explosion of noise came from overhead, making Rhea jump, and a cloaked vessel dropped, landing one-hundred meters from her position into the valley below. It was anyone's game at this point, and she suddenly regretted parking so far away. Rhea scanned the area, keeping her place behind the boulders. Her visor detected the five life signs of the men circling the ship, but another red blip blinked within the craft.

"Somebody help me!" a voice cried out from the ship's intercom system. Analyzing the vocal tones, it proved to match the voice from the SOS. It was the Exterminator.

Rhea narrowed her eyes, finding it odd that the assassin waited while the bounty hunters surrounded him. Scanning and zooming onto the cockpit window, she caught sight of the man seated in the pilot chair, his hand pressing against the console.

"None of this shit feels right," she huffed.

A proximity alert signaled to her right, fifteen feet below. Rhea readied her rifle and peered over the edge, aiming directly at the figure that shuffled across the unsteady rocks below—another bounty hunter. It seemed he had the same idea—watch and observe. However, something shimmered by his foot, and as he motioned to step forward, Rhea jumped, crashing into him. They tumbled to the side, and she abruptly stood, aiming her plasma rifle at the hunter's head. She groaned when she recognized the man's face through his visor. It was Alek.

"I knew it had to be you. You're the only one careless enough to give up your position right off the bat."

"I didn't want to be late to the party, seeing as all the guests have already arrived," he replied with a smirk as he slowly raised his hands, eyeing the giant weapon.

Rhea ignored his statement and tapped his helmet with the rifle's barrel. "You should watch where you step, dumbass. You nearly triggered a boobytrap."

"Aw, isn't that sweet? You do care about me." Joking was Alek's obnoxious forte, but he also knew Rhea wouldn't hesitate to kill him if necessary.

"I don't give a shit about you. I have no idea what's on

the other end of that trap, and I was too close to want to find out." She risked a finger to point, and Alek looked over his shoulder, squinting. A harsh wind tossed a cloud of dust over the area he previously walked, revealing a cloaked wire. Rhea then nudged toward the group of hunters roughly two hundred meters away. "Those assholes out there, I don't care what happens to them. Since this place is thoroughly baited, I would say we all just walked into a trap." Rhea kept her aim.

"How 'bout we lower that gun, and then we can discuss the situation, hm?" Alek sat up, dusting himself off as he eyed the group. "Yer most likely right. The whole thing has been suspicious from the start, but I did see and hear the target inside his ship. So, he can set up all the traps he likes. One of us is gonna get him."

A loud squeal of electronic feedback erupted into the air. "We have you surrounded! Come out with your hands up. No funny business. You ain't getting out of here alive!" one hunter from the group shouted through the loudspeaker feature of his helmet. If there were any other trackers out there, they now knew their location.

"Just shut up and get down," Rhea snarled, tugging Alek behind a boulder.

The five men eased closer toward the ship, tightening their circle. Suddenly, chaos erupted. One man set off a tripwire. A netted trap, invisible to the eye, curled around him, the strands squeezing his body. It sliced through his armor like butter, doing much quicker work with his flesh, leaving chunks small enough to be dog food. At the same time, a spear shot from nowhere, piercing a second man through the chest. A large blade plunged into another man's helmet, coming out the opposite side, lodging into a rock not far from where Rhea and Alek hid. A large weapon shaped like a shuriken circled the air from the opposite end of the field. It caught the fourth bounty hunter, carried him across the dust, and pinned him harshly against the ship. His helmet cracked from another ricocheted blade, breaking in two. The acidic rain sizzled as his face melted to the bone, cutting off his scream. And the final man barely had time to react as his head exploded in a spray of murky red.

It all occurred within seconds, annihilating each bounty hunter before all but one could even scream.

"Holy shit!" Alek grabbed the sides of his helmet, hunching closer to the ground. "What in the fuck was that?!"

Rhea lowered herself, eyeing the blade a few feet away. She recognized the weapon and how the men were killed. It was all a setup, but not in the way she expected. This wasn't the Exterminator's doing, but someone far more sinister.

"A fucking Predator, that's what!" Rhea caught her breath, trying to stabilize her pulse.

Her visor flickered with new data, bringing her attention back to the field. Alek received the same alert and peered at the gruesome scene. A shimmer of a form apparated in front of the Exterminator's ship. Indeed, it was one of the famed alien Hunters. She was massive, wore gold-plated armor, and sported a red and black painted helmet. A clicking snarl echoed from behind her mask as she moved toward the corpses. Doing quick work, the Predator salvaged the skulls from her victims, strung them together, and attached them to her hip with a clatter. With two giant strides, she approached the body missing its head, removed the spine, and took a hand as a souvenir. Securing an invisible cord around the limb, she let it hang around her neck.

"Fuck this, I'm getting out of here," Rhea said with a shaking voice, wondering why she lingered at all.

"What are you talking about? All those fuckers are dead! That means the prize is ours!" Alek gestured toward the ruined craft as if it were a pot of gold at the end of a rainbow.

"You're nuts. You can't fight a Predator, let alone... *her*! Did you not see what just happened? They all died before they could even fire their weapons." Rhea looked in the opposite direction toward her ship. If she made a mad dash for it, perhaps she could make it back safely before the Predator found her, but even she knew that was wishful thinking.

Alek snatched her by the elbow as she prepared to climb the rock wall behind them. "You ain't going anywhere."

"The hell I'm not," she snarled.

Suddenly, the man held up a familiar, shiny piece of machinery. "Not without this," he chuckled.

"What the fuck did you do?" Rhea reached for the item, but Alek pulled away, wiggled it between his fingers, and then tossed it over the rocky wall. The device was the connection joint for the zero-point injection rod. Without it, Rhea's ship wouldn't start. In fact, the engine would seize up as it tried to suction the aether that couldn't flow into the system. "That better not be from my ship!"

Alek was a sneaky bastard. Before falling into the realm of bounty hunting, he was a top-notch mechanic for space vessels. He was also a master thief. With his knowledge and swift hands, he could dismantle the trickiest of machines within minutes. Rhea knew this, as he bragged about it once at headquarters while she was trying to enjoy a quiet drink at the bar.

"Oh, it is, honey. You know, those newer models are so easy to sabotage. Pull a plug here, remove a pin there, and you got yourself a useless machine."

Rhea shoved him into the dirt and pressed a forearm against his throat. She twisted his arm in a way that made him squirm and groan, but it still didn't give her pleasure. Only his death would at this point. "I was ahead of you. How did you have the time to do all of this?"

"I know you always play it safe. You shouldn't have parked so far out. Also, you're not the only one who recently upgraded." His mouth curled into a sly grin. "My last bounty provided more than enough for a new engine."

"Whose kill did you steal this time, you vulture?" Rhea shook her head. Arguing with Alek was a waste of time. "You're taking me back to my ship, and you're going to fix it. Then, I'm going to shoot you and leave your ass behind to become the Predator's next target. It's almost tempting to stay and watch the slaughter," she hissed as she released him.

"I have a better idea." He laughed, lifting his free hand to reveal a tiny black device, and Rhea thought it was a detonation remote. His thumb flicked the switch, and instead of an explosion, a piercing alarm rang from the direction of her ship.

"You son of a bitch! Are you crazy?" she screamed behind her teeth.

The Predator lifted her head, looking toward the noise, and disappeared. Rhea pressed against her visor, desperate to catch a reading of the alien's form. However, she didn't have time to spare and dashed to the side, hiding within a billowing cloud of toxic gas. Her helmet chimed in alarm at the rising temperature, warning her not to stay put for long as it would damage the suit. Alek joined her side, and she desperately wanted to blast him in the face with her rifle. Unfortunately, she needed him.

Rhea couldn't see the Predator, so she closed her eyes, listening for footsteps while also giving a silent prayer—an unusual behavior. No noise came, but the blade that had plunged itself into the rock near their hiding place suddenly ejected and vanished, telling her that the Hunter had passed their location. Alek thankfully remained silent another minute before opening his unpleasant mouth once again.

"You're working for me now," he laughed. "Help me capture the Exterminator, and I'll give ya twenty percent."

"Fuck you, Alek. I'm not helping you. I'll just take your ship."

"You ain't getting anywhere without my keys." With a pat at his waistband holding an arsenal of grenades, a pouch jingled, revealing the desired item's holding place. Rhea couldn't help but notice the explosives.

"You would be dumb enough to bring grenades down here, too. Did you even analyze the planet?" she snapped.

"Course I did. If shit hits the fan, I'll let off one of these babies."

"You'll cause a chain reaction that would also blow your ass to bits."

"Consider it a last resort if I can't retrieve my target. If I can't have him, nobody can." Alek gave a smug grin, and Rhea raised her weapon. He did the same, and they threatened one another, the alarms of their suits simultaneously beeping. "We can threaten each other all day, honey. The longer we wait, the more time we waste. Now's our chance to get the target while the boogeyman is away."

Rhea bit her lower lip, eyeing a digital outline of the target through the yellow smoke. She couldn't go to her vessel now that the Predator headed that way. Besides, who knew what else Alek had done to her ship. She could kill him now and take his keys, but he was also correct. It was now or never. Was the money worth it?

"We fucking move in and out. No bullshit, Alek, or I will kill you. And when this is all over, you're buying me a new ship."

"Only the biggest, brightest, and pinkest." He nodded, dashing out of the smoke without another word.

Rhea growled in frustration and hurried, sprinting toward the target. She suddenly regretted her actions. What if there were more boobytraps? What if more Predators waited in hiding? It wasn't worth it. If anything, she would at least receive the pleasure of killing Alek if his actions screwed her over. She promised herself that.

It was both the fastest and longest thirty seconds of her life. As Alek neared the ship, he crouched. The vessel lay in the open with no surrounding cover, and Rhea slowed beside him, looking in each direction.

"I say we barge in, guns blazing," Alek suggested, examining the door.

"And if it's boobytrapped?"

"Help me," a tired voice called from the intercom.

"That's him, alright." Alek plodded forward.

"Alek! Wait!" Rhea called out, but the man didn't pause. He approached the door, and it slid open, but he waited to the side of the entry ramp as the woman joined him. Silence filled the air other than the occasional puff of smoke and spray of scalding geysers. Rhea gripped her weapon, anxiously searching the landscape.

"Hello?" the voice called out. The Exterminator sounded frightened.

Alek held up his hand, signaling one, two, three, and they both dashed up the ramp into the ship. Together, they aimed their rifles, but the Exterminator remained seated, not concerned by their presence. Rhea and Alek exchanged cautious glances. He motioned for her to move forward and kept his rifle locked on the man. Carefully, Rhea approached with her finger on the trigger.

"Put up your hands," she commanded.

Nothing.

"Do it now."

No movement. Not waiting a moment longer, Rhea aimed low and fired. The plasma rifle burned through the Exterminator's knee, severing the leg. Still, the man didn't move.

"What the fuck?" Alek tensed.

Rhea approached the chair and quickly spun it. The Exterminator's glossed eyes and pale skin were a surprise, and already the corpse reeked of rotten fruit. A singed hole burned through his chest, revealing bits of bone and muscle and the leather seat behind.

"He's already dead," Rhea said. One arm slipped off the chair's armrest, revealing the hand was severed just above the wrist. "And his data chip is missing."

Without the data chip, a microchip that allowed access to confidential information along with a person's vitals, they couldn't prove the Exterminator was dead unless they carried the rest of his body or head back with them.

"So much for the easy way," Alek murmured. "Take his head."

Wanting to hurry, Rhea reached for her knife. Before she could start working, a triangle of red dots appeared on the dead man's forehead. She turned, tossing the blade directly behind her, catching sight of a red glimmer at the back of the vessel. Just as she dove, a dark blue laser beam shot past, and the Exterminator's head exploded, splotches of chunky red painting the front window.

"Get down!" Rhea screamed, tugging Alek back as a second blast fired toward the front, whizzing by his head to burn a hole through the canopy. Alek toppled over, and Rhea rolled across him, shoving him down. "Just get out of the way!"

The Predator's body flickered as his cloaking deactivated, and he paused only for a moment to peer at the blade lodged within his shoulder. He reached for the handle and tugged it with a growl, green blood spattering the grated metal floor as the knife dropped with a clang. Rhea fired her rifle, slipping to the opposite side of the doorway, but the Predator sidestepped, the plasma melting through the wall instead. Raising his arm, the creature shot from his gauntlet. A large blade plunged through the wall and emerged inches from Rhea's face, taking a chunk of her shoulder instead. Immediately, her suit worked to repair itself with nanotech fibers to prevent outside contamination.

Rhea shouted, backpedaling toward the console as she gripped her arm. She fired multiple times, the Predator rushing toward her as his cloaking dropped, revealing splotchy skin beneath netting and armor. A tiny smear of black and red on his facemask matched the female's—most likely his mate. One blast hit his right shoulder, green blood bursting from the wound as sparks flew from his ruined shoulder-mounted cannon. The Predator's arm hung uselessly at his side while the other swiped at her. Rhea lifted the gun, blocking the hit. However, it knocked her off-center, and she stumbled to the side as the Predator retrieved a metallic disc and threw it, slicing the air. Rolling, she barely avoided the hit, the blade cutting through the pilot's chair and the deceased Exterminator's body at an angle, exposing a tangle of intestines.

"Will you help, already? " Rhea screamed.

Alek shot, but his weapon was much weaker than hers. He managed to hit the Predator, but it didn't slow him down. Distracted by the human man, the Predator swung toward Alek. Rhea fired again, but the enemy ducked and twisted, cutting her weapon in half as she used it to block her body. The force knocked her away toward the back of the vessel. Alek tussled with the beast, shooting while clumsily dodging the attacks, cornering himself. The man froze as the alien raised the blade, readying for the kill. Rhea snatched up her knife, sprinted to the front, and leaped onto the alien's back, stabbing his chest. She didn't relent, removed the blade as he screamed, and reached for the mask, gripping the metal beneath his chin. With a tug, she planted the knife directly into his throat and cut across. With his dying breath, the Predator flung the woman over his shoulder and collapsed. Rhea crashed into Alek, and they tumbled together into a pile of green ooze mixed with the Exterminator's remains.

"Holy shit," Alek gasped. "We made it."

"For now. Congratulations, we risked our lives for nothing."

"What do you mean? We got a body!" He pointed at the gruesome remains of the target.

"They wanted either the head, data chip, or full body. Not pieces!"

"Come on. We have a blood sample at least." Reaching into a small pouch on his belt, he removed a glass tube. Retrieving a sample of blood and other visceral materials didn't seem to bother the man, proving it was something he had done before. He pocketed the sample and then moved toward the exit. "Come on. We probably don't have much time before the female shows up again."

Just then, an alert popped up in Rhea's visor. She stopped, reading the message. Her vessel was damaged. "Damage report," she firmly stated. Another series of stats proved that her ship had caught fire. "Alek! Did you do this?"

"Do what?"

"Set fire to my ship!"

"Not me. I assume that was the other Predator, which means we're still in the clear. Let's go!" He stomped down the ramp.

Perturbed about the demise of her overpriced vehicle, Rhea didn't want to leave completely empty-handed. She reached down and yanked off the Predator's color-smeared mask with a hydraulic whoosh. If Alek's samples weren't accepted or he went against his word, she would at least have something to cash out on. Inspecting closer, she noted that the creature was hideous, reminding her of an overgrown insect.

"Not a face I would want to wake up next to," she grumbled, turning toward the exit. She walked halfway down the ramp and paused, looking down a barrel. "Alek, you bastard."

"You ain't got no ship. You don't got any samples. And you've been a pain in my ass since you joined the association.

Women like you shouldn't be playing with boys like me." Alek chuckled. "You're just too soft."

Rhea ground her teeth. She'd hesitated in killing him first, and now she would pay the price. "I should have let you die."

A peculiar clicking sounded from above, and Rhea smirked. They weren't alone. She hopped over the side of the ramp just as a projectile flew by. A large spear plunged through Alek's shoulder, the tip spreading to latch onto his scapula. The female Predator stood atop the ship, snarling in rage. She yanked on an invisible cord, and Alek soared through the air, dropping his rifle. Rhea snatched the weapon and aimed.

"Fucking shoot the bitch already!" he screamed.

The Predator tugged the spear from the man's torso and raised it in the air, roaring with victory before finishing the kill. Clamping a large hand around his throat, the Predator lifted Alek until his feet dangled.

"You know what, Alek?" Rhea looked down the sights. As the man flailed and screamed, she eyed the set of grenades on his belt. "Us bitches got to stick together." She fired, and the collection of explosives went off, tearing Alek into a dozen pieces. The ignition struck a billowing cloud and set it aflame, which created an even larger eruption that led to a series of blasts underground. Rhea flew back as bits of Alek, the ship, and other materials landed beside her.

Her hip ached, and blood gushed from her torn shoulder, wetting the inside of her suit. Struggling to stand, Rhea limped toward the wreckage. Trapped beneath a chunk of metal and covered in glowing green blood, the female Predator somehow survived the blast. It wouldn't be long before she took her final breath.

"Fuck all of you," Rhea hissed. She turned and spotted a string of skulls—the Predator's trophies. "Hm… lucky me. Who knows, maybe they're worth something." She seized the reward, tying the male Predator's mask to the bunch, and continued in the opposite direction, removing a set of keys from her pocket—Alek's. She knew he would screw her over again somehow, so she had taken the opportunity to do a little pickpocketing of her own while pulling him to safety inside the Exterminator's ship. She only hoped she could make it to his craft before any more surprises showed up.

"Fucking shoot the bitch already!" Alek's voice called out.

Rhea froze, looking back toward the injured Predator, whose helmet had cracked in half. The alien pressed a series of buttons on her armband, side-eyeing the human woman.

"Don't… you… fucking… dare," Rhea warned.

"Fucking… dare," the alien repeated, mimicking her voice through the bio-helmet.

"Goddamnit!" Rhea didn't wait and took off toward Alek's ship, clicking a button on his box-shaped key set. An alarm chimed in the distance, and a hologram popped up from the black rectangle. She entered a series of commands, hoping to God that his craft remained in working condition, selected the auto-start feature and disengaged the lock mechanism to allow the ramp to lower so all would be ready for her departure from the accursed planet.

Rhea counted down the seconds in her head, knowing that if the Predator had activated the self-destruct bomb, she would have little time to escape before a series of underground explosions would cause the ground to collapse. Would the entire planet turn into one massive bomb? Would it implode and become a ball of fire? She didn't want to stick around and find out.

Tramping up the ramp, Rhea anticipated the devastating blow. "Computer online! Alek's dead. Scan for his data chip to confirm," she shouted as she entered the cabin. The ground tremored, sank, and then blew outward in a series of massive explosions rushing in all directions from the site of the Exterminator's ship. It wasn't as devastating as expected, most likely a chain reaction caused by Alek's grenades. Which meant she still had time to spare if the Predator's bomb hadn't triggered.

"Confirmed," the computer spoke.

"I'm your new owner. Engage shields!" Rhea stumbled to the pilot's seat, strapping herself in. "Liftoff! Now!"

The vessel lurched into the air as a wall of flame rushed forward like a tidal wave. The shields ignited in colors of blue and green, absorbing most of the damaging blast. However, something impeded the ramp's closure, and a rush of heat filled the interior, nearly cooking Rhea within her suit.

"Obstruction in the ramp zone. Door cannot close. Entrance into high atmosphere halted until obstruction cleared," the computer warned in an overtly sexual feminine voice. Everything about Alek was insufferable.

Rhea, in a panic, fumbled with the straps and stumbled toward the back. Gusting winds pushed against her as she eyed a strange piece of metal caught between one of the hinges, preventing the joint from bending to allow closure. As she gripped the object, her blood ran cold. It was a Predator blade, the same one that had previously embedded into the rock near her and Alek's hiding place. An ominous clicking echoed behind her just as the female Predator decloaked.

Rhea ducked and turned, using the alien blade to knock aside the Predator's broken spear. The creature appeared gravely injured as globs of green melded with her shattered armor, a trickle of similar hue dripping from her mangled mandibles. The blast had damaged the Predator's shoulder cannon, and Rhea's gun lay on the floor next to the pilot's chair. It was to be hand-to-hand combat, blade against blade.

They both swiped, repelling each other's weapon. "Bitches... stick together..." the Predator repeated fragments of Rhea's words. They clashed again, pressing against one another as they locked intense gazes. A quiet beeping caught Rhea's attention as the self-destruct device finally activated, but fewer symbols appeared across the band. She assumed she had mere seconds to get rid of the extra cargo before they were both blown to bits.

"You are a freaky bitch!" Rhea snarled. "I won't die with you!"

The woman jumped back on the ramp, avoiding a swipe from the spear, but the door sloped as it readied to close. Rhea somersaulted between the giant's legs and rolled to her feet, ready to parry. However, another explosion occurred directly beneath them, and the ship careened to the side. The Predator would have flown overboard, but the door had nearly shut. It was a split-second decision as the countdown neared, and Rhea dove forward as the Predator steadied herself, palming the edge of the entryway. Rhea sliced through the Predator's arm with a quick swing, cutting clean through, but the spear tip met her in the oblique. An ear-piercing shriek filled the vessel as the arm with the detonation device slipped through the crack just as the door closed. The appendage spiraled toward the devastation below.

Despite being injured, Rhea didn't hesitate. She was no longer frightened but angry. The Predator gripped her forearm as green ooze saturated the floor. Yellow eyes glared at Rhea, and the monster screamed, bits of neon blood and slobber spattering the human's armor. With a grunt, Rhea lodged the blade into the crease where the alien's neck met the collarbone, removed it, and stabbed again.

"I... did... not... come... here... for... you!" she screamed between jabs until there wasn't much neck left.

An enormous rumble shook the craft, and Rhea dashed to the pilot's seat, sheathing the blade to grab the rifle instead.

"Shields at twenty-five percent," the computer droned.

"Keep rising! Full thrusters! Use as much fuel as you need to get out of orbit ASAP!" Rhea screamed as she faced the Predator's body, aiming.

"That would require overriding the safety protocols of this ship. Do you wish to do so?"

"Fucking yes!"

She felt her heart slam into her lungs as the vessel lurched forward through blasting waves of fire and yellow gas. The explosive roar pained the woman's ears, and she thought she had gone deaf. Within seconds, the sky shifted from muddy colors to the beautiful hues she had forgotten about upon her descent. The shades swirled, contaminated by the chaos below. And as the view turned into the blackness of space, an enormous explosion pushed the vessel further away. A series of sparks shot from the control panels on either side of the ship as an alarm blared. Rhea didn't care. She would worry about rescue once she caught her breath. An extinguishing system worked to put out the tiny flames and cool the overheated circuit boards while the woman sat rigidly, her hands clenched over the harness straps. She gasped for air and looked into the darkness as the ship swirled in a circle, alternating between the view of a black palette versus one of a churning ball of light with rocky debris.

"Holy shit," she exhaled sharply, relaxing in her seat.

"Backup power at fifteen percent," the computer hummed as a pale orange light lit up the cabin.

"Send out an SOS to headquarters," Rhea spoke softly. She felt the burn of stomach acid in her throat as she undid the harness. Going limp, the woman waited for her nerves to calm. She eyed the alien body. It lay lifeless, but she didn't want to take any chances. Rhea pushed to her feet and approached the body. With one final, deep cut, she decapitated the Predator and lifted the head to stare into its dead eyes. Overkill? Perhaps. Still, Rhea didn't feel bad one bit. She knew, deep down, there was something fishy about the mission, but she never expected this.

A deep hum erupted as the cockpit suddenly lit up from an outside source. With a jerk, the ship drifted through space, not of her control. Rhea jumped, dropping the severed head, and stared in awe as a massive craft intercepted her vessel.

"Fuck me," she shakily whispered. She didn't recognize it, but the look told her it was Predator in design—a mothership perhaps as it appeared capable of retaining multiple transports the size of her own.

Rhea had no weapons that would stand a chance against a Clan but took her gun and the blade as she hobbled toward the back of the ship, gripping her side injury. The ramp creaked loudly as it forcibly lowered, and a dense fog rolled through the opening. Rhea numbly waited with the collection of skulls and Predator helmet tied to her hip. After a solid minute of complete silence, she felt irritated. Nobody entered, which told her they awaited her outside.

"Fuck it," she muttered as she stomped down the slope and followed a long winding corridor to a rotunda. Various skulls and weaponry from countless lifeforms decorated the alien walls. Nothing surprised her, even as a group of invisible forms suddenly appeared within the mist, surrounding her.

"I have a little fight left in me, but I'm willing to bargain if you'd like," she said with a tired chuckle, tossing the strung-together trophies onto the floor.

No response came. Instead, a holo screen appeared before her, replaying multiple recordings that seemed to come from the two Predators she encountered. Each one ended in blackness at their defeat by her hand. Rhea wasn't sure what it meant. Indeed, she had killed two of their hunters, which didn't register until now. She wanted to boast but kept her mouth shut.

One entity stepped forward, uninterested in her offering. He was larger than the others, with lengthier dreadlocks. He wore no helmet and proudly displayed countless scars and war markings over his body. She assumed he was an Elder. Golden eyes stared down at her while his mandibles clattered in a language she didn't understand. Then, he shoved a severed hand against her chest and turned away. Rhea grabbed it with slippery fingers, and she stared in utter surprise as the Elder disappeared. One other member of the clan grabbed the trophies and helmet, but something else caught her eye. She recognized her prized weapon, the Little Destroyer, equipped at his side. He was the one who set fire to her ship, which made her wonder how many Predators had been on the hunt. They made eye contact for only a moment before he fell in line with the others, each one trailing into the mist. Rhea remained stunned for an undecipherable amount of time until a roar of an engine told her it was time to leave.

With a gasp, Rhea sprinted to Alek's ship. The ramp slammed shut behind her as she clambered into the pilot's seat. The deceased female Predator was missing, and power had returned to the vessel. As the craft spun back out into space, the computer taking over the controls, Rhea stared at the severed hand given to her. She identified part of a tattoo by the thumb from her bounty reports. Then, it clicked. Predators were proud warriors, and she had bested not one but two of their kind. As a reward, they had spared her life, given her enough fuel to return home, and presented her with the ultimate trophy—the Exterminator's severed appendage with his data chip. She would soon be one of the wealthiest people in the galaxy.

Then, she frowned. She would also be known as one of the most dangerous and skillful hunters. It would only be a matter of time before someone placed a target on her back. And since Predators liked to select dangerous prey, she felt this wouldn't be the last she would see of them either.

"Where to, New Owner?" the computer asked.

The woman smirked. "Headhunters Association. And the name is Rhea Ortega."

THE MONSTER

BY MICHAEL KOGGE

The night we went Squatching we should've turned back. We had plenty of chances. We were even given fair warning on multiple occasions. Still we rushed ahead—brash, stupid, and willfully ignorant as to what we were actually doing. When you go looking for monsters, it's almost inevitable you'll find them.

The moon was full on that crisp October night and shone through the sunroof of Reynolds' truck. He was at the wheel, rocking out to '70s metal on the car stereo. I sat next to him up front, displeased with the choice of music but pleased with myself for the preparations I'd made to mount this expedition, from hollowing out Louisville Sluggers for our Squatch sticks to locating the most favorable patch of forest in Mendocino County. In the back, Flannagan played with his cameras while Schaller played with her phone, earbuds lodged in her ears, oblivious to us all. I'd brought together an odd bunch, truth be told: a brawny, tatted-up Army vet seeking one last adventure; a gangly weddingographer desperate for a viral video to make his name; a Fjällräven-wearing Gen-Z grad student on an anthropology practicum; and little old me, Jane Lisbon, tenth-grade biology teacher moonlighting as a famous cryptozoologist (at least on internet message boards). But odd is what you get when you're searching for the Sasquatch.

Despite Black Sabbath rattling my bones and hurting my ears, all seemed well when we turned off the highway onto the forest road. The trees that lined the sides could be found all across the West Coast. Oaks graced with autumn leaves. Firs green with long needles. Bushy junipers of every shape and size. Yet the farther we drove, the older—and wilder—the forest around us became. Fronds of large ferns swiped against the truck's windows. Pine cones as husky as water bottles bounced off the roof. Towering redwoods soon dominated all other species of trees, reaching so high they blocked out the moon.

We had entered a primeval world. A world tucked in the mountains of northern California where inexplicable things happened and people often went missing. A world where the fabled giant primates of North America were said to still live.

I had Reynolds dim the headlights. This reduced visibility considerably, but it was best to keep our presence a secret if we wanted to find any of the mysterious creatures.

The hand-drawn map I'd paid a pretty penny for showed a split in the road. Reynolds slowed, and sure enough, we came across a gravel road that didn't appear on the GPS. According to the old hippie who sold me the map, cannabis farmers back in the '90s had made the road to access hidden patches where they'd planted their then-illegal crop. After taking my money, the man warned me to stay away from the area. People had been killed there recently. In ways not reported by the local news. Strung up, torn apart, flayed—and those were the least gruesome of the deaths he'd mentioned.

"Those are quite some nasty pot farmers," I'd said.

"Not farmers," the old hippie said. "Bigfoot."

His answer was music to my ears. I hadn't informed him of my true pursuit, instead introducing myself as the head of an extreme hiking group that wanted to explore the redwood forest. But his unprompted revelation about Bigfoot—the name the Sasquatch were universally known as because of the supposed size of their feet—helped assure me that his map might be indeed the best path to finding the most elusive creature in the world.

I must admit I wasn't in the least concerned about his warning. My research had convinced me that the Sasquatch were not highly aggressive. Like other cryptids, those creatures of legend long overlooked by science, the Sasquatch had survived for centuries because they stayed far away from humans. Yes, if you encroached on their territory, they might try to scare you away, but they weren't mad, murderous beasts. If they had engaged in mass slaughter, mankind would've hunted them down to extinction long ago. Humans had to be behind the killings the hippie described, not Sasquatch.

We were about a mile down the gravel road when all of a sudden the racket on the stereo became a deafening squeal. At first I thought it was an electric guitar solo gone way too long until Reynolds himself cringed. He changed tracks and tried to lower the volume, yet the assault on our hearing continued, blaring though the truck's speakers. "What the fuck," he said, smacking the unit. "Must be some kind of electronic interference ..."

"Better than that shit you call music," Flannagan shouted from the back.

Reynolds cocked an eye at the rearview mirror. "What's that, Slim Jim?"

I thumbed the power button, ending the wail. "Focus on the road, please."

Reynolds huffed but didn't argue. Schaller, meanwhile, continued tapping away on her phone, earbuds in place, as oblivious as before. She hadn't looked up even once.

Though I didn't say it aloud, the squeal was an encouraging sign. Electronic interference was often reported in the proximity of cryptids like Sasquatch. We could be near our objective.

Overgrowth soon took much of the road. Clearly no one had ventured this far in a long time. Reynolds didn't mind; in fact, he seemed to enjoy plowing through the brush. It gave him an outlet for his temper or A.D.D. or whatever bee was buzzing his bonnet.

"Like being back in Guatemala," he said with a smile

"What were you doing down there?" I asked.

"Lots of shit. Special Ops. Killing commies. Huntin' for the CIA." He looked wistful. "The things I seen in those jungles..."

Flannagan snorted. "Bet you don't even know where Guatemala is."

"Sure do. It's the same place your mama is," Reynolds snapped back. "'Cause she's got one mighty thick jungle—"

There were two pops as loud as gunshots and the truck jostled so much Flannagan banged his head against the ceiling. He banged it again when Reynolds slammed on the brakes and shifted into reverse.

"Dammit," Flannagan said, rubbing his crown, "you trying to kill us?"

"Just you, asshole." Reynolds parked and got out, shutting the door behind him.

I glared at Flannagan. I didn't need to remind him that Reynolds had a short fuse. It would do him no good to have Reynolds' fist in his face. "Get your cameras ready. And please keep your comments to yourself."

I strapped on my helmet, grabbed my Squatch stick, and left the truck. Flannagan did the same, slinging his camera bag over a shoulder. Schaller stayed inside, lost in her phone. I wasn't going to bother her at this point.

Reynolds was inspecting the driver's side tire, now a flat and wedged up on a log. "Fallen redwood," he said. "Blew both tires—fuck me. Just bought these last year. If I had my lights brighter, could've seen it."

"I'm not so sure. This log seems pretty well hidden." I switched on my helmet lamp, ensured it was on its dimmest setting, and kicked away brush that had been laid over the log. "Almost intentional."

"Check this out." Flannagan turned on his helmet light and pointed at the underside of the log where jagged rocks jutted out like spikes. Two were chipped, likely the ones that punctured the truck's tires. He touched a rock—and sliced his index finger. "Jeez that's sharp." He sucked on the finger.

"Probably some old farmer's booby trap. To stop rip-offs of the crop," Reynolds said.

"Maybe." I didn't venture my opinion, that this was a trap laid by Sasquatch to prevent outsiders from driving too far into the forest. "You have any spares?"

Reynolds nodded. "In the truck bed. But they're big. Take a while to change."

"Then we can change them in the morning. This is prime time for our target to be up and moving. We should start the search."

A brilliant blue light flicked on from the car. Schaller leaned out of the door, earbuds in her ears, pointing her glowing phone at the surrounding forest. It did little to penetrate the darkness.

"Turn that off!" I yelled. "You'll scare away the creature!"

"I saw it," Schaller said. She lowered the phone, her fingers working on their own to power off the light.

"Where?" I asked.

She gestured past the log. "Up the road. Between the trees."

We all looked. There was nothing. Reynolds laughed. "Kid's already seeing ghosts."

"It was there," Schaller said. "Two orbs... like eyes. Burning in the dark. Watching."

Flannagan glanced at me. "Sasquatch eyes are known to glow."

"They are." I looked back to where she'd pointed. I wasn't surprised I didn't see anything, since Sasquatch were notorious for keeping themselves unseen. Some Squatchers said their brown-black coat was a natural camouflage that allowed them to blend into the forest and the shadows. Others posed the creatures had developed an extraordinary power to blink in and out of visibility. And there were a few who advocated the Sasquatch weren't real at all, but phantoms projected into the minds of susceptible humans by a global paranormal phenomenon responsible for everything from poltergeists and ghosts to leprechauns and UFOs.

As a biology teacher and a scientist, I fell firmly in the first camp. I studied flesh-and-blood organisms, not ectoplasmic apparitions. Those things could exist, but the Sasquatch wasn't one of them. I knew that because I'd encountered a live one. When it had caressed my cheek, that was no manifestation of my mind. Its touch was real.

Yet as eager as I was to prove the creature existed, I recognized the forest was full of wildlife often mistaken for something else. "Owls and opossum also have eyeshine."

"Bet it was some crazy doper with night vision goggles," Reynolds said. "Plenty of them still around planting crop, don't want to pay the fucking taxes."

"No. These eyes… there was intelligence in them. They wanted to… to kill us." Schaller looked at me as if I could give her support.

I'd picked her because we needed a skeptic among us. Flannagan was one of those cryptid super-geeks who had watched every Bigfoot movie and reality show, collected plaster casts of alleged footprints, jarred possible scat, and owned a library of books and DVDs devoted to the subject (like me). Reynolds, on the other hand, didn't give a shit whether there was Bigfoot or not; he was just along for the ride.

Schaller had joined us for academic reasons. I didn't know her exact age, maybe early or mid-twenties, but she seemed much wiser than her years. During our interview, she told me her doctoral dissertation was titled "Hairy Men in the Woods: The Cultural Impact of the Sasquatch Phenomenon on the Populations of California's Mendocino and Humboldt Counties" and made it clear at the outset that she was not a believer in cryptids or the paranormal.

"I'm coming at the subject from a purely scientific and sociological angle," she'd said. "I want to know why people believe in something they can't prove."

"People like me," I said, smiling.

"People like you," she said, all serious. So sure of herself she'd been.

Now her confidence was gone. As was her skepticism. It had taken but one peek into the darkness to shatter them. "We should go back," she said.

"Back?" Reynolds said. "Maybe you should stop being chickenshit and take those fucking things out of your ears for once..."

Schaller didn't respond, her gaze locked on me. In her eyes I saw a fear I was quite familiar with. I knew what she was feeling, the dread deep churning her gut, as if she had seen something she wasn't ever supposed to see, something far beyond this reality. I'd experienced it myself, years ago. It was what had led me here.

"Don't worry. Sasquatch don't kill. What they do is scare the crap out of people." I came up to her and patted her shoulder. "Grab your gear and let's go."

To her credit, Schaller did as she was told. She put on her helmet, hoisted her backpack onto her shoulders, and took her Squatch stick from the truck. She then headed up the road, where she had seen the eyes. It was as good a direction as any from here. Reynolds got out his machete to cut brush and then we all followed her.

Judging from the hand-drawn map, I approximated we had sprung the trap about two miles from the end of the road.

I was proved right about forty minutes later when the road terminated abruptly in a wall of forest, as the map showed. That was fine by me. Our main goal was to go as deep into the forest as possible, which was what Roger Patterson and Bob Gimlin did when they captured their famous footage.

As the legend goes, the two cowboys wandered around these forests for weeks in October 1967, searching for Bigfoot yet coming up short-handed. They were about to head home when they spotted a black-haired simian striding along the bank at Bluff Creek. Patterson took out his movie camera and shot almost a minute of film, including the remarkable moment when the creature turned and looked back at the camera.

Skeptics often questioned the legitimacy of the footage, criticizing it for being blurry or disregarding the creature as nothing but a man in a gorilla suit. While I had my own doubts about Paterson and Gimlin's real motives, I never had any about the reality of the Sasquatch. I knew the creature existed because I had seen it with my own eyes, thirty-five years ago at the tender age of nine.

At the time, my dad and I were hunting and camping in these same woods. Late one night I woke to the faint sound of crying—or maybe it was cooing. Call it youthful curiosity or whatnot, I left the tent to investigate what was making the sound.

When I had taken a few steps into the brush, I heard a snuff and leapt back. Two red pupils blazed in the darkness like balls of fire. A massive nine-foot figure of wiry black hair and ropy muscle rose over me. I was so terrified I choked on my own scream. The creature bared its white fangs at me, and when I didn't move—I was, as they say, scared stiff—it did something I'll never forget. It reached out to trace a finger along my cheek. Its nail was long and chipped, yet the creature was gentle and didn't cut me. Its touch lasted all of a few moments before it withdrew its hand from my cheek and let out a horrendous wail so loud I covered my ears and closed my eyes.

I remember standing in place for many minutes, despite the discomfort of having wet myself. When I opened my eyes again, the creature was gone.

Shaken by the experience, I returned to my tent. My father was dead asleep and I didn't wake him. In the morning, as we prepared our hunting gear, I mentioned to him what had happened. He hadn't heard anything during the night. He said I must've been sleepwalking or dreaming and we never talked about it again. But those eyes burned themselves into my memory as no dream had ever done. Now here I was in the same forest to prove to myself that little girl hadn't been imagining things.

My team didn't have the luxury of time to roam the forests like Patterson and Gimlin had—it was Friday night and we all had to be back at our jobs by Monday morning. But at least we could go deep into a part of the wilderness that few had visited. If the Sasquatch was going to be anywhere, it was going to be here, far away from human civilization.

The plan was to hike until midnight, then set up camp near the waterfall drawn on the map. Cellphone service was non-existent except for GPS, which we used to pinpoint our location and record a route back to the truck. As we went along, Flannagan staked low-light cameras and infrared flashbulbs every thousand paces or so. Because it was so dark in the woods, and that Sasquatch seemed to evade most normal photography, we had decided that infrared would be the best way to image the beast. To have this happen, Flannagan had configured the bulbs to trigger on significant motion and the cameras to record video in both the visible and infrared spectrums. This would allow us to acquire the highest resolution image possible of any bipedal simian loping by without disturbing them.

We hadn't ventured all the way out here to add just another fuzzy photo to the thousands of others already taken. For ordinary people to accept the Sasquatch as real, they needed extraordinary evidence—fur, eyes, arms, legs, and body.

Midnight arrived and the most we had seen or heard was the howl of a coyote. We did come across a fast-moving river and this we followed until we came to the waterfall marked on the map. The drop was a good twenty, thirty feet, and made a tremendous sound, pounding the rocks below.

In a nearby clearing, we pitched our tents just before a storm hit. All the weather reports had predicted almost zero percent chance of precipitation. But this was one of those nights, I soon learned, when the percentages were against you.

Reynolds, obstinate as he was, had refused to bring a tent, desiring instead to "sleep under the stars." When the drizzle became a downpour, he crammed himself into my two-person without asking and proceeded to sip whiskey from his flask. His B.O. was so strong I considered collecting it and deploying it outside to attract Sasquatch.

As the night went on, he sharpened his machete and rambled on about his time in Guatemala hunting for the murderer of three buddies from his old unit. "The thing that chopped and skinned them, it got these vicious, searing eyes," he said. "Could jump you from nowhere, right out of the dark. Butcher you without ever giving you a chance. No sense of honor, this thing. From a killer clan, one CIA spook told me, though no idea what that meant. Heard it might be in California, so came here to look. I ever find that motherfucker, I tell you, I ain't going to give it any mercy."

"Are you talking about the Sasquatch? Because if that's why you joined us—"

He laughed. "What I'm talking about is a demon."

His response didn't reassure me at all. "Sasquatch aren't demons," I said. "They're primates."

"Yes, primates, yes. No debate here."

"Just remember this is a peaceful expedition. We're here to observe, capture some pictures, say hello if possible. Nothing else."

"And that's all I want. Peace," he said, taking a swig. "Peace and fucking harmony."

I didn't believe him. But there was not much I could do except keep an eye on him.

An hour passed. The storm did not let up. Flannagan monitored the camera sensors from his laptop, to check if any had been tripped. None had. Schaller charged her phone from a battery and napped. Reynolds drank from a second flask. He offered it to me. I declined. Some said that Sasquatch had the ability to mess with one's perceptions. I needed mine intact.

The moment the rain slowed, I grabbed my Squatch stick. "Let's go knocking," I said to Reynolds. He gulped the rest of his whiskey and came after me, sheathing his machete and taking Schaller's stick. She stayed asleep and never noticed.

Studies said that Sasquatch communicated with each other primarily by shrill vocalizations and a behavior called knocking, which was basically banging two pieces of wood against each other. Our "Squatch sticks" were handcrafted to make the most resonant sounds. That's exactly what they did when Reynolds and I struck them against the trunks of redwoods. The reverberations went far into the night.

A couple of knocks was all that was needed. Any more and the Sasquatch would know they weren't being made by a member of its species but an imposter. Replies were rumored to take a long time, so we waited. And waited.

Without any hesitation, Reynolds unzipped his trousers and started to piss on a bush. "You have any shame?" I asked.

"Me? Ashamed?" He swung his stream up and down and laughed. "Come to daddy, Mister Sasquatch, let's see how big you really are…"

Disgusted, I turned and walked to the camp. In his tent, Flannagan noticed me and shook his head. Nothing yet had been picked up, it seemed.

Then I heard it. An echo from faraway, yet distinct from the other sounds of the forest. The hollow rapping of wood against wood.

Knocking.

A Sasquatch had heard our call—and had replied.

That sound was drowned out by a gunshot. "Die, motherfucker!" Reynolds screamed.

I ran back into the forest. Reynolds had a pistol in one hand and his machete in the other.

"What the hell are you doing?" I yelled. "You trying to kill someone?"

"It took my stick," Reynolds said. "Didn't kill it in Guatemala, but tonight this devil dies." He fired again into the darkness.

I was stupid to let him join us. I thought having a little muscle might help—and he offered to drive his truck—but I never even considered he'd come packing. I mean this was Bigfoot we were looking for, not some demonic butcher.

Reynolds cocked his pistol, but never got the chance to fire again. He fell back, losing hold of his gun and machete. I saw a blur in front of me, as his waist was sliced open. Guts spilled out. Blood sprayed everywhere.

I jumped away, looking around me. Saw nothing more but trees and foliage and darkness. Heard nothing but my own breathing and Reynolds' gurgles. What the fuck had happened? What had attacked him?

My mind landed on the only possibility I could conceive. A Sasquatch must have done it. But a Sasquatch wouldn't have attacked without being attacked first. Reynolds must have shot the creature or cut it with the machete.

I bent down to Reynolds, the stupid prick, and tried to revive him, slapping his face, calling his name, yanking at the dog chain around his neck, knowing it all was futile. He was dead. The Sasquatch had killed him.

The old hippie's warning came to mind. Stay away.

I thought of the others. "Flannagan! Schaller!"

No one answered.

I rushed back to the camp. The tents were still up. Our gear was untouched. Yet Flannagan and Schaller were gone.

I searched the surrounding forest. It did not take long to find Flannagan—or what was left of him. His severed head stared at me with wide open eyes, spiked atop a branch pole. His body hung upside down from a tree branch. Blood dripped from his ruptured neck.

Somehow I'd held it in with Reynolds, but now—

I threw up.

When I had nothing else in me, I continued forward. I did not look back.

I heard Schaller's earbuds before I saw them. Something on the forest floor seemed to emit the same high-pitched squeal from the truck, without the volume. I glanced down to find two little white rods.

I picked up the earbuds. The squeal was coming out of their tiny speakers. Electronic interference no doubt. Whatever was causing it must be nearby. I was probably being watched.

I looked all around me Again, nothing.

The fact that the earbuds still outputted sound meant they remained connected to the phone. I owned a similar pair at home, and the wireless range couldn't be more than a hundred feet or so. Schaller—or her phone—had to be somewhere in the vicinity.

I put the right earbud near my right ear, cringing at the squeal, and double-tapped the rod. "Find my phone," I said.

Something pinged behind a fern ahead.

I pocketed the earbuds and held my Squatch stick before me as I approached the fern. The blue square of a smartphone glowed between the fronds.

I probed the plant with my stick, ready for anything.

A pair of hands grabbed the end of the stick. Schaller peeked through the fronds. "Get down!" she whispered, rather loudly.

I dropped to the ground.

A whirling metal disc spun through the air where I'd been standing and thunked into a redwood beyond. From what I could see, it looked like the blade of a table saw, its points more wicked and curved.

Sasquatch were notorious for hurling rocks, but I'd never read or heard of them using edged weapons. Certainly nothing like Japanese throwing stars.

Schaller emerged from the bush and yanked me by the arm. "Run!"

We ran, away from the camp, deeper into the forest. I chanced a look behind me, but the darkness blurred. Probably from the sweat in my eyes.

Schaller stumbled. I let go of my Squatch stick and caught her. Only then did I notice the gash in her leg. "You're hurt."

She groaned, couldn't go much further. I took her behind a tree. It was big enough for both of us to hide behind it.

I took off my jacket and began to wrap it around her leg. The gash was deep and surgical, hardly the work of an animal claw. Were the Sasquatch more advanced than previously thought? Was there someone else out here? Crazy dopers as Reynolds had called them, armed with machetes and ninja stars and causing interference to muck up our electronics?

"The thing that did this to you. What did it look like?"

"Only saw… its eyes," Schaller said. "Yellow, burning, like before. Then something slashed my leg, out of the dark."

"You attack it?"

She shook her head.

"Flannagan?"

"No. It came at us—and we just ran."

So the old hippie was right and I was wrong. The Sasquatch were killers. It was possible the one that I'd seen as a kid was not, but I shouldn't have assumed that others weren't. My blind faith that they were gentle giants had now led to injury and death.

"I should've listened to you," I said to Schaller. "We should've gone home."

"You didn't know," she said. "I didn't even believe until I saw…" Fear returned to her face. Her own eyes went wide, staring at something behind me. I turned.

Two hellish yellow-orange orbs shone in the darkness, then winked out.

They were not like the eyes I had seen as a kid. Those had been curious. These were filled with contempt. As if it viewed us as inferior. An annoyance.

"You go," Schaller said. "I'll—"

"Shut up." I put her arm around my shoulder and started to move. But not quick enough.

A blue bolt of energy struck the tree, blasting Schaller and me off our feet. I scrambled up, pulling Schaller with me.

Only half of Schaller.

The other half tumbled away as a large blade whizzed through her waist and cleaved her in two. She never had the chance to scream. Her eyes never closed. Fear forever fixed on her face.

I wish I could say I was shocked or expressed some kind emotion. I didn't even vomit. She was dead but I was still alive, whether deservedly or not. At this moment, all I cared about was my own survival.

I dropped the upper half of her body and dove to the forest floor. Mostly out of instinct, because when something is shooting or throwing ninja stars at you, going to the ground seems like the safest course of action.

Down there, I found her phone. I grabbed it before I was grabbed myself.

An invisible hand lifted me into the air by my neck and a

figure shimmered before me, revealed in the dim light of my helmet. Not a crazy doper. Not a human.

A monster.

But not the monster I was searching for.

It was as tall as a Sasquatch, yet that was where any resemblance ended. Lacking fur or hair, its skin was rough like that on a reptile, a dull yellow and green. It wore dark gray armor, including a full chest plate, gauntlets, and shoulder and leg greaves. Its eyes glowed yellow through oval lenses of a giant metal helmet and its breath rasped through a filter. Around its neck hung a string of cracked skulls, human and animal. Long tendrils, ornamented with metallic bands, dangled from the back of its head like rubbery braids. Its two hands were spotted and its black nails were manicured into sharp points. It brought to my chin a hooked blade like the kind my father used to gut fish. From its filter a wet, gravelly voice rasped "*Saasss—qquaatch*?"

I couldn't answer, its grip on my neck was so tight. The monster holding me was beginning to flicker in and out of view. I was beginning to pass out.

If there's one thing about me, it's that I'm a pragmatic person. Go ask the kids at Lewis Wilson High. Practicality is the hallmark of our species, I teach. During moments of crisis, we improvise with what we have in order to survive.

What I had was Schaller's phone.

With a downward glance, I jiggled the phone, bringing up the lock screen. I didn't know the code, but what I was about to do didn't need it. I touched the emergency flashlight icon at the bottom of the lock screen, turning it on at its brightest setting. Then I raised the phone and planted it right onto an eye-slit lens of the creature's helmet.

I didn't know what reaction, if any, it would have to the phone's bright blue light. All I knew was that if it was shone directly in my eyes, I'd have to look away.

Luckily, this species had the same reaction.

The creature roared an inhuman sound, recoiling its head from me. Its grip loosened as it struck the phone out of my hand with its knife. I levered my feet against its chest to wrench myself free.

I hit the ground running.

I had no weapons, not even a Squatch stick, nothing to defend myself against this beast. My only chance was to find a place to hide. But where would I go? Behind a rock? Up a tree? I'd be blasted apart by whatever firearms this thing had. Plus, this thing had somehow noticed Schaller and me behind that redwood. Reynolds had joked about the eyes being night-vision goggles, but maybe he'd been right. Maybe the helmet the creature wore had the capability to see in the dark, maybe even see my heat signature from a distance. Problem for me was, when I looked back, I couldn't see it. It had become invisible again.

Except there was one thing about it that wasn't invisible to me. The question it had hissed at me had revealed why it was here, what it wanted, its intentions. It could've killed me quite easily but didn't. It wanted to find out something that it thought I had the answer for.

That could only be the Sasquatch.

But it wasn't just searching for evidence or trying to capture images, like we were. One doesn't bring weapons and armor in a search.

It was *hunting* the Sasquatch.

I went down the trail Reynolds had cut, looking back

every so often. I still couldn't see what was behind me. But I knew it was there. And if it wasn't, when it heard me, it would be.

"You want Sasquatch," I shouted, "I'll show you Sasquatch!"

Of course I wasn't going to bring this hunter to Sasquatch. That would be morally repugnant and against every ethic I held dear. I couldn't do it even if I wanted to because I didn't know where one was.

What I did know was where our cameras were.

I hurried along the trail, and by doing so, set off audio and video capture from the low-light cameras. I might never see the footage, but that wasn't why I took this route. At the first interval mark where Flannagan had staked the infrared LEDs, I did a little skip-hop, high enough to avoid triggering the bulbs.

About ten seconds later, my pursuer did not. The bulbs flashed, though the light was dim and red to the naked eye. But to someone who could see in the infrared, it could be blinding.

The invisible hunter made a clicking sound that I assumed was an expression of surprise. I didn't stop to ponder, veering off the trail. If it was tracking my heat signature, there was perhaps one place where I could hide.

Coming to the riverbank, I jumped off the edge into the stream.

The water was freezing and probably lowered my body temperature a couple degrees immediately. It was also deeper than I expected due to the heavy rains. All that was fine by me. Water both reflects and refracts, and the deeper I went, the more difficult it would be to detect me in the infrared.

What I wasn't prepared for was the undertow. It yanked

off my helmet, dragged me about, then shoved me forward. Soon I was caught in the rapids, hurtling toward the waterfall. Even if I survived the drop, I'd be pummeled by the power of the flow.

My head popped above the river's surface. Water roared around me. I inhaled a deep breath, then was pulled under again. I smacked a boulder, felt my rib cage crack. I was going to die before I fell over the side.

Then I saw those eyes.

Two red orbs, as if plucked from memory. They glowed in the dark waters and held my gaze. A pair of arms reached out and circled my waist. I was pulled backward by a force stronger than the undertow, lifted out of the rapids, and hoisted onto the bank.

There I lay, in pain, coughing, alive but barely. I raised my head ever so much and spat out water. Above me loomed the monster from my childhood.

It stood taller than I remembered, maybe nine feet tall, covered in brown-black hair. Its arms were thick and long, reaching nearly to its knees, and its feet—my God, its massive feet!—lived up to its species' popular name. Its head rose like a cone that had been cut off at the top, and though it bore the body of a beast, its face was almost human. A mane and beard framed a ridged brow, a flat nose, and lumpy lips. Then there were its eyes, scintillating like opals, with red embers for pupils that sparked in the night.

Here was the object of my quest. I had come to find the Sasquatch, yet the Sasquatch had found me. More than that, it had saved my life.

It hunched over me and its stubby fingers stroked my cheek. Its touch was warm and inquisitive. It seemed fascinated by my smooth skin and poked at my freckles. Was it the same creature that I had encountered as a child? I wanted to ask it so many questions but then I remembered what else lurked out there.

I pushed myself up. "You must go..."

The Sasquatch leaned back, its eyes narrowing at me. I could only assume its expression meant it didn't quite understand.

"There's a hunter—"

I was too late.

A net of ultra-thin wire unfurled over the Sasquatch, wrapping around it from head to toe. The creature bulked out its muscles and tried to wrench the net off, to no avail. The more it fought to remove the net, the tighter the net constricted around it, biting into its flesh. It looked at me, panicked, as if I'd betrayed it.

"No, no, it's not me—"

The net was yanked back and the Sasquatch fell on its rear.

A ghost materialized in the darkness. It was the hunter, no longer shimmering or camouflaged, but as real and as huge and as mighty as the Sasquatch. It holstered a gun-like device that must have shot the net, then pressed a button on a glowing panel on its wrist gauntlet. The net retracted toward it. The tangled Sasquatch fell on its back, and was dragged, kicking and flailing and shrieking, toward the hunter.

I came to my feet and cried out, pain erupting in my chest. I must've broken some ribs.

The hunter pointed its other arm at me. Some kind of small cannon slid out of its gauntlet. It aimed. I knew it wouldn't miss.

I dove onto the Sasquatch.

The razor-sharp net cut my skin in a hundred places. But the hunter never fired its weapon. If it had, it would've risked hitting the Sasquatch too.

The result was that I was also pulled back to the hunter. But I was on the outside of the net, so I had a freedom the struggling Sasquatch did not. And I used that freedom to do something no human in their right mind would ever do. It was the one action the hunter never anticipated. No one expects a mouse to attack a tiger—certainly not the tiger, right?

Levering my legs against the Sasquatch, I launched myself up at the hunter. The hunter was so astonished by my daring—which it likely viewed as stupidity—that it didn't realize my true goal.

I reached for the glowing panel on its wrist gauntlet and pressed every single button on it, hoping one would do what I wanted. One did. The wire net went slack and dilated.

The hunter swatted me with its other arm and sent me flying. I struck a tree, breaking more than a few ribs this time. But my desperate act worked.

The Sasquatch, its hair coated in blood, its body a lattice of cuts and slices, crawled free of the net and lifted itself up to face the hunter. It was a foot taller and probably the same in width. It bared its white fangs and bellowed in rage.

The hunter stepped back to aim its cannon. Before it could get off a shot, the Sasquatch grabbed the hunter's arm and snapped it at the joint. The hunter screamed, a sound like a nest of hornets enraged, as it fired a blue energy bolt.

It missed.

A limp arm wasn't going to stop the hunter. It extended

a blade from its other wrist and jabbed it into the Sasquatch's side. The Sasquatch shrieked, so loud it probably could be heard for miles.

I wanted to do something, but I could hardly move from my injuries. At this point I was just a spectator.

What a spectacle to behold.

Instead of trying to extract the blade, the Sasquatch locked the hunter in a tight hug. With its weapon arm pinned to its side, the hunter couldn't stab again. Nor could it push away with its other arm, as that had been rendered useless. The hunter kicked but couldn't get its legs or knees high enough to make a difference. All the hunter could do was move backward along the cliff and strain its muscles to break free of the Sasquatch's squeeze.

It appeared as if the Sasquatch was going to wring the life out of the hunter when electricity crackled around the gauntlet of the hunter's pinched arm. The energy shocked the Sasquatch, and the creature relaxed its arms and released its victim. The hunter whipped around, popping out a blade on its other gauntlet and slicing open the Sasquatch's chest. Then it backpedaled away onto a ledge over the waterfall. The Sasquatch followed, swinging furiously and wildly at its adversary.

"It's a trap," I yelled out, hoping to be understood. "It's trying to lure you over the edge!"

The Sasquatch must have partially understood because it hesitated. The two monsters stood apart from each other on that cliff ledge, silhouettes against the full moon. Both were heaving their chests, the cool air steaming around them. Both were hurt and bleeding, the Sasquatch's blood red like mine, the hunter's glowing chemical green.

The Sasquatch snarled, baring its teeth once again. The hunter answered by flicking a button on its helmet. A faceplate opened to reveal a hideous, wet crab-like face. Four curved mandibles opened at the corner of its mouth like the stomach of a starfish. The ear-piercing hiss it let out was not of this Earth, but something inhuman, infernal. A battle cry from hell.

The Sasquatch was not afraid. It leapt at the hunter, who in turn leapt at it. In mid-air they caught each other in a deadly embrace, from which they never broke free as they wrestled and fought and clawed and bit.

Predator versus predator.

As one, they plunged over the side of the cliff.

I plunged into unconsciousness.

When I awoke, it was morning and my condition had improved slightly. I was still in pain, yet I could move. I gathered enough energy to stand and hobble over to the side of the cliff.

The waterfall pounded the rocks below. The waters fumed and foamed. In this violent display of nature, there were no signs of the hunter or the Sasquatch. There were no bodies, no bloodstains. No discarded helmet or broken net gun or tuft of hairs.

I had the most dreadful thought that the Sasquatch had been taken away, but I didn't have any proof. Just like I didn't have any proof that I'd seen either of the creatures. The only proof I had that something terrible had happened was a chest full of broken ribs and three dead colleagues, which is no proof at all, not in the court of popular opinion.

Like I said, I should've turned back that night. It would've saved me a lot of pain and my team might still be alive. But

I didn't turn back and here's the kicker: I don't regret it. I wanted a glimpse of the unknown and did everything I could to get it.

When you go looking for monsters, inevitably you'll find them. Here I am.

GHOST STORY

BY JOSHUA PRUETT

They called it the "Ghost That Kills."

The Demon Butcher of Camp 'Blood.

It started summer of '71.

Five kids. Mutilated. They were the first.

They weren't the last.

Folks had been visiting "Camp Blueblood" for almost a hundred years. Good spot to bed down under the constellation-covered black blanket of night. Only, not too long now. Best not to overstay your welcome.

Something wrong with the ground.

Story goes, plenty of blood was spilt in this area for a long time before, on the border between the Choctaw and Chickasaw nations, then more blood when the English and French moved in, then again during the Civil War.

Union Blues spilled their guts here, ground underfoot by Confederate Grays, and someone thought they were being clever when they coined this place Camp Blueblood—back in the late 1870s and '80s when they started carving up state parks and campsites. Name just stuck.

But that bad ground kept earning its name come summer of '71. Hottest summer on record.

Late August, three boys and three girls set up camp down under the trees, and got busy doing what boys and girls do when no one's watching but the stars.

Only this time, someone was watching. Some*thing*.

Things were quiet until these kids got itchy trigger fingers and went hunting. They used the headlights on their truck, spooked a few buck, got their rocks off and their shots too, all fun and games until one of them noticed something moving in the glare of the lights.

Something big. Bigger than a buck. Bigger than a man.

They tried to get a shot off, but it was too fast.

It shimmered like water on two legs, like a ghost.

The Ghost of Camp 'Blood.

Then they heard it pound into the brush.

The others fired their weapons, but it was long gone.

Only it didn't stay gone very long.

Later that night, cicada were calling, night birds responding and everyone was sleeping but the youngest, little Sofia, underaged and feeling like she shouldn't have lied to Mama and Daddy about where she was headed that night. Sofia hated lying and only did it on the rare occasion when it served her. She sat up, nervous, while her much older boyfriend slept like the dead next to her.

The thing in the woods, that thing in the lights had

spooked her. Spooked her bad.

The rest of them, they'd decided it was nothing, laughed and drank it off, *a trick of the light*. But she knew better.

Her heart was beating so loud she didn't notice that the insects and birds had gone very still.

All around her, the forest held its breath.

Then she heard a strange gurgling howl.

First it came from one side of her tent, then the other—circling her, brush and branches moving in its wake.

Then nothing. Silence, and the fear pounding between her ears.

Then, a broken growl, deep and guttural, only this time, it was inches away from Sofia's face, the top of the tent fluttering in its breath.

Sofia broke, arms flailing, screaming, pitching herself out of the tent and into the humid air like a wild thing, falling forward before her legs managed to get beneath her, sliding like a newborn foal.

There was a loud cracking sound, like a firework going off and the forest lit up around her, blazing like a summer day.

Sofia stumbled to her feet, running, glancing back in time to see the large shimmering shadow standing amongst the tents as Sofia's friends hollered and panic charged their way into the night, doomed.

But Sofia didn't slow down, putting as much distance between herself and the terror behind her as she could, the sounds of gunshots, terrible screams, and violence echoing into the forest. When her legs finally gave out, Sofia fell hard, weeping and shuddering onto the ground.

Hours later, she woke up, cursing herself for abandoning her friends. It was still dark. The night seemed to last forever.

Shaking and weak, she slowly padded back the way she came, everything hurting.

Finally, she made her way to the camp, but it was too late. Much too late.

Sofia had walked into hell.

She found her friends strung up like gutted game—bodies naked, bare, and broken open.

Some of their heads were missing.

Everything smelled like iron, stomach acid, and gun smoke.

Sofia gagged, biting the back of her hand to choke back the horror.

She hobbled over to her boyfriend's body, hanging a few feet above her head, upside down, leaking dark liquid and steam. His gun lay close by in a puddle of his insides. She reached out for him, then froze.

A sound. Branches breaking underfoot.

Sofia turned and the forest walked toward her.

No, not the forest. Something wrapped in the forest, wearing it like a cloak.

Transparent but not. A mirror thing. A *ghost*.

Sofia wasn't thinking anymore. She wasn't in her body. But something, some shred of self-preservation pushed her to grab her boyfriend's gun, still covered in his blood.

Her hands shook, slipping as she tried to aim.

Then Sofia dropped the gun.

Suddenly, the Ghost was upon her and—

"Boo!"

The whole team jumped, all four of them, Kim, Wayne,

Jules and Darpan, all in their mid-twenties but hollering out like grade-school kids. Even Wayne, who'd been telling the story, the same story his *Paw* had told him and *his* Paw had told him before that, had freaked when he heard the new voice.

Kim and the gang sat in front of three tents and a four-passenger pickup truck, dirt bike in the back, still visible in the orange light, just away from their campfire. A few coolers made workable seats. The forest fencing them in was pitch black.

The new voice in the dark belonged to a tall man bundled in plaid and a three-day beard.

"Hey man, not cool," said Wayne. "I peed a little."

"Sorry, folks," said the man. "Couldn't pass up that opportunity, you telling ghost stories and all…"

"Can we help you with something?" asked Kim.

She stood with her back to the fire, light hoodie and jogging shorts wrapping her lean build. She was light on the balls of her feet, a runner, but pumping herself up to be a bit tougher, a bit bigger than she was. Kim was the oldest, and this trip was her idea. She felt responsible. The man cocked his head at her question, his eyes giving her the once over, catching Kim's tone and posture.

"Sorry, miss," said the man, offering his hand. "Name's Colby."

"Kim."

Kim took his hand, sure to give it back just as firm as she got it.

"You stalk campsites at night professionally, or is this just a hobby?"

Kim wasn't smiling.

"No, sorry," said Colby. "Meant no harm by it. Just

looking for a friend. Me and the boys were out for some late-night hunting and..."

Suddenly, there were gunshots cracking the night, followed by hoots and hollers.

Two more men ran by quickly, rifles held up to their crotches like rejects from an Hieronymus Bosch painting—one heavyset, the other a stick on two legs. They exited into the dark, joining the voices of others off in the distance.

"Wilson! Brady! Cut that shit out!" hollered Colby. "Shoulder those rifles, you damn fools!"

"Shit," said Darpan. "Hunting? Through our campsite?"

Darpan went to stand up, but Jules pulled him back to his seat.

"God damnit, Kim," said Jules, leaning into her boyfriend. "You bring us out for a turkey shoot or a research trip?"

Darpan put an arm around Jules. Darpan was an all-arounder at the university, on the small side but as brilliant an athlete as he was a budding scientist. Jules was on scholarship for geology and field hockey, born and raised in California, and came complete with red hair and a fire in her belly. They were a power couple, when sufficiently motivated.

"College credit isn't worth getting shot at," continued Jules.

"Speak for yourself," said Wayne. "I need the units."

Wayne was a local, southern raised, but metropolitan, head topped with curly hair, quick with a smirk and a joke.

"You're from the university?" asked Colby. "College kids?"

"Grad students," said Kim. "Geology."

"Geology," said Colby. "As in, dirt?"

"Dirt *science!*" said Wayne.

"Erosion. Climate change," said Darpan. "Maybe you heard of it?"

"Saving the world," said Jules.

"With dirt," said Colby.

"We thought we'd have the place to ourselves this weekend," said Kim.

"We'll be gone by first light," said Colby. "Soon as we find our friend."

"You lost a whole person?" asked Wayne.

"Pretty sure Robby lost himself," said Colby. "Green hat, red beard. Damn fool. If you see him, please send him our way."

"Will do," said Darpan.

Colby nodded and turned to leave, but Kim wasn't letting him go that easy.

Kim stepped after him, raising her voice. "And we'd appreciate you keeping your boys and their guns away from the flat lands out behind the old cabins. We're surveying some local erosion levels… wouldn't want to get mistaken for a wild and dangerous, I don't know, bunny rabbit? And get shot."

Colby's face went hard in the campfire light.

Then he pivoted and left the way he'd come.

"Have fun with your ghost!" said Colby. "Welcome to Camp 'Blood!"

Then he was gone, the night swallowing his voice.

"You wanna punch him, Kim, or have his babies?" asked Jules. "Hard to tell in this light."

"Weekend warriors and wannabe militia," said Kim, staring into the dark. "Trophy jockeys collecting deer heads. Not my type."

"Wasn't your father a hunter, Kim?" said Jules.

"Had my fill of trophies," said Kim. "Thanks."

"I got a bowling tournament trophy once," said Wayne.

Wayne offered to return to his story, but everyone just groaned.

"It's bedtime, and my man needs his beauty sleep," said Jules, squeezing Darpan's cheeks together like a taco in her hand. Darpan motioned to his face.

"All this handsome is hard work."

Jules and Darpan tickled and giggled their way back to their tent.

Wayne turned his back to their foreplay and pouted at the fire. "But I didn't get to finish my story."

"She was trying to shoot a ghost. A ghost. You can't shoot a ghost," Kim said.

Wayne's fingers padded the air like spiders at the ends of his sleeves.

"But it's not just *a* ghost. It's the 'Ghost That Kills'!"

Kim yawned and stretched, warming herself by the fire. "Whatever. She dropped the gun. Like one of those girls in a horror movie. They always drop the weapon."

"But..."

"We got worlds to save tomorrow. Bright and early. Good night, Wayne."

Kim crawled into her tent and zipped the flap.

Wayne spat into the fire and the flame hissed back at him.

"But, it's a true story," added Wayne. "I think."

"Good night, Wayne."

Robby had made a mistake.

His blood had been up, having fun with the fellas, shooting off his mouth and his gun too, chasing the dark like the boys in that Peter Pan cartoon. The Lost Boys.

Robby chuckled, holding his rifle closer to his chest as he picked his way through the brush.

Least he got the "lost" part right.

Robby scratched his red beard, picking a bit of barbecue out of it.

He pulled his green hat off his head and fanned himself like an old woman.

Robby hadn't planned on coming out tonight. The Wife had encouraged him. Maybe just to get him out of the house or away from her. Both worked for Robby. But coming out to Camp 'Blood in the middle of summer? Not a great idea. Not after the stories he'd heard.

The stories about the Ghost.

But Robby wasn't really scared until he noticed the woods had gotten quiet.

Carefully, he slid a bullet into the rifle's chamber.

Then, movement. On his left.

He spun. Nothing.

Then movement again, on his right this time. Robby spun back the other way, getting dizzy, one hand on the rifle, the other trying to keep his pants up.

Horns.

Robby squinted. A buck. Big one.

He breathed, relieved.

"Lost Boy's gotta eat."

He caressed the rifle's trigger, once, twice, three times, casings twirling through the air and back over his shoulder.

Only, the buck didn't move.

Before Robby could react, the antlers flew right at him, and he fell on his ass.

The horns poked and scratched his face and arms and

hands as he fought back, until Robby realized the buck wasn't attacking. It wasn't a buck at all.

Just its severed head, antlers still attached.

Its tongue and bloodied neck were still warm.

"What the fuck!?" hollered Robby.

He tried to get to his feet, but it was too late.

There was something huge standing over him, shimmering in the dark like a man-shaped mirror on two legs.

Robby brought his rifle up, fired, missed, then a whistling sound turned the rifle and his forearm into splinters.

He tried to breathe but couldn't.

He had bits of his own bones in his mouth.

The figure, the thing, the Ghost, sprouted two large knives from its arm.

Robby put up a hand, the only hand he had left, to try and stop it.

But the knives passed through his palm, breaking his wrist, and went into Robby's guts, wedging into his ribs, hooking him like a fish.

The Ghost dragged Robby away, into the hot dark.

"When was the last time someone was out here?" asked Wayne the next morning.

They were a few hundred yards behind Camp Blueblood's cabins, sun-bleached and ancient. Kim and Wayne scouted near some fallen trees uprooted from depleted soil, while Darpan and Jules took measurements from opposite ends of a wide field using two yellow surveyor tripods. Jules sunned herself and Darpan looked bored.

"Decades," said Kim. "Darpan, try to pretend you're still

interested and not considering a change of major."

Kim made her way across the field, shielding her eyes from the sun. She joined Jules at her station, stealing a swig off her cantina.

"Copy that," said Darpan. "This dirt…"

"Honey," said Jules.

"I mean, this sediment is old," said Darpan. "Real old."

Kim leaned down into the surveyor's lens, lining up her field of vision with the instruments, then she spun it around the other way, pointing deeper into the woods.

"Topsoil's been washed away," added Wayne. "Wouldn't be surprised if we found dinosaur bones out here."

"What is that, now?"

Kim pointed for the others to follow her finger.

Something was shining, catching the sun back in the woods, half hidden.

Wayne and Darpan looked where Kim pointed as Jules leaned over Kim's shoulder, noting the elevation levels on the equipment.

"Someone's truck, maybe?" asked Darpan.

"Old construction?" said Wayne.

"Not at this angle of elevation," said Jules.

Kim looked over the numbers on the surveyor and did some quick math.

"Whatever it is, it used to be buried pretty deep," said Kim. "Come on, let's get out of this sun and check it out."

The ship was some sort of metal, scored and scarred by heat and time. It was hard to make out a recognizable shape, but there was an elegance to the lines. At its height, it was two or three times as tall as Jules and probably as wide as two semi-trailers.

Front to back it looked like a kind of metal fish with a wide forehead and stubby fins or wings. There were places that had to be for venting air, heat or propulsion. And it was beat to hell. "Darpan, you still bored?" asked Kim.

"Definitely less bored now."

Wayne could barely keep on his feet, feeling lightheaded and wobbly. Kim put a hand on his back.

"Just breathe," said Kim.

Darpan and Jules were ten to fifteen feet below them now, circling the wide pocket of Earth the ship nested inside. Kim could track with her eyes where the flood waters had invaded this place and cleared away the dirt and sediment that, at one time, had kept the thing hidden. From her vantage point, you had to look down to even see the thing. Five years ago, it probably would have still been hidden from sight, buried, but climate change was revealing all manner of secrets once buried in the earth.

"How long you think it's been here?" she asked.

Jules ran her hands around the walls of the great wide hole, she and Darpan still keeping their distance from the thing itself.

"It ain't deep," said Jules. "Maybe, fifty years. Maybe."

"Maybe it crashed here," said Kim.

"Forget college credit, Kim," said Darpan. "This thing's gonna make us rich!"

"We might actually be able to buy a house," added Jules.

"Not in this market." Wayne belched, then sat down.

"Feeling better?" asked Kim.

"We found some kind of UFO," said Wayne. "Hell yes, I feel better."

They studied the thing for hours, taking notes, measurements. Wayne was on fire, throwing out theories, ideas. It was exhilarating. Before anyone had noticed, it was dusk.

"Alright, gang," said Kim. "I think we gotta wrap for the day. We're losing the light."

"Nope," said Wayne. "Find of a lifetime. I can still see my hand in front of my face, and we've got cellphones with flashlights. Staying."

Kim laughed and shook her head. She didn't really want to leave either.

Wayne put his hand on the hull of the ship.

"Just, no touching," said Kim.

"No touching," said Wayne, backing off.

She called Jules and Darpan over.

"You two head back, get the camp packed and meet us at those cabins," said Kim. "Try to avoid any of those good ol' boys if they're still around. Wayne and I will wrap up here."

"We're already gone," said Jules.

They headed out, practically skipping.

Then Wayne gasped.

"Kim!" said Wayne. "Eyeballs. Here. Now!"

Kim slid-walked down the side of the dirt bowl to where Wayne was standing.

"I thought I said no touching," said Kim.

"Fuck that and fuck you, no touching," said Wayne. "It's a fucking spaceship, and I'm gonna touch it all day."

Then she gasped herself.

A panel of the ship had slid back to reveal a small room

or antechamber. It was raw and humid inside, metal walls painted dark, deep colors.

It was filled with bones. Animal skeletons and the remains of things that didn't look anything like any animals you'd find on this planet.

Then she spotted the human ones. Skeletons and skulls. Hung up all over the room, stretching further back than she could see.

"How long did Jules say this thing could have been here?" Wayne asked, a tremble in his voice.

Kim squinted, noticing that one of the human skeletons looked fresh, blood and gore still staining the white bone.

"Fifty years or more," said Kim.

"The '70s," said Wayne. "It crashed in the '70s…"

Wayne grabbed Kim's shoulder. "The Ghost, Kim. That's when the Ghost first killed those kids."

Kim leaned down and picked something up off the floor.

It was still wet. Bloody.

She showed it to Wayne. "Green hat. I think we found Robby."

Running into Colby and his boys on the way back to camp didn't make anyone friendlier than the night before, but Colby at least seemed thankful for some lead, any lead, far-fetched as it may have been. The rest of the boys didn't seem as grateful.

"A fucking ghost ate him?" said Wilson, the biggest of the group, face going red.

"We don't know that," said Colby. "All we know is that they found his hat."

"And it's got blood all over it!" said Brady. He was the skinny one from the night before.

"We can replace a ruined hat," said Colby. "We can't replace Robby."

The others gathered around the two beat-up pickup trucks the hunters had arrived in, one yellow, the other blue. A few sat in the back, in the truck bed. There were more of them than Kim expected, close to sixteen total, so she played it cool. They all had guns in their hands and looked ready for a fight.

Wayne hid his eyes as Kim pointed away from the ship, lying that they'd found the hat closer to the lakebed, very far away from the ship. She knew Robby was dead. No point in giving away the scientific find of the century too.

"Now let's get out there and get *whatever ruined* Robby's hat!" said Wilson. He spat when he spoke, glaring at Colby, then he climbed onto the nearest truck like a horse and it sped off, the men hooting and hollering and firing their weapons.

They could hear Wilson call out as the truck dropped him and a few others off, then sped away. They were forming some kind of half-assed perimeter. Kim's stomach turned.

Colby turned to Kim, his expression serious. He pulled a handgun out of his belt. 460 Smith & Wesson. Oversized barrel.

Kim flinched.

"It's just a gun," said Colby.

"We've met," said Kim.

Colby loaded his weapon, then put it back in his belt.

"You and your friends should leave," said Colby. "These boys… they, uh…"

He shook his head, then looked after the truck.

"I wouldn't want anyone getting mistaken for a

dangerous, I don't know, bunny rabbit?"

Colby smirked, turned and joined the others, the engine of the second truck revving like a caged animal as he climbed aboard.

"You lied to them," said Wayne as they watched the rest of the men drive off, shooting at the night. "And the Ghost, Kim. What about the Ghost?"

"Ghost or no Ghost, those men have blood in their eyes," said Kim. "The further they are from us and our *find* the better. Now, where the fuck are Jules and Darpan?"

If they'd waited a moment longer, she would have devoured him whole.

As it was, they'd taken the long way back, *forget packing, that could wait—they were gonna be rich and they were gonna celebrate!*

The only reason they'd signed up for this research trip was to find a memorable place to fool around. They'd have some fun *and* get a few more credits toward their degrees. Bonus. But the prospect of fame and fortune and more after finding that ship made them positively vibrate with excitement.

They pulled at each other's clothes, the fire of the chase in their blood, the warmth of the night coaxing water from their skin.

She led him, almost running, tripping, stumbling into the dark like teenagers anxious to earn their expulsion from Eden.

Jules giggled and laughed as Darpan fell then recovered quickly. He shushed her with a finger, pressed to her lips, and she opened her mouth, closing her lips around his knuckle. He grasped her head in his hands, bit her neck, and they cascaded to the ground like water.

They were galaxies away, lost in their own gravity, and didn't notice the figure approaching until it was too late.

It had hung back, watching, taking in the show. Then it got bored.

The sound of cracking brush beneath its feet was like an alarm clock, shocking the couple from their bliss.

Darpan rolled to the side, putting his body between Jules and the figure in the dark.

*Someone had followed them. Someone or some*thing.

Flashes of the stories they'd heard dried his tongue.

The Ghost.

Darpan stared into the trees, squinting so hard it made him dizzy, heart kicking the inside of his chest like a donkey. He'd gone from horny as hell to terrified too quickly, and he couldn't breathe.

"Darpan..." said Jules.

Her voice sounded hollow. Shaken.

Darpan reached back for her hand as the figure stepped forward and belched.

"Maybe you two should find a room," said Wilson.

He snickered like a cat through his teeth, then took a swig of the light beer dangling from his fingertips.

Jules covered herself as they both felt immediate relief followed quickly by anger.

Not the Ghost, but Wilson, the biggest of Colby's troop of militia wannabes, and the last person Darpan would have wanted to meet in the middle of a haunted fucking forest at night, but that didn't stop his engine from revving into overdrive. Sex and adrenalin pushed Darpan to his feet.

"Hang the fuck back," said Darpan.

Jules roared over Darpan's shoulder as she stood up. "Get the fuck out of here, asshole!"

"You need to show a little respect, bitch," said Wilson. "I'm looking for the thing that killed Robby."

"Killed Robby? The fuck are you talking about?" asked Darpan.

"Who you calling, *bitch*, you fat fuck?" spat Jules.

They both immediately wished Jules could take her words back, but it was too late.

Wilson snorted then leveled his rifle at them and fired.

He missed, barely, the bullet kicking up dirt and grass by Darpan's foot.

"You should watch your mouth," said Wilson, slurring his words. "Or I'll take it from you."

"Hey!" said Darpan.

"My god!" said Jules. "Stop firing your goddamn gun at us!"

Suddenly, there was a sound from the surrounding trees. An engine gunning. A truck.

"Those are my boys," said Wilson. "I'm gonna have me some fun tonight!"

He fired again, narrowly missing Jules this time.

Then another sound, a different sound, got Wilson's attention—hollering voices and gunfire.

All three turned to see the headlights of the truck dancing behind the dark trees. More gunfire, then a strange whistling sound from overhead and the truck exploded, filling the black night with flashing light like fireworks.

"What the fuck?" said Wilson.

Darpan saw a window and took it. Lunging forward, he grabbed Wilson's gun with both hands, but the huge man was even stronger than he looked.

"Darpan!" cried Jules.

The two men wrestled with the gun, until something new caught Wilson's attention. Something moving, high in the trees.

Wilson shoved forward with the gun, knocking the wind out of Darpan and pushing him back into Jules, the two of them collapsing to the ground.

Wilson pivoted with his weapon, the deeper, still sober part of his brain clicking into gear. He fired.

"You bring back my Robby!" said Wilson. "Where's the rest of Robby?!"

He aimed and fired again at the shimmering thing in the trees.

And then it fired back.

Something like the sound of thunder cracking filled the night and there was a blue flash, and suddenly Wilson's arms were gone, his bloody gun falling at Darpan's feet.

Darpan and Jules looked up just in time to get showered with Wilson's blood, as what was left of Wilson's body buckled, then crumbled to the ground.

They barely had time to react before something huge and heavy dropped down from the trees behind them and charged. It felt like a stampede was headed their way.

Fumbling with the gun, Jules and Darpan turned to face their assailant. Jules fingered the trigger and it fired, kicking the rifle up into Darpan's face, breaking his front teeth.

Then the thing was on top of them.

"The Ghost," said Jules. Then her head was separated from her body.

Kim feared the worst.

She and Wayne could hear explosions and gunfire and screams.

"What the fuck is going on out there!?" hollered Wayne.

"We've got to get out of here."

"What about Jules and Darpan?" asked Wayne. "And the ship?"

"The ship will keep," said Kim, dropping the tail gate and pulling her dirt bike out of the truck bed.

"They were supposed to meet us at the cabin," said Kim. "We can hide out there, and wait for them, but not for long. We hunker down, stay out of sight. If they show, great. If they don't, the keys to Jules' truck are in the glove box where she left them. Reasonable people doing reasonable things. This ain't a campfire story."

"But the Ghost," said Wayne.

"I'm not worried about the Ghost, Wayne," said Kim. "We stay, we're gonna get taken out by those fucking hicks."

"B-b-but Robby's hat," stuttered Wayne. "The ship. And the stories. What if it's really out there?!"

Wayne stared at her as Kim's mind rolled back to Wayne's story, then up to the present, collecting details.

"Kim?" said Wayne.

He watched her shake it off, then she turned to look him right in the eye. "No, Wayne. Nobody's gonna be a final girl tonight. Ain't nobody got time for that."

Wayne stopped loading supplies into his bag and removed something heavy and metal.

"Where the fuck did you get that pistol, Wayne?" It was a revolver. A Colt.

"My uncle! He thought I might need it, just in case, you know?"

"You can't kill a ghost with a gun!"

"But something killed that Robby guy—"

"Put the gun the fuck away and get on," said Kim. "No guns. Not ever. If that thing is out there, all the gun's gonna do is bring it to us. We're leaving."

The Ghost stood tall in the brush, lit only by the fire of the burning truck, surrounded by black. There were bodies in every direction and the air smelled like death, a perfume of blood and gunpowder.

The Ghost would have many souvenirs from this hunt.

Suddenly, a roar ripped up out of the trees, speeding its way.

Kim and Wayne rode the dirt bike through the forest, headed for the refuge of the cabins, the bike's headlamp bouncing light across their path.

They turned into the clearing, revealing the burning wreck of the truck to the right and nearby, a tall shimmering figure.

The Ghost.

Kim swerved wide to the left, trying to veer away, Wayne clinging hard to her chest and back.

Then she felt Wayne's right arm pull free.

Kim glanced back just in time to see Wayne pointing the revolver at the thing.

"Wayne! No!"

Wayne fired.

And just like that, the Ghost turned their way; the bullet, like a signal flare, begging for its attention.

One moment, Kim had her eyes on the cabin two hundred yards ahead, then there were two quick bursts of blue light and heat, the first turning most of Wayne into a fine red mist, the other focused on the bike, the front tire vanishing in a tight explosion of rubber and metal shards.

Kim flipped forward, bucked like a cowgirl from an ornery steed, tucking before her head and neck collapsed, eating dirt and grass until her momentum finally slowed to a painful stop.

Barely conscious, Kim could hear the Ghost coming at her.

She scrambled behind the wreck of the bike, burning her hand on the exhaust pipe.

Kim peeked over the bike as the Ghost shimmered, an odd clicking filling the air as its invisible cloak vibrated and shorted in and out like an old television.

Her mind jumped away for an instant—*yes, this is a simulation, all of this is programing, this ghost nothing more than a glitch in the matrix*— but then a terrible roar tore her back out of her thoughts and into her body again. Kim fell back, pedaling her arms and legs like a toddler as the figure of the ghost thing rose over the temporary shelter of the bike.

Its shimmering arm rose, and the birdsong of engaged metal signaled a weapon; knife-like extensions appearing at the end of its fist. Her mind spun again—*what the hell was this thing*—from forest ghost to digital demon to knife-wielding knight from hell.

Then, the twin blades hurtled toward the earth, slicing the air, then splitting the bike—the motor bleeding oil and gas like a stuck pig. Its mechanical blood covered Kim's face and forehead, stinging, and she rubbed it in, trying to rub it away, watching through bleary eyes as the bike was torn in two pieces, parting like a violent, smoking curtain to reveal her hunter.

Kim watched through blurry, pain-wracked eyes as the Ghost's shimmer shorted one last time, then dissolved or simply turned off, revealing a monster in armor. It stood over eight feet tall, flexing clawed hands and feet, its broken helmet merged with its terrible face, old, battle-worn and damaged shielding no longer covering much of the battle-worn creature beneath.

It was like a nightmare on two legs, like nothing she'd ever seen or imagined, a chimera—one part a child's grotesque daydream, the other, a dark, hellish soldier with armor-covered muscles, yellow splotchy skin covered in combat netting and long, snake-like dreadlocks.

The thing bent down to grab her, and a car horn called out in the night.

The monster turned as the front end of a pickup truck lifted it off its feet and slammed it into a tree.

Kim could see the thing over the hood, back half of the beast embedded in the tree, the front of it wedged into the broken hood, strange green blood leaking from its helmet and torso.

Suddenly, the truck door opened, startling Kim. Colby hobbled out, 460 Smith & Wesson in hand, leg black with spilt blood. His own. There was a piece of Colby's thigh missing, cut, torn or blasted away. He was pale and battered, just this side of death, but refusing to give in. Colby had already been at war with this thing, this ghost monster; Kim was just catching up with the end of their battle.

Colby started toward her, then the truck moved.

Kim and Colby turned to see the monster physically pushing the truck back. Locked tires dug into dirt as the thing roared and pushed harder, trying to free itself.

"Come on!" Colby screamed. "Run! Run!"

Moments later, Kim and Colby collapsed in the cabin.

The inside was a relic from another time, posters from the '80s on the walls, metal cots draped in disintegrating fabrics and cobweb blankets.

Kim looked around for shelter, a place to hide—something, anything—but the cabin was so empty it could have been a tomb. Or soon would be.

She turned to Colby. It looked like he was bleeding out on the wooden floor.

He had stopped moving, face down, fingers loose on his gun.

Then she heard the pounding of the monster's clawed feet, headed their way.

Kim crawled forward, pushing the cots out of her way, but she didn't get very far.

She stopped, then pushed Colby. "Wake up! Wake the fuck up!"

Keeping her eyes forward, Kim pawed at the cabin floor, almost reaching for the Smith & Wesson in the red puddle, but then stopping herself.

A single thought whispered through the back of her head.

If I pick the gun up now, this is all over. She had to wait.

Instead, she turned toward the alien.

The thing filled the doorway, then marched forward,

cracking the top of the door jamb, old wood splitting and spitting dust into the moonlit air.

"Colby, wake up!"

It moved toward her. The hunter, hunting for big game.

She looked at the gun again and bit her lip. Not yet.

Colby moaned and turned, barely getting up to a half-sitting position.

"Colby!" Kim needed him awake.

The alien kicked the fallen cots out of its path, the entire cabin complaining at its weight, at the wrongness of the thing.

Colby coughed. "The gun! Where's the gun?" He coughed again, grasping at the hole in his leg. He sounded like an old man, years dripping from his mouth in black blood like paint.

The Ghost stared down at the scared, broken things.

There was a hissing sound, a snake's warning, a valve releasing, or both as it reached for its broken helmet.

"Get the gun, you chickenshit," said Colby. "Shoot it."

Kim set her jaw.

The alien pulled what was left of its old broken helmet free. Kim could see its breath billow in the air as the mandibles on either side of its jaw spread like a startled fleshy insect, bright green blood dripping from its teeth glowing in the dark of the cabin.

Colby gagged. Kim stared.

The alien looked half-dead.

Everything about it was strange—almost the shape of a man, hands of a lizard, face and skull a hodgepodge of animal, insect and crustacean taxonomy, but that wasn't what was strange.

It was *beat up*. Broken. There was history there.

The ship they'd found had crashed and this thing, the pilot, the hunter, had taken a beating and like a vet wounded too far from home, never healed quite right.

With its broken mask on, it had looked like a mix between the Phantom of the Opera and a robot, but now, it looked more like a soldier to Kim's eyes. Someone who'd seen too much, been through more, and only had this one thing left.

The kill.

"Shoot it!" hollered Colby. He gestured for the gun, stretching for it.

"I—I can't," said Kim. There was only one way this was gonna work, if it worked at all.

The alien gurgled then roared at Colby, but then turned back to Kim.

It was waiting for one of them to make the first move. It didn't have to wait long.

"Fucking bitch, I'll do it!" said Colby.

Why take off its helmet?

He snatched the gun off the floor.

So, it could see its prey with its own eyes.

And whoever had the gun, was the prey. Big game.

And the game was almost over.

Colby raised the Smith & Wesson and the monster pivoted with mechanical precision, turning all its attention to Colby. He was the big game now.

"Oh shit," said Colby.

He sounded like a little boy using words too big for his mouth.

The alien was on Colby like a wild animal, tearing at him in a fury.

But it didn't forget Kim, backhanding her with its

gauntlet and rolling her hard into the cots, bouncing her off the wall and onto the wooden floor.

Kim froze, on her stomach, gritting her teeth at the pain, but careful to keep the creature in sight.

The alien held up one arm, silhouetted in the moonlight of the open door behind it and engaged its talons. Then it removed Colby's arms from his body in three quick movements, drawing a backward capital "n" over his body—down, across, then down again.

The gun spun from Colby's dismembered arm and slid toward Kim, slowing to a stop on the floor.

Kim didn't budge. Not yet. Her eyes darted from the gun to the alien, then back again.

The alien stayed focused.

The wet shimmer of its killing knives froze in Kim's mind's eye as she watched.

The Ghost That Kills. The Demon Butcher of Camp 'Blood. The killer in the horror movie, the butcher with his long knives.

And she was the final girl.

Only this time, when the girl dropped the weapon, or at least *played* like she couldn't pick it up, she did it to save her own life.

Images flashed in her head.

The stories of the Ghost and its victims, all of them with weapons. All of them big game.

The strung-up bodies, the bones at the ship weren't leftovers or remains, they were trophies.

This wasn't just a monster. It was a thinking creature. An alien with an agenda. Rules.

A hunter.

Just like Kim's dad. Like her whole family had been.

In the stories, and in the last twenty-four hours, the thing only went after people with weapons. Big game. That's what drew it out of hiding. The heat, the guns, the hunt.

She watched, as the Ghost cut a slit under Colby's throat, unzipping his skin like the zipper on a hoodie, then flipped Colby over onto his stomach, the alien still straddling him like farm stock. Instinct. Experience.

Colby grunted. He was still alive.

Kim held her breath and looked up at the alien, steam rising off its body. Carefully, she pulled her legs up beneath her, getting into position.

The alien grabbed the back of Colby's scalp and pulled, tearing the skin from his face, back up and over his head like tissue paper, and hurled it across the room, splattering against the wood wall like a wet T-shirt. Then, with both hands, it started to pull Colby's skull and spine out of his body.

That was her cue.

She rolled forward, curling her body, tucking her head.

Kim exhaled, coming up with the bloody gun in her hands, thumbed the safety off and fingered the trigger. Just like she'd been taught.

Like she'd practiced over and over. On family vacations and holiday weekends. At shooting ranges. She'd never liked guns. But she knew what to do with one. This was instinct and experience.

Finally, the thing paused and turned to face her.

Kim looked into its eyes.

She wanted to see the expression on her prey's face when the game was over.

And it was over.

Daddy taught her to never point a gun at anyone unless you meant to kill them. And she meant to.

She didn't feel the blades of the beast's gauntlet in her thigh until they'd already pushed well past her skin, glancing the bone.

Kim felt blood in her throat.

The thing smiled at her, its broken, wriggling cheek bulging and wrinkling with the effort.

Then it closed its eyes.

Kim emptied the large Smith & Wesson into the alien's face at point-blank range, fire, smoke and green blood bursting like wet rockets against the nearest wall. Then its body went limp.

She let the gun fall and stumbled back, then howled.

The creature's arm blades were still in her thigh, its nearly headless body still clinging to hers, tethered by pain.

Kim bit hard, exhaled and yanked the blades free.

Blood poured like water from a spigot.

Kim got dizzy.

She fell to one knee, wobbling, trying to keep her other leg straight, a desperate, long-limbed bird that forgot how to walk.

With the last bit of strength she had, Kim pulled off her shirt, tore it from the collar down and tied it around her thigh, stanching the blood.

Then she collapsed, her head bouncing off the wood floor.

When Kim woke up, half a day later, she removed the alien's gauntlet from its arm and used its own blades to separate what was left of its head from its body.

Cleaned up, it was gonna make one hell of a trophy.

SLY DARK IN THE DAYLIGHT

BY YVONNE NAVARRO

Val Wilson was pulling weeds in her backyard when she saw the Rosales boy next door get yanked off his feet and hauled up into a tree.

She stayed where she was, on her knees with sweat rimming her lips and stinging her eyes, as she squinted and tried to decide if she was hallucinating. Everyone kept telling her to stop overdoing it—"For God's sake, Mom, you're seventy years old. Can't you just hire someone?"—but she liked to get out in the fresh air and move her joints. Besides, she didn't feel like she was *that* old. When she woke up in the morning, her mind was refreshed and excited, looking forward to whatever she had planned. It wasn't until she got out of bed that her body reminded her of her age.

Val wiped the sweat away with the back of one gloved

hand, still staring over at the yard. She had just about decided to go back to weeding when she saw a line of blood flow straight down from the branches to the ground.

Nope, not a hallucination.

Val hurried inside and called 911. Sheriff Wayne York came by himself, because why would he believe she'd seen a kid pulled into a tree and presumably killed? He stopped to talk to her and then lazy walked over to the Rosales yard while she stayed where she was. She'd seen plenty of blood during her time as a field nurse in Vietnam. Had she been bitchy, she would have voiced a smug *I told you so* when Wayne scanned the area below the tree, then looked up and reeled backward. Instead she felt sadness thud through her. Robbie Rosales was a decent kid and loved by his parents; this was going to be tough. It wasn't long before three more cruisers raced up, then a fire truck and an ambulance. A black station wagon arrived shortly after the area was taped off, but she turned away from the window when she saw someone unfolding a black body bag. While she waited for York to come back and talk to her, she made a chicken casserole to take to the Rosales family that evening. When her doorbell finally rang, it was Deputy Bo Lawley who came to question her. He said Sheriff York had been called to the scene of another murder four blocks away.

Swift, Colorado—named for a bird, the white-throated swift—was anything but. Life was slow and sleepy and mostly lower-income, with an old train depot and a two-room museum made of beer cans as its only tourist attractions. With a population of 647, it was a big deal if someone died. A murder was unheard of, let alone two.

Jack Menendez had been a good guy with a burly build who added to his social security by selling firewood. Sheriff York's complexion was gray-tinged as he stared down at what was left of the man everyone in town called Old Lumberjack. Menendez had been in his late sixties but in damn good shape. He'd cut trees with a chain saw but still hauled out the logs and loaded them by himself.

"What the hell coulda done something like this, Sheriff?" Deputy Frescura's eyes were carefully trained on a tree about three feet to the left of the mangled body. York couldn't blame her. She'd been with the department about four years, long enough to see some pretty extreme stuff on the highways, but this was insane. Some kind of animal? Because if a human had done this... shit, they needed to call in the Army.

On Tuesday afternoons the high school football team met for practice on the field behind the school. Swift High had kids from a few other towns in the county, but the team wasn't more than a conglomeration of students across all four grades; they only had enough to play mini-games against each other. Football was just something to burn energy—they didn't even have a coach. As usual, the best players were those with the most brawn and the prettiest girlfriends. They were also the biggest jerks. Some things never change.

"Come on, Holland," Danny Fischer yelled. "Maybe someday you can *catch* the fucking ball instead of dropping it."

At sixteen, Owen Holland was built more for track.

Twenty yards away from the muscled, self-appointed quarterback, he sighed and picked up the football. He tried to act indifferent and toss the ball from hand to hand, but only dropped it again. As he retrieved the ball for the second time, he heard hoots and groans from the sidelines, where Danny's girlfriend Claire and her cronies were hanging out. A girl's voice shouted "Geek!" but he couldn't tell who. He threw the ball underhanded back to Danny, which only garnered more derision. The only thing he wanted was to be at home, where he could grab a snack and work on his science paper, maybe go for a run later along Pine Forest Trail. Instead he was here, where his parents insisted he'd "make friends." Right.

A Sheriff's SUV with its lights going pulled into the parking lot, then drew up next to the stands on the east side of the field. Owen didn't know the name of the deputy who got out, but Fischer headed over like they were old friends. As many times as the kid had been pulled over for speeding, they probably were.

Fischer had a shit-eating grin on his face. "What's up, Watson?"

Owen wandered over with the rest, not getting too close. The others, even the girls, took advantage of his quiet, resigned personality; staying out of reach would save him from being shoved and other shit.

The deputy sent Fischer a long-suffering glance. "It's Malik, Danny. Deputy Malik." The officer turned and addressed them all. "Listen up. I want you all to head home and stay inside until further notice."

They stared at him, then Chris Edwards, Danny's best friend, stepped forward. "No way, man. This is our practice time."

"It's not a request," Deputy Malik barked.

To Owen, it was an answer to his prayers, but Ray Ockert, another jock who thought he was all that, wasn't having it. "We didn't do anything wrong," he protested. "You have no right—"

Deputy Malik's two steps put him nose to nose with Ockert. "The badge on my chest gives me that right, kid. Head home on your own or I'll take you there in the back of my vehicle."

When Ray looked like he was going to mouth off again, Owen decided to step forward. "Did something happen, Deputy Malik?"

The officer turned his way, frowning, then decided Owen wasn't being sarcastic. He inhaled. "Yeah," he answered. "Two people in town have been killed. We don't want anyone on the streets until we figure this out." His gaze sharpened. "Go home. *Now.*"

Lourdes Rosales sat at the kitchen table with her back to the window that looked out on the yard. Her cellphone was in front of her, but she hadn't called Miquel. She didn't know *how* to do that. Miquel was on the road, headed home after delivering a shipment to Colorado Springs. He'd picked up cargo on the way back, so he had one stop to make in Pueblo. Then another two hours would bring him home. Four hours max, driving an empty thirty-five-thousand-pound semi-tractor trailer.

Maybe she should wait until he got home to tell him his only son was dead.

Lourdes came from solid, hard-working Mexican stock,

the kind that didn't back down from problems or difficult situations. Her grandparents had immigrated to the United States in the late 1800s, bringing seven kids and their own parents. They had faced discrimination and hard times but they had stayed. And if they hadn't precisely prospered, they'd managed a decent life, passing good values to their kids and making it through spells that today's world couldn't imagine. Losing her child wasn't something Lourdes had ever even considered—right now the clichéd saying wrapped its words around her heart in barbed wire: *Children aren't supposed to die before their parents.* She knew what needed to be done—call the family, funeral arrangements and the like—but she didn't know what to do about the fact that Robbie had been *murdered*.

She was damned well going to do *something*.

The chicken casserole was in the oven and Val Wilson gazed out the window again. At four in the afternoon everything was still soaked in early September sun. The crime tape in the Rosales yard was clearly visible, as well as a deputy watching over the scene. Bad news spread fast and she'd already had a bunch of calls telling her about Jack Menendez. She turned her head when the sound of sirens floated over from Highway 285. Before the noise faded, her phone screen flashed an incoming call from Juliet Engle, a friend who worked at the Food Mart.

Val felt her gut tighten up as she answered it.

Lourdes didn't have any plans beyond putting her loaded twelve-gauge in the front seat of their pickup and driving somewhere. She figured the whole town knew about Robbie by now, yet her phone hadn't rung once. That was strange, but she was too numb to be hurt. She looked left before starting to pull out of the driveway onto Twelfth, glimpsing strobe lights three blocks south; she turned that way instead and eased the old Ford to the side of the road at the corner of Aspen. With the engine running, she stared at a cluster of emergency vehicles blocking Old Lumberjack's driveway. People from the Sheriff's Department hurried everywhere. When one of the deputies ran to a cruiser on the street and raced away, taking the turn at Aspen so fast he almost spun out, Lourdes decided to follow him.

After all, she didn't have to make lunch for Miquel.

Swift Town Park was a small area that blended into the forest on its west and south sides. It had standard playground equipment, half a dozen picnic tables, restrooms, plus a multi-use path for the occasional jogger and bicyclist. Most houses in Swift didn't bother with fenced yards, so a few folks walked their dogs around the park and let them wander in and out of the trees. Sandi Lawrence was a regular, letting her German Shepherd, King, haul her along Pine Forest Trail every afternoon in a useless attempt at training him.

Sheriff York rubbed his cheeks then reluctantly put his glasses back on. He had two deputies and one of the doctors from Valley Health Clinic standing next to him, but none moved closer to the figure on the ground.

Finally Silvia Varley—Dr. Silvia to everyone—let out a

long breath. "Wayne, where's her head?"

"I don't know," he answered. "I've got four deputies and the county crime investigator searching the woods but no one's found it yet." He winced. He hadn't wanted to say *her head* but somehow *it* sounded worse.

Dr. Silvia nodded at something lying at the base of a pine about ten feet away. "And that?"

"Her dog," said the deputy standing next to York. His name tag read *Pacios* but she'd never seen him before.

"King," York put in. "Big German Shepherd."

Pacios shook his head. "Doing that to a dog is fucked up." The doctor gaped at him at the same time York scowled. Deputy Pacios cleared his throat. "Sorry, that came out wrong."

The Sheriff's face was grim. "Your division told me you're an expert," he said to Pacios. "So do your stuff."

The deputy nodded, then pulled off his hat and scanned the ground around the body. After a few moments he made his way over to King's corpse. The grass from Sandi Lawrence's remains to King was trampled. He studied the dog, then turned toward where the bushes and scrub became heavier around the trees before the foliage became the forest proper. "Here," he said at last, and gestured to the left of the tree. "Something came out of the woods. The dog must've seen it."

Dr. Silvia nodded but didn't come any closer. "There's significant bruising around her wrist. The leash?"

"No doubt," Sheriff York said. "Everyone knows how King pulled her everywhere, no matter what she tried."

"He perceived a threat," Pacios said. He pointed at the Shepherd's bloody lead twisted in its mangled remains. "Yanked free and attacked, trying to protect her."

"Well, that didn't work," York said.

"Obviously," Pacios responded without sarcasm. He indicated a path along the ground. "It took care of the dog, then went for her."

"Why do you keep saying *it?"* the Sheriff demanded. "It had to be a man."

Pacios hesitated. "Of course... assuming it—*he*—is almost seven feet tall." When neither York nor Dr. Silvia responded, he pointed to the ground more emphatically. "Stride length," he said by way of explanation.

"He was running," York said. "I don't think—"

"No," Pacios interrupted. "There are no deeper indentations indicating that was the case." He straightened and gazed at them. "There are also signs that the attacker had long claws on *his* feet." This time the deputy's voice was definitely cutting. "Four long claws, to be exact, grouped in two on each side of the foot."

"What kind of shit are you trying to pull?" Sheriff York's voice was thick with anger. "Next you'll be claiming it's fucking Bigfoot."

Pacios put up his hands. "I'm just telling you what I see on the ground. Any tracker will tell you the same. You want the takeaway to be a hairy monster, that's on you."

"You little snot, wait till I call your—"

"Both of you get a grip," Dr. Silvia snapped. Her tone was enough to silence them and her gaze was hard when it met York's. "Believe whatever you want, this will make three bodies—and a dog—in the basement of my clinic. I don't have room for another one, so find whoever, or whatever, did this before I end up with more."

Despite being ordered to go straight home, after driving away while the deputy watched, most of the kids ended up at the DQ. Danny and Claire ordered burgers and shakes, and the lot of them talked about what was going on. Most figured it was some kind of military thing, although no one found anything on Google or the news stations. Owen Holland suggested alien invasion and regretted it immediately when the other kids screamed with laughter and pelted him with French fries. That ticked off the manager, Bill Ellison; he gave them five minutes to finish eating and, as he put it, "Clean up the mess you made or get the fuck out and don't come back." They were gone in four, Owen heading home with his face and shirt spotted with ketchup.

When Danny Fischer took his girlfriend Claire back to her house, the teenagers found her father at the kitchen table. In front of him were three guns: a.357 revolver, a 9mm pistol, and a .45 automatic. Dave Lawrence stopped what he was doing when the kids wandered in, but instead of looking up, he just kept staring down at the disassembled weapons.

Something in the way he was sitting—straight-backed and stiff—made Claire frown. "Hey, Daddy. What's up?"

"Your mother is dead," he said. "Someone killed her in the park." Lawrence had always been a man who kept his emotions tamped down and he delivered this announcement as though he was telling his daughter that the car wouldn't start.

Claire froze. "What?" Her voice came out as a wheeze.

"King tried to protect her. He's dead, too." He went back to work on his guns. Almost as an afterthought, he added, "The murderer cut off her head."

Claire had no problem expressing her feelings. It was Danny who held her when she started screaming.

Ajax Beck and his boy Tom—not a boy anymore at twenty-six—were working in their shop, the Hunting Depot, when someone crashed through the heavy glass door instead of opening it. Ajax was stocking ammo boxes behind the counter fronting the back wall; when he spun toward the sound he saw Tom fixed in place behind the main counter with his mouth hanging open. Sharp pieces of annealed glass surrounded an over-sized freak in some kind of costume who was just standing there, head cocked as he looked around like he was assessing the place.

Ajax was a retired Army staff sergeant with three Iraq deployments and an unhealthy dose of PTSD. In a microsecond the scene flipped from the store to a desert battlefield. By the time he bellowed *"Get down!"* at his son he was in a firing stance with a loaded Mossberg twelve-gauge pointed at the crazy guy. "Freeze, asshole, or I'll blow your head off." The intruder turned and stared at Ajax, but Ajax stood firm and didn't lower the shotgun. Even as his eyes processed what he was seeing, his brain couldn't make sense of the elongated helmet that came to a point halfway down a face mask that covered the eyes and had no opening for a mouth. The helmet was ringed in black spirals like hair sprouting around the skull of a bald man; they hung to shoulder length, falling behind some kind of steampunk contraption on one shoulder. With a quick scan he saw that the rest of the skimpy costume was leather, more metal, and netting covering mottled spots.

"That's the ugliest fucking costume I've ever seen," Ajax said. His voice was cold and flat. It pinged in his thoughts that this was the killer working his way through town. "Take off the mask." When the man didn't move, Ajax clenched his teeth. "I'm not asking, fucker."

Instead of complying, a red laser light came out of the helmet, the shoulder apparatus extended upward on a metal arm, and rotated toward Ajax. As it passed Tom it momentarily blinded him.

"Dad, get down!" Tom shouted. Years of following military orders kicked in and Ajax dropped just before a blast of heat hit where he'd been standing, destroying everything around it. The counter exploded, shards of glass and chunks of wood pelting him where he crouched on the floor with his arms instinctively covering his head. Misshapen boxes of ammunition, their contents destroyed, were flung in all directions, thudding painfully onto Ajax's arms and back. Smoke, debris, and the smell of gunpowder surrounded him, so much like when he was in Iraq. For a precious moment, he froze... then muscle memory kicked in. Ajax found the Mossburg under the wreckage and dragged it with him as he combat-crawled along the wall and around the corner.

"Eat this!" his son screamed as he came up from behind the register with a .50 Desert Eagle. The first round hit the costumed man in the shoulder and knocked him backward at an angle, where he staggered to the right of the shattered door. Tom fired again but his target was down and rolling to the right. Ducking below the counter, Tom tracked him through the glass, hoping for a money shot as the asshole rounded the far end. He saw Tom fire again, then his wife charged out of the office with an AR-15 rifle and right into the killer.

"Lana, no!" Ajax scrambled toward her, slipping on the

fragments on the floor. He slipped and fell hard, fingers smashing against broken glass beneath the stock of the shotgun, at the same time one knee took a deep, three-inch gouge from a jagged chunk of wood; the old soldier in him slammed a mental wall between the pain and his brain and he kept going, clawing back to his feet as he heard his wife's two shots. When he was finally upright again, he was sure she'd ended the guy—no one could survive two point-blank 5.56mm rounds. It wasn't until he was able to focus past Tom that he realized Lana wasn't standing there.

"Mom?" Still crouched, his head just above the top of the counter, his son sounded like a small child.

Lana didn't answer. Of course she didn't, because she was dead. She lay on the floor at the intruder's enormous feet, her blood painting the wall and the office door and dripping from two long serrated blades extending from one wrist of the freak's bizarre costume. There had been a time in Ajax's life that he could survey an area of attack and immediately know his next move. That time was gone, and right now he was as frozen in place as his son had been when the killer first crashed into the store.

It was a fatal mistake.

The object on the intruder's shoulder shifted in his direction. Ajax had a millisecond to register the sound of sirens—help was coming—then a blast of heat blew him into scarlet mist.

Tom jerked toward his father just as the older man disintegrated in front of his eyes. When Tom dropped onto his left side, it was more because his body felt boneless rather than a tactic. Although it didn't take him out of the killer's line of sight, it did give him time to bring up the Desert Eagle and fire as rapidly as he could across the twelve-foot space. With each heavy shot the attacker whacked hard against the wall, yet he still didn't go down. Tom squeezed the trigger until the .50 was empty, but he didn't have another clip—no burglar would be upright after a single hit, much less multiple ones. He could see liquid leaking from small injuries in the man's arms and legs—*spotted like a lizard's*—but although there were smoking holes all over his chest, none of the bullets had gotten through. He must be wearing some kind of armor.

The wall behind him was hung with more than a dozen rifles, but none were loaded; the counter Tom crouched behind was bulletproof and locked, and there sure as hell wasn't time to get the key. He wasn't the biggest guy in town, but he was in damned good shape. So be it: this guy had killed his mom and dad. He was going to kill this murdering fuck with his bare hands.

The youngest of the Beck family launched himself toward the attacker like the former high school linebacker he used to be. Tom had great strength, good momentum, and fierce anger on his side. None of that helped him when the guy snapped out some kind of spear and shoved it right through Tom's sternum and out his back. It happened so quickly there was almost no pain and he had time only to gape at the crazy bastard before his vision began a fast dwindle at the edges, then closed to a pinhole and winked out.

With the building now empty, the Predator closed his combistick and hooked it back onto his belt. His helmet display found no other lifeforms, so his fun was over. Most of his wounds were inconsequential, but a few could not be dismissed. Standing amid the rubble of the pyode amedha weapons structure, he chose the appropriate implements from his medicomp. A lesser Yautja might be grateful for the insignificant punctures and small glass and wood pieces in his flesh, since more substantial cuts would have required the scorching blue medication and cauterization. But he was not afraid of discomfort, no matter the level. He was *Kwei Lar'ja*—Sly Dark—and he would take the lessons learned on this secret hunt and use them to pursue more difficult prey. On the homeworld, it was believed that humans were high on the list of challenging foes, but so far this hunt on Earth had made Kwei Lar'ja think them weak and unimpressive.

Finished, Kwei Lar'ja stowed the medicomp and turned away from the bodies. The older male was nothing but fragments and he already had trophies from his earlier kills, including the skull of the woman whose animal protector had been so pathetic. The humans had some weapons of note—Kwei Lar'ja would admit to no one else that his form was sore from those final hits—but still... nothing remarkable. It was time to return to his drop pod and depart.

He was about to step outside when a number of differently painted vehicles careened into the concrete area at the building's front. Kwei Lar'ja's helmet had been noting many high-pitched sounds growing in intensity, and now he grasped they were alarms. His display registered a least a dozen, with more arriving. He slipped back and to the right, taking cover as the noises stopped and humans rapidly exited and crouched behind open vehicle doors. He heard weapons being readied at the same time one of the males raised a speaker.

Mandibles clicking in anticipation, Kwei Lar'ja flicked out wristblades on one arm then pulled the combistick off his belt. The plasmacaster on his shoulder rose to its full height, program ready.

Maybe he would *finally* face a worthy opponent.

Sheriff York thumbed on the bullhorn and lifted it above the open door of the SUV. "We know you're in there. Come out with your hands up." York waited, his gaze trained on the destroyed entrance to the Hunting Depot. There didn't seem to be much of anything left of the place—besides the entrance, all the windows were shattered and from his position, he could see that the back wall was blown to shit. The rest of the interior was likely the same, and he had a real bad feeling about the Beck family.

York saw movement to the right of the doorway. He tensed, the bullhorn in his left hand and his right resting on the Glock in its holster. As had always been true in his twenty-six year-career, the cold metal offered no comfort. He didn't have a lot of hope in his next words, but tried anyway. "Is that you, Ajax? We got you covered—just give a holler so we know."

The man who stepped outside was not Ajax Beck.

"You're kidding me," Ryan Malik said. He partially rose from his crouched position by his own cruiser. "Asshole must think it's Halloween. He—"

Before the deputy could finish his sentence, a blue beam cut across the space and he and his cruiser blew up.

York didn't have to tell the other deputies what to do. Along with smoke, bits of metal and concrete and Malik's blood and flesh, the air exploded with gunfire. As the old brick front of the Hunting Depot shattered under the onslaught, their target dove to the right and—

—disappeared.

No one stopped firing. A hundred, two hundred rounds, and finally York aimed the bullhorn at the sky and screamed into it. *"Cease fire, damn it! Cease fire!"*

The gunfire stopped slowly, like a bundle of fireworks petering out. The silence that followed was pointedly short.

"Where'd he go?"

"Find the bastard."

"Don't let him get away!"

Abandoning their cover, the deputies spread out, some heading around the sides of the building while others fanned across the parking lot. York backed away from the car and turned slowly, trying to find something—*anything*—that would indicate where the guy was or how he'd gotten away. His gaze paused on a deputy a couple of cars over just as the armed lawman suddenly stood straight up, as though someone had shoved a hot poker up his butt. Before York could process this, the deputy's throat split, opening wide like a mad clown's wide, red grin. Blood geysered out of it and for a second, the guy still stood there, jittering. York thought he saw movement, a quivering like the air over hundred-degree pavement. Then it was gone and the deputy collapsed.

The Sheriff sprang toward the young man even though he knew it was too late. As he bent to check the body, he felt something brush past. A breeze... what? He'd never believed in a so-called sixth sense before, but now it kicked in and he ducked, at the same time throwing himself over the body and rolling under the car. He came to rest and stared out at...

Nothing.

York saw the air between himself and the deputy's corpse shimmer, that same phantom undulation. Sparks pelted down as metal screeched across the closed passenger door, then he scrambled farther back as the driver's door was wrenched off and knocked a good eight feet away. Finally York heard heavy footsteps heading away—the long stride of a large man—but again, he saw...

Nothing.

Around the parking lot people were screaming amid bouts of gunfire and what sounded like explosive rounds. Dust and smoke obscured York's vision as he pulled himself from under the car. Glancing at the door, he swallowed as his saw deep furrows ripped across the metal. Had he not dropped and rolled...

York didn't let himself finish the thought.

"There!" someone shouted. "I saw movement. He's headed around the building toward the train cars!"

"There's nothing there," someone else yelled in response.

"Shoot at it anyway—I'm telling you, it's there!"

At least half a dozen deputies headed in that direction. More ran to their cruisers as they pursued. York let them go as he took stock of the carnage in front of the store. Three, maybe four down, but all were being tended. He heard more sirens coming. Trusting the others to handle it, he jogged to the shop, watching his step as he carefully stepped over the sill.

There wasn't much left inside, but a fast scan confirmed what he'd known all along: a Rorschach splash of scarlet on the back left wall, a pile of blood-soaked clothing and skin to the right of the front counter, and Tom splayed across the heavy glass top directly across from where York stood. An entire family—a good one—wiped from the face of the earth.

On his belt, York's radio crackled. He listened, then thumbed on the speaker. When he spoke, his gravelly voice was filled with fury.

"Let's go get this motherfucker."

Val Wilson pulled her late husband's Remington 700 hunting rifle out of its case and loaded it. The sirens had started after Juliet had called and not stopped. She'd heard enough sirens and gunfire in Vietnam to give her a lifetime of nightmares, and she wasn't acting on a whim when she decided the town was under some kind of attack. She might be old but her aim was still almost as good as back in 'Nam, and if Swift had somehow ended up in a war, she was gonna fight for it.

Lourdes had given up following anyone. There were too many, all going too fast, and she didn't know which to choose. Thinking about Robbie, Miquel getting home, and trying to tail a sheriff's car was just too much. Her last attempt led her to the park, where she finally pulled the Ford over and stared numbly at the latest scene in the murderous spree that had apparently started with her son.

That had been a couple of hours ago, and while the action had moved elsewhere in Swift, a couple of deputies were still standing watch. Being a trucker, Miquel had installed both a CB and a police scanner in the F-150. Lourdes had never bothered before, but years of riding with her husband had taught her how to turn on the scanner and tune in to the local frequency. The words were filled with static but after a while she was able to pick up that the killer was working his way back into town.

She listened, the thumb of her right hand absently rubbing the carefully oiled barrel of the twelve-gauge.

The .38 special weighed more than he expected.

He probably looked stupid fast-walking south on Pine with a sweater tossed over one arm like a girl, but the gun didn't have a safety and Owen was paranoid about blowing his balls off if he tucked it into his waistband. His emotions were a mix of grief and anger since he'd talked to his mom and found out his best friend, Robbie, had been murdered. It was probably the worst news he'd ever had, then he learned that whoever did it was still loose, going through town like some kind of fucking serial killer. Owen had already gotten the loaded gun out of his dad's nightstand when he saw Mrs. Wilson get in her car and leave; then he realized Robbie's mother had done the same thing earlier. Mrs. Wilson had headed south into Swift proper. Owen followed the same route, still wearing the ketchup-stained shirt; it was a bitter reminder that Robbie had been his only friend in this miserable place.

Yeah, it was a far-fetched fantasy, but what he wanted most in the world was to shoot the guy who'd killed his friend.

There were plenty of radio reports for Sheriff York to process on his way toward the park. The killer was moving fast diagonally through town, no longer concerned about keeping a low profile. They'd seen some crazy shit at the gun shop, so no call-in was dismissed, no matter how strange; when one of the customers at the cannabis dispensary reported backing into something he couldn't see that then smashed in his trunk, York didn't even question it. He didn't know why, but the murdering son of a bitch was aiming for the park—maybe he'd put a getaway vehicle in the forest to the west, an ATV or off-road bike that could move through the heavy trees.

At Fifth and Spruce where the park started, York kept going, bouncing over the curb and onto the grass. He ground his teeth when he saw that word had spread and way too many folks had gathered, every damned one armed like this was some kind of old west bounty hunt. Men, women, and more than a few veterans had joined the deputies. York's cruiser halted near the park's center, where he could go either south or west depending on circumstances. His window was rolled down, but there was zero conversation. Now and then he heard a radio squawk, but nothing beyond that. The crowd's silence and the thick line of trees made the dense forest that bordered the park on two sides suddenly become downright terrifying.

The Sheriff got out of the car and rubbed his hand over his face hard enough to make his skin sting. He couldn't wait for this day to be over. Preferably with no one else dead.

Kwei Lar'ja knew the humans were tracking him. His cloak was working but there were places where it didn't operate at its full potential and the humans had picked up indications of his presence. No matter. Just across the deforested area they used for relaxation—they called it a *park*—was the wilderness in which he had landed his drop pod, now stocked with illicit trophies. Once he left Earth, he would reconnect with his scout ship and then rendezvous with the mothership. After pre-loading the drop pod onto the scout ship, he had managed to ease the scout ship out of its mothership slip without being detected, but returning would require the most extensive of his stealth and technological skills. If he were caught, the traditionalist, narrow-minded Elders on the homeworld would execute him. He knew he was too advanced for that to happen, but the danger heightened the thrill of the challenge.

Kwei Lar'ja's attempt to cross the park without being detected failed immediately.

The playground was on the south side. It had half a dozen metal and plastic climbing contraptions, swings, see-saws and other things that made Sheriff York think it was a path the killer might use. He was scanning it for perhaps the twentieth time when a sudden chorus of frenzied howling made his teeth grind. He spun and saw Paul McCoy's hounds standing up at the ends of their leads, struggling to pull free of McCoy's solid grip. The dogs—of *course*. York had been too intent on catching the madman to think of them, but someone else had. McCoy lived the farthest outside of town on a small dairy farm. He had cows, chickens, and horses, including a mean chestnut stallion very protective of the mares sharing his corral. Watching over the entire farm were his dogs, a bloodhound and two redbone coonhounds. Here those canines had a bead on something only they could see, right where York had guessed.

What he *couldn't* have predicted was the surge of townspeople in that direction. He lost a couple of seconds staring, then started shouting as loud as his lungs would allow. "You all stay back! Let law enforcement handle this. I say again—"

He might as well have been shouting into his coffee.

York saw a series of shimmers move through the playground equipment and McCoy running with the hounds as they dragged him toward whatever was causing it. McCoy wasn't armed beyond the dogs, but there was a shitload of people following him who were, and York wasn't surprised to see Dave Lawrence in there. He caught a glimpse of Lourdes Rosales, then one of the dogs snarled and snapped at the air. It got teeth into something because York heard a harsh cry at the same time the dog jumped away and shook its head. An instant later a wound opened across one of the dog's front legs and it yelped. McCoy jerked back on the leash so hard that he fell on his butt in the dirt and all three dogs tangled on top of him. In the now empty spot, there was a clang and sparks flew from the outside metal support of the jungle gym. Green liquid gushed out of nowhere and outlined the shape of a foot, oversized and ugly.

McCoy's tumble turned out to be a good thing. Before York could do anything, Dave Lawrence sprinted forward, a .357 bouncing in one outstretched hand while another big gun swung wildly in the other.

"Dave, you stop right now!" York bellowed. He took off in the same direction, but Dave was closer and there was no way he or any of the other deputies were going to intercept him. Dave skidded to a stop twenty feet short of the equipment, and dropped the other gun. Then he brought up the .357 and fired it at whatever the hell was attached to the bleeding foot.

He hit *something* because dirt flew up from the ground right afterward and the grass suddenly flattened as something heavy fell on it. A cry that sounded like a huge, agonized animal cut across the park as more green stuff—blood?—abruptly circled a large gunshot wound. The fluid spread in all directions, defining a netted, heavily muscled chest with armor on the other side. The exposed skin was gray-white and weirdly spotted, and more of it showed as the green blood spread and blue flashes, like electrical sparks, began following what was undeniably its shape and destroying its camouflage. In only a few seconds, the killer became completely visible, and York's mouth went slack as he finally realized it wasn't fucking *human*.

Dave Lawrence was gaping at the creature, like everyone else in the damned park. York got his legs moving at the same time a red light shot out of the thing's helmet and focused on Dave's upper body. York didn't need a lesson to know what that meant.

There was a *boom* and fire spewed from its shoulder apparatus. But Dave Lawrence wasn't there—Owen Holland, of all people, had done a football tackle and taken the older man to the ground.

"I knew it!" Owen screamed. "It's an alien, just like I said. I was right! I told—"

The rest of his words were drowned out by a heavy, hot wind that came out of nowhere and crazily whipped the tree limbs. The ground shook as York's hat sailed away, but he didn't care as he watched a giant ship materialize above them.

In the park's southeastern quadrant Val Wilson was next to Lourdes Rosales, which made sense considering they'd been neighbors for twenty years. Both women were crouched, and when that *thing* shot at Dave Lawrence, Val grabbed Lourdes before she could run toward it. If anyone deserved revenge it was Lourdes, but Val thought losing Robbie was enough. She didn't want to see his mother die, too.

Then there was the ship and everyone stopped moving and just gawked as it silently landed a few yards from where that green-blooded creature was fighting to get back up. It made it to one knee when a ramp lowered from the ship and another being just like him came into view. It ignored the sounds of weapons being primed all around and strode purposefully toward its injured comrade.

The first creature managed to stand just as the other one joined it. The second one, incredibly, was almost a foot taller and seemed older, more experienced. The smaller one tried to aim its shoulder weapon as a defense, but the instant the mechanism moved, a massive hand shot forward and wrenched it free; it hit the grass and he crushed it underfoot. Then, in a single powerful move, the big one grabbed the other by the back of the neck and hauled him up until his feet dangled above the ground.

The dangling one shot a set of serrated blades out of one wrist, but his captor trapped that arm and snapped it. An attempt at grabbing something off its belt ended just as quickly, and the struggle went out of him when the larger one shook him like an oversized rat and turned back toward the ship.

Lourdes started forward but her friend Val suddenly had a death grip on her arm. She knew her friend had been watching her, but assumed that like everyone else, Val was caught up in the aliens'—Owen's description—drama.

Wrong.

Lourdes tried to yank free, but Val wasn't having it. "Oh no, you don't," Val said. Her face was grim. "Enough people have died today. For God's sake, Lourdes—Miquel will come home to find out about Robbie. Please don't make that bad news include you, too."

"Let me go," Lourdes hissed. "There will be no human justice otherwise."

"It doesn't matter—"

"Yes, it does!" Lourdes screamed. She wrenched her arm free and spun away.

"Then I'm going with you!" Val yelled. When Lourdes ran forward and planted herself between the two foreigners and the ramp of the ship, Val was right by her side. She had no idea whether she would help or die in the process.

"Stop!" Lourdes brought up the twelve-gauge and pointed the barrel toward the creatures. "You don't get to take him—he killed my son!" The taller alien looked at her and tilted his head, as though considering her words. Lourdes felt her face go scarlet with rage. Her voice escalated to a shriek as she focused on the smaller one. *"He was just a boy and you killed him for no reason!"*

She tried to lunge at them but found herself hauled backward when Val's fingers hooked into the back of her jeans. "Wait," Val ground out.

Without warning, the bigger alien reached over and snatched off the smaller one's helmet. *"M-di yin'tekai."* The sounds he made were a sort of guttural clicking, then he pulled some kind of bladed weapon off his belt and slapped it into the smaller one's hand before pushing the bare-headed creature in her direction.

Val gasped. Lourdes would never know the incomprehensible sounds meant *"No honor,"* but she understood immediately that she would have to fight for the right to kill her son's murderer.

"Time to let go," Lourdes told Val.

For a second, Val hesitated. Then her voice dropped low enough that only Lourdes could hear it. "If you fall," she murmured, "I'll kill it for you." She released her friend.

Lourdes had barely enough time to register how horrible the thing's face was. She saw a thick, deep pink mouth holding elongated incisors and large pointed bottom teeth bordered on four sides by fangs as long as her fingers. He looked at her with tiny eyes and roared, his cheeks and huge fangs spreading open as wide as his face. With a twist of his uninjured wrist, the sharp weapon doubled its size and he spun it dangerously. Even when he leaped toward her and all she could see was his larger-than-human body hurtling toward her, Lourdes was not afraid.

"You murdering fuck," she said, and shot it in the face.

There hadn't been much left of the alien's head besides luminescent green blood and shreds of tissue. As Lourdes had stood there, smelling gunpowder and scorched flesh, the remaining alien had leaned over, grabbed one foot, and dragged the body up the already closing ramp. Thirty seconds later the ship lifted straight up, then literally vanished. She got in the Ford and went home, assuming the Sheriff and everybody else set about doing whatever they needed to get past this unspeakable day. She didn't care one way or another.

When Miquel walked in an hour later, Lourdes stayed where she was and didn't say anything. He closed the door and turned around, then stopped, shocked. She was sitting in his recliner with the shotgun leaning against the wall beside her. Her face, hands, clothes, and the shotgun were splattered with the alien's green blood, and she imagined he didn't know what the hell he was looking at. She thought she should dread the coming conversation, but she didn't. She felt oddly out of it, like a narrator in someone else's story.

"Sit down, Miquel," she said. "I have to tell you what happened today."

DEAD MAN'S SWITCH

BY SCOTT SIGLER

PROJECT YELLABEAST MARKETING COPY
Version 8-f: *CMO, CLO review*

ACCESS (review only)
- C-Level
- Bioteam

Imagine stalking the most savage animal in the galaxy, while that same animal stalks you.

Imagine a hunt so exclusive you need references from established big game guides. No amateurs allowed here. ~~Only the best of the best may apply for a permit~~. *(CMO: Let applicants find this out on their own. Outrage at being denied establishes exclusivity)*

~~Imagine a five-star lodge so advanced it includes a world-class trauma center that requires your stem cell deposit a year in advance, so replacement organs are waiting if needed~~. *(CLO: Counsel wants this less specific)*

Imagine being on a distant moon, the only hunter on a sprawling, private island covering over five hundred square kilometers.

Imagine being protected by the Pollinator℠, ~~the cutting edge~~ of hunting technology. *(CLO: change to: "the highest level," per Sibester lawsuit settlement)*

Can you imagine? If you can, then your imagination becomes reality with Kivi Safari~~, a subsidiary of Nyyrikki Ltd~~. *(CMO: per Memo D16-4b, references to parent company are to be removed)*. Our packages include round-trip travel to Kivi, which orbits Perko's World (KI-612), lodging, and five days (local) solo field time (groups allowed with up-charge)

We won't lie, this is dangerous. *Beyond* dangerous. So dangerous that customers must sign a waiver absolving Kivi Safari of legal obligation.

Yeah. *That* dangerous.

Contact our sales department now to apply for a permit.

"Do alarms really need to be so *piercing?* It's a sound meant to alert us to problems. I think we could know there are problems without going deaf."

Lewis knew Brunka had a point. The alarms were, indeed, piercing.

"We'll take it up with C-Suite when this is over," Lewis said. "Complain later, focus your attention on following our threat protocols."

She complained a lot. It was annoying, even though, more often than not, her complaints were valid.

This particular alarm was one of the more concerning ones in the facility's repertoire. Not as bad as *wall breach,* or *subject loose in facility*, but definitely not good. Not good, because in a facility as remote as this, tucked away in the jungles of the moon Kivi, *intruder alert* did not bring with it a single iota of positivity.

"RFID sweep clear in Pens A and C," Brunka said. "Pen B shows two staffers."

Lewis ground his teeth.

"I assume Colmeyer is one of them?"

"Yes, Doctor," Brunka said. "And Pung."

No surprise there. Colmeyer acted like the rules didn't apply to her. Pung was undoubtedly trying to get her to move to a secure area.

"Lock down A and C," Lewis said. "No access without your signature or mine. *Make sure* to deactivate Colmeyer's access to all three pens. Once Pung gets her out of there, we can keep her out."

"On it."

The fucking alarm felt like it was coming from a tiny, needle-shaped speaker driven through Lewis's tympanic membrane. The shrill tone warbled between 3.75 and 4.25 kHz. The low end of it, which wasn't "low" at all, was a good 500 Hz above the Yellabeasts' hearing range. That was important. A calm Yellabeast was still an incredibly dangerous beast. When agitated or angry? They were death on four legs.

Colmeyer thought she could ignore an intruder alert? Lewis would have fired her months ago save for two things. First, she was the only one who understood all levels of his work. Second, replacing her would take months, *if* the home office got lucky and found a candidate talented enough to replace her, and that candidate was willing to spend eight months in hypersleep.

Lewis minimized his protocol windows, called up camera access to Pen B. Sure enough, in Pen B's observation bubble, Aquina Colmeyer stood like an overconfident fool. She was too tall for the bubble; she had to stoop slightly and tilt her head a bit, even in the bubble's apex. She was the tallest person on staff, almost a foot taller than Lewis. Her height was the least of the reasons he hated her, but it was a factor nonetheless.

The small bubble sat in the center of the one-acre, high-walled, octagonal pen. Colmeyer hadn't even opaqued the bubble's ballistic glass, which remained perfectly clear, letting the two Yellabeasts see her and Pung. Even without the bubble's mics activated, Lewis could see the wide-bodied Pung angrily gesturing at her—*come on, come on, we can't be here.* Pung's hands clutched at a stubby M39 submachine gun, the standard arms for an on-duty guard.

Two Yellabeasts crouched nearby, primitive brains likely thinking the pen's ochre bushes and underbrush hid them from sight, as it did their far smaller ancestors. The animals' wide, stubby, triangular eyes fixed on Colmeyer.

Lewis activated comms to the bubble.

"Doctor," he said, "what in the hell are you doing? We have an intruder alert."

Colmeyer kept her eyes locked on the Yellabeasts.

"I'm staying until their food is delivered," she said. "I have to make sure Omi and Tau are fed. Hibernation season is coming."

Epi, short for Epsilon, four meters long from snout to tail-tip, 861.8 kilos of muscle and violence. Epi's eyes moved independently of each other, giving her almost 360-degree vision horizontally, and 0- to 90-degree vision vertically. On Kivi, *everything* was potential prey to something else. Yellabeasts needed the forward-facing sight of a predator, but also full awareness to avoid the things—swimming, walking, *and* flying things—that wanted to eat them.

Both Omi and Tau had mottled, slate-gray fur, solid legs that ended in claws adept at both burrowing and shredding prey, and bulbous protrusions at the front of their heavy heads, between the eyes, just above pincer-like jaws that ended in jet-black shovels of serrated bone.

Those protrusions hid the Yellabeasts' deadliest weapon, a barbed "tongue" that could stretch out almost six meters to first hammer prey with a 15,000 kPa concussive blow, then drag the prey back to where those claws could pin it, allowing the serrated jaws to rip free chest-sized chunks.

That god*damn* alarm, screeching in his ears. This god*damn* woman stating the obvious.

"We are on total lockdown, Doctor," Lewis said. "No one is bringing in a damn side of beef during an intruder alert.

We'll catch up on feeding when this situation is resolved. Get to your safety zone, *now*."

Colmeyer checked something on her wrist-pad. Was she *ignoring* Lewis?

"Problem," Brunka said, her voice tight. "The staff door to Pen B just opened."

Lewis glanced her way. "I told you to lock it down tight."

"I did," Brunka said. "Something overrode the lock."

An intruder alert. An open door.

"Find out why," Lewis said. "Quickly. While you do, call Barnaby, tell him we have a door we can't seal and that Colmeyer won't leave Pen B."

Lewis looked at the monitor.

"Pung, be advised the intruder may be heading your way. Get Doctor Colmeyer out of there, by force if you have to."

Pung turned, suddenly, looking back down the tunnel that led into the bubble. Lewis saw the man raise his M38, then Pung's back blew outward in a spray of gore and fire. Blood spattered on the inside of the ballistic glass.

Thin smoke filled the dome, obscuring what Lewis could see.

Lewis slapped the *all-comms* button. "The intruder is in Observation B. I repeat, the intruder is in Observation B."

Lewis watched, there was nothing he could do but watch, waiting for Colmeyer to die. She stood there in the swirling, contained smoke, her head slightly tilted, her body shaking, her hands raised.

The intruder didn't shoot her.

And in that instant, Lewis knew why.

He again slapped the *all-comms* button, this time so hard he felt pain shoot up his wrist.

"All staff, all staff, follow Protocol three-twenty-four, I repeat, follow Protocol three-twenty-four. The intruder may be a Hunter."

ALERT 27A-4
ACCESS:

- C-Level
- Exoplanet Senior Administrative
- Exoplanet Security L4 & Above

SUBJECT: Threat from nonhuman sentient species

The Competitive Intelligence Department (CID) has obtained information from Chigusa Corporation regarding a dangerous sentient race known as "Hunters."

This species appears to hunt for sport. Prey includes humans, and predatory species of sufficient size and ferocity to predate human adults.

Hunters appear to have interstellar ships with abilities beyond every known military state-of-the-art technology. Hunter ships may possess advanced stealth capabilities allowing them to enter planetary atmospheres undetected and remain undetected even when landing a few kilometers from settlements or facilities.

Unverified reports claim that Hunters are humanoid, 210 to 243 centimeters tall, weigh approximately 200 kilograms, and are substantially stronger than a typical human.

Reports also include mentions of advanced camouflage, as well as lethal ranged weaponry. However, most reports indicate Hunters prefer to kill using hand-to-hand or thrown weaponry. The assumption is that close-in killing requires more hunting skill than taking down prey at a distance.

PROTOCOL: 324

If Hunters exist, it is highly improbable that staff will encounter the species. If one should be spotted in or near a company facility or vessel, however, the following protocol must be followed:

- The species hunts for sport; the less of a threat you present, the higher your chances of survival.
- Do not aim weapons of any kind at a Hunter.
- If you have weapons, discard them.
- If you encounter one in person, *do not run.* Doing so may establish you as prey.
- Lie prone with hands and feet outstretched.
- Tactical units are exempt from these instructions, and should instead follow Protocol 342-B.

Lewis's own words rang in his ears. How did he sound so calm, when his insides churned like a lava lamp?

A *Hunter*.

Maybe it wasn't. He hadn't seen it; it had been too far back in the observation bubble's access tunnel. But the observed data fit the intel: it hadn't killed until Pung aimed a weapon at it. It hadn't killed Colmeyer, who was unarmed. At least, it hadn't killed her *yet*.

Lewis switched through the monitors, a fast-click scan of

the facility's rooms and corridors. A few people held weapons, but most were following protocol, sealing themselves inside assigned safe zones, then lying flat, arms outstretched.

"Brunka," Lewis said, "how did the intruder get through the door to Observation B?"

The *locked* door. Only admin had that kind of master-leave access.

"A root-level bypass code was used." Brunka said. "Looks like some code has been overridden at the core level, I don't know how to block it out."

"How could the intruder do that?"

"A sniffer, maybe," Brunka said. "Manual attachment collecting data over days, even weeks. Maybe a man in the middle picking access changes, I don't know."

Days? Maybe *weeks*?

If it was a Hunter, how long had it been on Kivi? Watching, waiting, gathering data...

Lewis saw the fear in Brunka's eyes, fear he felt just as intensely. "Doctor Yellan, do you really think it could be a Hunter?"

Despite her fear, she kept her voice fixed and level. Brunka was a good hire.

"I didn't see it," Lewis said. "I can't be sure."

Brunka glanced at the monitors showing staffers lying prone.

"If it isn't," she said, "if it's mercenaries or something like that, then following Protocol three-twenty-four is a really bad idea."

Maybe a Hunter wouldn't kill an unarmed staffer, but corporate mercs would. And yet, would a rival corp really kill people to steal research for a game preserve?

Unlikely.

"No incoming ship warnings," Lewis said. "No air traffic warning. Mercs would have had to land in the ocean, then come onshore and travel at least six kilometers on foot."

On Kivi, even a battle-hardened, fully armed marine wouldn't make it more than a half-kilometer on foot. The Yellabeast's dog-sized ancestor was only one of hundreds of predatorial species. In Kivi's thick jungle-swamps, a soldier stood zero chance. *Hundreds* of soldiers stood zero chance. Only fully sealed, all-terrain tanks promised any chance of survival, and those gave off signals—*if* they could traverse bogs where even the plants wanted to eat you.

Lewis's company had dropped bombs, *big* bombs, to clear the island of indigenous life long enough to build the main research facility and landing pad, the three large pens, and the shell for the eventual construction of the hunting lodge.

Lewis clicked through monitor coverage. Some people had reached safe zones. Others had not; they'd stopped where they were, stopped and lay prone, just as Protocol three-twenty-four instructed.

Then, all the internal doors slid open.

He stared for a moment, trying to process what he saw, trying to understand it. An instant to think there was a malfunction, but that instant vanished. If the intruder had opened Observation B's doors, what was to stop it from opening *any* door.

Half of his monitor changed to static.

"Working on camera dropout," Brunka said before Lewis could order her to do so. "Sixty percent of our coverage gone. Make that seventy percent."

A new alarm sounded, also high-pitched but different, a harsh warble that made the lava lamp churning inside Lewis speed up.

"Brunka, tell me that alarm is a mistake."

She gripped the sides of her console.

"Pen B interior doors open," she said. "The… The Yellabeasts can access the main corridors."

The research facility was the island's second-largest building, a hub with four spokes: three short passages leading to the three octagonal pens, and a fourth passage that led to the Pollinator. To save on building materials that had to be shipped from other worlds, the same main passages that allowed staffers to move around the facility were also used to move young Yellabeasts from research to pens, or to move adult Yellabeasts from pen to pen, or move them to the Pollinator.

If Yellabeasts were in the main corridors, right now…

"Impossible," Lewis said. "There are five levels of safeguards before test subjects can enter the corridors."

Brunka blinked. "The safeguards were overridden."

A blur of motion on a monitor covering the northwest corridor, a blur like liquid glass in the shape of a man. A *big* man. The blur ran toward two people lying prone in the corridor.

"Eighty percent of coverage blocked," Brunka said.

It couldn't be, and yet, Lewis's mind began marking the data, cataloging what had to be done to provide the greatest chance for survival.

"Focus on the Pollinator coverage," he said. "Protect those views, do it *now*."

The alarms, and the heavy clacking of Brunka's fast-moving fingers.

Those people on the floor. Lewis recognized them. Peter Van and Carla Abadi.

"Run," Lewis said, even though they couldn't hear him.

The blurry figure leapt over them.

From where the blurry figure had come, more movement.

"No," Lewis said.

Omi barreled down the corridor like an agile bull with stubby eyes for horns, eyes aimed at Peter and Carla. Thick muscles rippled beneath mottled fur. Carla heard Omi, or saw it—or both—and scrambled to her feet to run.

The tongue hit in the lower back, so hard it almost snapped her in two. Before she hit the floor, the barbed tongue yanked back, pulling her along like a broken rag doll. Claws pinned her to the ground.

She lurched violently when the Yellabeast bit into her side, snapping ribs and spine as it tore free a chunk.

Peter didn't get up. He didn't run. He seemed trapped there as if the corridor's gravity was ten times that of Kivi's.

"Run!" Lewis said.

Peter did not.

As Omi ate, Tau rushed in. Tau didn't have to use the tongue, because Peter didn't move, unless you counted a convulsive shudder of fear as movement. Tau reached him. Tau bit into his thigh.

Carla hadn't screamed, but Peter certainly did.

"It's a Hunter," Brunka said, her fingers still flying. "It didn't kill them because they weren't a threat, but it… it…"

Lewis tried to parse out what he'd just seen, balance it against the limited information he'd had before this shitshow began. He was a scientist. He prided himself on his ability to observe, to analyze.

One person with a gun: the Hunter had killed him.

Three people without weapons: the Hunter had *not* killed them.

The observed data, the intel from CID… it matched up.

Lewis knew what was happening.

"Pollinator cams locked down," Brunka said. "I think my changes will hold, but I don't know. Doctor, what are we going to do? Should I grab rifles?"

At least two Yellabeasts were loose.

The Hunter had opened internal doors. Staying in research was as dangerous as staying in the corridors, or the pens themselves.

If Lewis and Brunka grabbed M39s, the Hunter might kill them. If not, Yellabeasts certainly would.

They could run for the landing pad, but would they make it? If they did, would any of the three atmospheric ships still be there, or had others already taken them, already evacuated?

Every option held little hope for survival, but one held slightly more than the others.

"We go to the Pollen room," Lewis said.

PROJECT UPDATE 42–L-12

ACCESS:
- C-Level

Lodge Project Admin reports that Bioteam is projected to hit targets for subject length, weight and ferocity.

The current Yellabeast generation, Gen6, is the largest yet.

Individuals are trending 18% heavier and 12.5% longer than Gen5. Gen6 is, on average, 693% heavier and 418% longer than indigenous specimens of *T. hateicus*.

Extrapolation models indicate Gen6, when mature, will satisfy all project targets. If that projection proves accurate, Lodge Project Admin will move the Project to Phase 4: Hunt 1.

Screams echoed through the corridors. Screams, occasional gunshots, and the excited grunts of Yellabeasts.

Lewis sprinted through the corridors. Or, at least, he *tried* to sprint. Corporate required staffers to maintain a level of physical conditioning. Lewis had ignored that requirement. Who was going to call him to task? Without him, there was no Yellabeast project.

His lungs burned. The facility was big, but not *that* big. He'd run less than a half-kilometer. Lewis cursed himself for his arrogance.

"It must have hacked our system," Brunka said.

She wasn't even breathing hard. She didn't have his cachet with Corporate; she maintained her conditioning, and it showed.

"It opened pen doors," Brunka said, so nonplussed from the sprint she looked at the tablet she'd taken from Control as she ran. "That's the highest-level access we have. It overrode the safety measures. I don't think I can lock it out of the Pollen Room."

"If we make it, you'll have to try."

"I know code but I'm not a programmer," Brunka said. "I don't understand why the Hunter let them out."

She was smart. One of the smartest people Lewis knew. And yet, she couldn't see the obvious logic.

"The protocol," he said. "It must have realized most of us wouldn't fight it, wouldn't run from it. There's no sport in murdering unarmed people. It let the Yellabeasts loose to kill us."

Which, in a way, was *very* sporting. Lewis wondered if anyone might survive the Yellabeasts. If so, would the Hunter let those people live? Was there some kind of honor code, or something?

Lewis and Brunka turned a corner, she with ease, he almost careening into the far wall.

"But *why*?" she asked. "What does the damn thing want from us?"

It was obvious. Obvious, and terrifying.

"We made a hunting preserve," Lewis said, forcing out the words with what little breath he still had. "We made an apex predator. The Hunters *hunt*. I think it wants the Yellabeasts, and the preserve, for itself."

In a way, that made Lewis immensely proud of his own work."That's insane," Brunka said.

Sanity was a relative thing. Lewis wouldn't pretend to understand what an alien race considered normal, considered *sane*. If he survived, he could spend mental cycles philosophizing about the moral implications; he didn't think it likely he'd get that chance.

Up ahead, the wide, heavy, sliding door to Pen C. Rho, Psi and Kap were in there. Would the Hunter let them out, like it had done with Pen B?

Lewis skidded to a halt just past the door, holding tight to Brunka's arm to make her do the same.

"Pen C," he said. "Can you change the code? Lock it down?"

Brunka looked at her tablet, shook her head.

"I don't know," she said. "I can try."

"Figure it out, fast. If we can control Pen C access, it increases our chance for survival."

Yellabeasts ate fast, like all species on Kivi did. They could easily eat half their body weight and keep hunting, keep killing. If Omi and Tau had found other prey, though, if they'd found other *staffers,* the two monstrous beasts might be full.

Rho, Psi, and Kap would not be.

Movement caught Lewis's eye, movement from back down the hall. Movement that was there and was *not* there. Movement from a blur of color and light that made a segment of wall seem to flutter and ripple.

The Hunter.

Lewis froze.

The there-not-there humanoid stood still.

It wanted Lewis to fight, to run.

A sentient alien being. The scientist in Lewis wanted to know more, so much more, wanted to celebrate this huge moment in human history, but the primitive ape in him wanted to *survive*.

Lewis spread his hands, palms out, made sure the there-not-there shape could see him do it.

"Brunka," Lewis whispered, "can you use the tablet to open the pen doors?"

She looked up from her tablet, looked at him, her eyes wide. She hadn't seen the danger.

"Yes, the safeties have been disengaged, but why the fuck would we want to open them?"

Lewis gripped Brunka's upper arm, started backing up, slowly, pulling her along with him, moving them both away from the shimmering there-not-there shape.

"When I say *now,*" Lewis said, "open it."

He felt Brunka stiffen; she saw it, too. She tensed as if to run. Lewis squeezed her arm as hard as he could.

"Slow," Lewis said. "Don't make it a challenge for it."

A ring of metal; two blades extended from the shimmering Hunter's arm. Parallel half-meters of death.

Brunka leaned away from him, tried to pull free without lurching.

"Let me go," she said.

Lewis did not.

The shimmering shape strode toward them, dragging the blade tips against the corridor wall. From within the shimmer, red eyes flashed.

It was trying to spook them into running.

"*Lewis,*" Brunka said through gritted teeth, "*come on.*"

In response, Lewis squeezed her arm even harder, silently told her she would move at his pace or she would not move at all.

He kept backing away, *slowly* backing away.

The Hunter closed the distance.

Five meters and closing.

The shimmer sparkled, then vanished, leaving behind a walking monster, well over two meters tall, thick with muscle. A metal helmet with narrow, black eyes. Long, thick strands of hair, or perhaps decorations of some sort.

"Get ready," Lewis said.

The Hunter drew abreast of the door.

Lewis let go of Brunka's arm.

"Now," he said.

There was no warning. No *beep* of alarm—the Hunter had disabled those.

The doors to Pen C slid open.

Three Yellabeasts rushed out, three metric tons of hunger and brutality. Two leaped for the Hunter, which didn't run as Lewis had hoped. Instead, the Hunter drove its paired blades deep into Rho's thick chest. Lewis heard the thick breastbone crack. Such *power*. Even as the blood sprayed, Kap's jaws bit down on the Hunter's other arm.

That was all Lewis had time to see, because Psi didn't attack the Hunter—the beast's thick head turned toward Lewis and Brunka.

"Run!" Lewis screamed, but Brunka was already moving, already turning the corner.

Lewis turned his back on the carnage, on the corridor filled with murder. His legs seemed to pump in slow motion, his out-of-shape ass doomed to feel Psi's barbed tongue drive into him, drive *through* him. There would be no warning sound, no chance to duck aside, as a shooting tongue made no noise. On Kivi, predators had to be silent, both to catch prey, and to avoid becoming prey themselves. He turned the corner an instant too early, slammed into the edge and spun away, unbalanced, just as the tongue smashed into the wall, kicking out a spray of broken plastic.

Psi had missed.

Lewis righted himself and sprinted—just down the corridor, the door of the Pollinator's narrow chute hung open. In he rushed, knowing his lifespan would be measured in seconds if he didn't make the control pod.

PROJECT UPDATE 43–L-8

ACCESS:

- C-Level
- Marketing Level 2 & above
- Sales Level 3 & above

CoS reports that Phase 4's five hunting permits are sold out, at double the projected retail package price. This round alone has paid for 38% of the project development costs. When the Main Lodge opens for business (Phase 5), Admin expects to achieve ROI by Hunt 6, after which each hunt will produce a profit of 288% above operating costs.

The ferocity, vision, and predatory instincts inherent in unaltered specimens of *T. hateicus* remain in Gen6. We believe the Yellabeast is among the most dangerous game animals in history. This best-of-class advantage will justify our premium price point.

Correspondingly, Legal has determined the Pollinator[SM] safety system sufficient to merit the full litigation waivers required of customers. This advanced hunter-safety system preserves the inherent risk of hunting a genetically modified apex predator.

For more on the Pollinator, see Project Update 16-P-4.

The shaft had been built so that a one-ton Yellabeast could enter but not turn around. Lewis weighed less than a tenth as much; while he could have turned around, nothing in the universe could have made him do so.

Stomach churning, lungs burning, he sprinted for his life. He passed the pollinator jets, hoping Brunka wouldn't panic and let loose the charge on him.

He heard Psi's grunting, felt the reverberating footsteps as the big animal thundered down the shaft behind him. Lewis again waited to feel a crushing blow drive into his back, to feel the barbs punch through flesh and bone.

He was too slow.

He would not make it.

He would die horribly.

The shaft vibrated.

He heard the hissing whine of the jets spraying out the charge behind him.

Lewis reached the shaft's end, launched himself to the right, heard the whisper of air driven by a tongue that had missed him by centimeters.

He landed hard. Dull pain in his knee. He kept that pain at a distance, because to feel it, to think about it, to *slow down*, to slow was to die. On his feet. Moving through the round chamber, toward the angular, windowed egg that was the Pollinator control pod.

The pod hatch hung open.

Brunka, inside.

Psi's guttural roar bouncing from the metal walls—the Yellabeast was out of the shaft.

Brunka shouted words Lewis couldn't process because there was only the pod door and nothing else. He leapt forward. Through the open hatch. Hard thump against the floor. Smashing into a console.

The hiss of the hatch.

The whir of steel bolts sliding home.

Psi's roar again, now distant, muted.

Hands on him, shaking hands, searching hands.

"Lewis! Are you hurt?"

He let Brunka help him up. His knee wouldn't hold his weight. He looked out the pod windows, saw Psi on the other side, not even a meter away. Fleshy, barbed tongue smearing saliva on the glass. Jagged black jaws snapping together so hard they sounded like two baseball bats smashing against each other.

The beast wanted him.

It wanted Brunka.

It wanted *food*.

"The pollen charge," Lewis said.

Brunka's hands kept searching, sliding, gripping, checking for blood.

"I got it," she said. "Fifty percent coating, at least."

A hundred percent would have been better, but fifty percent was enough.

Lewis slapped Brunka's hands away.

"Give me the detonator," he said. "And prep another charge. Hurry."

She pointed to the console. Amidst the monitors and keyboards and controllers, there was a black nylon wrist harness attached to a small black plastic box. On that box, a single red button and two small dip switches.

Brunka's hands gripped the dual black joystick that controlled the Pollinator. Her finger trembled on the blue trigger.

Lewis wrapped the harness's nylon around his right wrist, sealed the Velcro tight.

"Charge loaded," Brunka said.

Lewis ignored the desperate roar of the hungry beast trying to claw its way into the control pod. He pushed both dip switches to *on*, then watched the red button. Four seconds seemed like forever. The red button began to flash, flash faster than he would have thought.

That's what he got for being so out of shape.

"Oh my god," Brunka said. "I can see it. The Hunter, it's in the shaft. The Hunter is coming!"

She stared at a monitor. Lewis wanted to see, didn't dare look. Brunka had hit Psi—she would hit the Hunter as well.

Lewis saw the rack of detonators. One missing, the one on his wrist. He grabbed the second, wrapped it around his left wrist.

"Do not miss," he said.

He had to look, he had to see.

In the monitor, the long, narrow shaft. The Hunter, one arm hanging limp, ran down its length.

"It shut the outer shaft door behind it," Brunka said.

Were Omi and Tau still out there? Had the Hunter fled Kap? How many Yellabeasts were in the halls, shredding the staff? The Hunter wanted to protect its back, to face one enemy at a time.

On the monitor, Lewis saw glowing green blood trailing behind the Hunter, dripping down from the wounded arm.

"Here it comes," Lewis said. "Don't miss."

The Hunter stumbled but kept going. When it neared the nozzles, it was all Lewis could do to not take the controller from Brunka's hands.

When it drew abreast of the nozzles, Brunka pulled the trigger.

In the shaft, a cloud of pollen sprayed out, obscuring the view for a moment. Then the Hunter sprinted out of the descending droplets, as if it thought the cloud was poison.

In a way, it was.

"Keyed to your left-hand detonator," Brunka said.

On that detonator, Lewis slid both dip switches to *on*. The red button flashed a stuttering light, then it blinked steadily, in the exact same rhythm as the light on his right-hand detonator.

Lewis looked out a patch of pod window not covered in thick spit. He saw the Hunter walk out of the shaft and into the chamber, saw Psi turn and scramble toward it. Something at the Hunter's shoulder blazed; Psi's front right shoulder ripped away in a burst of flame and blood. The big monster tumbled, fell, already trying to right itself.

Lewis reached out, slapped the *emergency release* button. The pod door hissed open.

"*Lewis, what the fuck*?"

Brunka's self-control had finally vanished. Her held-back horror let loose in her throat-ripping plea/accusation.

Lewis raised his hands, palms out, then stepped out of the control pod.

The Hunter saw him, looked away from Psi to him, the weapon on its shoulder matching the move of the Hunter's head, wide-bore barrel now aimed at Lewis's face.

Psi, blood jetting from the gaping wound that used to be a shoulder, tried to balance itself. Even with one leg gone, slipping in its own blood, it tried to move toward the Hunter.

The wide barrel swung back to the Yellabeast. A blue flash, a spray of blood and bone and brain. Psi slumped to the floor. The three remaining legs twitched. Its three-meter tongue lolled out, wiggling spasmodically.

The barrel again aimed at Lewis, but it did not fire.

The Hunter's left arm dangled, limp and broken. Glowing green sheeted skin and armor alike. The alien glanced at the slight sheen on its hands, its legs.

A sheen caused by the pollen.

"You're hurt," Lewis said. "Do you speak my language?"

If the Hunter did, it did not say so.

It had flown a spaceship to this planet. It had hacked the facility's systems. If Lewis could make things obvious enough, the Hunter *would* understand.

Lewis moved slowly. So slowly. With his left hand, he pointed to his right wrist, to the flashing red button, then he put his fingertip to his own sternum, tapped to match the button's rhythm. Did Hunters have hearts? Of course they did, something had to pump that green blood.

Lewis then pointed at the twitching Yellabeast. Then, slowly, *so* slowly, sure he would die at any moment, Lewis gripped the Velcro on his right wrist, slowly peeled it loose, then tossed the harness aside.

Psi's still twitching body exploded, a snapshot burst balloon of fire and meat. Lewis blinked against the spray of blood that splashed against him, splashed against the walls and ceiling, that splashed against the Hunter.

Lewis trembled. He waited for death.

Death did not come.

Half-cooked organs inside Psi's meaty skeleton smoldered and bubbled. Bits of the Yellabeast dripped from the ceiling. The room smelled of burned hair and singed rubber.

Slowly, so slowly, Lewis pointed to the black box on his

left wrist, to the flashing red light there, then to his heart—then, he pointed at the Hunter.

The soulless black dots stared out from the gore-smeared helmet.

The Hunter glanced back down the shaft, stared for a moment, then the eyes again fixed on Lewis.

It understood.

"Get us out of here," Lewis said. "Get us to the landing pad, or you die."

PROJECT UPDATE 16-P-4

ACCESS:

- C-Level
- Bioteam, all

Bioteam reports a successful deployment of the Pollinator. The device was used on Subject Theta-2, resulting in the subject's immediate death.

All Yellabeasts entering the hunting range will first pass through the Pollinator chute, where the "pollen grains" are applied via a proprietary spray application process.

Each pollen grain consists of 2200mcgs of DitSP, a proprietary explosive compound. A Pollinator charge consists of 800,000 grains, plus 100,000 proprietary RFID detonators. Therefore, each pollinator charge contains 1.98 kilograms of DitSP, with an explosive power equal to six sticks of TNT (1140 grams).

Pollinator charges are distributed in a spray via 36 ejectors, assembled in 3 rings of 13 ejectors each. Upon ejection, all grains of each charge are keyed to a specific "detonator unit," which is worn on the customer's wrist. Upon activation, all grains detonate simultaneously.

Even a 50% coating of a pollen charge contains sufficient explosive power to instantly kill a 900kg Yellabeast.

Detonators have dip switches that code for three settings:
Setting 1: Pollen is detonated when the detonator's trigger button is depressed. If customers feel threatened, they have the option of instantly killing the Yellabeast. This setting may be turned off if the customer wants a true challenge.
Setting 2: Pollen is detonated if the wearer's heart stops. This is the "dead man's switch" setting.

Corporate strongly recommends setting both dip switches to "on."

"So, it can't understand us?"

"No," Lewis said. "I don't think so."

Lewis kept drawing. He wanted Brunka to shut up, but she kept asking questions, whispering them as if secrecy lay in low volume, not in lack of understanding of English.

"Then push the fucking button," Brunka whispered. "Do it."

She made it so obvious, the Hunter probably didn't need to understand English at all.

"There could be up to five Yellabeasts loose in the halls,"

Lewis said. "We stand no chance, not unless the Hunter escorts us out."

A Faustian bargain to say the least.

Lewis put his pen down. He held up his crudely drawn map so the Hunter could see it: the chamber they were in, marked by stick figures of Lewis and Brunka, and a larger stick figure of the Hunter; the path to the landing pad, marked with stick figures of Yellabeasts; a ship on the landing pad.

"You get us *here,*" Lewis said, tapping the ship. "Or you die. Understand?"

The black eyes stared out for a moment, then the head nodded.

That human expression, at least, the Hunter understood perfectly.

The Hunter's finger, still dripping with Yellabeast blood, pointed to Lewis, then to the ship, then at Lewis's wrist band.

"Un... der... stand," it said.

No upward inflection, but a question nonetheless. A question, and a command.

Lewis nodded.

Without another word, the Hunter strode to the Pollinator shaft entrance, ruined arm still trailing blood.

It was as simple as simple could be. No need to ask if the Hunter would honor the bargain.

"If it gets us to the landing pad," Brunka said, "and if there's still a ship, what do we do about other survivors?"

Were there other survivors? Part of Lewis, a big part, hoped there were not, because if there weren't, he and Brunka could simply fly away.

And if there were, they might do that anyway.

"We'll burn that bridge when we get to it," Lewis said. "Let's go."

He and Brunka followed the Hunter into the shaft.

Lewis wondered if he should feel sadness at seeing his work blown to bits. He didn't wonder long.

His creations would have killed him like they'd killed the rest of the staff. The corridors had become an abattoir. Torn corpses, body parts and blood everywhere. He wouldn't have thought a bit of intestine would stick to a wall, and yet, there it was. Who had it belonged to?

Lewis didn't want to know.

Surely the beasts had eaten their fill, yet they'd kept on killing. Perhaps they'd instinctively realized there were no other predators here to steal their trophies? No carrion eaters that might drag away the corpses?

Whatever the reason, the only still-living beings Lewis saw were himself, Brunka, the Hunter, and the Yellabeasts—although, when seen, the latter did not live long.

The Hunter strode down the corridors. It had activated its camouflage, which seemed to work as it had before despite the thin yet thorough coating of pollen.

Lewis found he recognized only about half of the human corpses that he'd worked with for years, yet he knew every Yellabeast on sight.

The Hunter used its shoulder blaster to kill Kap, blowing the beast's head into bloody pulp.

It killed Mu and Nu the same way. Somehow, they'd gotten out of Pen A, either because the Hunter let them out, or because the system hack had cascaded into multiple failures.

When Omi came, the Hunter had stopped, extended its parallel blades, and waited. Omi's tongue lashed out—the Hunter severed it in mid-air, the fleshy, barbed end rolling down the hall like a half-inflated basketball. Or was it a football? Lewis could never keep the sports straight

Omi rushed on, enraged, muscles twitching, looking to kill. The Hunter ran to meet it. Lewis could do nothing but watch as the Hunter slid at the last moment, right under the rushing Omi, and gutted the beast, from neck to hips. When Omi's blood and some lacerated organs splashed to the floor, the tall Hunter was already past, already standing.

"Magnificent," Lewis said.

He couldn't help it. The word just came out.

"He's going to kill us," Brunka said.

Lewis gave that eventuality a 50/50 shot.

At the door to the landing pad, Lewis saw Tau, chewing away on a torso. The person's severed head lay nearby, staring out. That one Lewis did recognize: Colmeyer. Pen B was on the other side of the facility. How had she made it this far? She knew the Yellabeasts better than anyone, save for Lewis, so perhaps she'd put her knowledge to work and made a smart dash for safety.

She'd almost made it.

Tau had been her favorite. Now, perhaps, she was Tau's favorite.

The Hunter took a step toward the beast, but stumbled.

"Oh, shit," Brunka whispered. "Has it lost too much blood?"

Again with the quiet talk. As if it mattered now.

Tau twitched its head, opened its jaws—Colmeyer's

mangled body flew down the hall, a broken, bloody, headless rag doll.

The Hunter fell to one knee.

Tau roared. Tau rushed.

The Hunter's shoulder blaster fired. It missed.

Tau came faster, closed the distance.

The Hunter seemed to gather itself, to think, perhaps to *aim*. The blaster fired again; Tau's front right leg fell off at the knee. The creature fell. It howled. The blaster fired a third time. Tau's guts exploded in a ball of fire, splashing against the walls and ceiling.

The beast seemed to gulp for air once, twice, and managed half a third before falling still.

"So much for hunting season," Brunka said.

The moment of truth.

Lewis stood on the boarding ramp of the last ship. The other two were gone, which meant at least two staffers had escaped. Hopefully, both ships had been full, but for now there was no way to know.

The Hunter stood at the base of the ramp. It waited.

"Push the button," Brunka whispered.

She was already inside, prepping for liftoff.

Lewis wondered: could he push the button before the Hunter realized what he was doing? Before the shoulder blaster blew him to bits?

Maybe. Maybe not.

He decided he didn't want to find out.

Slowly, so slowly, he slid both dip switches to the *off* position. He undid the Velcro. Then, slowly, *so* slowly, he removed the harness, and tossed it at the Hunter's feet.

With no drama, the Hunter bent, picked up the harness, then walked back into the facility.

Lewis Yellan walked up the ramp.

"Close it up," he said to Brunka. "See if we can do an RFID scan from in here. If anyone is still alive, we'll wait for a bit, see if they can reach us."

The door began to close.

"If there are survivors, and they *can't* reach us," Brunka said as she flipped switches, "what then?"

Lewis watched the door seal tight. He was safe from Yellabeasts, but not from the Hunter. What if that creature changed its mind?

"I'm not going back in there." Lewis said. "For anyone. Will you?"

Brunka paused mid-flip. She stared at the ship's controls as if they were a convenient excuse for her to not meet Lewis's eyes.

"No," she said, quietly. "I won't go back inside."

She was braver than he was. Stronger, faster, in better shape. That she wouldn't risk herself to help others made him feel just a little bit better. Just a little bit less cowardly.

"Do the scan," he said. "Then let's get the hell out of here."

EDITOR BIOGRAPHY

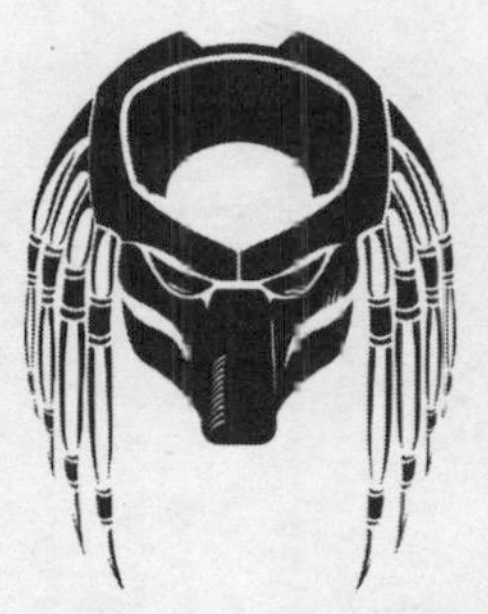

Hugo-nominated **BRYAN THOMAS SCHMIDT** is the national bestselling editor of nineteen anthologies including *Aliens vs. Predators: Ultimate Prey* (with Jonathan Maberry), *Predator: If It Bleeds*, *Infinite Stars*, *Monster Hunter Files* (with Larry Correia), and *Joe Ledger: Unstoppable* (with Jonathan Maberry), and the author of ten novels and numerous short stories, including the forthcoming *Shortcut*, The Saga of Davi Rhii trilogy, and The John Simon Thrillers. He was first editor of Andy Weir's international bestseller, *The Martian*, and books by *New York Times Bestsellers* Angie Fox, Todd McCaffrey, Mike Resnick, Frank Herbert, and many more. His previous works in the expanded universe include the story "Drug War" co-written with Holly Roberds for *Predator: If It Bleeds*, "First Hunt" for *Aliens vs. Predators: Ultimate Prey*, and "Aftermath" in this volume. He can be found online via his website at www.bryanthomasschmidt.net.

AUTHOR BIOGRAPHIES

LINDA D. ADDISON is an award-winning author of five collections, including *How To Recognize A Demon Has Become Your Friend*, and the first African-American recipient of the HWA Bram Stoker Award®. She is a recipient of the HWA Lifetime Achievement Award, HWA Mentor of the Year and SFPA Grand Master. Her work has made frequent appearances over the years on the honorable mention list for *Year's Best Fantasy and Horror* and *Year's Best Science-Fiction*. She has a B.S. in Mathematics from Carnegie-Mellon University and is a member of HWA, SFWA and SFPA. Catch her work in *Black Panther: Tales of Wakanda*, *The Magazine of Fantasy & Science Fiction*, *Weird Tales Magazine*, and anthologies *Giving the Devil His Due*, *Don't Turn Out the Lights* and *Classic Monsters Unleashed*. Her site is www.LindaAddisonWriter.com.

A British-born member of the Writers Guild of America, **PETER BRIGGS** jumped careers from assistant film cameraman to motion picture screenwriter with the overnight sale of his *Alien vs. Predator* spec script to 20th Century Fox in 1992. Probably best known for co-writing the 2004 *Hellboy* movie with Guillermo Del Toro (which opened number one at the US box office), Peter's been hired-on or sold projects to just about every major Hollywood studio, in addition to having work produced for television. His screenplays have featured in numerous authors' "How-To" screenwriting books.

Off the silver screen, Peter's a published comic book writer; been an on-air correspondent for BBC television and radio; and penned journalism for the *Los Angeles Times* and other publications. When not trying to wrangle his own projects out of Development Hell, he continues to contribute to educational screenwriting tomes; lectures on screenwriting panels; and tutors and mentors aspiring movie scribes through both online script consultancies, and directly via his Twitter page.

A lifelong *Star Wars* fan, Peter is averse to glowing green rocks, and likes pink very much, Lois.

ROBERT GREENBERGER is a writer/editor of numerous works for readers of all ages. His media tie-in work includes cowriting with Michael Jan Friedman *Predator: Fire & Blood* and the Scribe award-winning novelization of *Hellboy II: The Golden Army*. He has worked on staff at DC Comics, Marvel Comics, Weekly World News, ComicMix, and Starlog Press. A member of the Science Fiction Writers of America and the International Association of Media Tie-In Writers, his résumé includes novels, short stories, essays, and reviews. A cofounder of the digital imprint Crazy 8 Press, he continues to write and edit original fiction.

Additionally, he teaches high school English in Maryland where he makes his home with his wife Deb. For more, visit his website: www.bobgreenberger.com.

Though **AMMAR HABIB** was born in Lake Jackson, Texas, in 1993, his family originates from Pakistan and South Asia. He is the author of nine books, including *The Heart of Aleppo* and *The Orphans of Kashmir*, along with many other shorter works. He presently resides in his hometown with his family.

STEPHEN GRAHAM JONES is the *New York Times* bestselling author of nearly thirty novels and collections, and there are some novellas and comic books in there as well. Most recent are *The Only Good Indians* and *My Heart is a Chainsaw*. Up next is *Don't Fear the Reaper*. Stephen lives and teaches in Boulder, Colorado.

GINI KOCH writes the fast, fresh, and funny Alien/Katherine "Kitty" Katt series for DAW Books, the Necropolis Enforcement Files series, and the Martian Alliance Chronicles series. She also has a humor collection, *Random Musings from the Funny Girl*.

As G.J. Koch she writes the Alexander Outland series, and she's made the most of multiple personality disorder by writing novels, novellas, novelettes, and short stories in all the genres out there and under a variety of other pen names as well, including Anita Ensal, Jemma Chase, A.E. Stanton, and J.C. Koch, all with stories featured in excellent anthologies, available now and upcoming. Reach her via: www.ginikoch.com.

MICHAEL KOGGE is a screenwriter and bestselling author from Los Angeles. His original work includes the graphic novel *Empire Of The Wolf*, a werewolf epic set in ancient Rome. He's also written books for many high-profile properties such as *Star Wars*, Harry Potter and Fantastic Beasts, *Game Of Thrones*, and *Batman v Superman*. His adaptation of *Star Wars: The Rise Of Skywalker* won the 2021 Scribe Award for Best Young Adult Novel. You can find him on the web at www.michaelkogge.com.

TIM LEBBON is a *New York Times*-bestselling writer from South Wales. He's had over forty novels published to date, as well as hundreds of novellas and short stories. His latest novel is the eco-horror *Eden*. Other recent releases include *The Edge, The Silence, The Family Man,* and *Blood of the Four* with Christopher Golden. His new eco-thriller *The Last Storm* is due for release in 2022.

Tim has also written extensively in existing universes, including *Alien, Predator, Star Wars, Firefly,* and *Hellboy* novels. He also novelized the movies *30 Days of Night*, *The Cabin in the Woods*, and *Kong: Skull Island*.

He has won four British Fantasy Awards and a Bram Stoker Award for his original fiction. He was also awarded the Dragon Award for his novel *Firefly: Generations*, and a Scribe Award for *30 Days of Night*. He has been shortlisted for World Fantasy, International Horror Guild and Shirley Jackson Awards.

The movie of his novel *The Silence* debuted on Netflix April 2019, and *Pay the Ghost* was released Hallowe'en 2015. Tim is currently developing several more projects for TV and the big screen. Find out more: www.timlebbon.net.

JONATHAN MABERRY is a *New York Times*-bestselling author, five-time Bram Stoker Award-winner, Inkpot Award winner, anthology editor, and comic book writer. His vampire apocalypse book series, *V-WARS*, was a Netflix original series. He writes in multiple genres including suspense, thriller, horror, science fiction, fantasy, and action; and he writes for adults, teens and middle grade. His works include the Joe Ledger thrillers, *Ink*, *Glimpse*, the Rot & Ruin series, the Dead of Night series, *The Wolfman*, *X-Files Origins: Devil's Advocate*, *Mars One*, and many others. Several of his works are in development for film and TV. He is the editor of high-profile anthologies including *The X-Files*, *Aliens: Bug Hunt*, *Out of Tune*, *New Scary Stories to Tell in the Dark*, *Baker Street Irregulars*, *Nights of the Living Dead*, and others. His comics include *Black Panther: DoomWar*, *The Punisher: Naked Kills*, and *Bad Blood*. His *Rot & Ruin* young adult novel was adapted into the #1 comic on Webtoon, and is being developed for film by Alcon Entertainment. He is the president of the International Association of Media Tie-in Writers, and the editor of *Weird Tales* magazine. He lives in San Diego, California. Find him online at www.jonathanmaberry.com.

KIM MAY has always been a storyteller—just ask her mother. On second thought don't. She knows too much. Kim writes fantasy, sci-fi, thrillers, historical fiction, steampunk, and a bit of poetry because she collects genres like a cat lady collects strays.

Kim's debut novel, *The Moonflower*, was a 2017 Whitney Award nominee. She also won first place in the Named Lands Poetry Contest with a haiku. Kim's short stories can be found in *Monster Hunter Files, Straight Outta Dodge City, Eclipse Phase: After the Fall, Put Your Shoulder to the Wheel, Particular Passages, Sanctuary*, and several issues of *Fiction River*.

Kim lives in Oregon where she works at an independent bookstore and watches a lot of anime. She's a retired stage actor and has a penchant for fast cars, high heels, and loose screws. To find Kim's works or to follow her on social media go to https://linktr.ee/KimMayDay.

YVONNE NAVARRO is a multi-genre author and artist. She has written numerous media tie-in novels, including *Elektra, Species, Species II, Aliens: Music of the Spears, Ultraviolet, Elektra,* and the first *Hellboy*. Her most recent original tie-in novel was *Supernatural: The Usual Sacrifices*, published by Titan Books. With her husband Weston Ochse, she co-authored the novel *Aliens vs. Predators: Rift War* forthcoming from Titan Books in 2022.

JOSHUA PRUETT is an Emmy Award-winning TV Writer and the only human being on Earth to have written for both *Mystery Science Theater 3000* and *Doctor Who*. Best known for his work as a writer on the Disney Channel series *Phineas And Ferb*, and the feature film *Candace Against The Universe* for Disney Plus, Joshua has worked in feature and TV animation for over 15 years, inflicting laughter and monsters on others, most recently writing on Onyx Equinox for Crunchyroll and the Emmy Winning adaptation of the *New York Times* bestselling series *The Last Kids On Earth* for Netflix. His first original middle grade novel *Shipwreckers: The Curse Of The Cursed Temple Of Curses, Or We Nearly Died. A Lot.* with Scott Peterson debuted May 2019 from Disney/

Hyperion. He is also co-author of *The Jungle Book: The Strength Of The Wolf Is The Pack*, an adaptation and expansion of the 2016 live action feature film, the original horror short story collection *The Misery Company*, and *Avatar: The Last Airbender: Legacy Of The Fire Nation* from Insight Editions. Joshua grew up as a monster kid and writing *Predator* is a dream come true.

A. R. REDINGTON (formerly A. R. Crebs) is a native of Kansas. At a young age, she dove into the creative world, focusing on art and storytelling. Her passion for gaming and creating characters led her to pursue a career in art and design. After taking art classes throughout her academic life, she attended the Rocky Mountain College of Art + Design, receiving a BFA in illustration/children's book specialization. With experience in graphic design, formatting, illustration, editing, and writing, Redington creates and designs everything for her novels while working freelance on the side. She is the author and illustrator of the sci-fi/fantasy series, *The Esoteric Design, Masters of the Ellem* (fantasy), *Trouble with Mystery* (romantic thriller), and *Whispers from Beyond: 30 Miniature Tales* (horror). You can find out more about A. R. Redington at her website: www.ARRedington.com.

#1 New York Times best-selling author **SCOTT SIGLER** is the creator of eighteen novels, six novellas, and dozens of short stories. He is an inaugural inductee into the Podcasting Hall of Fame.

Scott began his career by narrating his unabridged audiobooks and serializing them in weekly installments. He continues to release free episodes every Sunday. Launched in March of 2005, "Scott Sigler Audiobooks" is the world's longest-running fiction podcast.

His rabid fans fervently anticipate their weekly story fix, so much so that they've dubbed themselves "Sigler Junkies" and have downloaded over fifty million episodes. Subscribe to the free podcast at scottsigler.com/subscribe.

Scott is a cofounder of Empty Set Entertainment, which publishes his Galactic Football League series. A Michigan native, he lives in San Diego, CA with his wife and their wee little Døgs of Døøm. His website is www.ScottSigler.com.

ACKNOWLEDGEMENTS

Gratitude goes out to Aaron Percival and Adam Zeller, webmasters of AVPGalaxy.net, which is the definitive source of research online for this book and many authors, for once again going above and beyond the call of duty in helping us navigate the complicated worldbuilding of the Expanded Universe. Their advice and insights were invaluable to keeping us on track.

Thanks to Disney/20th Century Studios Franchising, especially Nicole Spiegel, and Titan Books, especially Steve Saffel, our editor, for letting us play in this fun universe we're fans of, Paul Simpson, copyeditor with a keen eye, and to all of our authors for their hard work and dedication to getting it right.

Many thanks to the legion of fans of *Predator*—for enthusiastic support and nit-picky technical info. I hope we did better this time. Every effort was put forth to bring you the new, interesting takes on the old theme and add new, exciting tidbits and possibilities to lore.

And last of all thanks to the cast, crew, and writers of the original 1987 *Predator* for creating such a memorable universe thirty-five years ago that continues to be worth celebrating time and again.

And thanks to May for bringing new joy and music and love to my life.

ALSO AVAILABLE FROM TITAN BOOKS

ALIENS:
BUG HUNT

"These colonial marines are very tough hombres. They're packing state-of-the-art firepower. There's nothing they can't handle."
Burke to Ripley (from the movie *Aliens*)

When the Marines set out after their deadliest prey, the Xenomorphs, it's what Corporal Hicks calls a bug hunt—kill or be killed. Here are fifteen all-new stories of such "close encounters," written by many of today's most extraordinary authors:

DAN ABNETT • RACHEL CAINE • LARRY CORREIA
KEITH R.A. DECANDIDO • DAVID FARLAND • MATT FORBECK
RAY GARTON • CHRISTOPHER GOLDEN • HEATHER GRAHAM
BRIAN KEENE • PAUL KUPPERBERG • TIM LEBBON
JONATHAN MABERRY • JAMES A. MOORE
YVONNE NAVARRO • WESTON OCHSE • SCOTT SIGLER
MIKE RESNICK and MARINA J. LOSTETTER

Set during the events of the first four *Alien* films, sending the Marines to alien worlds, to derelict space settlements, and into the nests of the universe's most dangerous monsters, these adventures are guaranteed to send the blood racing—one way or another.

ALSO AVAILABLE FROM TITAN BOOKS

AVP: ALIENS VS. PREDATORS
RIFT WAR

by WESTON OCHSE and YVONNE NAVARRO

The planet LV-363 is scarred with deep rifts as if torn by gargantuan claws. It teems with exotic life, much of it lethal—including a plant that grows in the shadows. The plant's flower yields an addictive narcotic for which people will pay any price. Criminal cartels—the worst of humanity—force desperate workers to harvest it.

When a Predator ship arrives to prepare for a hunting ritual, its occupant seeds the rifts with Xenomorph eggs. The aliens emerge, attack indigenous fauna, and produce bizarre and deadly hybrids. These ravenous creatures—some of which can fly—swarm out of control.

A second ship lands, carrying young Predators who must prove their skills by hunting the Xenomorphs. What they find, however, may prove more than they can handle. A bloody conflict ensues, a Rift War, with the humans caught in the middle.

TITANBOOKS.COM